THE NIGHTMARE NEVER ENDS

When Ruth awoke, she was drowning in blood. She gagged, mindless, her arms and legs churning in the hot, coppery brew. But could it really be blood? All of *this?*

She couldn't think. She didn't even know who she was yet. Only instinct fired her nerves: the will to survive.

It didn't occur to her just yet that she was already dead.

Her thoughts screamed: *Where am I? What is this? Somebody help me!*

She desperately breast-stroked, but more madness shrieked through her psyche when glimpses upward showed her a sky that was as red as the blood she was swimming in, and smudged clouds idling across a black moon shaped like a sickle.

I'm having a nightmare! She managed to think. *I'm seeing things. The sky isn't RED, and the moon isn't BLACK, and it's IMPOSSIBLE for me to be swimming in a LAKE of blood!*

Just keep moving. Eventually the nightmare will end...

EDWARD LEE

HOUSE INFERNAL

LEISURE BOOKS NEW YORK CITY

A LEISURE BOOK®

October 2007

Published by

Dorchester Publishing Co., Inc.
200 Madison Avenue
New York, NY 10016

ISBN-10: 0-8439-5806-5
ISBN-13: 978-0-8439-5806-5

Printed in the United States of America.

Visit us on the web at www.dorchesterpub.com.

HOUSE INFERNAL

Prologue

Blood bricks were used to construct the district's most prominent edifices and roadways. For thousands of years, the City of Abandoned Hope churned as a diabolical microcosm that could be likened to an endless jigsaw puzzle, and one of the puzzle's biggest pieces was this district—the Boniface District—and the reason it could be seen from a hundred miles in any direction was because it had essentially been built with blood.

A thousand cauldrons boiled ceaselessly, each filled to the brim with the blood of abducted citizens, fugitives, Demons, mongrels, Hybrids, etc., and even occult-engineered blood, a more recent technological breakthrough. As the cauldrons boiled, their levels reduced. Water was distilled from the steam, of course, but eventually, when the blood had boiled down to paste, it was blended with lime and milled bone, then pressed into foundry molds. When the bricks dried, they were later disenchanted by specially trained Warlocks from the district's Collegium of Sorcerial Sciences. These spells would not only bolster the bricks' resistence to stress and deterioration but also strengthen any wall against the occasional malcontents and anti-Luciferic terrorists trained in the black arts.

A hundred yards long and fifty wide, Fortress Boniface was the first structure to be built with blood bricks. When humidity was high, the bricks would "bleed" slightly, and district residents would touch their fingers to the fortress's walls for good luck.

Boniface gazed south over the parapet. Hot winds carried smoke and a thousand screams as the sky churned blood-red behind a black sickle moon. Beyond, the city extended into its wondrous, demented infinity. Griffins and Caco-Bats swept down out of bruise-colored clouds to tear limbs off unsuspecting inhabitants, including children and infants. Gargoyles lurked about the crestwork of the higher buildings, hunting for vermin, weak windows, and ledge jumpers. Lower, in the nooks and crannies of the city's guts, Boniface could see the everyday life: Broodren—the demonic young—cooking horned newts on sticks over flaming sewer grates; taloned Ushers with faces of slag disemboweling the helpless in a regional Mutilation Zone; nine-foot-tall Golems standing watch on every corner; rows of chained mongrel slaves hauling great two-wheeled limbers full of body parts to the district De-Boning Line and Pulping Station . . .

Perfect order, Boniface thought.

He moved farther down the parapet of this macabre, dark scarlet edifice that comprised the Exhalted Duke's Fortress. A glance over the edge showed him the Boniface District itself, his first gift from the Lord of Lies. *Oh, Lucifer, my great god, I give thee thanks,* Boniface sang in his head. Damnation and status had changed his features to something stolid and blocklike, while his face, long ago consumed by Bapho-Rats, remained covered by a mask fashioned from the salt of the Valley of Siddim. This was the same salt that Lot's wife, Edith, had been changed to when she ignored Gabriel's warning and dared look behind her as the two most vile cities on the earth were razed in flame.

The scarlet sky cast a long shadow at the Exhalted Duke's feet, which gave him satisfaction. Boniface had been a short man on earth, and he remained short in Hell. Dressed in his gilded white cassock, the shadow seemed like a huge chess piece made even longer by the anti-pontiff's miter hat emblazoned by a gold inverted crucifix. His squat fingers were embellished by pyrite rings which bore the unglimpsable faces of Lucifer and the premier Fallen Angels, and in his left hand he bore a pastoral staff made from the arteries of past concubines. The blood vessels had been twisted, hexed, and then desiccated in a sulphur kiln. Boniface would add to its girth on occasion, when he wearied of a doxy.

"My lord," Willirmoz announced as he approached. "recently, I divined what I am about to tell you."

Boniface's nearly fleshless skull beneath the salt-mask grinned. "The Usher Squads have found the fourth Oblation? Tell me it is so. . . ."

Willirmoz' face was nearly fleshless as well, but from another symptom. The Exalted Duke's personal adjutant and fortune-teller had lost his countenance—and a great deal of the rest of his flesh—to fire. In the Living World, Willirmoz had been burned at the stake in St. Claude, France, in 1680 for black magic and molestation. Since the time of his Damnation, he'd risen to the rank of High Priest in the Guild of Lithomancy. The totems of his trade were in constant evidence, as they had been stitched into every square inch of his gown: the most mystical of crystals, namely ophite, bloodquartz, and deadly Lapis Baetullum stones, just to name a few. His most recent imperial training had taken place at the Oppenheimer Monastery, and one condition of induction was for all Lithomancers to mimic the conditions of their deaths in the Living World.

Yet the High Priest's skills were incontestable. "Indeed, my lord. The fourth Oblation has been procured." A charred finger pointed over the parapet. "Bear witness . . . and rejoice."

Now Boniface gazed down into the courtyard, whose cabalistic geometry provided its power. The courtyard was a great rectangle; limestone blocks the size of coffins sat at each of the yard's four corners, and on top of each stood a stone font—called a *Morte-Cisterna*—full of moldering blood. The blood in each basin had come from the slit throats of three Human sacrifants.

"Is the blood sufficiently corrupted?" Boniface asked.

"Yes, my most atrocious lord. It is rotten, spoiled, brown from curdling—the perfect consistency. Come, to the Watch-Turret."

Boniface followed the vile magician to the fortress's fourth corner—the southeast corner—from which a turret with ramparts bulged. Boniface stood behind the pulpit and looked down into his courtyard between the stone merlons. It was this point that would afford him an optimum view of the ritual. . . .

"Be ready, my lord," Willirmoz whispered from within his hood, "and watch."

Boniface's sickly eyes began to go teary behind the mask. *It's all coming together, my great Satan. . . .* Below, the platoon of hideous Ushers—with their eyes and mouths like knife-cuts in meat—hauled the final sacrifant from the jail-wagon.

A lone feminine shriek pierced the open air.

The creatures that hauled the wagon were known as Metastabeasts, something like a horse, only twice the size, that had been placed under a mutation conjuration. Cancers had been implanted into their musculatures and stimulated rampant growth, so the beasts could haul astronomical loads. Eyes bulged from mutated sockets over long snouts of bone, while irregular fangs twisted from their mouths. They were hairless and gray, and webbed with veins.

By psychic command, the beasts stopped. A slug-skinned Usher opened the wagon's door of iron bars and pulled out its only occupant.

"She's quite comely," Boniface observed, surprised. "Are you certain she's chaste?"

The wagon's prisoner fainted the instant she glimpsed the Usher's face. The young blond-haired woman was flipped over the Usher's runneled shoulder; eighteen years old, perhaps. Strips of rags comprised her clothing, between the gaps of which showed a supple, fresh physique.

"She is quite chaste, my lord," Willirmoz assured. "Six teams of Channelers and Tactionists have examined her memory. She's untouched. Unblemished."

"She can't have been Damned long, judging from the excellent condition of her Spirit Body. . . ."

"A relatively new arrival, which is how she managed to avoid being raped. It was a Golem on Ghettoblock duty who reported her. The dead thing could smell her virginity issuing from the alley crevice she lived in. That's when the nearest platoon of Ushers was summoned; they took her posthaste to the De Rais Asylum for psychic inspection." The High Priest's crusted black lips turned up. "She was Damned for murdering her parents—for a land inheritance. And her father . . . was a Methodist minister."

"Lucifer, bless her!" Boniface chuckled.

"Another inmate murdered her in prison . . . then she came here."

"It's our good fortune, Willirmoz. Finding virgins in Hell is no easy feat. Simply finding the first three took long enough."

"And now we have the fourth, and final, sacrifant, my abhorrent lord. It's providential that she be so stunningly attractive."

Boniface watched as the girl's limp body was laid on the fourth Dolmen and stripped of the rags. Were she not so essential for the rite, he would've liked to go down there and eat her alive, but not before a fastidious carnal ravaging.

Below, from one of the De-Vestry arches, scarlet smoke began to pour and fill the courtyard, but when the smoke thinned, a coven of Arithmetrices stood around the fourth Dolmen, where the fainted girl had now been tied. These occult mathematicians belonged to a rarefied sorority of witches known as the Cultes des Pythagorae, and they'd existed in damnation for thousands of years. All of these ancient women were obese and grimly stood naked, every square inch of their pallid bodies branded with tiny numbers and equations. Even the whites of their eyes were inscribed with the most minuscule numerals. The Arithmetrices were masters of the conversion of number systems into quantifiable abyssal energy.

One, the fattest and squattest, began to read from the only existing copy of the *Book of the Involution*, perhaps Hell's rarest tome. But it was not words that drifted from the witch's branded lips but theorems, in a language known only to the Culte.

"I can feel it," Boniface whispered.

"Indeed, my lord." Willirmoz's charred gaze held fast to the nearly silent spectacle below. "Only through the skills of the Arithmetri does metaphysical ideology become palpable, as solid as the blood bricks lain to erect the walls of your fortress."

Boniface felt his immortal skin crawl beneath his vestments; the intonations below made the air churn, and the remnant censer-smoke left hanging in the yard began to draw out in long vermillion lines and then began to spiral inward. . . .

When the witch fell silent and closed the unholy book, Boniface saw with some startlement that she was no longer hideously obese—none of the coven were now. Instead they stood *emaciated*, the rigors of the secret spells having converted all that body fat into energy.

Then the entire coven looked up to Boniface in the Watch-Turret. In the air, Boniface made the sign of the inverted cross and nodded. The coven turned and straggled back to the De-Vestry.

Willirmoz mouthed something in total silence, a psychic command to the Sergeant at Arms below. This Sergeant, armored in demonic hide and with a great bronze helm, came from the lauded Diocletian Brigade. These conscripts were the most loyal Human-Demon Hybrids in the city, and proved their allegiance to Lucifer by murdering—and devouring—their families. In a voice like heavy wood splitting, the Sergeant ordered, "Render of the House! Front and center!" and from the sacristies a Cutter-Demon emerged. The tall, chock-faced thing wore nothing but wrist-cuffs and a chain mail kilt while his arms, legs, back, and chest remained all bare black-green skin and muscles. Renders were experts with the blade, and hand-forged their own cutting instruments, and on this one at least a dozen blades were in evidence. There were no scabbards, however; instead each knife was buried to its hilt in the Render's own flesh.

He followed the Sergeant to the Dolmen. The Human girl remained unconscious. An attending Usher hung her head over the Dolmen's edge, and directly below this point stood the wide stone Cistern, like a birdbath, waiting to be filled.

"In the name of the Lord of Lies, once God's bringer of light and now Hell's bringer of darkness!" shouted the Sergeant. "And in the name of Boniface the Exalted—commence!" And then the Render withdrew a small paring knife from his left pectoral and very quickly slid it against the side of the girl's throat. Even in unconsciousness, she hitched on the slab, released a garbled scream, but then the Usher's taloned hand grabbed her hair to hold her head down. Meanwhile, the Sergeant had straddled her, pinning her down.

And the blood poured like a tapped keg into the Cistern's stone basin.

It drained quickly, rife with rich, red bubbles. When the flow began to retard, the Sergeant pumped the victim's bare chest—a heinous CPR—to coax more blood into the font. Eventually four Soubrettes approached each corner of the Dolmen, their wanton faces wide with grins. The Soubrettes were Boniface's chambermaids, bred for sexual appeal, breasts, privates, and other features hexegenically enhanced. Each woman, all dressed in clinging pink tongue-gowns, raised one of the victim's limbs and massaged it from top to bottom. Smaller gushes renewed at the gash.

"Lovely," Boniface whispered.

When no more blood could be squeezed out, the Sergeant climbed off and dismissed the others.

"It is done, Exalted Duke!" he barked upward.

Boniface's salt-mask nodded. "Give what's left to the streets of my proud District, and cover the precious blood. Post guards."

The Sergeant snapped orders, then more teams of Conscripts and Ushers came into the yard. A field Archlock slid a stone lid over the Cistern, so that the blood would rot properly, while Golems and Ushers were posted at all four corners of the courtyard.

Still more attendants tightened a noose around the girl's ankles; then she was hoisted up to the rampart and expeditiously thrown over the side. She wasn't "dead," of course; as one of the Human Damned, her Spirit Body could never die unless completely destroyed. But drained of all blood?

She'd lie paralyzed in the streets. Now that her virginal blood had been secured, her body didn't matter. She'd likely be raped and eaten in short order, or perhaps some crafty Broodren would get to her first and sell her body parts to various vendors. . . .

Boniface looked at the Hasdrubal Clock Tower in the distance. All clocks in Hell had no hands on their faces. "It is nearly time," the whisper escaped the lip slit in his mask.

"Another week, perhaps; little more."

Boniface grasped the sleeve of his High Priest as if desperate. "I *must* succeed, Willirmoz. I must achieve for Lucifer what has never been."

The charred face within the hood could barely be seen. "You will, my revolting lord. In the visions of my mances, I've already seen that it will all be so."

"Swear to me, Priest."

"I swear, my lord. If I'm wrong, I shall feed myself to a Ghor-Hound."

Boniface allowed himself to relax; he sighed through the mask. "It's so difficult to be patient in Hell, Willirmoz. And that doesn't make sense, does it? Where everything is forever?"

"It makes *perfect* sense, my lord. The four Cisterns have been filled. All that remains is the final conditioning of our most important visitors." The charred hand bid his underlord toward the stone stairs. "Let us go to the Lower Chancel . . . to bid them our best wishes. . . ."

Boniface and his Priest went down the spiral stairs to a very special place deep in the bedrock of Hell.

Chapter One

(I)

"I'm familiar with all the rectories, monasteries, and theological academies in New Hampshire, but St. John's Prior House?" Venetia commented from the backseat of the Cadillac SUV. "I've never heard of it."

"I don't even know what *it* is," her father remarked from the driver's seat. Richard Barlow, as he'd aged, reminded Venetia of the father on that old black-and-white show called *Dennis the Menace*, but just a bit more cynical. He and Venetia's mother seemed perfect for each other in their oblivion. A pipe—which he wasn't allowed to light anymore, due to blood pressure—hung from the man's mouth. He chewed its end while he talked. "When your mother told me about the assignment, at first I thought she said *fry* house. I thought, That's just great. I put my daughter through college so she can work the fryer at a fish-and-chips joint."

"Your father's being ridiculous, as always, dear." Maxine Barlow thrust her bosom between the seats. Venetia's mother would be called "pleasingly plump" now that she'd arrived into her midforties: a stereotypical New England housewife who was always preparing for a Tupperware party or the Saturday night spaghetti dinner and fund-raiser at the church. She always wore smocklike print dresses and old-fashioned Earth Shoes. "Motherly" was a good word for her, chunky but still curvaceous, and with a hefty bosom that still turned heads. Her shoulder-length hair was a mix of blond, brown, and gray. "A prior house, or priory as they're sometimes called, is like a monastery. Surely, Richard, you know what a monastery is."

"Yeah, our bedroom." Then Venetia's father broke out into a very uncharacteristic round of laughter.

All Venetia's mother did was smile and bat her eyes. "See what happens when you let animals out of their cages, Venetia?" Her smile beamed. "We'll see how hard he laughs tonight when I stick that absolutely *ludicrous* pipe right up his—"

"Mom!" Venetia exclaimed.

Her father smiled back over his shoulder. "Don't worry, Venetia. Your mother thinks of herself as far too cultured to use the word '*ass.*'"

"He's right, honey. And after we drop you off, I'm going to spend the whole ride home thinking of a nice alternate word for the thing I'm going to *kick* tonight."

Richard Barlow chuckled through the pipe. "Sounds like it might be a pretty good weekend after all."

Jeez, Venetia thought. *Those two.* She'd only been back home for several days, and her parents' jovial sniping was already wearing her out. But it had been her mother who'd gotten Father Driscoll to send the recommendation to the university. Most field studies for theology students involved little more than endless research at church libraries and diocesan archives. But . . . *restoring a Prior House by a famous Vatican architect?*

The prospect sounded fascinating.

Since she'd been back, the neighbors had all parroted the same sentiment: "Oh, my gosh, Venetia, we're so proud of you! You're about to get a college degree after only two years! That's amazing!" It seemed, however, that the only person *not* impressed by this feat was Venetia herself. *Big deal*, she concluded. *If I'd worked harder, I could've gotten it in a year and a half.* She was at least proud of her discipline to remain goal-oriented. *The rest of life will come later. For me, now, it's school, and then . . .*

That's what she wasn't sure about yet. The *then*.

She'd been worrying too much, and that wasn't like her. Why worry? She'd only just turned twenty-one. *I'm young,* she reminded herself every day. *I don't have to decide right now if I really want to become a nun. . . .*

Up front, Venetia's parents were bickering over radio stations. "Come on, Maxine, the Sox have the damn Yankees at home!" "Just . . . shut up, dear, while I find the gospel station." Venetia was grateful for the break. A bad night's sleep left her limp in the backseat. She tried to let her thoughts disband by watching the beautiful New Hampshire countryside sweep by in the window. *Thank God it's summer.* The summers up here were a marvel of nature; it was the winters that had dragged Venetia down during childhood and adolescence. Too depressing. She thought that going to school in Washington, DC, would be something of a relief from all the snow . . . but all she got instead were ice storms and rain. At least the weather—not to mention the crime wave—had kept her inside most of the time, to focus on her studies.

Eventually, she caught herself nodding in and out of sleep as she tried to watch the rolling green fields beyond the window. *That weird dream,* she groaned to herself. *I barely got any sleep last night.* She rubbed her eyes, then briskly shook her blond head in hopes of rousing herself.

"Honey, are you all right?" her mother's face hovered between the seats again.

And her father added, "To tell you the truth, you don't look too good."

"Thanks, Dad," she said with a smirk. But she knew he was right. "I tossed and turned all night. I had this weird dream, and then I couldn't get back to sleep."

"I'll stop at a convenience store so you can get some coffee. It'll perk you up. You don't want to fall asleep in the middle of your interview with Father Driscoll."

Her mother: "It's not an interview, Richard. She's already been accepted for the assignment. They can't very well turn down a twenty-one-year-old *senior* with a four-point-oh average."

Venetia groggily leaned up. "I know, but that's still a good idea, Dad. I could use some coffee now that you mention it."

"Good. And I could use a chili dog." Richard looked to his wife. "No offense, sweetheart, but your hash and eggs didn't quite cut it this morning."

Maxine Barlow smiled. "You get that chili dog, Richard. Get several. Because they'll be following that ludicrous pipe right up your . . . you-know-what."

Venetia winced. "You two really are a scream today."

"Don't listen to your moronic, stick-in-the-mud father, dear," her mother urged.

"Hey. I admit I'm a stick in the mud, but I'm *not* moronic."

"I'm sorry, dear. I meant imbecilic." Maxine turned back to her daughter, concern in her eyes. "But what were you saying before your thoroughly uncouth father interrupted? Oh, yes—it was a nightmare that kept you awake."

"Not a nightmare, really . . ."

"Thank God," her father interrupted yet again. "Your mother's breakfast was nightmare enough."

Maxine's smile just kept growing. "I'll put the leftovers in the fireplace bellows . . . and can you guess where I'll stick *that?*" The robust woman fingered the small gold cross around her neck and again addressed her daughter. "So it *wasn't* a nightmare, then?"

"No, Mom. It was just a weird dream. Nothing scary about it—it just bothered me for some reason."

"What happened in the dream?"

Venetia let her thoughts slide back. She dreamt of standing in a red-tinged darkness. All she could see before her were six boxes. Were they small coffins or vaults of some sort?

Then they vanished, and a voice from nowhere jolted her. It was a man's voice, and he'd spoken loudly and with obvious alarm: *"This isn't a dream! You must understand! You have to understand!"*

The exclamation arrived as a half shriek, with an undertone of dread. It was sourceless.

The voice faded with these words: *"Everything's opposite here. You must understand . . ."*

And that was it.

But now that she'd replayed it in her mind, it seemed weak, petty. *A voice in a dream . . . telling me it* wasn't *a dream? Stupid . . .*

"Can't really say why the dream kept me awake. Now that I think of it, it was kind of stupid."

"Oh, you mean like those soap operas your mother watches all day," Richard Barlow remarked.

"No, Richard, she means *stupid* like that ridiculous wrestling you watch all day," Maxine cut in through gritted teeth. "Venetia? So we can actually have a practical mother-to-daughter conversation, ignore everything that comes out of your father's mouth. It's easy. I've been doing it for twenty years—"

"To make up for what you *haven't* been doing for twenty years." Richard chuckled and boorishly elbowed his wife.

What did I do to deserve this? Venetia wondered through her fatigue.

"The Prior House is simply a piece of Vatican-owned property," Maxine began to explain. "It never functioned as a monastic domicile—Father Driscoll said that in the past the Church used it for important priests to take respites, a vacation between pastoral assignments."

Venetia tried to focus on the topic. When she'd done a quick Internet search on St. John's Prior House, she'd come up blank. "That's interesting. There are a lot of old priories in the DC area, but they changed most of them into hospices. I read somewhere once that dedicated monasteries are declining. Men don't want to become monks anymore."

"What about nuns?" her father piped up.

"In America? Interest in convent life is declining too.

The overseas assignments are pretty rough—Third World countries, high death and disease rates, stuff like that."

"But that doesn't bother you?" her mother asked.

Venetia gave her textbook answer. "I just want to do what God wants me to do. The problem is, He's not exactly shining His guiding light in front of me these days." She rubbed her eyes again. *I need that coffee. Now.* "I'm not going to worry about it until I get my master's." She managed a grin. "Who knows? Maybe I'll just get a job in a fry house."

"What? What?" her father snapped.

"And it was great to see Father Driscoll after all these years," her mother went on. "If anything, he's more handsome now than he was fifteen years ago."

"He always struck me as a young punk," Richard felt the need to remark. "Now I guess he's—what—a *middle-aged* punk?"

"And you're an *over-the-hill* punk, darling," Maxine said.

Venetia shook her head. "I don't remember him."

"He was the seminarian at our church for a year or two, the nicest man, very earnest, and serious about his devotion to God. You were only five or six when he became a priest. When he stopped at the service two weeks ago, he looked almost exactly the same. Handsome, even kind of dashing."

"Sounds like trouble," Richard murmured. "I can't wait to tell my bowling team my wife's got the hots for a priest."

Maxine sighed. "I wish I knew how to say 'shut up' in Latin."

"*Silere,* I think," Venetia said.

"Richard? Would you please *silere?* Thank you."

Her father looked over his shoulder again. "Hey, Venetia? How do you say 'pain in the ass' in Latin?"

"You two are impossible," Venetia groaned.

"But Father Driscoll certainly remembered you, and he was very impressed when I told him you were at Catholic University and wanted to become a nun."

"*Might* become a nun," Venetia corrected.

"Or a fry cook," her father said.

"He said that the only true theology student is the student who devotes their life to God. 'The Evangelists of the modern age,' he said."

"You'll be fine," her mother assured. "All through high school and now college, I don't think you ever got a mark lower than an A."

"A master's curriculum in theology and Christian thesis at a religious college is another story altogether." Venetia paused and wondered again why she was worrying about it. *I feel confident, I feel ready. . . . So why am I fretting?*

Could the sudden nervousness have something to do with this field assignment at the prior house?

What's wrong with me today?

"Here's a Qwik-Mart," Richard announced. "Let's get some coffee"—he winked at his wife—"*and* some chili dogs."

Maxine nodded as if an exciting idea had struck her. "I read once on AOL News about a man who unknowingly poisoned himself to death in his sleep because he broke so much wind. . . ." She glanced swiftly to her husband. "Richard, get yourself a dozen of those chili dogs. I'll sleep in the spare room tonight."

"Oh, that's great. I'll finally get a break from your snoring." Richard cocked another snide grin to Venetia. "Your mother snores so loud it sounds like a chain saw crew in the room—"

"You two are killing me!" Venetia yelled, hands to her ears.

Her parents continued to bicker as Venetia followed them into the store. A man in his early twenties, with a black mop haircut and HIGHWAY TO HELL T-shirt, was tending the register. His eyes widened when they all entered. He took obvious glances at Maxine's bosom, and then at Venetia's. *Eyeball us to death, why don't you?* Venetia thought; but she scarcely cared. Even at a fairly rigid Catholic college, Venetia had learned to deflect the ever-rising tide of male sexism, but, conversely, she knew that a tiny bit of herself was mildly flattered by the boy's appraising glance. Venetia hadn't inherited *all* of her mother's mammarian allotment, but with a 36C, she supposed she was two-thirds there, and two-thirds was enough.

"Hey, son?" her father asked. He looked over the rims of his black-framed glasses. "You heard a Red Sox score?"

"Yankees are leading six to zip in the fourth," the kid answered.

"Goddamn—"

"Richard!" Maxine objected.

"God-*dang!* I was going to say god-*dang!*" Then he stalked off to the chili dog rack. "Those goddamn, money-belching Yankees can kiss my ass."

"Excuse me," Venetia asked. "Where's the restroom?"

The kid pointed to a corner. "Right back there."

"I'll get your coffee, dear," her mother said.

Was it jealousy she felt next? The lanky clerk's eyes shot to her mother's bosom, not Venetia's, as Maxine bounced toward the coffee station. Venetia's eyes thinned when she turned toward the corner. *I don't believe it!* Maxine didn't appear to be wearing a bra.

I guess that happens when you get older, she reasoned. *You do things to feel vital again, to reclaim some youth even though you know it's behind you.*

But if that were so . . . then how did *Venetia* feel, barely twenty-one?

Did she feel vital? Or desexualized since she'd been considering a nun's vocation?

All I feel right now is tired, she thought.

When she flicked on the bathroom light, the room filled with white light. It was a unisex bathroom. She locked the door, then washed her hands, fearful of all the germs on the doorknob, and when she recalled the shiftless clerk, she put toilet paper down along the seat's rim. *That pervert probably pees on the seat deliberately, because he knows women will sit on it.* A strange thought but, then, she knew she was in the real world now, for however briefly. On the wall someone had penned, NOT TO BE BORN IS BEST. *That's Sophocles,* she knew at once. *I'll bet the guy at the register didn't write that one.* While she relieved herself, something on the floor caught her eye, like yellow cellophane but with a ring. *Oh, gross,* she thought when she realized it must be a used condom.

A moment later, she caught herself jolting awake.

This is ridiculous! I almost fell asleep on a convenience store toilet!

She flushed with her shoe, then vigorously shook her head. Her fatigue seemed to be compounding. *Get it together. You're about to meet a priest who's had assignments at the Vatican. Wake your butt up!*

Tired eyes looked back at her in the mirror. She took a moment to appraise herself.

No wonder that creep outside was staring . . . It occurred to her that the simple white blouse, which she'd only bought a year ago, was now tight. *I guess they're still growing.* She stepped back for a longer view and felt comfortable with the conservative attire: a pleated, black knee-skirt to complement the white blouse, and a cross about her neck. A white-blond ponytail, shining and straight, hung to the bottom of her shoulder blades. Her bosom straining the blouse was the only thing that might nix the austere Catholic schoolgirl–look she'd hoped for.

Just as she'd been rousing herself, more graffiti snagged her eye. *What in the name of . . .*

She knew it was vulgar before she even looked at it all: a drawing in black ballpoint, craggy like a grade-schooler.

But no grade-schooler had drawn this.

It was a crude sketch of a nude woman, thighs spread, squiggles for pubic hair. A dot for a navel, and a pair of circles with dots for nipples. The mouth gaped, with ink droplets at each corner—presumably a depiction of semen. The woman's eyes were a pair of Xs.

A just-as-crudely-drawn knife was cutting the woman's throat. The artist, though completely without talent, had been conscientious enough to bring a supplemental red pen to denote blood pouring from the woman's throat.

However vulgar, Venetia wasn't shocked by the sketch. She read the online news everyday as well as the local Washington papers. Murder, rape, and molestation dominated the headlines most days. Her exhausted eyes shifted over the sketch. *It's a sick world,* she thought, *full of sick people.* As a nun, she would likely have to tend to such people often with compassion.

Immediately below the sketch was a senseless diagram:

A rock group emblem? she guessed.

She turned on the faucet at the sink, cupped her hands beneath it. *Gotta wake myself up . . .*

And she almost screamed when the distorted voice from her dream shouted, *"Don't put water in your face! Keep yourself fatigued! It's the only way I can maintain communication!"*

The voice sounded flayed but high-pitched, like a blown speaker.

"Everything's opposite here! You must understand! Your moon is white—ours is black. . . ."

Venetia collapsed to the corner, hands to her ears.

But she could still hear the voice.

"Enchantments are dis-enchantments! Compassion is atrocity! You must understand! You have to understand!"

The voice, somehow, raised vibrations in her guts; she began to gag as she willed herself to crawl toward the door.

"I'm speaking to you from a city called the Mephistopolis!" A bristling pause.

She didn't make it to the door; the black oscillations in her belly shot upward and brought a headache like a spike in her brain. The harder she pressed her hands to her ears, the deeper the spike sunk.

"Get out of my head!" she gasped.

"I'm about to be captured by Scyther Detachment in Pogrom Park! I don't have much more time, so—PLEASE—just listen. . . ."

Venetia was hyperventilating one cheek pressed against the dirt-specked floor. She was drooling.

The flayed voice blared one more time. . . .

"This is not *a dream! In the name of God on High, be careful at the—"*

An inhuman shout cut the macabre sentence short; then the ghastly oscillation in her gut ceased. Venetia passed out on the bathroom floor.

(II)

Captain Ray Berns felt as dilapidated as the tiny police station looked when he pulled in after the all-day drive. His sports jacket was covered with creases, and when he got out of the cruiser his knees wobbled from fatigue. He'd scarcely heard of the town he'd just entered. The white sign read LUBEC POLICE DEPARTMENT in faded black letters. The building itself looked like it might have been a gas station in the fifties—Esso, maybe—and the roof looked like it might fall in with next winter's first snow.

I hope this isn't a bunch of crap, he thought.

This far north, he was surprised how hot it was—over eighty. He was even sweating when he crossed the lot and pushed into the small brick building.

The local cop behind the booking desk had a goatee just like Berns'. *Hope that's not a bad omen.* He flashed his badge and ID. "I'm looking for a sergeant named—"

"Lee. That's me. And you must be the captain from New Hampshire." The sergeant was slim, in a dark blue police uniform. The Maine accent instantly rubbed Berns the wrong way, and so did the goatee, even though Berns had one himself. *Just doesn't look right on a uniformed cop.*

"You want some coffee? It's really lousy."

"Sure," Berns said. Anything. "And I gotta tell you something. The roads in Maine *suck.* I feel like I've been driving on square wheels since six this morning."

Sergeant Lee looked at his watch. "You *drove?* You guys got a helicopter; why didn't you take that?"

"Loaned it to Manchester PD for the Fire Quackers Parade."

Lee arched a brow. "Well, you made good time. And you're right, the roads here suck, but I think they're worse in New Hampshire. You guys ever going to get with the program and start a state income tax?"

"Probably about the same time Maine gets the death penalty."

Did Lee have a limp? *How tough can duty be in this postage stamp tourist town?* Berns wondered. He took the cup of coffee and winced at the first sip.

"Funny you should mention the death penalty, Captain." Lee grabbed a ring of keys like you'd see in the sheriff's office in an old Western movie. "That's what part of this guy's spiel is about."

Berns tossed his crumpled sports jacket over a chair below a poster: WELCOME TO THE LOWEST CRIME TOWN IN THE PINE TREE STATE. "I don't follow you. Your teletype said you've got him cold on molestation and attempted murder of a child. I don't have shit on him. What's his name? Freddie Jackson?"

"Johnson."

"My people ran a check and say he's never been a resident of New Hampshire."

Lee shrugged. He seemed to relish every sip of the awful coffee. "He's itinerant—a waterman. Let me put it this way, Captain. The guy's white trash, just goes from town to town working for any boat that'll hire him. But here's the rub. He wants to cop a plea—in *reverse.*"

"Look, I'm brain-dead after driving all friggin' day on your shitty roads. I saw more lynx and porcupines than people, and three hundred miles of spruce trees have got me half hypnotized. Spell it out for me."

"He's confessing to a couple of sixty-four's in your juris, Captain. Wammsport."

"The two women—"

"Right, one was a nun and one was some kind of church custodian. That happened a couple months ago, didn't it?"

Berns nodded.

"Johnson wants to confess to that. Says he'd rather die by lethal injection in New Hampshire than do life with no parole in Maine at Warren. How's that sound to you?"

"It sounds more fucked-up than a tube of crickets. Lemme see this guy."

Lee jingled the keys on purpose, unlocked one service door, then took Berns down a long hall with a bare cement floor. Berns frowned at another poster that read LUBEC POLICE—TO PROTECT AND SERVE. "Let me ask you something, Sarge. How many murders do you get up here in this rough and tumble town of yours?"

"None. Ever. Barely any severe crime. We're a pretty vigilant police force, Captain. The thing two nights ago with Johnson was the closest we've ever come to a hard-core murder."

"Burying a little girl? Yeah, I'd call that hard-core."

Lee was shaking his head. "We were *all over* him, just minutes after the nine-one-one. Took the scumbag down before he even got three shovelfuls of dirt in the hole."

"He say why he wanted to bury the girl?"

"Oh, yeah. Said he did it for the same reason squirrels bury nuts."

Berns felt an inner twinge.

Lee stopped to unlock another door. "State PD's crime shrink says he seems for real, wants to MMPI him. But the psychologist from Washington County detent thinks he's Gansering."

"Doesn't make sense to Ganser—"

"In reverse? Damn right it doesn't."

A row of three jail cells extended past the next door. Two cells were dark but in the third sat a lean, cockily grinning man in orange prison utilities. Thirties or forties, it was hard to tell with watermen; the elements weathered their faces prematurely. Long, greasy blond hair, clean-shaven, and—*Jesus,* Berns thought—a gold tooth up front.

"Freddie, this is Captain Berns, from the Rockingham County Sheriff's Department in New Hampshire," Lee said.

"Hey, Captain. You think you could get me a TV in here?" Johnson's tone was cool, easygoing. "I been watchin' paint peel in here for a couple of days."

"It's called domestic behavioral indoctrination, Freddie," Berns said. "They're just breaking you in, see? You'll be watching paint peel for the next fifty years, so you might as well have a taste now."

Johnson slumped on his cot. "Aw, now, man—that ain't cool. I'm tryin' to give you something and you're already steppin' on me. And you dudes wonder why folks call cops pigs."

"Oink, oink." Berns glared through the bars. "Listen. I just drove all the way up the coast of Maine to listen to you. Please don't tell me I've wasted my time. Why am I here, Freddie? Make it good."

Johnson stood up from the cot and held out his hands, gold tooth flashing from the amped-up grin. "I wanna do you a *big* favor and confess to—"

"And don't slide me any bullshit about confessing to the Wammsport murders. You could've heard about that anywhere. Shit, I've got no reason to even believe you ever even *lived* in Wammsport."

Johnson looked offended. "The boarding house on Fifth, man. Room three, a bill and a quarter a week. I paid three months in advance, by the way—ask my landlord, Mr. Cotton. Told him I'd be traveling. Oh, and I used to drink at Abny's all the time, too."

"All right, so you know the name of a bar. Who'd you work for?"

"I was a day-hire for any boat that needed help. Ask anybody on the town dock if they heard of me. Old redneck named Desmond hired me most 'cos he had the biggest boat. Peekytoes and Jonahs run best in the spring."

"What the hell's that?"

"Crabs, man. Sweeter than blue. Shit, the guys who owned the crabbing boats all wanted me 'cos whoever I went out with got the most crabs." The white teeth shimmered. "See, I know the secret."

"What's that?"

"The bait, man, the bait. I never tell no one this but, shit, since my goose is cooked now, I'll tell you. You use cat food for Jonahs and salmon scraps for Peekytoes. You do *that*"—Johnson pointed—"and you'll fill every trap you drop."

"I drove all the way up here for you to tell me about crabs?" Berns tried to sound disgusted. So far, though, the story was level. "Five seconds before I walk out."

"I'm trying to confess to the nun thing, Captain. It's no jive."

"Right, those two nuns—"

"Only one was a nun, I think."

Still. He could've heard that somewhere. Berns spoke like an irate father scolding his child. "Don't insult me by trying to confess to the nun thing. We already caught the three guys, and they all confessed."

Johnson sat back down and winked. The big smile never left his face, to the extent that Berns was amazed. *How can this loser be so happy when he knows he'll be getting life with no parole?*

"Shame on you, Captain. You are a card, you know that?" Then Johnson laughed. "It wasn't three guys, it was just two: me and another dude, a boat hand. And one chick."

Another wink.

"The state shrink says you're Gansering, Freddie. That means you're lying through your face to snatch a lower sentence."

Johnson shook his head in disbelief. "You need to eat more fish, Captain, 'cos fish, they say, is *brain* food. I don't want no lower sentence—I want a higher one. I want capital murder in a state that'll execute me."

"I'm leaving, Freddie. You're full of shit."

"What? Are you crazy?"

"No, Freddie, but that's what you want the jury to think—because only a crazy guy would *want* to be executed for a crime he didn't commit."

Berns started for the door.

"I don't believe this shit, man. I killed those two gals—stripped 'em naked and cut their throats! I'm handing myself to you on a silver platter, man!"

Berns turned back around. "Then tell me why you buried that little girl two nights ago." He tried to surprise him.

Johnson calmed down, cocked his head. "I didn't bury her. I *tried* to bury her." He edged a shoulder toward Lee. "Until John Law here and his town clown supercops rained on my parade."

Berns lit a cigarette right beneath the NO SMOKING sign. "Who would do something like that? What kind of man would rape a ten-year-old girl and then try to bury her alive?"

Johnson's smile switched to a sneer. He jumped up and banged the bars so hard both Berns and Lee flinched, hands instinctively hovering over their holsters.

Just now, the happy-go-lucky crabber looked scary. "I ain't no kiddie-diddler, pig. I ain't a sicko, and I didn't do *nothing* sexual to that girl."

"I'm supposed to believe you took her clothes off but didn't molest her?"

"She had to be naked, man—it was part of the thing, see?" Johnson banged his fist against the bars. It had to have hurt yet he betrayed no sign of pain. "Fuck you, man. I'll just hang myself in Warren. Why should I give you credit for a double-murder when you treat me like this? Bet you ain't been doing nothing your whole career except writing traffic tickets for tourists and scarfing free coffee."

"Won't argue with you there, Freddie."

"And I *resent* you, man, for sayin' I'd do something sexual to a kid. You got doctors who can tell that I didn't, and you damn well know we didn't do anything sexual to the nun either, and that other woman last spring."

Berns gave him a long look.

"They can't be sexually tainted, but I don't expect you to get that. And I bent over backwards to be careful with the little girl. She was unconscious the whole time, 'cos I didn't want her all terrified and shit. I made it so she'd have smothered to death underground, never would've regained consciousness."

Berns glanced to Lee, who stood with his arms crossed. "He's not pulling your leg on that one, Captain. He knocked the girl out with ether he stole from a veterinarian. He must've been casing the trailer park she lived in because he knew when her parents would be gone. Knocked out the fifteen-year-old brother baby-sitting, then knocked the girl out, both with the ether. He already had the hole dug in the woods."

"How'd he get fingered?"

Lee smiled. "Next-door neighbor saw him hauling the girl out the window, so he called nine-one-one." He looked to Johnson. "Pretty bonehead move, Freddie. Maybe you're the one who should eat more fish."

"Damn straight," Johnson said and got his smile back.

"And the good news is the girl didn't remember anything that happened. Didn't even remember getting snatched or being in the hole. Shrink says she won't be all screwed up in the head later. I guess we at least have to give Freddie some credit. For a flaked-out demented sociopath and would-be child-killer, he's pretty considerate. Oh, and here's something. When we searched Freddie's pad, we found forty grand in cash."

Berns raised a brow. "That's righteous bucks, Freddie. How's an itinerant crabber get forty grand?"

The big shuck-and-jive smile returned in full. "Let's just say that my boss appreciates loyal employees."

"Tell the Captain your boss' name, Freddie," Lee urged.

"Eosphorus," Freddie said. "But trust me. You wouldn't understand."

Eosphorus? What the hell is that? "Back to the girl you

tried to bury," Berns said. "What do you mean, she *had* to be naked?"

Johnson lay back on the cot, crossed his feet. "The revelation of her innocence, Captain. It's an epiphany, see? It's transpositional. We'd call it a precursory oblation."

Epiphany? Oblation? Berns wondered.

Johnson held up an elucidating finger. "And you already know—the nun and the church woman? Their bodies were naked, too. And I killed 'em on March twentieth, the night before the vernal equinox. But I'm just trying to make it easy for you, Captain. You wouldn't understand what I'm all about, so just leave it . . . and charge me with capital murder." He shrugged in the bunk. "I'll take a polygraph any time you say. Type me up a confession. I'll sign it right now."

What's making this guy tick? Berns wondered. *He's not crazy, and he's not fucked-up from drugs. What gives?* "So you had two accomplices for the Wammsport job?"

"That's right. Another dude and a chick."

Berns whipped out a notebook. "Names."

"Uh-uh. It was me who did the cutting anyway. They just helped. Forget them. It's me you want. They were just help on the side. Adjuncts."

Johnson's recent selection of words began to bother Berns. "Equinox, adjuncts, oblations—shit, Freddie, that's a mouthful for a guy like you, and it bugs me. They can't be *sexually tainted?* You talking about sacrifice? Is that what this is all about—you're some kind of Satanist?"

"Let's just say that I'm an Eosphorian, man." Johnson winked again.

"The occult, huh?" Lee remarked. "He's got a pretty creepy looking tattoo, by the way."

"Oh, yeah?"

"Freddie, you want to show the Captain your tattoo?"

Johnson hopped back up. "Shit-yeah, man. I'm proud out it," and he unbuttoned his utilities, dragged his arms out, and began to drag them down past his waist.

Berns signed. "I did not drive all this way to see this guy's dick, Sergeant."

"Freddie, please. Just the tattoo. I'll Taser anything else you whip out."

"I believe you would, Sarge." Johnson grinned. "I believe you would."

Johnson pulled the utilities past his navel and stopped just above his pubic hair. "Check it out . . ."

The tattoo, the size of an index card, was between Johnson's navel and crotch:

Berns didn't know why but there *was* something sinister about it. "See what I mean?" Lee said, then, "Art show's over, Freddie. Hoist 'em back up."

"Is that cool or what?" Johnson shouldered back into the jail-cell pajamas.

"It looks new."

"Got it less than a year ago. Hurt like hell, too, and I think the chick doing the work was digging that."

"Fine. So what is it?" Berns asked.

"It's . . . my trademark, man." That gold-toothed grin seemed to hang in the air. "And that's all you need to know. So how about it? I've leveled with you. Level with me. You gonna help me out?"

"Believe it or not, I'm thinking about it," Berns told him.

"I mean, come on. You guys are *cops.* Cops hate the idea of murderers having rights, and I'm a murderer. Dudes like you believe all hard criminals should be executed without trial—save tax dollars for better things. Get the shit out of the gene pool, right?"

Berns and Lee traded smiles.

"You're speaking our language, Freddie."

"Well, here I am. I confess to the Wammsport murders. Transport me to New Hampshire and charge me. I'll plead guilty and deny my appeals. And since I'll be on death row I'll be on the PC block. They'll punch my ticket in a month, and I'll have a smile on my face."

Berns stroked his goatee. *I don't think this scumbag is lying. . . .*

For the first time, Johnson seemed distraught. "Captain, in two days they're gonna haul me out of here and take me to my arraignment. Then my ass lands in central-processing at the Warren supermax until my trial. Warren's the worst state cut in the East—I'll be hamburger there after five minutes."

"I know," Berns said.

Johnson's eyes beseeched Berns with an earnest plea. "Help me out, man. And you get the collar for busting a guy who murdered a *nun.* You'll be the local hero."

"You really do want to die, don't you?" Berns leaned closer. "Why? You're not crazy. You're not suicidal."

Johnson sighed, as if exhaling cigarette smoke. "When the party's over, it's over, man. That's my philosophy. But don't make me off myself in Warren. Help me out, Captain." Freddie paused, grinning again. "Who knows? You might be rewarded someday."

Berns let his thoughts tick. Then he said this: "I'm going to come back and see you in a week, Freddie. And in the meantime, I'm going to ask the Sarge here to request an arraignment delay for pending evidence analysis. I'll fax up your confession tomorrow, and you sign it, and then I'll talk to the New Hampshire state attorney's office and have them prioritize your charge. Then your smiling redneck ass gets to stay in this cushy cell until you're transported to protective custody in New Hampshire. How's that sound?"

Freddie's grin turned huge. "I *knew* you were a cool guy!"

"You can thank me at your execution."

"Damn straight!"

Lee added, "And maybe I can even scrounge up a TV so you won't have to watch any more paint peel."

Johnson clapped his hands and whistled. "You guys are the *bomb!*"

"When I come back here next week, I'll have some more questions, all right, Freddie?" Berns said.

"Hell yes, Captain."

"I'm gonna want to know about your accomplices on the Wammsport job."

Johnson leaned forward on the cot, hands clasped. "Captain, those flunkies don't matter for shit. *I* did the cutting. *I'm* the murderer. I don't even know their last names—that's how we worked. You want descriptions, I'll give 'em to you, but you won't be able to find 'em anyway."

"Why?"

"The day after the murders, we all split."

"All three of you left the state?"

"That's right. That's what we agreed, and we agreed not to tell each other where we were going. *I'm* the guy you want. Those other two? Ain't nothing but a pair of pissant rednecks. They could barely even hold down jobs—*I* had to buy their fuckin' beer!"

Berns looked at him.

Freddie's tooth flashed like a mint commercial. "But when you come back to see me? I'll tell you *all* about the blood."

"Okay, Freddie. Don't fuck me over on this one."

"Ain't gonna happen, Captain. See ya next week."

Berns and Lee returned to the front office. "Are you okay with that arraignment delay?" Berns asked.

"Piece of cake."

"Thanks—and do me another favor, will you? Have your guys go over Freddie's pad with a fine-tooth comb. Look for anything out of place."

"More out of place than forty grand in cash?"

"Anything . . . occult," Berns clarified.

"Sure. But what was that business about the blood?"

"When we found the bodies of the nun and the church custodian, they were drained of blood. I think what Freddie's promising to tell me—if I keep my end of the bargain—is the blow-by-blow."

"Dead bodies with no blood means they were killed in another location," Lee said.

"Yeah, and maybe it means more than that."

"Something occult . . . ?"

Berns shrugged. "There's a lot of delusional people in the world. They believe in fucked-up things because—"

"Because they're fucked up." Lee was pouring more coffee. "You want my gut feeling?"

Berns sat down, suddenly exhausted. "Your gut feeling is probably the same as mine. Freddie's not lying about committing the Wammsport murders, but he *is* lying about his accomplices."

"That's the read I got too. Which means his accomplices are *still* in your jurisdiction." Lee smirked after the next sip of coffee. "Happy trails, Captain. It looks like you've got a real murder investigation on your hands . . ."

Chapter Two

(I)

When Ruth awoke, she was drowning in blood. She gagged, mindless, her arms and legs churning in the hot coppery brew. But could it really be blood? All of *this?*

She couldn't think. She didn't even know who she was yet. Only instinct fired her nerves—the will to survive.

It didn't occur to her just yet that she was already dead.

Her thoughts screamed. *Where am I? What is this? Somebody help me!*

She desperately breaststoked, but more madness shrieked through her psyche when glimpses upward showed her a sky that was as red as the blood she was swimming in, and smudged clouds idling across a black moon shaped like a sickle.

I'm having a nightmare! she managed to think. *I'm seeing things. The sky isn't fucking* red, *and the moon isn't* black, *and it's fucking* impossible *for me to be swimming in a lake of blood!*

She tried to stabilize herself: dog paddling now, then floating on her back, etc. Her thoughts spun like a whirlpool. Every time her head pitched above the surface, her eyes strained but could see nothing, nothing but the tossing, endless expanse of scarlet.

Just keep moving. Eventually the nightmare will end. . . .

Hours later she was still paddling . . . and wearing out. Then . . .

Did she hear a voice? Was someone calling her name?

Something white bobbed on the low surf, fifty yards ahead.

A boat!

It looked like a canoe or lifeboat, but that didn't matter. It was something that could get her out of all this blood. And, though she wasn't sure, she thought she could feel things swimming below her.

Fifteen more minutes of alternating breaststrokes and dog paddles got her to the little white boat. Stenciled letters on the bow read PROPERTY OF S.S. *NEFARIOUS*.

Ruth had no idea that the S.S. stood for "Satanic Ship."

When she finally hauled herself up onto the tiny skiff, she looked once—

And screamed so loud she thought her throat might explode.

Collapsed at the end of the boat were two corpses half-bloated by decomposition. Flies that were red and the size of bumblebees buzzed in abundance. Ruth stared frozen at the two congealed masses. Of course their skin would be discolored—the effect of decay—but . . .

Each corpse seemed to have a pair of horns on their heads.

"Help me! For God's sake, I'm over here!"

Ruth sat hunched at the bow, mortified. *I did hear a voice. . . .* All that she'd seen so far, in her first twenty minutes of Damnation, had reduced her sense of reason to something as thin as tracing paper, and through that metaphorical paper, she could glimpse nothing but a raging madness.

"Ruth Bridges! In the name of *God*, would you *please* just look over here!"

"My name," she gasped to herself.

She looked off the port-quarter and indeed saw a head bobbing in the bubbling red surf.

There's a man out there. . . .

She was trying to pry the oars from their paste of dead blood and heat-baked bilge, but they were stuck to the floor as if glued. The current suddenly changed, and now . . .

The man tossing in the water began to drift toward Ruth rather quickly.

"Grab me!" he bellowed. "And pull me in!"

Ruth had no desire to do anything of the sort but—

Who is he? How does he know my name?

"For God's sake, you better get ready to grab me! I'm the only one who can help you!"

Help, her thoughts sputtered.

The current was bringing him closer, faster. "Your name is Ruth Bridges! You're from Collier County, Florida! And right now, you're terrified because you don't know where you are. I can tell you! I can tell you everything, but that ain't gonna happen unless your *stick your hands down* and *grab me!*"

Ruth figured the command made sense. She looked for his hands to grab but didn't see them under the rushing blood.

"Grab me! Grab me!" he gargled just as he would drift beneath the boat.

Ruth thrust her hands down, grabbed onto something that felt like it might be his collar, then she pulled.

She screamed again—louder than the first time—when she saw what she'd dragged aboard: a man in a black jacket . . . with no arms or legs.

"Calm down, Ruth," the head on the torso said. The blood from the impossible sea ran down his face. He was wearing a Roman collar.

"You're a living torso!" she shrieked.

"I know. My name is Thomas Alexander. I'm a Catholic priest." At least the head on the torso was handsome, not like those horned *things* festering at the other end of the boat. Short dark hair with some gray, intense eyes, leaned-faced. But still . . .

"This is fucking impossible!" She desperately pointed out into the endless sea of blood. "That's impossible!" She pointed to the scarlet sky and black sickle moon. "That's impossible! And *you're* im-*fucking*-possible!"

The torso-priest slouched against the bow. "Unfortunately, Ruth, none of this is impossible. It's all very regrettably real. Right now we're both floating on the Sea of Cagliostro—a sea of blood. About an hour ago, you died, and now you're in Hell."

Ruth sat paralyzed in the bobbing boat as the priest talked.

"It's impossible to explain everything, so I'll just tell it as we go. It was foreseen that you'd be here. I've been waiting for you in the city for a while now. I'm supposed to hook up with you—I'm on a job, so to speak. There is a great power that needs your help, and mine."

Ruth's eyes bugged, as if to pop out. "I don't know what the fuck you're talking about!"

The priest sighed. "Just listen. And believe. This isn't a nightmare that you're going to wake up from. This isn't a hallucination or some aspect of insanity. It's real. You're what's called a Newcomer. You're one of the Human Damned. You have a body identical to the one you had on earth—the Living World—but here that body is called a Spirit Body. The soul inside is immortal. In Hell, it's very difficult for your Spirit Body to die, but when that happens, your soul continues to live. It moves to the closest Hellborn life-form. Do you understand?"

"I don't know what the fuck you're talking about!"

"Oh, man," Alexander muttered to himself. "This ain't gonna be easy." His gaze snapped back to her. "What's the last thing you remember before you found yourself here?"

"I-I-I . . ." Her teeth chattered in spite of stifling heat. "I'm . . . from Florida. I was . . . helping two guys pick up some pot, but then—uh, shit, I can't remember!"

"You will. It takes awhile." The boat pitched slowly back and forth. The stumps of the priest's arms kept moving like he was one of those people who talked with their hands but he'd forgotten he didn't have any. "Here's the scoop. For your worldly sins and your rejection of God, you've been condemned to Hell. My story's a little bit different, though. I'm not like you, I'm not one of the Human Damned, but I didn't go to Heaven when I died either. I went to a place called Purgatory—it's a city in one of the Netherplanes. It's not as bad as Hell, but . . . it ain't that great. And I have to be there for five thousand years before my sins are purified and my Spirit can transcend to Heaven."

"Five thousand years!" Ruth wailed. "How long do I have to wait before *my* sins are purified?"

Alexander didn't answer.

Ruth's face fell to her hands; she began to blubber like a baby.

"There is hope, and I'll tell you about it in time," Alexander added.

Ruth wasn't even listening now. She was—quite understandably—inconsolable.

"Ruth, listen. There's more—a lot more. I need you to get yourself together—"

"How can I fucking get myself together? I'm sitting in a boat in a sea of blood listening to a priest who's a torso tell me I'm dead and in Hell!"

"One thing at a time!" the priest yelled. He was getting irate. "You and I have a job to do. But I need your help and you need mine."

Ruth paused at the words . . . then her eyes bugged. "I need *your* help? How can you help *me*? You're a fucking *torso!*"

"Tell me about it," the priest lamented. "It only happened yesterday. Like I said, I knew you'd be arriving. I have an intelligence source, you might say. This current is going to take us to a port town—"

"A town?" Her lower lip quivered. "But you said we're in Hell. Hell doesn't have *towns*. It's like . . . fire and brimstone and shit, right? It's caves and rocks and lava and flames and holes in the ground that devils come out of, right?"

"Not anymore, Ruth. Think about it. Ten thousand years ago, what did America look like?"

Ruth's not-terribly-powerful mind churned. "I don't know! Just woods, I guess!"

"Right. Just one great expanse of wilderness. Hell was the same way, just with different natural attributes. But ten thousand years later? America's the most industrialized nation on earth, and most of its population lives in big cities, and the same for lots of other countries on earth. It's because during that time the human race *evolved,* Ruth. Human beings learned things, then passed that knowledge on to the next generation. Over the ages people got smarter and smarter, and became more and more resourceful. They turned the wilderness into a mechanized, sophisticated society. Get it?"

Ruth stared at him. "I don't know what the fuck you're talking about!"

Alexander tried to rub his temples, then sighed when he remembered the reason he couldn't. "Ruth, the same thing happened in Hell. Just as the human race evolved on earth, the demonic race evolved in Hell. It's not a smoking sulphur pit anymore. It's a great big industrialized *city.* And that city is called the Mephistopolis."

Ruth sat and let the words sink in.

"Here, look for yourself. Take my Roman collar off and reach into my shirt."

Ruth raised a brow. "You putting moves on me?"

"Just do it!" Alexander yelled, his patience draining.

Ruth fumblingly did as she was told. "What are these?"

"They're several pendants around my neck. Pull them out."

Ruth yanked upward, and out came one pendant that was attached to some sort of horn, another with a little bag on it, and another with a small wooden box on it.

"Open the box and take out the Abyss-Eye."

"The what?" Ruth asked, her knees in some indescribable muck.

"You ever heard of a monocle, Ruth? You know, like Colonel Klink wears?"

"Hey, I remember him on TV!"

Alexander nodded, smirking. "Well this is the same thing, only it's—well, you can think of it as magic. You put it over your eye, just like Colonel Klink, then . . . you look."

Ruth opened the box and howled. "You fucker! It's an eyeball! What kind of a sick fucker are you?"

The priest groaned. "It's a *magic* eyeball, Ruth. Okay? Things here are magic. In the Living World it's science. Here it's magic."

The object was indeed a raw eyeball, but smaller than human and with a vertical iris. It had been set in a brass ring the size of a silver dollar.

"Abyss-Eye," she said very slowly and turned it in her fingers. "So that's . . . a *demon's* eyeball in it?"

"Not quite. It's the eye of an Dentata-Vulture. It's a Hellborn bird that's sort of Hell's equivalent to a bald eagle. They have extremely good vision."

She kept looking at it. At one point, the eye blinked and Ruth yelped, bobbling the Abyss-Eye in her hands.

"Be careful! That thing was very hard to get! It's irreplaceable!"

Ruth put a hand to the YUCK FOO T-shirt-plastered to her chest, letting her heart slow down. "Fuck . . . So I'm supposed to—"

"Just put it to your eye, Ruth."

Her fingers faltered as she raised the bizarre device to her eye, and—

"Holy ever-loving shiiiiiii . . ."

She was looking out past the bow, then—

She went rigid in a silence that lasted quite a while.

In the distance, there was a craggy line between where the scarlet sea and the bloodred sky came together. When she strained her own eye, the Abyss-Eye zoomed. That's when she saw the city. . . .

Crooked skyscrapers shot up into the soot-tinged horizon, interspersed by lower, squat buildings whose chimneys gushed smoke of all colors. From some buildings she saw heads on spikes, and between others, from things like clotheslines, squirming bodies hung from nooses around their necks. Several of the lines were probably a mile long. One Gothic spire had a clock just below its oddly angled and skull-ornamented roof.

But the clock had no hands.

Lower, she saw churches, or things *like* churches, that seemed to shudder as if alive, with black steeples marked by inverted crosses and cryptic symbols. Things like bats plunged down from the soiled sky to pluck screaming figures from rooftops, and along the sides of the tallest skyscrapers, hairless gray-skinned creatures crawled up and down, fast as field mice defying gravity. A group of black-winged flying beasts were harnessed together to pull a carriage of some sort. Ruth almost threw up when she saw the faces of the things within the carriage. From high ledges, figures jumped, most to be captured in the claws or beaks of Griffins before they hit the ground, and from windows she thought she saw smaller figures— *babies? children?*—being cast out to take a similar plunge.

And when she zoomed closer to a street—

"My God . . ."

She saw the masses of the Damned.

Ruth collapsed against the boat's edge.

"See what I mean?" Alexander said. "Hell is a city now, Ruth. That's what it's evolved into since Lucifer was tossed out of Heaven. But it's a city that's as big as a continent. It's a city that never ends."

Ruth sat in glum shock. She looked over the bow and momentarily dipped her hand into the sea.

"This really is blood, isn't it?" her voice cracked.

Alexander nodded.

"And I really have been condemned to Hell, haven't I?"

"Yes."

She began to cry.

"You need to prepare yourself, Ruth," the priest said in a fragile tone. The wind sifted through his hair as the red sky continued to bristle. "Forget about logic, common sense, and every basic speck of knowledge you ever learned on earth. In Hell, two plus two doesn't equal four, it equals six. In the Living World, there's science. Here there's sorcery and black magic. A blessing is now a curse, love is now hate, and white is black."

Ruth listened, eyes wide, mouth open.

"Knowledge is disinformation. Democracy is *Demonoc-racy*, and death is life." He blinked. "Everything's opposite here."

Chapter Three

(I)

"You passed out, honey." A hand was patting her face, then a cool damp rag covered her brow.

Venetia's eyes opened and eventually the two blurred forms sharpened into the faces of her mother and father.

"There she is," Richard Barlow said, smiling.

A third face came into view, back a few feet. It was the scroungy kid at the register. "Everything all right? Want me to call an ambulance?"

The question jerked Venetia out of her drowse. "No, no, I'm all right. . . ."

"Are you positive?" her mother asked.

Her father: "And what happened?"

"Like I was saying before, I didn't get much sleep last night." She leaned up in the big SUV's backseat. "I probably haven't been eating enough either. Been studying a lot."

"Of course, dear." Maxine's voice offered motherly comfort. She turned to her husband. "Richard, where's that piece of paper with the map? I think Father Driscoll's cell phone number is on it. We'll have to call and tell him Venetia can't make it today."

More alarm. Venetia straightened herself. "I'm perfectly fine, Mom. I can't miss this opportunity at the prior house. It's a lot of extra credits."

Her mother looked hesitant. "Well, if you're sure."

"Oh, she's okay." Her father seemed convinced now. "Our daughter's got a lot of spunk. But let me ask you something, honey. I thought I heard talking in that bathroom. There wasn't someone else in there with you, was there?"

She didn't allow herself to reflect. "No, Dad, just me. I may have muttered something to myself when I started to feel dizzy. . . ." A stab of guilt then, but only a tiny one. She didn't like to lie to her parents, but what could she say?

"All right, then. It's off to the prior house. Buckle up!"

A minute later they were back on the road. Maxine handed Venetia a cup of sweet coffee, which perked her up after only a few sips. The rushing scenery of another winding road through forest-backed grasslands invited her to reflect.

What did *happen in there?*

The voice, of course. Grating, tinny, like someone talking over a very old radio. And she remembered what it had said: *Everything's opposite here.* But she had to wonder *where.* And: *In the name of God on High, be careful at the—*

Be careful at the *what?*

Why did she have the dreadful impression that the voice meant to say, *Be careful at the prior house?*

"It's just so wonderful that Father Driscoll is back," Maxine remarked. "He's so—"

"Handsome," Richard repeated. "And kind of dashing. You already told us, dear."

"I only meant that he's barely changed at all in the fifteen years that he's been away."

"Neither have your boobs. That's what's worrying me. Once he gets a load of your milk wagons, he'll probably leave the priesthood and run off with you. Then I'd have to eat Chef Boyardee every night."

"Where has Father Driscoll been all these years?" Venetia broke in, desperately trying to change subjects.

"I'm not sure," Maxine replied. "He said that he took some classes at the Vatican for a year or two, but he never mentioned if he got his own parish after that."

"He's probably into clerical education," Venetia said. "Some priests never become parishional. This job at the prior house is a good clue."

"Sounds more like janitorial duty in the name of the church," her father said. "You'll probably be taking out more garbage cans than studying"

Maxine had to contribute: "And you could perform a *welcome* duty for the church yourself, Richard. By getting *into* one of those garbage cans."

"Do you two always have to cut each other down?" Venetia complained.

Her father looked back and winked. "It's just your mother's way of letting me know she's hot to trot."

"Oh, is *that* what it is?" Maxine said, but she unconsciously pulled at the V of her blouse. Her bosom jiggled as a result.

"Careful with those, dear. I'm driving, remember? If you keep distracting me like that, I might have to pull over, and poor Venetia'll have to sit in the Caddy by herself while you and I disappear into the woods for a half hour."

"Really, Richard. A half hour? I'll give your virility a break and refrain from further comment."

This was driving Venetia nuts. "Dad, are we going to be there soon? Please say yes."

"Yes." Richard pointed to the right.

An ornamented wooden sign with gothic letters read: ST. JOHN'S PRIOR HOUSE—EST. 1965. NO TRESPASSING - APPOINTMENT ONLY.

Thank God! Venetia thought.

"And getting back to what your mother was saying," Richard continued with a sly grin, "she wasn't complaining about my virility a couple Fridays ago. I forgot to close the bedroom window, and the next day the neighbors asked me what all that noise was about—"

Maxine put a hand over his mouth, then looked back at Venetia. "Your father gets this way every now and then, honey. You know. Like a cow that needs to be milked?"

"Mom, please, I can't handle that image. . . ."

Then her mother lowered her voice to a quick whisper. "But I'll ball his brains out tonight. That'll keep him simmered down for a while."

"Mom! Please!" Then Venetia looked out the windshield and saw the prior house loom into view.

Richard pulled around a circular drive surrounded by grievously untrimmed hedges. They all stared at the building.

"Well, there it is," Richard said breaking the silence. "I must say, it's . . ."

"It's . . . well . . ." Maxine hesitated.

"It's the dullest, most lackluster looking church building I've ever seen," Venetia ventured.

"Took the words right out of my mouth," her father remarked.

What a letdown. Venetia scrutinized the long two-story edifice. She'd been expecting an Edwardian masterpiece with gables, Doric columns, and intricate cornice-work. *This is the work of the Vatican's master builder of the twentieth century?* "You know what it looks like?" she considered. "An old English hospital from the twenties."

"Yeah, only duller," her father added.

"I thought it was designed by someone important in the Vatican," Maxine posed. "I remember Father Driscoll mentioning something like that."

Venetia grabbed her purse and laptop case. "It was, the Pope's favorite modern architect, a man named Amano Tessorio. For decades he built the most spectacular churches, convents, and monasteries all over the world."

"I hope he didn't get paid much for this one," Richard said, drawing on his unlit pipe.

"Tessorio was a Vatican-schooled priest," Venetia said. "He got the same paycheck as all priests—a couple hundred dollars a month. God's work isn't supposed to be a big payday. But Tessorio was quite famous in his time."

The three of them got out and stared some more at the unremarkable structure: simple brick and cement outer walls interspersed by side-sliding windows, and it was topped by a low-peaked roof with standard shingles. Indeed, the place more resembled an old school or institution whose designers either lacked any architectural creativity or were more concerned with function than appearance.

Maxine perked up, pointing to a pair of steel double doors more suited for an urban high school. "Here he comes!"

Venetia looked past several other parked cars, including a shiny black Mercedes. A man nearly six feet tall in traditional black slacks, black shirt, and a Roman collar approached them. He had intense blue eyes, and could've been a Marine with his blond buzz cut. *Mom's right. He is handsome.* She sensed a very serious demeanor behind an expression that wasn't quite a smile . . . which Venetia also found weirdly alluring.

"Mr. and Mrs. Barlow, it's wonderful to see you again," he said, and then there was an exchange of pleasantries. The blue eyes drilled into Venetia, "And you, young lady . . . sorry to sound clichéd but the last time I saw you, you were a yard high."

"Hi, Father." She shook his hand, which she found strong and callused. "I'm sorry I don't remember you."

"Well, maybe you will after a couple of days here." The comment seemed cryptic. "Back then, I wasn't much older than you are now. And, a four-point-oh at Catholic U? I graduated there myself."

"Really? I didn't know that."

"And I'll admit, I'm a bit jealous."

Jealous? "Why's that Father?"

"I barely got out of there with a three-point-five." His gaze leveled, and again he seemed to be *trying* to smile while never really doing it. "I only hope that a superior student like yourself won't be too disappointed when she realizes the true nature of this field study option. There won't be a lot of academics going on here, but we *will* be working our behinds off: painting, wallpapering, and a lot of yard work."

"That's fine with me, Father. I could use a break from the books anyway, and if God wants a paint roller in my hand instead of a midterm, then so be it."

"Excellent response." The priest turned and cast a quick glance at the building. "As you can all see, the prior house won't win any awards for beauty in architecture but now that I think of it, the Church might've been better off choosing utilitarian designs like this all along."

"What do you mean, Father?" Maxine asked.

"Think of all the money the Vatican would've saved over the last two thousand years. God doesn't care if His house is ugly as long as it works. But just for formality's sake, we'll have it looking a little *less* ugly before reopening."

"How long has it been closed?" Venetia wondered.

"Well, it's never been *totally* closed. For decades it's served a variety of uses for the Church: book repository, warehouse, and sometimes parish priests would board here while their own churches were refurbished. There was a small maintenance staff the whole time, but they all retired recently. So did the previous prior."

Venetia didn't want to sound nosy but she *was* suddenly curious about this man. "What were your duties before you received this assignment?"

"A lot of teaching, plus some counseling," the priest responded. His gaze flicked up when a seagull sailed by. "Rome, France, India, Brazil, and all around the U.S. The church has given me a lot of opportunities to travel. But now the diocese wants me to reopen this place, so here I am. It'll be different, that's for sure. I only wish I'd been able to recruit more girls like you."

"Like me, Father?"

"Students of theology. It's my favorite subject. I put fliers out at the theology departments of some of the nearby colleges but no one replied. I was lucky enough to run into your parents at my old church in Dover, and when they told me that you were at Catholic U, I thought it couldn't hurt to ask you to apply."

Suddenly Venetia became self-conscious. *I hope I don't look too ragged from lack of sleep.* She felt driven to make a good first impression. "I just want you to know that I'm very grateful, Father, for giving me this opportunity."

"Don't thank me yet." He turned with that same failed smile. "Thank me at the end of the summer"—he swept his hands across the cul-de-sac's unkempt excuses for flowerbeds—"when we've gotten all these weeds pulled. Sounds like fun, huh?"

"At least it's a bit more interesting on the inside," Driscoll said once they entered. "A bit more interesting and a bit more dirty."

Venetia stood just inside the doorway, her bags tugging at her arms. The inside floor layout was an immense atrium surrounded by four walls of offices and libraries on the first floor and presumably living quarters on the second. Two drab stairwells on either side led upstairs, and a stair-hall wrapped around the atrium as well. A variety of throw rugs, some quite large, covered the floor, on which couches, arm chairs, and writing tables were arranged. In between each lower-level office door stood rows of book shelves festooned by cobwebs.

"Wow," Venetia said. "This is going to be a big cleaning job."

"Sure is. But at least the upstairs is already spic 'n span and ready for painting."

"I noticed cars parked outside. How many others will be on the job?"

"Three others—you'll be meeting them soon."

Three others? she thought with little enthusiasm. *That's not much of a work crew for this big dirty dump.*

"I see you've brought your laptop," he added. "If we're lucky enough to find a working phone line, maybe you could e-mail some of your fellow students at the university. We can use all the help we can get, and it's an easy three credit hours."

Easy? She doubted it. And she doubted that any of her friends at school would want to abandon their summer for such a job.

"While I'm thinking of it . . ."—the tall priest handed her a key on a cord—"wear this at all times, and any time you exit the building lock the door behind you."

Venetia put the key around her neck. *Is he afraid of burglars?*

"This area's never been known for much crime," Driscoll elaborated, "but there are a lot of valuable books in here, some quite old." He briefly showed her the front doors. "First thing we did was put high-quality locks on all the exit doors, and alarm tape on the windows."

It seemed undue paranoia to Venetia. *This is New Hampshire farmland, not downtown DC.* "I suppose in this day and age we can never be too security-conscious."

"Exactly," he said, and led her on.

Before her parents left, her mother had made her promise to call every night on her cell phone. Venetia wondered what her parents' reaction would be if they'd seen the *inside* of the place. But she truly believed that things happened for a reason, and that God was often behind those reasons. *God must really want me to get dirty,* she mused.

"I can guess what you're thinking, Venetia."

"I'm sorry, Father?"

"You're thinking that you've walked into a real clunker of a job. I can see it on your face."

Venetia laughed. "It's nothing like that. I'm just a little shocked. It's not what I expected from a Tessorio building."

"So you're familiar with his work?"

"I have several picture books of his monasteries and convents—"

"They're magnificent, aren't they?"

"Yes."

"And this place . . . isn't."

She giggled. "No, it isn't. Tessorio was known for fancy Gothic Revival and Edwardian designs, right?"

"Pretty much." Driscoll frowned, wiping his brow with

a handkerchief. "And I'm afraid what he *wasn't* known for was air-conditioning."

Venetia only noticed that now. It was very hot inside. More self-consciousness assailed her. *Am I sweating? Are my underarms damp?* "At least the nights are usually cool. They don't even have window units here?"

"Nope. The boiler's fine for heat in the winter. My boss at the diocese says he's going to have some fans sent out, but who knows when that will happen. We have a lot of hot work waiting for us, I'm afraid."

Venetia didn't mind. As a child she'd always looked forward to the brief New Hampshire summers; warm weather always made her feel purged. "So the prior house was built in 1965? I think that's what the sign said on the main road."

Driscoll led her around the atrium's outer skirt, passing bookcase after dust-filmed bookcase. "That's right. It only took eight months to build, even as big as it is. The atrium alone is almost five thousand square feet."

Venetia gazed across the great expanse. There were probably several dozen couches and chairs set out, some covered with sheets, some not. "Pretty simple design. It's just not what I expected. I went to services once at the Convent of Regina Pacis just before it closed, and I've visited the Gomang Monastery in Nashua several times— oh, and also the abbey at Saint Anselm College. They're all beautiful pieces of architecture."

"This isn't supposed to be anything more than a place for priests to decompress. The burnout rate's pretty high."

"I know. I remember reading about it in the *Catholic Standard*. High suicide rate, too, I think."

Some of the tile flooring could be seen between the throw rugs; the dust was so thick, Driscoll's shoes left footprints. "The older a priest gets—and the more of his life he gives to God—the more he becomes subject to basic human frailties. Self-doubt, depression, wavering faith. The prior house isn't intended to be a home for sick or elderly priests—it's just sort of a rest stop, in between jobs."

He pointed to all the chairs and couches filling the atrium. "That's what all that's for. Our guys can come here and just sit around, read, meditate."

The way Driscoll talked seemed to humanize the sterile exterior—referring to priests as "our guys," for instance. The gesture reminded Venetia of his smile—something that struggled to be seen.

Statues and busts on pedestals stood intermittently between the bookcases, set back in tall sconces. Venetia examined each one as they walked, and found that she recognized most before having to look at the nameplates. Thomas Merton, Aquinas, Soren Kierkegaard, St. Augustine . . .

"Here's one of my favorites," Father Driscoll said, touching a granite bust of St. Ignatius of Antioch. "How can anyone not admire him, even atheists?"

"The earliest progressive Christian philosopher," said Venetia. "I guess you mean you admire his distinction of the relationship between body and soul, and being the first Christian writer to use the name 'Catholic?'"

"I forgot about *that* part," Driscoll admitted.

Venetia found the faux pas amusing. "What then?"

"His martyrdom. You can't deny the devotion of a man who smiles as his body is being ravaged by dogs."

"The same for St. Stephen," Venetia said as they moved to the next bust. "The first Christian martyr."

The next sconce stood vacant.

"Who's supposed to be here?" she asked.

Driscoll wiped off the dust-smudged plaque: FR. AMANO TESSORIO.

"The statue was never delivered, believe it or not, but Tessorio built this recess and even mounted the nameplate when the prior house was completed. He had a . . . lofty ego, I guess you could say."

Venetia stalled over the comment.

"St. John's Priory was Tessorio's last assignment before the Vatican discharged him," Driscoll added in a manner that seemed hesitant.

"I had no idea he was *discharged*. What was the reason?"

"Well, the Catholic record says he was discharged due to poor health."

What's he hedging? Venetia wondered. "It's curious how you phrased that, Father. It implies that poor health wasn't the real reason he was dismissed."

Driscoll nodded through an awkward pause. "The real reason is he was caught attending a Black Mass in 1966 or so. He was charged with heresy, banished from the Church, and died of late-stage syphilis several years later."

Venetia snapped her gaze from the empty recess to the priest. "You're kidding me."

Did the priest snort a chuckle? "The details may be exaggerated but it's essentially true. For years, Tessorio was leading a very blasphemous double life."

Venetia was waylaid. "You're telling me that the Vatican's official architect was a Satanist?"

Driscoll led her away from the sconce, past more busts and statues. "That's putting it a bit harshly. Sometimes when priests get old, they become cynical and lose faith. They believe that celibacy to God caused them to miss out on aspects of their humanity. So they rebel. I don't know that he was a bonafide Satanist, and I'm not even certain that there is such a thing. It was probably a case of a bored, bitter old man who joined a devil club to put some spice in his last years."

"How . . . bizarre."

The priest unconsciously raised a finger. "But there's no real telling how long Tessorio was secretly participating in such things."

Venetia thought further. *No telling how long? A secret double life?* "So it might not have just been toward the end of his life? He could have been doing things like that for—"

"For decades, sure. Who knows? But it hardly matters."

She knew he was right but she was still intrigued. Venetia followed Father Driscoll on his quick tour of the prior house, and as her eyes took in the building's features she couldn't quell the macabre fascination.

The house I'm walking through now was built by a Satanist. . . .

(II)

"You fuckin' gotta be motherfucking shitting me, man," Ruth grumbled.

She sat huddled next to Father Alexander's torso. The small boat rose on each swell of blood. Everywhere she looked, she saw red: the sea, the sky. She was snow-blind by blood.

"You really have terrible language, Ruth, not that I'm one to talk," the priest remarked.

Ruth barely heard him. "Aw, fuck it. I know. I've always said the F word. Can't fucking help it."

"Sure you can. I was the same way. Even when I was a priest I used profane language, and that's just not cool for a priest but I did it anyway. It's actually kind of funny: Several times I got reprimanded by monsignors for cussing. I got reassigned from cushy counseling posts in nice cities, got transferred, got kicked out of quality clerical jobs—all for cussing. I guess I was trying to be a 'hip' priest, I was trying to be real-world, but it was all a sham. Foul language defames God—that's why we shouldn't use it. Foul language separates us from Grace."

"Who's Grace? Some chick you had the hots for?"

"Never mind . . ."

He's giving me shit about cussing. I'm in fucking Hell . . . It was ridiculous. She squinted hard, shielding her eyes from the scarlet glare.

More quiet words came. "I have a lot to tell you. Might as well start now. I'll try not to overwhelm you."

"I'm already fuckin' overwhelmed."

The boat swayed on another swell of blood. The torso turned his head to her. "Something's in the works, Ruth—that's the best way to look at it. And we need your help."

"We?"

"I told you earlier, I have an intelligence source that's very powerful. And don't worry, you're not expected to work for free. There's something in this for both of us."

"What's in it for you?" she said sarcastically. "New arms and legs, I hope."

"Not quite. But if we succeed, my sentence to Purgatory gets revoked, and I'll be transferred to Heaven."

"Oh yeah? And what's in it for me?"

"You own Condemnation to Hell gets commuted to a Condemnation to Purgatory."

Her eyes snapped to him. "Purgatory's, like, not Heaven but—"

"But a lot better than this, trust me."

Her trashy yet pretty face beamed. "That fuckin' rocks, man! I'm in!"

"I mean, well," he stumbled on something. "There's a little bit of a catch."

Ruth's happy smile turned to a knife-sharp frown. "There always fuckin' is."

"Yes, you get to go to Purgatory but—"

"But what!" she yelled.

"But you have to wait a thousand years first. . . ."

Ruth wanted to dump the human torso overboard. "A thousand fuckin' years!"

"It's not that bad, Ruth, considering the alternative," he added hastily.

"And how long do *you* have to wait to get transferred to Heaven?"

"Well, what I mean is, if you and I succeed with this mission, I get commuted to Heaven . . . instantly."

"Oh, that's real fair!" Ruth started to get up. "I'm pushing your ass overboard, you fucker! Fuck this shit! Spent my whole life on earth getting shit on by men, and now I'm still getting shit on! By *you!*"

"Ruth! Listen to what you're saying! Don't blow your only chance to ever get out of here. You've been offered something that no one else ever gets down here: hope."

That prospect simmered her down. "A square deal—no bullshit, no snow jobs?"

"A square deal, Ruth. And these folks *never* BS."

Ruth thought on that one. Maybe the reason she'd never been a good person was because she'd *never* gotten a square deal. *I guess it's better than a poke in the eye with a sharp stick*, she thought.

"We've quite a journey ahead of us. First and foremost, we'll have to be very careful," he said. "I wasn't and . . . well, you can see what happened to me."

Again, she looked at his chopped stumps. "What *did* happen to you?"

Something like a toad with leathery wings flapped overhead. "My source did foresee your arrival at the Sea of Cagliostro, but unfortunately she didn't foresee me being dismembered."

Ruth caught that. "She?"

The priest ignored the query. "It's not foolproof, not even with the most powerful Celestial Magic. There are pockets of Hex-Fluxes all over the Mephistopolis. It's like an electromagnetic field in the Living World that interferes with radio waves. These Hex-Flexes interfere with telepathic wavelengths. We have to take what we can get."

"You still didn't tell me what happened to your arms and legs!" she yelled.

"Sorry, I ramble sometimes. I'd been staking out an area on the mainland for several months—a place called Pogrom Park, as well as some other places. I was preparing for your arrival. But as my lousy luck would have it, I walked right into the middle of a Municipal Mutilation Zone and a Scyther Detachment got me. Remember, here everything is opposite. In the Living World, they have street cleaners to clear dirt and garbage from the roads, right? Well, here they have Mutilation Zones. Government agencies clean *people* from the streets. They butcher anything that moves, and it's legal."

Ruth stared at him.

"Ordinarily they shovel the corpses and body parts into wheeled hoppers when the exercise is over, then take it all to a District Pulping Station, but they made an exception for me."

"Why?" she asked, wide-eyed and in a very low voice.

"Because they saw my Roman collar. They knew I was a

priest, and seeing that I'm one of the Human Damned—
or so they thought—they knew that my Spirit Body
couldn't be killed by mere dismemberment. So they threw
me into the Sea of Cagliostro to further my torments."

The boat rocked. Ruth looked down in the blood . . . and
could swear she saw things swimming in the red murk.

"It's best not to look, Ruth," Alexander advised.
"There's stuff down there that you don't want to see.
Fifty-foot lampreys, Phleboto-Fish, marine Gigapedes . . .
Just . . . don't look."

Ruth shuddered and shot her gaze away.

"There's what I want you to look at instead." He mistakenly raised his stump as if to point off the port side.
"We're closer now. Put on the Abyss-Eye and look toward
the shore till you see the port."

Ruth brought the hideous thing to her eye again and
looked.

She stared in breathless silence as she beheld a strange
cityscape rimming the edge of the sea. Before it, there
were myriad docks full of boats in slips, and larger ships
moored there. In the background, things like condo buildings rose, but they looked . . .

"What *is* that place?"

"It's called the Port of the Vulgaressa, the priciest sector
of the Rot-Port District. See all those condos? If you
thought there was a real estate boom in Florida, that's
nothing compared to this place. Rot-Port is the most expensive bloodfront property in all of Hell."

Ruth zoomed the Eye. The high balconied condos
seemed . . . fuzzy in some way. No clean edges or lines
like normal buildings.

"The place looks really fucked-up," she articulated as best
she could. "Like the whole town is made of something . . .
spongy."

"The town is made of rot, Ruth," the priest clarified.
"That's why they call it Rot-Port. Every primary district
has something unique about it, to distinguish it from
the others. You know. Maryland's the Crab State, New

Jersey's the Garden State. Same thing here. Rot-Port's made of all manner of rot, every square inch of it. Mold, fungus, putrefaction, slime, muck, et cetera. It's all cultured onto every beam, block, and plank in the District."

Ruth slowly lowered the visual aid. "I'd rather drown in this—this . . . sea of fuckin' *blood* than go to that town!"

Alexander gave a patient nod. "But, see, you *can't* drown, Ruth. You *can't* die. You need to remember *everything* I tell you. Your soul will continue to live in Hell—it can *never* die. And as for your Spirit Body, it can cease to function but only if it's damaged to the point of total destruction. Then your soul moves on to something else."

Ruth's face fell into her hands again. "Fuck that shit, man!"

"It's our mission, Ruth. And it all starts by getting ourselves to Rot-Port."

Ruth rocked back and forth in silence.

"Your clothes are the first matter," the priest said next.

Teary-eyed, Ruth looked down at herself. *What the fuck is he talking about now? My clothes?* Her physique remained garbed in the last apparel she remembered putting on: the tight pink YUCK FOO T-shirt, thread-rimmed cutoff jeans that weren't much bigger than bikini bottoms, and pink flip-flops. "There's nothing wrong with my clothes. I look good, don't I?"

"You actually look great, Ruth . . . in a trashy kind of way."

"Thanks a fuck of a lot, you fuck."

Alexander smiled at the profanity. "What I mean is your body will work to our advantage. And as for your clothes, when you come here you only arrive with what you're wearing, along with any adornments, such as jewelry, tattoos . . . breast implants . . ." Alexander winked.

Ruth's hands defiantly rose to her 38D mammarian carriage. "Fuck you! These are real."

Alexander tsked. "Ruth, it's pointless to lie to me. Why bother? Abandon your vanity—look what it did for Lucifer. I know everything pertinent about you, via my intelligence source."

"Fuck your intelligence source," she muttered, disgusted.

"For instance, I happen to know that you received those implants absolutely free: gratis from a plastic surgeon you were shacking up with in Miami. Ultimately my point is, your trashy good looks are something we can exploit, because the Mephistopolis is quite a trashy city. But your current wardrobe—at the right time and place—will have to go."

"I don't know what the fuck—"

"Just listen." The priest staved a burst of impatience. "We have to get busy. We'll be at the port soon. What you have to do right now is search those two bodies at the front of the boat. Check them for implements of value."

Ruth's weepy stare moved forward, to the two corpses that shared the skiff. "What the hell are they? They don't even look Human."

"They're not. They're Demon Conscripts from the Satanic Naval Infantry. Sort of like the Marine corps but in Hell. By the looks of them, they're probably the *Pudendae Grosse* species, and they're tough customers. The name on this life boat says S.S. *Nefarious*, and that makes sense because I heard on the news recently that the *Nefarious* sank in an accident. It was one of the biggest prison frigates in the navy."

"How did it sink?" Ruth asked, hoping curiosity would cauterize some of the lingering horror.

"A thing called a Gorge-Worm capsized it."

"How can a *worm* sink a *ship?*"

"These worms are a mile long. They'll wrap around a ship and turn it over, then suck all the Demons and Humans into their feeding gills."

"Fuck!" Ruth's not-so-calculative brain whirred. "Then one of them might get us!"

"No, this skiff's too small, they only pursue big prey." The priest's eyes gestured to the corpses in the boat. "But if you don't get *those* things off the skiff right now, the scent of their decay might attract a Griffin or Dentata-Vulture. We don't want to have to deal with *that*. Now get over to those Conscripts. Get their belts. We'll need them."

"Why do I have to do it?" Ruth screamed.

"Because I've got no arms or legs!" the priest snapped back. "Hurry! Time's wasting!"

Ruth winced as she kneed her way to the bodies. Their ridged faces were running with slime; worms milled in empty eye sockets. She held her breath against the stench, then slipped off their belts. Two belts were ringed with supply cases and tools; a third had a holster housing a crude pistol.

"Better than nothing. A sulphur flintlock. That guy must've been an officer. The other one's probably a deckhand. Now check their pockets for money."

Ruth was revolted. "I'm not putting my hands in dead guys' pockets!"

"Not dead *guys*, Ruth. Dead *Demons*."

"That makes it better?"

"They'll have money. Get it."

Pus glimmered on the corpses' faces. "I-I . . . can't!"

Alexander shot her a chiding scowl. "You've picked pockets before, Ruth. You'd rip off johns all the time when you were turning tricks, and whenever those scumbag boyfriends of yours would mug some innocent guy—or even kill him—you'd be the one to go through their pockets."

"That sucks that you know shit about me! You're trying to make me feel bad."

"You *should* feel bad, Ruth, 'cos you were a pretty bad person. But now you've been given the chance to redeem a little bit of yourself . . . *so do it!*"

At last, the former grifter, drughead, sexpot, and party animal from Collier County, Florida, emboldened herself. She slithered her fingers into the rot-damp sailors' pants. She pulled several bills and coins from each. "Shit. That's all they had on them."

"Every little bit helps."

After a moment's rest, she was able to contemplate. Three belts, an old gun, and a couple of dollars were all the reward she'd received for rooting through the clothes of dead monsters. "That gun looks like a piece of shit," she snapped.

"It is, but it'll still kill a Demon or Usher."

"And what do we need belts for? I just had to put my hands on *Demons*. For a couple of lousy belts?"

"They're actually high-quality belts, Ruth. They're made from Lipo-Cow hide. And to answer your question, you'll wear the gun belt yourself. With the other two, you'll make a harness to carry me on your back."

Ruth smirked. "Can't fuckin' wait to carry a torso priest on my back like a fuckin' knapsack while we're waltzing through Rot-City."

"Rot-Port, Ruth. And it's coming up."

Ruth's eyes held fast to the approaching coast: the noxious port-city with its angles and lines all rounded off by spongy softness.

She could already smell it. . . .

"Now push those bodies overboard—"

"Stop ordering me around!" she shrieked.

The priest was getting fed up with her testiness. "Just do it! You're acting like a kid!"

A square deal, she reminded herself, and chewed her collagen-implanted lower lip. *Something in it for me . . .*

She flipped the detestable Demon-bodies over the side with a *splash!*

"Good girl!" Alexander rejoiced.

Then she threw-up over the side as well.

And the two of them sat in silence as the tiny boat rocked and bobbed toward Rot-Port. . . .

Chapter Four

(I)

"I'm very pleased to meet you, Ms. Barlow," the tall woman said, looking down. She spoke in a quiet yet firm tone.

"It's nice to meet you, too, Mrs. Newlwyn," Venetia said, momentarily taken aback by the woman's height, which was close to six feet. "And please, call me Venetia."

"Mrs. Newlwyn is the priory's new official house-keeper," Father Driscoll said.

After taking Venetia on the perfunctory look around, the blond priest had brought her to the spacious kitchen—which was like something one would find in a grade school—to begin the introductions.

Venetia could tell by Mrs. Newlwyn's narrowed eyes and curt, tight smile that she was one to take all church matters very seriously. Black hair dusted with gray was pulled back by a collar-length clip; she was likely in her early fifties, and due to her height and excellent physical condition, she reminded Venetia of some of the somber statues they'd just seen in the atrium. She wore jeans splotched with paint, and an equally splotched blouse hung loose around an ample bosom.

She talked while mixing something in a bowl: "I admire the zeal of your youth very much," the woman said. "I understand you're going to become a nun? In my younger days I wanted that as well, but I never quite got there. I'm afraid that motherhood won out in the end."

Venetia noticed there was no wedding ring on Mrs. Newlwyn's hand, just a cross about her neck, along with a key like Venetia's. "Actually I'm considering the vocation, but I'm not sure yet."

"You might consider waiting a while on that decision," Driscoll said, but it was strange the way he'd slipped in the remark while looking at a clipboard he'd picked up from the counter.

Before Venetia could comment further, though, Mrs. Newlwyn turned as a younger woman stepped through the entry. "And this is my daughter, Betta. Betta, this is Venetia Barlow. She's come all the way from Washington, DC, to assist us in the prior house."

Betta seemed sheepish: dark, wan eyes, hair pulled back like her mother's, and dressed similarly in scruffy jeans and blouse. She even had a few dots of wall paint on her cheek. Venetia shook her hand and noticed a timid smile. *Is she nervous meeting me?* Venetia wondered. She guessed Betta to be about thirty; she was much more petitely built than her mother, small-breasted and reedy, and stood six inches shorter. "Nice to meet you, Betta. Are you all ready for this big cleanup operation? I'm sure not."

Driscoll gave a dry chuckle.

Venetia expected an inconsequential response but then Mrs. Newlwyn explained, "Betta doesn't have the power of speech, I'm afraid, but she can hear fine. And yes, we're both quite ready for the tasks ahead—we're looking forward to them. Aren't we, Betta?"

The younger woman nodded, smiling.

"We've already been working here for a while," Mrs. Newlwyn continued. "Make no mistake, it's dirty work, but it is gratifying in its own way."

Driscoll made a joke. "We'll see how gratified Mrs.

Newlwyn is in about a month, when we're all done spackling the downstairs. I think by then we'll all be really sick
of this place."

"Betta and I will never grow weary of the prior house,
Father," Mrs. Newlwyn said with confidence. Her eyes
seemed to gleam in their slits, a known assurance. "This
is our home now."

"In that case, what time will *home* be serving dinner?"

"Seven sharp."

The priest nudged Venetia. "I'm going to show Venetia
to her room. Oh, and have you seen Dan?"

Betta pointed upward, which Venetia presumed to
mean upstairs.

"Good. See you at dinner."

She followed Driscoll back to the atrium, toward a stark
stairwell. "These stairs look terrible, too, don't they?" he
commented. "It's like an old hospital or something."

"You're the one who said God doesn't care if His house
is ugly."

"It's a good thing . . ."

"Who's Dan?"

"He's the last member of our little cleaning detail. He's
a seminarian—you'll like him. He might give you some
ideas about cloistered life."

Venetia frowned as she followed the priest up the dull
carpeted stairs. "What did you mean earlier?"

"What? About spackling?" He sighed. "Have you seen
some of these walls?"

He's deflecting on purpose, she thought. *But why?* "No,
Father, not the spackle. Were you suggesting that I *not* become a nun?"

"Not at all." His shoes snapped on the hard stairs. "We
really will have to carpet these, don't you think?"

Infuriating! "Father Driscoll, what did you mean when
you said—"

"All right. I only meant that the decision to become a
nun is a very weighty one. Isn't it possible that you're
maybe just a teensy bit too young to make a decision like
that? You're only twenty."

"I'm twenty-one, and I haven't made the decision yet. I want to get my master's first."

"Good girl. Then maybe wait ten years before going to a convent."

This was weird. "Is that clerical advice, Father?"

"No. It's just a suggestion." On the landing Driscoll stopped, leaning again the stair-hall's bannister.

Only now did it occur to her that she'd lugged her suitcase all the way up by herself. Driscoll hadn't even thought to help her, yet she felt certain it was from no lack of manners. *He's just distracted. His thoughts seem like they're all over the place.*

Up here most of the bedroom doors were open, along with their windows. The cross-breeze refreshed Venetia from the stuffiness of the atrium.

But the priest was looking at her with some unease. "Are you a virgin?"

Venetia's mouth fell open. "Father Driscoll, I can't believe you asked me that."

He seemed unaware of the misstep. "I'm a priest, for God's sake."

"Still, this isn't exactly a confessional."

"Venetia, I'm only suggesting that you live some of your life first. You can be just as devoted a servant of God without being a nun. I've seen it too many times. Girls go to the convent full of idealism, then are miserable for the prime of their lives. It doesn't do God any good. Things are different now, and God knows that. Twenty-one is way too young to even be thinking about stuff like that."

"So that's it," she replied. "I'm a kid? I'm not capable of making a life decision?"

"Don't be defensive." Again, he almost smiled. Almost. "When you're a nun, they're going to send you to places like Calcutta, Sao Paulo, Africa—"

"And I'm ready. I don't think I'm being naive by wanting to serve God. Part of my job is getting my hands dirty."

Driscoll nodded dismissively. He was looking down the long, empty stair-hall when he answered, "Yeah, *real* dirty. You'll be dealing with catastrophic human tragedy, Venetia. You'll be dealing with HIV victims, the starving, the abused, children with cancer, babies with tapeworms."

"I'm ready," she repeated.

"You'll be dealing with people on the crap end of life . . . and the only reason I didn't say *shit* is . . . well, I'm a priest." He looked at her deadpan.

Venetia laughed. She was figuring him out now. "You're saying I have to live life before I can help others live theirs?"

"Exactly. Life and all its very *human* bells and whistles. Humanity can be very grotesque at times. How can you help an AIDS-infested Calcuttan prostitute when you've never even experienced human sexual response yourself?"

It was a good question, but she was baffled by what it might be leading to. "Maybe I have, Father."

"Oh, so you aren't a virgin . . . ?"

"I didn't say that—not exactly. But I don't know that it matters. St. Augustine wasn't a virgin, either. Statistically, most priests aren't—they had plenty of experience with 'human sexual response' before they made their vow of celibacy."

"I'm not arguing with you there."

Her confusion now began to fascinate her. *Is he telling me I need to know what sex is like in order to become a fully aware nun?* "You have a way of evading your point, Father. If you want to give me clerical counsel . . . then just say it."

"All right. Get involved with a guy. Have a boyfriend. Date. Do like that, like everyone else your age. Know what it's like to be in love—"

"I—" she tried to jump in.

"—and I don't mean just a love of God. Have some relationships. Be human. Know what it's like to have a relationship you're happy with, and know what it's like to have a relationship that fails. It's all part of being human, which is what you need to be before you go to Africa and watch a hundred people die in a diphtheria outbreak."

"I understand what you're saying, Father—at least I think I do," she told him.

"And no I'm not suggesting you go out and lose your virginity just so you know what it's like."

"Good," she said with a long sigh. "Because that's what I *thought* you were saying." She blinked. "So . . . what *are* you saying?"

"You can have a perfectly acceptable relationship in the eyes of God, Venetia. You can date, you can be in love, et cetera, with—how do I say this? Without having sex out of wedlock."

Now she wanted to laugh out loud. "Really? How?"

"With . . . difficulty."

Finally he cracked a smile. "All I'm saying, Venetia, is live some normal life before you become a bride of Christ, all right? At least think about it."

"I will," she said, unable to resist. She knew it was iffy judgment but she sensed the unlikely conversation had broken enough of formality's ice. "But what about you, Father? Don't *you* have to live some normal life before you can be a good priest?"

"Hey, I go to baseball games all the time."

"Come on, seriously. Have you had all those things? Before you joined up, were *you* ever in love? Have *you* ever just dated a woman? Have you been in normal, healthy relationships?"

He maintained the inscrutable smile, and simply shook his head no.

Regrets, she realized now. That's what Father Driscoll had been getting at. *Make the right decision so I won't have regrets later in life.* He'd put it more clearly earlier when he'd explained that the prior house was being reopened for priests on respite. *The older a priest gets—and the more of his life he gives to God—the more he becomes subject to basic human frailties. . . .*

But now she had to wonder. *Does he have such regrets?*

Driscoll took her to a room in the corner. "Here it is."

Sunlight filled the newly painted room. There was a metal-railed bed, a desk, several lamps—including a black and very ugly floor lamp—and a dresser. Nothing else.

"Sorry it's so . . . unadorned," he added.

"It's fine, Father." She set her bags down, then looked around. "Where's—"

"The bathroom?" He shrugged. "Out your door, hang a right. The women's and men's bath- and shower rooms are at the end of the stair-hall. Kind of like the college dorm, huh?"

"Sure." She didn't care, but it would've been nice to have a private bathroom. "So what's first on my list of duties, Father?"

"Nothing much." He kept looking at his watch, as if late for something. "Just take a closer look around, go outside and check out the grounds. Get yourself settled. If you have any time to spare before dinner, you can help tape up the downstairs windows so we can start painting trim. The really grueling work beings in the morning." He eyed her severe black dress and white blouse. "And wear old clothes. We'll all be making a mess of ourselves."

Damn. The Catholic schoolgirl–look had been a mistake. "Stupid me—the only clothes I brought are all pretty much identical to these. I do have some sneakers, though."

"Good. Wear 'em." Looking befuddled, he glanced at his watch again. "I wanted to introduce you to Dan but God knows where he's off to."

"I'm sure I'll run into him."

"See you at dinner, then," he said, backing out of the room. "And thanks again for helping us out here."

"My pleas—"

Father Driscoll whisked out the door. *He's an enigma, all right,* she concluded. Cold on the outside—the rigid Catholic cleric—but then stiflingly human on the inside. Was the man inside being trammeled by his vocation? Unpacking, she pondered their odd conversation. *I still can't believe he asked me if I was a virgin.* Venetia confessed her sins appropriately on a regular basis . . . to priests, just like him. So why did his query shock her? *I know I'm a virgin, at least Biblically.* Indeed, she'd never been with a man, and even after that one time—when she wasn't sure—a GYN exam verified that her virginity had remained intact. She knew the temptations in the world outside of her faith, and Driscoll's additional comments made her suspect that he was probably more naive about those things than she was. Suggesting that she pursue love relationships while potentially remaining platonic was tricky indeed.

But maybe he's got a point.

Maybe she really should live her life some more before stepping into the nunnery.

Other than in dreams, she'd had one orgasm in her life, and it remained a sensation she'd never forget. *That party* . . . Just a typical college mixer, and they were always on the tame side anyway. In a Catholic university? She'd been nineteen at the time, and decided to attend only to talk to people and blow off a little steam after acing a 400-level Latin exam. She couldn't blame alcohol because she didn't drink—ever—and at the party it had been diet sodas exclusively. She hadn't seen the couple on campus before, even though they'd claimed to be seniors—a lie, she found out later. As the party wound down, Venetia realized she'd been enjoying the conversation with them—the girl a shapely, well-tanned blonde, and the guy a broad-shouldered jock with a delicate smile. They'd been discussing Immanuel Kant's Eight-Ball Theory and whether or not his "Transcendental Doctrine of Method" had as much practicality for the twenty-first century as it had for the eighteenth. The conversation had been invigorating.

Until about 2 A.M.

That's when Venetia had begun to feel sick.

Her knees felt rubbery, and her thoughts seemed to swirl in her head. "I don't know what's wrong with me," she murmured, bracing herself against the wall. The blonde took her arm: "Post-exam fatigue, hon. We all get it. You cram for a week straight, take the test, then—pow—it hits you all at once."

The guy took her other arm. "We have to go now anyway, but we'll walk you back to your dorm."

They took her to a van instead. Venetia had passed out, and when she'd choppily regained consciousness, she found herself sprawled naked on an air mattress, while the equally naked blonde was performing cunnilingus on her. Though Venetia's brain remained in a half-stupor, her body felt gorged by excited blood, breasts heaving, nipples tingling. When she'd seized enough cognizance to look down, she saw her own hands clasped to the back of the blonde's head, as the most delicious sensations began to crest. "Please, please . . . ," she murmured, all the nerves in her groin squirming for some incomprehensible release. At the same time, the jocky guy found her nipples to suckle. He was shirtless but still had his pants on, and when he grabbed Venetia's listless hand, he put it right to his crotch. The swollen bulge throbbed but felt unyielding as the end of a broom. "That's great, baby," he whispered in a voice as sweet as his counterfeit smile. "Let me take it out for you. . . ." But at the same time the blonde's deft skills brought Venetia to a back-bowing crescendo. Her orgasm didn't merely occur, it detonated, and then every nerve in her body began to spasm in an unloading of pleasure that she could only describe as unearthly.

"It's our turn now, right, baby?" The blonde grinned up between her legs. "You've been double-teamed before, haven't you?"

Somehow the climax had purged whatever chemical it was that they'd put in her soda. When she looked aghast to the guy, he was taking off his jeans.

Venetia never uttered a sound. She was up in a whir, dredging her clothes off the van floor, tumbling out, and running away.

"Oh, come on, hon," one of them said. "It's all in fun. . . ."

She dressed herself as she ran, however clumsily, through the empty parking garage, which happened to be just a block away from the entrance to her campus. The last she ever heard from them was the chirp of tires when the van sped down the ramp.

To her disbelief, outrage never occurred to her. It was confusion. *Technically a date rape,* she knew, just one that hadn't progressed to completion. And she also knew this: *That sort of stuff happens every day, but it's a lot worse than what I got.* Instead of feeling traumatized, she thanked God that she'd wakened when she had, and she even prayed that her assailants would find grace someday.

It was confusion that wracked her most of all. The climax had boggled her entire psyche. Even as she walked humiliated and barefoot out of the empty garage, her nerves thrummed in the post-orgasm. She'd left her bra and panties in the van, which left the tight jeans to cosset her bare pubis, and the ironic St. Gregory T-shirt titillated her nipples back to being gorged. The confusion arrived when all of those pleasurable sensations collided with her guilt.

She'd waited until *after* her orgasm was over to bolt from the van.

Did I do that on purpose? she'd asked herself a million times since then. She'd never told the police because rape would've been all but impossible to demonstrate. Anyone could've slipped something into her drink, and with no penetration, no semen? *Not in this age of slickster lawyers,* she realized. Instead of the police station, she'd gone to the confession booth, where an overbearing priest had scolded her for going to "parties full of nonbelievers" but said that her tardiness in leaving the van had been innate, not premeditated. "In the eyes of God, my child, you are still pristine," he'd said.

That's what Venetia wanted to be, but now, as she stood in her sterile bedroom at a dust-filled prior house, she admitted it. *I did, damn it. I waited on purpose . . . because I wanted to come.*

Yet she had been drugged—there was no doubt. Roofies, chloral hydrate, or whatever—it scarcely mattered. Such drugs affected judgment and artificially hindered inhibitions. Since she hadn't taken it willingly, she couldn't blame herself—*and neither can God . . .* In fact, it had been the only time in her life that she'd passed out.

Until today.

The spell at the convenience store. The voice, the rising pain in her head. *I collapsed. I was out cold. My father had to carry me out of the store.* She could still barely believe it. She felt fine now, but what might the cause have been, and the same bizarre voice that had ruptured her sleep last night?

A flashback? Was it possible for that sort of drug to produce temporary hallucinations that could recur? Venetia had never read anything indicative of that, but then she'd never researched it very much. *Don't worry about it. . . .*

She let the memory leave the room with her gaze. She was looking out the open window at scrubby grounds and tufts of unmowed onion grass that crawled up the hill to the woodline. She muttered, "What a mess. Can't decide what's uglier—the prior house or the land it's on." Just as ugly was the old redbrick supply shed or something way out in the back.

She brushed her hair out before the mirror and decided to leave the clip off. Seeing now how Mrs. Newlwyn and her daughter were dressed, Venetia's own appearance made her feel on the dorky side; with her blond hair unfettered she at least felt less parochial. When she left her room, a large, ornately framed oil painting stopped her halfway along the stair-hall.

The canvas was the largest of any upstairs, a yard by two feet. Dark colors and a sepulchral background seemed to thrust the painting's subject forward in a manner that seemed almost multidimensional: an elderly white-haired man, jowly, hard-eyed and scowling outward. He wore a cloaklike cope of some plush scarlet fabric, with a white liner. The black shirt beneath was buttoned to the top and joined by a Roman collar.

You have a good day, too, buddy, Venetia thought. Though the man in the portrait didn't exactly look hateful, his was clearly the most dour representation in the house. *Who is this crabby old guy?* At first she thought it might be the architect Amano Tessorio, but then doubted it when she recalled Driscoll's reason that the statue of the man was never even delivered. *Yeah, I guess it wouldn't be too cool to hang a painting of a heretic in a Catholic service building.*

A clattering startled her from downstairs, and a man's testy words: "Aw, damn it . . ."

Venetia looked over the stair-hall rail and saw a trim, thirtyish man in white painter's pants and a T-shirt dragging a cumbersome drop cloth across the atrium. He seemed to be walking on it more than moving it.

"Hi," she said.

He looked up as if distracted, short black hair and a face that was jovial and serious at the same time, like the class clown who always managed to get good grades in spite of his chicanery. He seemed to pause after focusing on her, and Venetia got the impression that he may have found her attractive.

"Dan, I presume? The seminarian?"

He stood erect, leaving the drop cloth. "Actually, I prefer *seminarist*, but you can just call me lackey, like Father Driscoll. Dan Holden, at your service, Miss—"

"Venetia Barlow."

"Oh, yeah," Dan said, enthused. "The girl from Catholic U?"

"That's me."

"Driscoll told me we'd have a real-live theologian on our crew."

"Well, you're a theologian, too," she reminded him.

"Not really. If you want to know the truth, the *real* reason I'm studying to become a priest is because, well"—he offered his paint-streaked arms—"it's easier than being a painter. Anyway, it's nice to meet you, Venetia."

"You need some help with that?"

"No thanks. We're going through these things like they're a dime a dozen. But you *can* help me set the table for dinner later if you want."

"I'd be happy to." For a moment, it was Venetia who paused at a distraction. *What a good looking guy. . . .* "Oh, but let me ask you something. Do you know who this portrait's of?" She thumbed behind her. "The scowling old man in the red cope?"

"That would be Prior Russell Whitewood. Looks about as friendly as a mad dog, huh?"

Venetia laughed. "At first I thought it might be Tesso-rio. . . ."

Dan grinned. "No, I'm afraid Whitewood's not *that* no-torious. Whitewood ran the prior house for twenty years."

"Is he the previous prior, who retired recently?"

The question caused Dan to arch a brow. "He's the previ-ous prior, all right. But what makes you think he retired?"

"Father Driscoll told me."

Another cocky grin. "Figures. He doesn't want you to get the heebie-jeebies."

"What?"

"Whitewood didn't retire. He . . ." Dan wiped at a paint splotch on his arm. "How do I say this without sounding overdramatic? Uh, Prior Whitewood disappeared without a trace, within a shroud of mystery."

Venetia squinted. "You're not serious?"

"Perfectly serious. Well . . . maybe the 'shroud of mys-tery' is an exaggeration, but, yeah, he walked off the job, disappeared. It was last spring."

Venetia subconsciously fiddled with a strand of hair. *Disappeared?* "Then why would Father Driscoll—"

"He told you Whitewood retired because it was easier," Dan said. "He didn't want to give you a reason to have second thoughts."

"About what?"

"About helping us get the prior house back in shape. He couldn't get any local theology students to join up for extra credits. Why? Because they were all in the area, so they knew what happened." Dan looked at her more in-tently. "Driscoll didn't tell you about the murders either, did he?"

"Murders?" she questioned with enough volume to cause an echo. "People were *murdered* here?"

"Two of them—two women. And one of them was a nun. They were murdered right here in this building last March. Whitewood ran off a few days later."

"So he was the perpetrator?"

"No, no, but he was a suspect until they found him. He

had an alibi, is what I heard. The cops say it was just a couple of creeps all crazy from drugs."

But Venetia's thoughts were blaring. This explained the new top-notch locks and Driscoll's emphasis on security. But why would he lie to her, and to her parents? "That's outrageous for him to conceal that."

"Well, it sounds more sensational than it actually was. People get killed in random murders every day. It just happened to be here on that day."

"I know that, Dan, but still . . ." She looked around and immediately felt a chill. "It's just quite a shock, you know? I haven't even been here two hours and now I'm being told that there were murders here."

Dan's grin turned sour. "And, if you're the squeamish type . . ."

"Yeah?"

"One of the victims was a devout churchgoer, a laywoman named Lottie Jessel. She was killed in the old accounting office, down here."

What was he working up to? "And the other victim? The nun?"

"Her name was Patricia Stevenson." Dan shrugged uncomfortably. "And she was murdered in your bedroom."

Chapter Five

(I)

The Angels, Boniface thought. *How I long to see them . . .
squirming . . . ready to burst. . . .*

He and High Priest Willirmoz had already descended
the narrow obsidian corridors deep below the Fortress, yet
even beneath all of this netherworldly rock, they could
hear the ceaseless screams resounding from his courtyard
above. The precursory executions had commenced—to
keep the air *saturated*—and they would transpire without
abatement until it was time.

"We're so deep now," the Exalted Duke whispered.
Was he afraid of his own catacombs? Of course not; he
was merely nervous, even in the cloak of all that hellish
power.

"Indeed, my lord. On the cusp of Lucifer's blessing . . .
Deep."

It was the esteemed She-Demon, Pasiphae, who led the
Duke and his High Priest through the twisting under-
crofts. Only she knew the way, which provided an effective
defense mechanism against intruders. In the torchlight,
Boniface let his gaze suck up the sight of her nude, jet-black

body—breasts jutting and perfect, legs, waist, and contours all bereft of error. Yet these features could've been composed of wet pitch, for it was not flesh that she was made of, but the ichor of Hell. The black body shined, gleaming.

Officially, Pashiphae was the Night-Mother and Queen of the Labyrinth. She commanded the Minotaurs and Minotauresses, who solely existed to guard these deep warrens.

She also commanded the lust of Voluptua, Boniface's favorite concubine. It enlivened the Exalted Duke to watch the two together on occasion.

At the last stone entry, Pasiphae turned with a black smile, and then she led them at last into the Lower Chancel.

"Why is it I can never comprehend the math?" Boniface complained, more to himself.

"It's the most complex black science, my lord," the charred Priest replied. "I have trouble myself. It involves manipulating the relationship between time and space—here, where there is no time, and in the Living World, which is calculable and finite. But take heart—thus far, no theorems yet devised by the Cultes des Pythagorae have ever been in error. We really must leave it to the Arithmetri."

The grinding of stone etched in their ears as the security wall rose.

"Ah. There they are."

The Angels. The booty of God's creation . . . blessedly tainted.

Boniface's eyes widened behind the salt-mask as he gazed into the Chancel's center. "Great Lord of Hell, they're so . . . *gravid.*"

"Yes, they are, my lord. They were all *very* fertile."

Squirming naked on the stone floor were the precious Angels, six of them, all female. Their wrists and ankles strained against the air, which was constantly charged by a Warding Spell that only a Class One Arch-Lock could relieve. Their wings lay paralyzed and collapsed behind their backs.

"It's still an unholy miracle that we were able to capture them in the first place," Boniface reflected.

"All by the grace of Satan, my lord."

"How long have they been here?"

"Just a day. But of course you're aware that the conditioning took a century."

Torchlight flashed on the inverted cross that was mounted atop Boniface's miter. "I'm *more* than aware of that, Priest. But how do we know they're sufficiently crazed?"

Willirmoz nodded to one of the helmed Conscripts, who in turn reached down through the invisible Warding Bonds, and loosened the gag.

The room shuddered. It was not a scream that leapt from the Angels' tumescent faces. It was a sound like a boulder grinding down a rocky hill. All the while, the Angels' sweat-glazed bodies heaved.

"Make it stop!" shouted the Duke.

The Conscript re-gagged the being and stepped back.

All of the Angels were from the arcane order known as the Caliginauts. It was this select order that frequently left Heaven to come here and wreak havoc. But Lucifer's personal diviners had predicted their arrival, and a brigade of Ushers and Bio-Wizards were ready for them. A trap was set in the Industrial Zone, and the most refined Obfuscation Spells had led all six Angels right into the clutches of the Constabulary, the Underworld's state security.

There, in the Constabulary's deepest dungeons, the Angels were tortured and tormented for the last hundred years.

Now, they were all insane.

And they were all something else, too.

Pregnant.

The final year of the torture regimen had included fastidious rape by all manner of Demons.

"Lucifer's dearest wish," Boniface whispered.

Willirmoz finished, "That they all be made pregnant with mongrels before we cough them onto the Earth."

All of the Angels were inexpressibly beautiful, breasts

sodden, limbs limber and toned beneath celestial skin. The Torturians had exacted psychic torment, not physical, so that the beings might retain every aspect of their physical beauty when they set foot in the Living World. Boniface watched in a dizzy glee as all six of their bloated bellies squirmed. *What wonders are waiting to be released from their soiled wombs . . . What monsters . . .*

"We've not long to wait now," Willirmoz said when he sensed his master's impatience.

"We must succeed."

"We will."

"The equivalent of two decades on Earth will transpire in one second?"

"Roughly, my lord."

Boniface's voice faltered. Was he having doubts, just as he had in 974 A.D. when he murdered Pope Benedict? "It's never been attempted before. How do we know it will work?"

"The most complex Necromancy has foreseen it, my wretched lord, just as *I* have foreseen it. The Involutionary Rites are now honed to flawlessness. When our hideous moon is in the proper hue, we will release the corrupted blood in your unholy courtyard, charge the Involution, and discorporate the Pith."

It was the Pith—the great stone slab on which the Angels shuddered—that Boniface's eyes held fast to now. The executions and sacrifices so far were already softening its tangibility. When he looked hard enough, he could see patches where the great black slab from the Valley of Death was growing translucent.

Willirmoz's crusted lips seemed to move around his words: "The most glorious day in Hell awaits . . . all by your hand, my lord."

I pray to Satan, Boniface silently implored.

Steadfast footsteps approached from behind. The Conscripts raised their hewers and dirks reflexively, but then lowered them when they saw the Sergeant at Arms enter the Chancel.

He did not dare look at Boniface but instead addressed the High Priest. "An urgent cipher from the Guild of Anthropomancers, sir."

Diviners of innards, Boniface thought with a pleasant twinge.

"Are you certain it's genuine?" the Priest demanded.

"It was delivered by Aldehzor himself, the Grand Messenger."

Willirmoz opened the corroded parchment, read the words, then stood silent.

"What, Priest!" Boniface roared.

"A potential problem has been predicted, my most revolting lord."

"Something threatens our endeavor?"

"No, my lord. I'd say not. A mere triviality."

Boniface had to rein himself; he wanted to strangle the High Priest then and there. "Explain, or die."

"Compose yourself," came Willirmoz's assured voice. "Just as our god has, the Morning Star for all these thousands of years—"

"What does the cipher say!"

"A brigade of Diviners has foreseen a minor matter, unholy one."

"That blasted Contumacy?"

"No, lord. Just a few petty insurgents. We'll simply heighten security just in case. And we'll notify the Grand Duchess Vulgaressa."

"That's already been done, great Priest," the Sergeant informed.

"See?" Willirmoz tried to assuage the Exalted Duke.

"The Vulgaressa is detestable and cunning," Boniface said.

"Yes, but she's loyal. She will heighten her own security, and I'm sure that will stem the paltry threat. The Diviners detected a few antithetic vibrations indicating the Rot-Port District. That's all it is, my lord."

Boniface looked back down to the imprisoned Angels. They continued to squirm in their mental horrors, perfect muscles straining under a sheen of Heavenly sweat.

"Rot-Port," the Duke intoned. "What of significance could possibly be brewing in *that* despicable pest-hole? The entire district is an open wound."

"We'll engage every Diviner, Clairvoyant, and Visionary in Hell to find out, my lord."

Willirmoz has never failed me, the Exalted Duke reminded himself. But still . . . "I'm feeling sick down here. Take me back to my fortress for some fetid air."

"Of course, my most unspeakable lord." Willirmoz took his master by the arm and followed Pasiphae back up to the catacombs.

With each step up Boniface fretted. *What in the name of Hell could threaten us from Rot-Port?*

(II)

"Rot-Port, huh?" Ruth griped, looking around with a wince. "Fuck. At least they picked the right name."

Docks spongy with colorful rot squished beneath her Day-Glo pink Teva flip-flops.

"It's just the first stop on our itinerary," Father Alexander said. "But every district in Hell is well-named: Tepesville, Osiris Heights, White Chapel—the Grand Duke there is a guy named Edward, Duke of Clarence. He's also known as Jack the Ripper. See, those who are born here—Demons, Trolls, Imps, et cetera—the Hellborn, have no creativity at all. The Fallen Angels themselves are pretty stupid in that department, too. I guess that's the deal when you don't have a soul. Everything here, since Lucifer's fall, every twisted science, every warped equation, all the architecture—every single thing that can be thought of as the product of innovation and creativity comes from the minds of the Human Damned. The Green River District, the De Rais Institutes of Occult Science, the Richard Speck Immemorial Medical Center. Hexegenic research, the Teratology Labs, where they use Human anatomical science to manufacture monsters, the Voudun Zombie Clinic—everything. It's all here because *Humans* are here. Even the restaurants have an interesting creative

flair that we can thank our Damned brothers and sisters
for. You'll see that one very soon."

Ruth huffed past a barrel full of clumps of mold and
slime. A sign read PLEASE RECYCLE YOUR ROT HERE. "What
do you mean I'll see that one very soon? Restaurants?"

"I'll tell you when we get there."

Ruth couldn't believe the visual spectacle as she
walked on. Rot as thick as sheets of ivy seemed to grow
over every wall of every building in the District, all burst-
ing with the most macabre colors. The road beneath her
feet, too, seemed to be tiled with different varieties of decomposed matter. *What the fuck is this?* she thought, stop-
ping at a shop. PICKMAN'S ART STUDIO, the rotten transom
read. Inside, a live female model—obviously a Ghoul—
posed for a man at an easel wearing disheveled 1920s
dress. The Ghoul was curvaceous and well-bosomed, but
emaciated nonetheless, meager strands of muscles taut
beneath gray, dust-dry skin. The artist was enthralled,
painting maniacally. When Ruth looked harder, she noticed the artist's palette contained not oil paint but daubs
of liquified rot.

"This place is really fucked-up," Ruth observed.

Of course, she couldn't see the priest frown behind
her. "Ruth, do you have any conceptions at all about
Grace?"

"Huh?"

"We should all pursue some aspect of Grace, shouldn't
we? Because it brings us closer to God. Just because your
sins have landed you in Hell doesn't mean you shouldn't
still seek Grace."

Ruth guessed her period was coming on; she was in a
bad mood. "I don't know what the fuck you're fucking
talking about."

"Your language! You have the foulest mouth of any
woman I've ever encountered."

Ruth had to keep reminding herself that Grace wasn't a
woman. She stopped and yelled over her shoulder at the
human knapsack. "Oh, yeah, listen to you! You throw

stones at me, and look at you! Priests aren't supposed to go to Hell, *or* Purgatory. But here you are, telling *me* I have no grace. Fuck that and fuck you."

"I'm just trying to give you some spiritual advice, Ruth. I am a priest, you know."

"Yeah, a fucked-up priest on some secret mission in Hell that you aren't telling me shit about." She stalked down the road that would lead them away from the piers. "You got no arms or legs, buddy. You *need* me."

"Yes, I do."

"So stop giving me shit! I feel bad enough as it is." She scanned down the road and could've thrown up at the sight of the place. "I wasn't that bad of a person. Sure, I partied a little, I did some bad things—"

Father Alexander laughed on her back.

"Oh, kiss my ass! Little Mr. Perfect back there." On the side of the rot-covered road, she spotted a canal and turned toward it. "Do I need this headache? Do I need you on my back for my first day in fucking *Hell?* I don't think so. I ought to throw you in this canal."

"Ruth." The priest's voice turned grim. "Don't get too close."

"Oh, scared I might do it, huh? Like on that boat?" But then she looked into the canal and saw that it was full of running waste, innards, body parts, and scum.

"The canals here exist to carry sewage into the Districts, not away from them. And they're full of Gore-Gators, E. Coli Snakes, and—"

Ruth screamed as something from the canal jumped out at her. The thing seemed half-invisible, only allowing a glimpse, but in that glimpse Ruth detected a chubby tubelike body ten feet long, two soft antennae, and a pulsating sucker mouth full of things like six-inch needles. She lurched back just in time.

"And Bapho-Slugs," Alexander finished. "Come on, Ruth. Don't ever go near those canals. Thank God that slug was a baby."

"A fuckin' *baby!*" She jogged away in haste, her high

breasts bobbing beneath the YUCK FOO T-shirt. "The fucker was ten feet long! How big's an adult?"

"Hundreds of feet," the priest apprised her. "When they get that big they either go out to sea or slip into the bigger rivers like the Styx."

"Fuck. I can't hack this shit, man."

"Be strong, Ruth. We've only just arrived. Let's both try to think more spiritually from now on."

"Easy for you to say," she said as her flip-flops were snapping onward over more multicolored scum.

"Your foul language, for instance. Work on that now. I'll help you."

"I don't need help controlling my language from a fuckin' torso who's stuck in the same shitty monster-filled slime-hole as me! All you religious guys are the same. You're all just a bunch of fuckin' hypocrites, condemning others for the same shit you all do. Maybe you really don't cuss out loud but I'll bet you still say cuss words in your mind, and if you say you don't, you're a fuckin' liar because even with that dumbass plastic collar you're still just as Human as me."

The priest's voice lost some of its punch. "I can't argue with you there, Ruth."

She passed a fungus-fat entrance sign:

WELCOME TO THE PORT OF THE VULGARESSA. BOATS MOORED WITHOUT PROPER LICENSE WILL BE IMPOUNDED AND THEIR OWNERS WILL BE SUBJECT TO SUMMARY TRANSRECTAL EVISCERATION.

Another sign quickly followed:

ABANDON ALL HOPE, YE WHO ENTER HERE.

"How's that for a welcome sign?" Alexander managed with a laugh.

"Fuckin' peachy." Finally out of the marina, Ruth marched on, the Port of the Vulgaressa behind them. "So who's this Vulgaressa person?"

"She's the official governor of Rot-Port, and to my knowledge the only Grand Duchess in Hell. If you thought women were discriminated against in the Living World, you haven't seen anything. She was one of Lucifer's first lovers after The Fall. He likes down-and-dirty women."

"Down-and-dirty, huh?" Some of Ruth's own past exploits sailed before her mind's eye. *Shit . . .*

"She's a Demonic nymphomaniac—has sex sixty-six times a day, they say."

"Holy shit. That *is* down-and-dirty."

"But get this, Ruth. The Vulgaressa deliberately keeps herself infected with every sexually transmitted disease in existence. The stuff they got here makes HIV, herpes, and syphilis look like a stubbed toe. Her body's pretty much just a great big bag of pus that's kept in feminine contours by her occult surgeons. That's her hobby. She infects people with this stuff. Sixty-six times a day."

Ruth had had a touch of gonorrhea and syph herself a few times. She didn't want to know what kind of cooties they had *here.*

Then Alexander whispered, "Holy shiiiiiiiii . . ."

"You almost said holy shit!"

"I know, but this is serious, Ruth. See that Steam Buggy up there? And those soldiers in Rot-Armor?"

Ruth saw them at the moldering intersection whose curbs were troughs of rot. "Yeah? Is that trouble?"

"Could be. That buggy is the Vulgaressa's personal coach. Just walk normally."

Ruth shook her head. *Walk normally he says. With a torso on my back in Hell . . .*

"Don't say anything and don't look at them. Just walk by like you don't see them," the priest warned. "There's something screwy here."

"I'll say. We're in a town made of *rot.*"

"I mean there's more Conscripts than normal," Alexander said, observing more Demonic soldiers prowling roofs and balconies. "And some of them aren't wearing Rot-Armor—it means they've been called in from other

Districts. And the Vulgaressa is never out at this time of night. It's almost like . . ."

"They're looking for someone?"

"Shhh! Just walk by."

Ruth loped ahead. Years of grifting and petty thievery had taught her to act inconspicuously, yet the priest's mysterious alarm was making her nervous.

"And *don't* be nervous," Alexander added. "They have Prism-Veils."

What the fuck! she thought.

She passed a large steepled structure fluffy with rot. It looked like a church but then she read the sign:

ST. BATHORY'S ABBEY OF CATHETERIZATION—JOIN ABBESS
JOYCELYN FOR BLACK MASS & GENITAL TORTURE.

Ruth just shook her head again, but then, as she passed a sewer grate full of pleading, twisted faces, she became dreadfully aware of the squishy *snap!* of her flip-flops. *Act cool,* she thought. *Don't blow this.*

She began to cross the intersection, right in front of the Steam-Buggy and platoon of horned and helmeted soldiers.

In the carriage window, Ruth thought she saw a pallid, shiny shape leaning out. *It's her!* she guessed. *And she's looking through . . . a veil. . . .* It was like the kind of veil women wore at funerals that only covered their eyes, only this one was glittery with bright, glassy colors.

Like a prism . . .

Then a wet gargle cracked through the intersection. "Stop them. Investigate."

Fuck, Ruth thought.

"You two! Halt in the name of the Grand Duchess Vulgaressa."

Three of the Rot-Soldiers approached, their armor like sponges soiled by cleaning toilets. Their helmets, too, were but blobs of rot with a slit to see through. Instead of swords, they carried large, rusted boat hooks.

"State your business," the lead soldier demanded.

It was all Ruth could do just to look at him. "Oh, hi, sir. We were just, you know, bopping through town."

He stepped closed, and put the point of his hook right against her exposed navel. "So it seems. Why, then, did your aura indicate prevarication when viewed through an Occult Sensor?"

What the fuck does that mean! She guessed it meant they looked shifty. "Oh, yeah, sir, see, because my friend here told me that the buggy belonged to the Vulgaressa."

The hook turned up and cradled a breast. One twist and she'd be punctured. "And why should that make you nervous?"

Ruth struggled not to tremble. "Because, see, everyone knows that the Vulgaressa is a very important person— one of the most important in all of Hell—and, well, I got nervous because I've never been so close to someone that great and important, sir."

There was a click, and in the corner of Ruth's eye she saw a figure getting out of the buggy. Then a mushy, wet gargle of a voice stated, "What an exemplary Human trollop to say such nice things about me."

"Yes, my Duchess!" the lead Rot-Soldier said. He lowered the hook and stood back at attention.

"So, what have we here?" came the splattery rattle.

"Newcomers, I'd say, my Duchess. A Human tramp and a torsoed priest."

The smell that approached with the figure almost knocked Ruth over, and when she got her first full look, she wanted to run away and jump into one of the canals.

"The only good priest is a torsoed priest," the strange voice continued. "And as for the tramp? Such an *attractive* one, I must say."

All that covered the Vulgaressa's body was a brassiere and a miniskirt fashioned from some manner of reptilian scales, and she wore a glittery headdress like Cleopatra. But the rest of her was indeed a containment of pus that had taken on the shape of a Human female. Her skin was clear as cellophane and through it Ruth could see bones and veins amidst a yellowish liquefaction. Blots of more infection comprised her eyes.

Then a hot, squishy finger stroked Ruth's cheek.

"Would you enjoy the honor of making love to me, pretty one?"

Ruth heard Alexander plead in the tiniest whisper, "Say yes!"

Ruth's teeth rattled but she managed to reply, "Oh, my great Vulgaressa, it would be the greatest honor!"

A wet chuckle. "What delights I could show you in my Rot Parlor. You could be my Under-Duchess of disease and infection but . . . lo, I haven't time. I and my security forces must embark on a problem. But please come back again." The pus-swollen face leaned close. "You *will* come back again, won't you?"

"Oh, you can bet I will, Vulgaressa." Ruth's stomach was turning itself inside out. "I can't wait to see you again. You're just so beautiful and important. . . ."

"That I am," came the rattle. "You're a lusty sinful little sexpot, I can tell, and your sin, I'm sure, could treat me to many pleasures learnt in the Living World. So do return, and until then, go in torment to love and serve the Morning Star."

"Thank you, Vulgaressa!" Ruth babbled, and began to stride away. "Have a peachy day!"

From behind, Ruth heard the Vulgaressa say, "There's certainly no threat to be had from a whore and a dismembered priest. Aldezhor's missive *must* be folly. There's no trouble afoot in *my* District."

"No, Grand Duchess!"

"But we'll continue searching all the same, and maintain the current alert level."

"Fuck fuck fuck fuck fuck fuck *fuck!*" Ruth almost shrieked when they were blocks away. "Did you *see* that woman?"

"Yeah, I saw her," Alexander said with a laugh from her back. "I thought we were cooked."

"Me, too. That fuckin' prism-thing!"

"But, Ruth, you did a fantastic job getting us out of it. I should've realized that—swindler, professional liar, and thief. Those traits will benefit us in Hell."

Ruth smirked. "Fuck."

"And remember, reclaim your Grace by toning down the foul language."

Ruth stalked down another rot-covered road, trying to avoid mites and worms feasting on the material that served as asphalt. "Now where are we going, damn it? I'm tired of walking around this shit hole!"

"You really are amped up today, aren't you? Period? Hormone imbalance?"

"Fuck off!"

"Just keep going down this road and take a left at Cadaverine Avenue."

"Peachy!" she grumbled and stalked on.

A block down a sign read CONSTRUCTION AREA - ALL WORKERS MUST NOT WEAR HARD HATS. A contemporary-styled house was being built on the corner. It almost looked . . . normal.

"I thought everything here was built with rot?" Ruth questioned.

"Rot's the treatment, the finishing touch. The basic building materials here are similar to those in the Living World. In the Outer Sector North, there's a nearly limitless forest full of Bone Pine and Druid Oak, trees that grow a thousand feet. And there's plenty of stone and mud for brick-making, lime for cement."

"So . . . where's the rot?"

"This is prime bloodfront property here, Ruth. Very expensive, like Naples in Florida. So only the best rot-cultures are used." Alexander wagged a stump. "See those Trolls there?"

Ruth saw half a dozen of the squat, bumpy things applying paint rollers to the outer walls of the house.

"It's not paint. It's patented rot-culture. There are several Culture-Stations in the district. They just fill these big cauldrons with body parts, blood, fungus, mold, lichens, and any kind of filth you can name, and toss it in the vat.

County Building Sorcerers cast Decay Incantations over the cauldrons, and then it all ferments for a while. When it's ready, they can it and ship it out. Just like Sherwin-Williams. Watch what happens."

Ruth watched, all right. As the Trolls pushed their rollers back and forth, each streak of liquefaction began to bubble, then grow.

"Holy shit! The rot's growing on the wood!"

"Sure is," the priest said. Another block down, beside some trendy town houses swollen with decay, he said, "Take a look in there."

Ruth peeked into the splotched window. *You gotta be shitting me. . . .* Inside, she noted carpets of rot, couches and chairs and tables all fat with rot. Pictures on the walls were framed with rot, and even the books on the book-shelves were bound in covers meticulously crafted by thin boards of desiccated rot.

"You can fuckin' have it!" she snapped, then treaded on.

"Oh, and check that out up there."

Ruth looked up. *Shit . . .*

In the center of the town square stood a column of rot a thousand feet high. Birds with leathery wings and dog faces flew circles around its peak, plucking smaller things out of the tinged sky. Ruth saw tiny windows at the very top, and from one of the windows, a gnarly figure—probably a City-Imp—jumped.

So much for him.

The body hit the street with a *splat!*

"Ever seen the Space Needle in Seattle? Well, that's the Rot-Needle," Alexander explained. "What do you think of that?"

"I think it's fucked-up."

"Hey, there's a public bench," the priest noted next. "Set me down a minute, will you? I'm tired."

Ruth wanted to laugh at his rudeness. *I'm the one lugging his hypocritical ass, but* he's *the one who's tired . . . ?* She groaned and unshouldered the priest, setting his torso down on the bench.

"That's better."

Ruth sat and stretched her shapely legs forward. She groaned again when she noted the area's details: trees covered with rot, sidewalks caked with it. In the small park before them, even the grass was rot, and the musky flowers were clumps of decay growing off stems. Something on a tree caught her eye and she jumped up. "Look! Coconuts! I'm starving!" and she reached up for the large, familiar seed. "We'd get these all the time in Florida after a hurricane."

Alexander chuckled. "That's no coconut, Ruth. It's an egg case for an Ova-Fluke. When it bites you, it releases eggs that swim through your bloodstream to your ovaries. That means any mongrel kids you have will be . . ."

Ruth glanced over in dread. "Fucked-up?"

"In a big way."

She rushed back to the bench. "Well, lemme tell you this, buddy. One thing I will *never* be in Hell is pregnant."

"Don't be too sure. Rape is the status quo here, so you have to be careful. Especially a Human woman with your looks. The way it works is two Humans can't reproduce, but other species? That's another story unfortunately. If you get raped by an Ogre, Imp, Gargoyle—anything Hellborn—you'll have a Hybrid kid. If you get snatched up by a Grand Duke to be in his harem, same thing. You'll be the vessel for his offspring."

"My ass!"

"And if an OP Squad gets a hold of you—"

"OP?"

"An Overpopulation Squad. They're select Conscripts who scour the streets for attractive females, then take them to do hundred-year tours at an FI Station."

"FI?"

"Forced Insemination. In the Living World, the big deal is stem-cell research and gene splicing. Here it's gene corruption. They keep you perpetually pregnant and experiment with what comes out. Overpopulation is a state law. Lucifer wants lots and lots of new births to keep the streets stuffed with turmoil and misery, and to keep the natural resource levels up. Blood's used for water, flesh is used for meat, bones for mortar."

Ruth's face twisted around. "That's hideous, man! It doesn't make sense."

"No, it doesn't. But remember, here everything is opposite. Everything that seems illogical and wrong in the Living World, like war, exploitation, addiction, violence, is logical and right here."

Ruth stared off. *Crazy,* she thought. *Do I really deserve this?* She reached instinctively into her pocket, then swore. "You don't have any cigarettes, do ya?"

"Sorry. I had to quit those, too. A penance."

"They don't even have *cigarettes* in Hell?"

"Sure, they do. Get some money from my top breast pocket, then buy yourself a pack. Get us some food, too."

Now you're talking! She fished in the torso's pocket and pulled out—

"Wow. Where'd you get this roll?"

"I stole it."

"Oh, that's super. A priest that steals."

"I told you, Ruth, I'm on an important mission here. I've been preparing for the equivalent of a year or so. Staking locations, marking routes, making connections. And . . . procuring funds."

"How?"

"Same way you used to do it. Ripping people off. Mugging them, jacking them, and taking their cash."

Ruth laughed, dark and hard.

"But there's a difference," he added. "I rip off Demons, criminals, and scumbags. You ripped off the innocent."

"Oh, bullshit, man! It's all the same. You're taking what doesn't belong to you. 'Thou shalt not steal?' Ever hear that one?"

Alexander exhaled as if wearied. "Just go over to that convenience store and get the stuff."

Such a hypocrite . . . Ruth sashayed to another rot-walled building, the door of which jingled when she entered. *Everything's opposite,* she recited, *but some things never change.* The man at the register wore a turban and looked Middle Eastern. But his beard was green rot hanging down to his sternum. A nametag said: HELLO! MY NAME IS ATTA. I AM UNHAPPY TO SERVE YOU!

"Hi," Ruth said.

The man glared. "You—how you say?—fuck you! You get out my store! We do not serve infidels! Death to all infidels and all enemies of Islam!"

Ruth was appalled. "Hey, buddy, I'm no enemy of anything. I just want to buy a pack of smokes and some food."

"You look like treacherous American prostitute, just like those cunning wenches we paid for in Boston before we fly the planes into the heart of your evil economy which is the Great Satan! You dirty American whore! One day my great nation will bury you all."

Even though Ruth had indeed participated in countless acts of prostitution during her life, she *did not* like to be called a whore.

She pulled the flintlock pistol from her belt and put it right in the proprietor's face. "Listen, spinach-chin. I didn't start any shit with you, so you got no right to start it with me. Now get me a pack of smokes, some matches, and"—she looked behind the counter and saw a grill—"are those sesame rice balls?"

The man shuddered with his hands up. "Yes, yes, miss. I get you all you want. Please no shoot me!"

"Just get the shit, sparky."

The man fumbled to put her purchase in a bag.

Ruth pulled out the wad of cash. "How much?" But then she reflected. "No—how *you* say?—*fuck you!* I'm not paying and if you don't like it, do something about it."

She saw now that the man had wet his pants.

"All the money, too, dickstain."

Tears in his eyes, the man emptied the drawer into the bag.

Ruth leaned over, waving the clunky pistol, big breasts settling on the counter. "And don't you even *think* about calling the police—or whatever the fuck you *have* for police in this ridiculous Satanic circus you got going here, 'cos if I even hear one siren, I'll come back in here and blow your shit away before they get me. Got it?"

"Oh, yes, yes, nice American lady."

"My ass." Ruth reholstered the gun and paused to squint at the trembling clerk. A button on his shirt read DEATH TO ISRAEL!

"Can't you guys do anything except blow stuff up and work in 7-Elevens? Get a life!"

Ruth tramped out of the store, breasts jiggling.

When Alexander saw all the extra cash, he said, "How'd you get that?"

"Same way as you. I ripped it off from that asshole in there."

"Good work!" He seemed pleased. Ruth fed him the rice balls, which he ate with gusto.

"Not bad."

"You're right," she agreed, munching hers. "Not as good as the ones back home but they'll do." She mused. "We used to get the best sesame rice balls at this place in Clearwater."

"I hate to tell you this, but those things we just ate aren't sesame rice balls. They're Imp testicles fried in Hell-Sow fat."

Ruth stared at him. "Oh, thanks for telling me *before* I went into the fuckin' store!"

"Down here, food is food, Ruth. You'll learn."

Ruth paused before lighting one of the cigarettes. "And now I'll bet you're gonna tell me there's no tobacco in these, but something fucked-up, right?"

"Shredded corpseskin and ground up dragon hair," he said.

Ruth tossed the pack into the garbage can right next to the rotten bench.

"Shouldn't have done that," Alexander muttered.

Within a second a great shadow crossed over Ruth. She looked up at the nine-foot-tall thing suddenly standing before her. It looked to be made of clay—like a giant Gumby, only the clay stank. All it had for a face were slits for a nose and mouth, and two thumb holes for eyes.

"Meet your first Golem, Ruth."

Holy shit . . .

Gray-brown fingers the size of Johnsonville brats handed her a slip of paper.

> *By order of the Constabulary, you are hereby ordered to remit a fine of $50 Hellnotes. If you elect not to pay, you will face immediate unlawful arrest or be subject to a public squashing. Officer's choice.*

Now it was Ruth's turn to wet her pants. She rummaged through the cash she'd just stolen and grabbed the first bill she saw with a *50* on it.

The Golem snatched it up and walked away, sidewalk rumbling.

"That's a *cop?*"

"One of them. Ushers and Conscripts are police, too, and certain Hybrids and Mongrels. You'll see them all in time."

"But what did I do? I thought he was going to bust me for robbing that store."

"You violated the citywide anti-littering law."

Ruth railed. "I didn't litter! I threw the damned cigarettes in the garbage can!"

"Ruth, here you're not allowed to *not* litter. Understand?"

"No. But that doesn't matter, does it?"

The priest chuckled. "You'll get the hang of it soon. Like I keep telling you, everything's opposite here."

Yeah, I guess it fuckin' is.

"Since we're taking a breather, check the gun belt," the priest said. "Make sure you've got some ammunition for the sulphur pistol."

Ruth frowned, fidgeting with the belt. She flipped up a leatherlike compartment. "Reefers!"

"They're not reefers, Ruth. They're powder cartridges. You pull the end off, dump the powder in the barrel, then drop in a sixty-nine caliber musket ball."

Just my luck. In the next compartment—"Holy shit! Are these giant pearls?"

"Yes, they are, Ruth."

She held one up, as big as the biggest marble she'd ever seen. "It's got to be worth a fortune!"

"It's worth one Antigonus piece."

"What's that? Like, a couple grand?"

"The equivalent of a quarter of a penny. It's the cheapest thing they can use for ball ammunition. Lead's way too expensive and gold is too soft."

"Huh?"

"Gold's worthless here, and so are diamonds. In Hell they have alchemists that turn gold into *lead*. Zircons, on the other hand, are worth millions."

Ruth was hating this more and more. "That's the dick-stupidest thing I've ever heard."

"Uh-huh. What's worthless in the Living World is priceless here, and vice versa. That's how Satan wants it."

Next Ruth looked in the bag of bills. "And what's with all this funky money?"

"Hellnotes are the official dollar here. Brutusnotes are worth fifty, Tiberiusnotes a hundred. Check out the Bonifacenote, the one with a thousand on it. There's one on my roll."

Ruth found one. "So this is a G-note, huh?"

"Yes. But look at the face. It's one you'll need to recognize eventually."

Ruth examined the odd portrait on the bill, which she guessed had been printed on some kind of skin. "It looks like a fat pope wearing a mask. Why do I need to know what he looks like?"

"Because you'll be meeting him soon."

Ruth didn't want to know.

Her eyes drifted to some other things around Alexander's neck, next to the Abyss-Eye: a pouch on one pendant and something like a decorative horn on another. "What's all that stuff? Hell-jewelry?"

"Hardly. The pouch is just . . . a pouch."

"Thanks."

"It's a goodie bag, sort of."

"You mean it's got special things inside, huh?"

"Yes." but his reluctance to talk details was plain.

Ruth glared. "So what's in it? Jesus! Why don't you ever tell me anything?"

"Because it's too much, too soon, Ruth," he said with some fatigue. "There's magic stuff in the pouch. It's too much for you to absorb all at once. You're still a New-comer. You haven't even been in the Mephistopolis for a day yet."

"Well then, what's that horn?" she asked next. A pang of hope. "Has it got booze in it?"

"No booze, Ruth." He frowned in resignation. "All right, take if off my neck and check it out. But be careful."

She took the connecting pendant off of him to examine the queer object. The horn was empty, its walls thin and bonelike. She imagined the last six inches cut off an ele-phant's tusk, which was then hollowed out. There was a hole at the small end too, and the horn had been intri-cately engraved—indeed, like ivory—but the characters were foreign to her.

"It looks like a hollowed out tusk," she observed.

"Close. It's the fore-horn of a virgin Demonness who hanged herself in rebellion to Lucifer's authority. Most of the words engraved on it are in a language called Enochian, one of the Angelic tongues, and some of them are in Zraetic, which is even older. It might have been the language originally spoken by God at Mount Sinai, but I'm not positive. They didn't tell me for sure."

"They?"

Alexander sighed. "My intelligence source, and some others, shall we say. The people who recruited me."

"And me, too, I guess, without even asking," she added.

Anger threatened his gaze. "You're not taking this very seriously. It's not a joke. You'll be transferred from Hell to Purgatory if we succeed."

"Yeah, but I have to wait a fuckin' thousand years!" she complained.

"It's better than a million. Believe me, Ruth, it's an offer you can't refuse. Purgatory's no picnic, but it's not"—he took a grim look around—"it's not . . . *here*. These are powerful entities we're dealing with. If you keep raising a fuss, keep complaining, keep being totally ungrateful for this historic opportunity . . . then they might just pull the plug on the whole deal, and you get nothing. You get to stay here. Forever."

Fuck, she thought. *Men are dicks.* "Chill, man." She used the horn to change the sour subject. "So *what's* this thing again?"

"It's called a *Vox Unterwelt.*"

Ruth didn't have a clue. "So you blow in it, like a trumpet?"

"No, but I can talk into it, to someone very specific, someone . . . in the Living World."

"You're shitting me!" The prospect sounded thrilling. "Who? Someone you know?"

"The ultimate purpose of our mission here is to relay critical instructions to this person I'm referring to."

"Who the fuck is it?" Ruth said insistently.

"Look in the fat end of the horn."

Ruth did so and saw . . . *someone's name?* She wasn't sure, because the writing was fat, murky, and black, like Magic Marker, only she had a deeper impression that the name was written in some kind of charcoal. She looked closer. "Is it . . . Veronica? Virginia?"

"The name is Venetia. From what I understand she's a theology student contemplating the convent. And she's chaste—a very important factor."

"Chased by what?"

"For pity's sake, Ruth—*chaste!* It means she's celibate."

Ruth's head turned. "Celebrating *what?*"

"It means she's a virgin!" his voice rocked.

Ruth turned furious. "Hey, fuck you and your stupid *Vox*-whatever-the-fuck this is! Just 'cos I don't know all the fancy words you do don't mean you can yell at me like I'm trash! So you can kiss my ass and shove this stupid thing up yours!" she bellowed and was about to throw the *Vox Unterwelt* at him.

"Ruth, Ruth, wait!" he snapped. "Relax, okay? I'm sorry."

"You better be, damn it. You can't even put this thing

back around your neck 'cos you got no arms. So stop treating me like shit 'cos I'm *not* shit!"

"I know you're not." He calmly paced his words. "You're a child of God."

"I ain't no child of God, either!" she continued to rage, hormones in havoc. " 'Cos God wouldn't send one of His children to this shit *hole!*"

"You sent yourself, Ruth, and I did, too. But I apologize. I guess I'm not a very nice guy in the long run, which is my reason for never making it to Heaven. Plus I'm cranky, irritable, and unreasonable sometimes. But let's both work together so we can *both* get out of this—what you just said."

Shit hole, she thought. *Fuck, I need a Pamprin, and they probably don't have that here either.* She continued to half-examine the *Vox Unterwelt* in her hands. "So somebody wrote this chick's name inside and that makes it magic?"

"That's the best way to phrase it, yes."

"Who wrote the name?"

Another long, weary sigh. "I can't tell you."

"That's great. That's just fuckin' great."

"But it works, so that's all that matters—er, I should say, it works some of the time. See, for the transmission to be unfazed, Venetia has to be tired. She can't be fully asleep, but she can be fatigued or about to fall asleep."

"Sounds like more bullshit."

The priest shrugged. "I think it's because her mental blocks are down when her brain waves are heading toward sleep. That's when I can actually talk to her. But you can *see* all the time. Take a look."

"What?"

"Put the small end to your eye, like a telescope."

Ruth did, then exclaimed, "Fuckin' *cool!* That's the world! *Our* world!"

"Yes, it is. We see everything she sees through her eyes. And when she's looking in a mirror, we can even see *her.* What's she looking at now?"

Ruth's eye opened wide. "Outside. She's looking out a window and it's nighttime and there's a big bright moon and there's, like, a weedy field and a bunch of trees way off, and—oh, wait, now she's walking out of some kind of room and . . . she's looking down over a rail and . . ."

"Yes?"

"She must be upstairs in a school or something, or maybe an old hotel 'cos now she's looking down at a really big wide-open room with a bunch of furniture all over the place, bookshelves surrounding every thing and . . . some of the furniture's covered by sheets and . . . looks like a bunch of old shitty pieces of carpet over this really big floor. . . ."

"It's not a school or hotel," Alexander informed her. "It's a prior house built over forty years ago."

"The fuck's a prior house?"

"Like a monastery, a rectory, an abbey. It's sort of a multipurpose building, for the Catholic Church to use as it sees fit. The reason Venetia's there is to help clean the place up—or at least that's what she thinks. Let's just say that my intelligence source has some better ideas for her."

Ruth didn't hear much of what he said; she was too excited to keep looking into this bizarre Demon-horn called the *Vox Unterwelt* and see little slices of the world she used to live in.

The world I took for granted, something caused her to add.

"Pretty cool little device, huh?"

"Oh, shit-yeah . . ."

"Can't even imagine how much energy and Celestial resources it took to make it and get it to me."

"Huh?"

"Just keep looking, Ruth," Father Alexander said with some contentment, "and let me know when it looks like she's getting ready for bed."

"What happens then?"

"That's when we get to talk to her . . ."

Chapter Six

(I)

"So you're telling me Freddie Johnson was a pretty straight-up guy?" Berns said.

The captain's name was Desmond, a proverbial salty dog. Old, bent, wizened, but tough from a lifetime of working the water. As he spoke with Berns, he was scraping small barnacles off a crab trap with a wire brush, and had an accent that sounded more like Maine than New Hampshire. "Ya mean did he steal? Naw, not that I ever heard. He was a partier, sure, but who ain't in this business?"

Berns gazed off the dock into a deep blue bay. "Drugs, you mean?"

"Naw, but he drank *a lot* of beer. Saw him with a bunch of folks once drinkin' at Abney's one night, and now that ya mention it, sure, *they* looked like druggers."

Important, Berns knew. "His friends. A girl and another guy?"

The leathery face squinted at the remark. "Yeah, I think ya might be right. Skinny girl, dirty-blond hair, looks forty but's probably thirty." Desmond picked up a chewed cigar end that had been sitting on the raw dock, and put it in his mouth. "Can't really recall the other fella."

"If I showed you mug shots, could you pick them out?"

A reluctance touched the old man's hooded eyes. "Wouldn't wanna do that, memory ain't what it used to be. Lotta folks come 'n go in this little town, lookin' for odd jobs—not just crabbin', mind you. All's I remember is the girl had tattoos, and the fella, too, I think. Gutter-mouthed, both of 'em. But I'd just be half-guessin' lookin' at pictures."

"I understand," Berns said. People always liked to talk, but never back it up. *Too much responsibility.* Not that Berns *had* any mug shots anyway. "Tell me more about Freddie Johnson."

"He was a damn good crabber—that's all we gave a crap about." Desmond moved the brush to another trap, gnawing the cigar butt. "Me 'n the other captains would damn near get in fights over him. But whoever's boat he went out on always came back with a full load of Jonahs and Peeky-toes. Some guys just have the knack, and that was Freddie Johnson. Said he tweaked the bait, that was his secret, but I just think he was lucky. He'd work for me a lot 'cos I'd always throw in a case of beer on top of his pay."

"How many commercial crabbers are there in Wamms-port?" Berns asked. He watched another boat pull in as its deckhands were sizing a trough of live crabs.

"Five or six—depends on the season. We're small-time here. The big boats trap outta Portsmouth. But we do all right. They got places in town that pay solid money for live bushels of Peekytoe, then get a buncha illegals to pick the meat 'n sell it to restaurants . . . er—aw, shit, guess I shouldn't have said that."

"Don't worry about it." Berns almost chuckled.

"That's why the crab cakes are so good 'round here—it's all fresh-picked meat. You eat a crab cake at Abney's tonight and you can bet the meat in it was alive 'n in the bay yesterday." The leathery face looked up. "You ever had a Peekytoe crab cake, Captain?"

"Actually, no. Not into seafood."

"Aw, that's a shame. But anyway, that's how it works. We sell off most of our Peekies around here. The Jonahs go inland. And since you're so interested in Freddie Johnson, I can tell ya, I ain't never had a bad day on the water when he was working my boat. He works *hard*."

Worked, Berns thought.

"I been doin' this over fifty years, crabbin' just like my daddy did. In alls that time I never saw a guy could fill traps like Freddie. If he weren't so damned unreliable, he could make a fortune in this business, have his own boat and crew."

Another interesting remark. "How was he unreliable?"

"He'd sign on for a week, two at a time, then the bastard wouldn't show up on his third or fourth day. He'd have a good night playin' poker, or hustle some fellas on the pool table or some such, and then he'd disappear for a couple weeks and I'd have to take the boat out myself. Like that, ya know?"

"Good old transient labor. They're great when they show up."

"Ee-yuh."

Berns found himself repeatedly distracted by the environment. *Forgot how beautiful New Hampshire is on the water . . .* Seagulls floated overhead, while smaller birds shot down into the water on a split second's notice, then shot back up with a minnow. He was taken aback by the clean salt scent of the sea coming off the bay. As a violent crimes captain, his duties almost never brought him to the state's meager sixteen-mile coastline. "All right, so Freddie worked hard but hardly worked."

"Pretty much."

"And beered it up."

"Ee-yuh."

"You see him out in the bars a lot?"

"Not that much but I know he threw 'em back on account he smelled like beer whenever he worked for me. But I never saw him out much in town, just that one night at the bar I told ya about, and maybe a couple, three more times. Come to think of it he hustled some guys on the pool table that one night, too—for a couple of hundred—and I was just sitting there with my beer thinkin' holy shit, with them winnings I'll bet my ass he don't show for work the next mornin'. Damned if I weren't right."

Berns knew the type—all cops did. But he needed something new. *The tattoos,* he remembered. *He mentioned the girl had a lot of tattoos.* He pulled out one of the booking photos he'd gotten, surprised by the Lubec PD's thoroughness of photographing all identifying marks on the arrestee. "The girl you saw him with—did she have a tattoo like this?"

The old man seemed to experience distaste when he looked at a close-up photo of the bizarre tattoo on Freddie Johnson's lower abdomen. "The hail's that? A fella's stomach?"

"Freddie Johnson, taken the night he was arrested in Lubec, Maine. Ever seen anything like that before?"

"You can bet not, son. The tattoos on that gal was all silly shit like I told ya, skulls and such. Don't know what *that* is."

"Neither do I." Berns reclaimed the photo and took a glance at the strange spiral within the bordered rectangle, and arrows pointing inward from three corners.

"Looks damned Satanic or somethin', don't it?" Desmond commented.

"Yes, sir, and I'm glad you mentioned that. Do you have any reason to believe that Freddie might have been involved in any cult activity? Devil-worship, something along those lines?"

The old man seemed addled by the question. "Like all that heavy-metal shit, upside-down crosses? Shit, I don't know. I never heard of nothing like that around here. It's all out in California, I thought."

Desmond's friendly demeanor was rapidly eroding. *Either I'm starting to annoy him,* Berns thought, *or the references to devil worship are getting under his skin.*

"We'se just a bunch of watermen here, son." Desmond slammed the lid down on a crab trap. "Northeast rednecks. That means hard workin' and hard drinkin'. There ain't none of that weirdo California shit here."

"How about—"

"And it ain't that I don't wanna cooperate with the police"—Desmond wiped his slimy hands on his pants—"but I'm a tad busy here. I told ya everything I know about Freddie Johnson."

That's all I'll get out of him, Berns decided. "Thanks for your time, Mr. Desmond. Oh, one last thing—"

The old man glared.

"Are there any tattoo parlors around here?"

Desmond began scraping the next trap, waving one arm but not looking at Berns. "Across the street, son. You're none too observant for a police captain, are ya?"

Jesus. Berns felt inept when he turned his head and immediately saw the shop. TATTOOS BY TERRY. "Thanks, sir."

"Yeah, yeah."

Berns walked quickly off the dock. *Am I that irritating?* The sun was baking him in his drab sports jacket, but he couldn't take it off due to his shoulder holster. While he waited to cross the pierfront road, a dented pickup rumbled by with its stereo turned up so loud Berns had a mind to write the driver a ticket for disturbing the peace. "Satan's just around the bend!" wailed the singer. *Great*, Berns thought. A shirtless, tattoo'd redneck in the driver's seat sneered. *Maybe that's one of Johnson's accomplices.* Then he realized how ridiculous the notion was. *This is a redneck waterman town, and watermen all have tattoos. . . .* Berns jaywalked a moment later, yet movement behind him caught his eye.

He stopped in the middle of the street and turned.

A dock bum in rotten clothes dug through a garbage can, but when his yellowed eyes caught Berns', he shirked away.

"Get out of the road, ass!" someone yelled, leaning on their horn. Berns almost shouted at the start, then felt himself blush as he jogged across the street.

"Chowderhead!" yelled the driver. The arm crooked out the window bore a tattoo of a grinning skull.

Great day so far . . . He took out the photo of Johnson's tattoo again. He remembered the convict's cryptic reply when asked what the tattoo was: *It's . . . my trademark, man,* with that big gold-toothed smile. *It's probably just some death-metal logo. Probably a million people have the same tattoo.* He sighed in relief when the parlor's AC seemed to suck him inside. Four walls and partition panels displayed hundreds of tattoo designs: flowers, crosses, Oriental characters, and the like. In the back was a counter and a chair almost like a dentist's.

Anyone here?

"Don't tell me a police officer wants a tattoo," came the voice of an energetic woman behind him. "That would be a first."

Berns didn't like the surprise, nor the comment. *One look and I'm made,* he thought, disgusted. But then a double take prevented him from saying anything right off.

A slim, very attractive woman in a blue bikini stood in front of him, off-blond, big eyes, her hair pulled back. She had no body fat at all, just tan curves and sleek, flawless skin, and . . . lots of upbeat tattoos. Big yellow, blue, and red stars crawled up her legs, while pink kiss marks crawled up her arms. Just above the waistband of her bikini bottom were the words WELCOME TO THE HAPPIEST PLACE IN THE WORLD! Just to the left of it, Mickey Mouse peeked out. Berns had to collect himself a moment.

"Are you the . . . tattooist?"

"Yes, I'm Terry," she said. "Are you going to let me ink you up, Officer?"

Berns finally shook off the initial shock. "How did you know I'm a cop?"

She giggled. "When that redneck almost ran you down on Dock Street, I saw the gun under your coat."

"Ah."

"And tell me why you seem surprised that the tattooist is a woman?"

Berns' thoughts bumbled; then he figured he'd just tell the truth. "Not that the tattooist is a woman but a woman in a pretty tiny bikini. I don't see many bikinis in New Hampshire."

She tapped a flip-flopped foot like someone who'd had too much coffee. "Officer, there's only three months a year when a girl can wear a bikini in this state. June, July, and August. So every June, July, and August, that's *all* I wear."

"I guess that makes sense. I'm Captain Berns, by the way, Rockingham County Sheriff's Department. I'm in charge of the violent crimes unit, and—"

She laughed out loud. "I'll bet that job sucks!"

"Uh . . ." Berns had no response. "I was wondering if you could—"

Before he could finish, the lissome woman's eyes darted to the photo in his hand. "That's not mine, is it?" and she quickly snatched it away from him and rushed to the wall.

Berns' thoughts bumbled again. *What the . . .* His eyes followed the sleek and almost-nude body.

"It's the same guy!" she exclaimed. "I have a picture here that's almost identical! The blond guy, right? With the gold-tooth, always smiling?"

Eureka! "He's a crabber named Freddie Johnson. Do you know him?"

"Oh, no, I don't know him, and I never got any of their names. But . . . why do you have a picture of his tattoo?"

Berns noted now that the tattoo samples on that section of the wall were actually polaroids. "It's part of arrest procedure, ma'am. He's in jail now, in Maine. And . . . why do *you* have a picture of his tattoo?"

"Most customers let me take a picture to display, if it's an original or unusual design."

Now she was leaning against the wall, arms crossed under pert breasts. *Jesus. This woman's body is killing me. . . .* Berns had to force himself not to stare. "So you're the one who gave him the tattoo?"

"Yeah, about a year ago, I think. He was a nice guy, too, and that's a little troubling."

Berns pulled his eyes away from her trim abdomen. "Troubling? Why?"

She looked at him, astonished. "Well, you're from the *violent crimes* unit, and you just told me he was arrested, so I don't have to be a brain surgeon to assume that he was arrested for a *violent crime*," she said very quickly. "And don't tell me what the crime was because I don't want to know! I don't want any negativity in my parlor."

Berns was grateful he didn't have to explain about the murders. "I see. But what did you mean when you said you never got *any* of their names?"

"It was weird. It was obvious they were all friends, but they came in a week apart, almost like they didn't want to be seen together. The three of them, I mean."

"Johnson and another man, and a woman?"

"You already know!"

The woman's energy level was knocking him off center, but above all he couldn't have been more encouraged. *My first real lead . . .* "Something Freddie told me himself when I questioned him. But he *didn't* tell me who these other two people were—"

"Oh, that's too bad because, well, like I said, I didn't get their names, and I never saw them much."

"The other guy was younger, right?"

"Yep."

"And the woman was slim and kind of a . . ."

"Beat-down weathered bar-tramp," she said blank-faced, then laughed after his pause.

"Took the words right out of my mouth. Could you pick them out of a lineup, or if I showed you mug shots?"

"Oh, I'm sure I could," she said, seeming eager.

Berns thought, *Eureka!* In less than a day he could have someone from the county records department print out photos of anyone in the area with priors who matched the descriptions.

She continued, talking quickly, her hands moving with her lips. "The first week, the blond guy came in. Then a week later, the other guy, and—"

"Then the woman, a week apart?"

"Right."

"But you figure they're all friends because they came in asking for the same tattoo," Berns supposed.

"Uh-huh, and they wouldn't let me stencil the design. They all insisted I ink it by sight."

Berns didn't know much about the art of tattooing but her comment raised a technical question. "So they brought their own *copy* of the design?"

"Same copy each time."

"What? Something from a book? It would be great if you could remember the name of the book."

"No, no, it wasn't a book. It was just a sheet of that lined, yellow writing paper. And I'm sure it was the same sheet of paper each week when the next person brought it in to copy."

Curious. "How can you be sure?"

"It had a lot of writing on it, scribble, really. I'm very interested in words, it's sort of my hobby."

"Words are your—"

"I love words!" she emphasized. "New words, different words. I belong to four different word-of-the-day Web sites."

What the hell is she talking about?

She grinned, aiming a finger. "You probably don't know what I'm talking about, huh? They have these Web sites that send you a new word every day so you can enrich your vocabulary, and they're cool words, like desultory and parsimonious and inviolate, you know?"

"Uh . . ."

She rushed off to her desk, a sylphlike blur, and returned a moment later with her business card. "On the back I wrote the Web address—check it out, it's free!"

"I'll . . . be sure to do that."

"But anyway, I just like words. And that's why I took a special notice of this sheet of yellow paper these people brought in. It had the diagram on it, for the tattoo, pretty much in scribble but there were also words all over the sheet, too. And they were words I've never seen before— that's why it caught my eye. Some foreign language."

Berns fiddled with his goatee, contemplating. *A foreign language. If they really are in some kind of cult, Johnson was clearly the leader, and Johnson's grade-A white trash. What's white trash doing with foreign words scribbled on a piece of paper?* "Foreign words," he muttered to himself.

"Creepy words, too—even though I couldn't read them," she said. The lithe body seemed to squirm around in the barely existing bikini. "What I mean is there was just something creepy about the way all that writing looked, along with that"—she shot a finger to the photo on the wall—"creepy diagram."

Berns thought further. "Do you know if they all lived in Wammsport? Freddie did up until last March, but I don't know about the others."

"I'm not positive, but I think I saw the girl somewhere once, the grocery store maybe."

More paydirt. Berns couldn't believe it. He was accomplishing something. "And what about Freddie? His landlord told us he lived in Wammsport most of last year."

"Oh, yeah. I'd see him a lot." Her slender, jubilantly decorated arm pointed out the window. "I'd see him working the docks quite a bit."

Berns nodded. "So it was only Johnson and his two friends you've done this tattoo for? No one else?"

"No one else, Officer."

For some reason, hearing this sleek women call him "Officer" made him feel silly. "Are you open year-round? I don't know anything about the tattoo business."

"I'm open six days a week all year long. Business is great, or—here's a good word! Business is *copious!* Isn't that a cool word? It was yesterday's word of the day."

Berns chuckled under his breath. "Uh, yes, it's a . . . cool word, and I'm delighted that your business is . . . copious."

"It sure is," she bubbled. She grabbed a bottle of Windex and began spraying the front window. "Oh, don't mind me, I multitask. And, yeah, you might not think a little eye-blink town like this would generate a solid tattoo clientele but it really does."

"All the watermen—"

"Exactly. Crabbers, clammers, lobstermen, oystermen. They move up and down the coast just like all those migrant illegals who pick seasonal vegetables. And they all want tattoos every time. There are guys out here even in the middle of winter dredging steamer clams and oysters. They're tough boys—and redneck to the max." Her body was almost a blur as she wiped the big window down, talking at the same time. "Every new port city means a new girlfriend, and that means a new tattoo. I had a guy in here once who had over two hundred hearts inked on him, and a name for each."

"That's what I call true love," Berns thought to say, staring at the compact rump hustling in the tiny bottoms.

Berns was becoming aroused. *Yeah, that's real professional. . . .* "I can't thank you enough for your time, miss. Hope you have a great day."

"Oh, you too." Now she was standing on the windowsill, her slender legs V'd and calves flexed, as she meticulously cleaned the upper casement. "And don't forget to check out the word of the day. Today's word, by the way, is 'providential'. Bet'cha don't know what it means."

Berns' eyes shamelessly slid up the back of her perfect thighs. "That's an insurance company, isn't it?"

Her high laughter filled the shop like a burst of finches. "It's something that happens as if through divine intervention or good fortune."

"I could use a little of that," he said, preparing to drag his eyes off her unknowing rump. Then a final question kindled in his head. "And one last thing before I take off."

"Uh-huh?" she said, the rag making squeegee sounds.

"Do you have any idea what that design actually is?"

The woman stopped on the sill as if frozen, hands poised. "Oh, oh! That's right!" and then she jumped down and faced him, her eyes huge with some kind of recollection. "They called it something!"

"The design?"

"Yes, they had a name for it and now that I think of it, it was a really cool word. . . ."

"Please tell me you remember the word," Berns said, almost a whisper.

She quickly sat down on the sill, foot tapping. Her elbow was on her bare knee, her chin in her hand as she clamped her eyes closed to think. *Tap-tap-tap,* the flip-flop went. The primal man in Berns' psyche could not be thwarted from looking down at the vulnerable pose. The cups of her bikini top hung down enough for most of her perfect lemon-breasts to be revealed, and their pert pink nipples.

I really am a shitty police officer, Berns admitted to himself.

"Oh, that pisses me off! It was such a cool word, and I *know* I wrote it down."

"Where?" he practically pleaded.

"I can't remember—fuck!"

There was something blatantly erotic about hearing her use the expletive. "Well, just think. You'll remember—"

"Evolution, revolution—that's what it sounded like but—damn, it wasn't either of them, they're too common."

Berns shot some wild guesses that might connect. "Institution, electrocution . . ."

"No, no, but that same sound. Locution? Damn, no, that means style of speech. Fuck!" she said again.

Of all the information she's given me so far, I need this the most, Berns thought.

"See, that's why I wrote it down, because it was such a cool word!"

"A cool word, right. But, just . . . What's the most natural place for you to have written it down?"

Then she shrieked and jumped up so fast Berns almost stumbled backward.

"It's been right here the whole time! How could I forget!" Her body spun in a blue and flesh-tone blur, back to the partition with the photos. She removed a pushpin and took down the photo of Freddie Johnson's tattoo. She handed it to Berns faceup, beaming at him.

"What . . ."

"Turn it over," she instructed.

He flipped the photo, and on the back in beautiful feminine handwriting was the word: *Involution.*

She sighed as if letting out a long-held breath. "Now I remember."

"I have no idea what this word means," Berns said, completely duped.

"Well, it's one of those words that has a bunch of meanings. It can refer to anything that's complex or involved, or it can mean an act of involvement, or an overly involved grammatical structure—"

Berns burned in disappointment. "How can that possibly—"

She shot out a silencing finger, standing on her tiptoes. "*Ooooor*, it can refer to a mathematical structure of raising a number to its own power."

Berns winced. *I should've known it wouldn't make any sense.* "I still don't see what that could possibly have to do with that screwy diagram—"

She shot out her finger again. "*Ooooor*, the last definition—from geometry, a curve that spirals inward."

Hmm, he thought, looking back at the face of the photo. *Just like the design itself.* "A curve that spirals inward, huh?"

"Like the number six," she added.

Chapter Seven

(I)

The unfaltering heat inside the prior house made Venetia feel prickly, and it only soured her mood after speaking to Dan Holden. Unpacking addled her nerves; she caught herself looking around the bedroom every few minutes and wondering exactly where the nun had been murdered. *Patricia Stevenson*, she recalled. Venetia's eyes locked down on the sparse metal-railed bed. *I hope she wasn't murdered on the same bed I have to sleep on!* At least some of her unease lifted when she left the bedroom.

It just infuriated her. *Father Driscoll . . . Why didn't he tell me?* A pair of recent murders wasn't easy to overlook. She busied herself in the atrium, changing the bags on several vacuum cleaners; then she began applying masking tape to some of the windows that she could tell hadn't been painted yet.

"Oh, I was just about to get to that myself," Father Driscoll said, appearing from an office doorway. Dust and plaster scuffs besmirched his black shirt. "We've still got a few minutes before dinner."

Venetia turned briskly. "What's this all about?"

"Pardon me?"

"You told me the previous staff retired. Now I hear they were *murdered*. That's an interesting definition for retirement."

He tried to deflect a wince. "Don't believe everything you hear."

"Oh, so Dan made it up?"

"Ah, the king of gossip. I should've known." Driscoll unreeled some masking tape. "Actually only half of the staff was murdered. Two women—the other two left."

"Oh, only *half* the staff," Venetia replied as sarcastically as possible. "And what about Father Whitewood? You told me he retired too, but Dan says he disappeared."

"Disappeared . . ." The dusty priest shrugged. "That's a bit melodramatic. He was old, Venetia. The murders traumatized him. He had a nervous breakdown, so he ran away."

Venetia studied him. She couldn't believe she was being this brusque with a priest. "So you're admitting that you lied to me?"

"Lie . . ." He winked. "That's a bit melodramatic, too. I merely left out some details that weren't pertinent—"

"Weren't pertinent!" Venetia almost laughed.

"And, yes, I'll admit that those details didn't serve my needs. So I . . . skirted the truth, for the good of the Church." He seemed totally calm as he applied more tape around the window trim. "If I'd told you everything, you might not have come, and I really need help here. Half a dozen other students signed up initially, but they all canceled when—"

"When they found out there'd been murders here," Venetia cut in.

"Yes," he said. "It's a terrible tragedy, but don't overreact."

Is he trying *to piss me off?* "Well, I'm sorry, Father Driscoll, but I don't think anybody would be overreacting to learn that a *nun* was murdered in her *bedroom.*"

Driscoll picked up a Red Devil razor knife to cut off some tape. "Murders happen all the time, Venetia. *Women* get murdered all the time. It's part of the world's evil. It was a random incident. The police think some drug addicts broke into the prior house looking for things to steal. They stumbled onto some of the staff and got scared."

"Happens all the time," she echoed.

"I don't know what you're all riled up about," he added. "You're a Christian."

Venetia gaped. "What's that got to do with it?"

"Lottie Jessel and Sister Patricia Stevenson are in God's house now—of that you can rest assured."

Was he trying to make a joke of it? Venetia just shook her head.

"I'm starving," the priest said when he finished the next window. "Let's go eat."

Venetia smelled something familiar when they entered the big, sterile kitchen where Mrs. Newlwyn and Betta were busy. Suddenly she *was* hungry, even after all the nonappetizing information. *Father Driscoll's probably right. I* am *overreacting.* "Is there anything I can do to help, Mrs. Newlwyn?"

The tall woman turned with a distinct frown. "Thank you, but no, Venetia."

Was she mad?

Betta smiled, pouring milk into glasses set on the long table.

Father Driscoll rubbed his hands together. "I'll bet you didn't know that Mrs. Newlwyn is quite a cook. She's won blue ribbons at the county fair and a lot of church benefits."

In fact, the tall woman looked like a proverbial New England housewife, the type to pride herself in her home-cooking talents.

But why is she frowning? Venetia wondered.

"Father Driscoll has quite an amusing sense of humor," Mrs. Newlwyn said.

Venetia sat down next to the priest. "Sorry, but am I missing something here?"

"Cooking is my pride and joy," the woman said, "and, yes, I've won many awards for my recipes. My New Hampshire Calm Casserole dish was even featured in *Gourmet* magazine several years ago."

"That impressive," Venetia said.

"But my skills in the kitchen will go unused as long as Father Driscoll is responsible for filling the pantry."

From the oven, Mrs. Newlwyn and Betta withdrew TV dinners and set them on the table.

TV dinners? Venetia was surprised.

"I'm always the bad guy," Driscoll said. "Sorry about the boring food, folks, but the diocesan coffers are quite tight. Every week I go to the grocery store in Wammsport and buy whatever's on sale: TV dinners, pork and beans, store brand soup, canned spaghetti."

Venetia chuckled. "Now I get it. And besides, anything we eat is a gift from God. Even TV dinners."

"A true Christian attitude if I've ever heard one," Driscoll said. "So let's dig in."

Mrs. Newlwyn and her daughter took their seats at the table. Venetia noticed six places set. "Isn't Dan joining us for dinner?"

"Who knows?" Driscoll said. "He's probably out hunting more gossip to poison your mind with."

Venetia smirked. "And who's the sixth place set for?"

"John Dyall," the priest said. "Right out there." He pointed out the window.

Venetia squinted to see a thin, dark-haired teenager standing on a ladder pruning some trees.

"Another helper?"

"John's an orphan," Mrs. Newlwyn said. "A church family took him in, and since he has such a green thumb he asked to help out with the gardening and such."

"Should I call him in?" Venetia asked. Now she saw the boy climb down and move the ladder. He appeared meek, withdrawn, about eighteen, she guessed.

Driscoll answered, "We won't see much of John. He's not really a people person."

"He has an anxiety disorder," Mrs. Newlwyn added. "He's nervous around others. But he's a fine churchgoing young man. Most nights he takes his meals alone."

"Oh." Venetia continued to squinted as the boy climbed up the other side of the tree with his pruners. She also noticed Betta looking raptly out the window.

"I'll leave their dinners in the oven on warm. Even if they dry out they won't be much less edible than they already are." Mrs. Newlwyn offered Driscoll another scowl.

The priest smiled. "You're a real knee-slapper, Mrs. Newlwyn. Now, who wants to say grace?"

Venetia elected to, reciting the dinner prayer she chose most at the university. Her TV dinner of starchy fried chicken and mashed potatoes was fine with her.

Mrs. Newlwyn eyed Venetia. "I'm curious about the father's remark regarding gossip, Venetia."

Venetia stalled with the pepper shaker. "It's not the best topic for dinner conversation."

"This miserly gruel can hardly be called dinner, my dear. And I suppose you must mean the murders that occurred here last spring."

"Yes, ma'am. It was something that Father Driscoll . . . didn't feel *pertinent* enough to tell me in advance. But since I'm so young and inexperienced in the real world, I guess I overreacted a little."

The tall woman nodded sternly, inspecting her food with a wince. "Get used to it. The good father has a knack for details left unsaid."

"I guess it's Gang Up On Father Driscoll Day," the priest said, and sloppily devoured half a drumstick.

"But you did say that only *half* of the house staff was murdered," Venetia said. "The other half . . . left?"

"They fled, my dear," said Mrs. Newlwyn, "for their lives. But we can hardly blame them. Two more fine nuns—Sister Ann McGowen and Sister Diane Elsbeth."

"They did their part here for a long time," the priest

said. It was clear he wanted to change the subject. "Now it's our turn. So forget about them."

Venetia tried to read his face more deeply. "You're not saying they quit the sisterhood?"

"I'm afraid they did," Mrs. Newlwyn verified. "The incident shook their faith to its roots."

"That's a bit melodramatic," Driscoll insisted.

His favorite word, Venetia thought. "What a shame . . ."

"They're just taking a break." The priest seemed frustrated now. "They're doing volunteer work just like they always have. Neither of them lost faith."

Betta looked at her mother, then dragged her glance back to her food.

Betta obviously doesn't agree, Venetia thought. *What is with Driscoll anyway?*

Mrs. Newlwyn pushed her half-eaten dinner away. "But it wasn't just the murders that urged them to leave, my dear."

"What else?"

Driscoll rolled his eyes. "Oh, please, Mrs. Newlwyn. Give me a break."

The tall woman's lips formed the most fragile grin. "Sisters Ann and Diane were absolutely convinced that the prior house is haunted."

Driscoll threw his hands up. "When it rains, it pours. On *me.*"

Mrs. Newlwyn lowered her voice. "They both swore that they saw the ghost a number of times, walking the stair-hall and the atrium, and prowling the grounds at night."

"Prowling," the priest mocked. "You sure it wasn't the meter man, Mrs. Newlwyn? By the way, what happened to those bottles of wine that used to be in the cupboard?"

Mrs. Newlwyn's grin widened, showing teeth. "The good father is always quick to jest. But *he's* only been here a few weeks. Diane and Ann worked at the prior house for *years.*"

Venetia had to ask. "You said *the* ghost, not *a* ghost. Who's the ghost supposed to be?"

The tall woman's eyes slowly scanned the table. "No one knows."

Venetia actually let herself entertain the notion. *Armano Tessorio, the defrocked Vatican architect? Didn't Father Driscoll say he died of syphilis?* But she knew it was all just a fanciful story. *It's starting to sound like Mrs. Newlwyn is the one given to tall tales.* "That's interesting, Mrs. Newlwyn, but tell me—have *you* ever seen this ghost?"

The woman's face hardened. "Finish your miserly dinner, dear. Before it gets cold."

"That's right, Mom," she said into her cell phone. "Two murders. Last spring."

"Good Heaven's, you're not serious."

" 'Fraid so."

"Oh, honey, I don't know what to say!" Maxine Barlow exclaimed. "Let me go tell your father, then we'll drive down there and pick you up."

Venetia laughed. *She's overreacting more than me. . . .* "Mom, really, it's okay. It happened months ago. It was just a random crime—it could happen anywhere. I'm going to stay up here all summer, do my job, and get my extra credits. The whole business was just kind of a shock at first. I was really mad at Father Driscoll for not telling me."

"And he should've told us, too," came her mother's stern reply. "I really wish you'd come back home."

"I'm fine, Mom."

"So they caught the murderer?"

Venetia paused. "Come to think of it, I don't know. I didn't ask."

"For goodness sake."

"But everything's fine, really. It's a big job, but the place is kind of interesting. The prior house is loaded with thousands of old books and a bunch of neat statues."

"How many other students are helping out?"

"Students? Just me."

"You're kidding! Does Father Driscoll want to work you to death? That place is huge!"

"But there are some other people here, a seminarian, a

groundskeeper, and this woman named Mrs. Newlwyn and her daughter. Mom, this lady is *old school* New England. At the dinner table she was implying that the prior house is haunted."

"Oh, for goodness' sake!"

"It was really funny."

"Well, at least I hope they're feeding you well down there. What did you have for dinner, honey?"

"TV dinners."

"Oh, for goodness' sake!" her mother exclaimed again.

"And there's no air-conditioning and no fans—"

"Venetia! You can't spend the entire summer baking in that stuffy old place!"

"It'll be fun, Mom. Don't worry."

"Did they give you your own bathroom?"

Another pause. "Well . . ."

"That's deplorable! You mean you have to share?"

"Mom, relax. No one ever said this place was a palace."

"Father Driscoll should have told us—"

"But it is God's work." Venetia tried to stem further objections. "I know that for all intents I'm a spoiled little rich girl, what with Dad's money and all. But I'm perfectly happy roughing it."

"Roughing it, indeed. I hope those other people with you are clean."

Venetia shook her head and laughed.

"And what about your spell yesterday?" her mother rushed on. "Are you feeling better now? Because if you aren't, we're driving down there right now."

My spell. She'd actually forgotten about it. "That's all passed, and I feel great now, Mom. I'm actually kind of excited to be here. It's a good break from the classroom."

"Well . . . you call me every night just the same."

"Mom, come on. I'm not a little kid."

"Well then every other night. But you call. Promise me."

"I promise," Venetia droned.

"I don't like this murder business and TV dinners—"

"Love you, Mom. Good night."

"Don't forget to call—"

"Tell Dad I said hi." Then she finally hung up. *Probably shouldn't have mentioned any of it,* she thought.

A meager breeze gusted in through Venetia's window; the smidgen of relief reminded her how hot it was inside the prior house. *I'll have to get into town to pick up a fan.* Along with the heat, she also felt exhausted, but in a gratifying way. *It's been a long day and I got a lot of work done. . . .* And after sleeping so poorly last night, her fatigue ensured a good night's sleep.

She'd stripped down to her bra and panties before she realized how bright the bedroom lights were. *Close the drapes, you numskull!* When she did so she peeked out her window at the vast property behind the building and noticed how much bigger it looked now that nighttime had arrived. The sound of crickets outside seemed as steady as electronic music. For a moment she thought she saw someone at the forest's fringe but noticed after another few seconds that it was just a pine tree branch bowing in another gust of breeze.

Or at least she thought so.

Am I paranoid?

She knew she wasn't. How could anyone be outside at this hour to peep up into her window?

When she was naked she caught her own eyes appraising her body in the mirror. *I guess I'm not bad looking,* she complimented herself. Humidity and sweat from working earlier made her belly and high bosom seemed dusted with a faint glitter.

But an unease began to itch at her right off. When part of her mind began to contemplate the grim fact that a nun had been murdered in this same room, she pulled on a white terry robe and hurried out.

The second-story stair-hall, which circumscribed the entire atrium below, was dimly lit now. Tulip-shaped lamps were mounted next to every door but less than half were actually lit. *Bad bulbs or Father Driscoll's trying to skimp on the power bill.* What amused Venetia more than Mrs. Newlwyn's ghostly implications were her more direct implications that Father Driscoll was a cheapskate. *I think maybe tomorrow night we'll skip the budget-brand TV dinners and I'll treat everyone to pizza,* she thought.

In the dark hall the oil painting of Prior Whitewood seemed to grimace at her. *He didn't retire,* she reflect. *He had a nervous breakdown and abandoned his own priory after the murders.*

Venetia wondered where the elderly man was now.

Should've known, she thought when she padded into the communal shower area. When she flicked on the overheads, only half of them came on. It left the long, tile-walled space diced by wedges of darkness.

Four showerheads branched out from the walls, like in a school gym. There were even lockers. Everything shined. *Looks like Mrs. Newlwyn and Betta have already taken care of the place.* The tile floor was warm beneath her bare feet when she entered. She arranged her soap and shampoo, then heard a muffled hiss. *Someone's taking a shower on the other side of this wall,* she deduced. *Must be the men's side. Dan or Father Driscoll, or—*

What's the young guy's name? John, she remembered, *the orphan. Not a people-person. Nervous around others. Did they also mention an anxiety disorder? I doubt that he'll be anxious around me.*

She cranked on the cold faucet and frowned. The water felt as warm as the floor; a cooler shower would have been much better. *Everything's so hot!* The water did cool a little after the pipes cleared. She sighed and let the water spray her breasts, between which her house key glittered. Then she began to soap herself up.

Much better . . .

She gasped softly as the cool water cascaded over her body, giving her immediate relief from the heat. She stood motionless, eyes closed, hanging her head in the jet. She let the water consume her as she concentrated on relaxing.

For some reason, she thought, *Dan.*

Then a noise alarmed her. She turned, her eyes shooting open and her hands flying to cover to her breasts.

A figure stood in the locker area in front of the showers. "Oh, Betta. You scared me for a sec."

The short but shapely girl—woman, really—seemed partially startled herself. Instead of a robe, she wore an oversized white blouse as big as a man's shirt, which hung down to midthigh. *Sorry,* she mouthed in silence. Then Venetia lip-read something like, *I'll come back.*

"You don't have to wait," Venetia told her. "I'm not bashful if you're not."

Okay. . . . Betta had on a shower cap covered with lady-bugs, like something a child would wear. In the open blouse, her own key glimmered in her cleavage.

"The water's not that cool, though, but I guess you already know that."

Betta smiled meekly, nodding. *Not enough lights on ei-ther,* she seemed to mouth. She didn't seem at all discomfited when she hung up the blouse and turned naked into the long stall.

Venetia subconsciously fingered her own key. "That was funny how your mother poked fun at Father Driscoll for being cheap."

Betta nodded again and cranked on the shower.

Can't make much small talk with a girl who doesn't talk, Venetia realized. When she rinsed the shampoo from her hair, she stole a few glimpses at Betta and found herself mildly jealous. She guessed Betta to be about thirty but her slim, curvy body seemed toned and much more youthful. Suds sluiced off her chest to reveal smallish peach-sized breasts. Her nipples poked out like tender pink cones while Venetia's were large and flat save for their papillas.

Why am I comparing my body to hers? Venetia asked her-self. *If she catches me looking at her, she'll think I'm a lesbo. . . .* The notion amused her. But she supposed it was instinc-tive for women in such situations to compare bodies.

Venetia rinsed off, then slipped out to dry herself. She put on her robe and combed out her blond hair before one of the mirrors. She turned her head away from the shower, then noticed she could see Betta's reflection off another mirror on a perpendicular wall.

Perhaps she was mistaken in the brief glimpse but Betta seemed to be caressing more than washing her small, tight breasts, and when her fingertips tweaked the nipples, her stomach sucked in as if in a gust of pleasure.

Something's on her mind, Venetia thought. *Hope it's not me!*

She felt guilty seeing it, as though she'd looked on purpose. But Betta couldn't possibly have known about the betraying mirror.

Could she?

This is too weird. I need to get out of here.

"See you tomorrow, Betta," she said quickly.

Bye, mouthed the girl, partially obscured by the shower stream. She waved and pulled her face back into the spray.

If anything, the slender woman had seemed more distracted than anything else.

Back on the ill-lit stair-hall, Venetia wondered which rooms the men were staying in. She scanned down each of the building's long walls and noticed a lot of rooms—mostly bedrooms, she presumed. There were just as many offices and supply rooms downstairs.

She passed her own door and padded to the corner. She heard a creak at the other end of the stair-hall, and a white blur caught her eye.

For a fleeting moment she thought, *Don't tell me that's the ghost,* but she smiled to herself when she realized who it actually was.

It was Betta, in her large blouse, going down the stairs.

I wonder why she's in such a hurry. . . . And where's she going?

Venetia peered over the rail just in time to glimpse the tail of Betta's blouse sweep into the kitchen.

"Is it the ghost?"

Venetia twirled, almost shrieking.

Dan chuckled, looking over the rail. His dark hair glistened from his recent shower. His own robe had a Boston

Red Sox emblem on it. "I saw it too, a figure floating down the stairs."

"You scared the . . . whatever out of me, Dan," Venetia snapped.

"My apologies."

"And it wasn't a figure *floating* down the stairs. It was Betta."

"Where's she going at this hour?"

"The kitchen, it looked like, probably to get something to drink before bed."

"Ah." He grinned at her. "Damn. I was hoping it was the ghost."

"I don't know who's worse, you or Mrs. Newlwyn."

"Don't laugh. Mrs. Newlwyn claims to have seen the ghost several times herself."

Venetia was finally recomposed after the scare. "It's baloney, Dan."

The seminarist turned and casually leaned against the rail. "Come on, Venetia. You believe in ghosts, don't you? The Holy Bible is chock full of 'em."

"Yeah, I know, but—"

"Oh, you're not a literalist, huh? It's these new theology professors who're infesting our colleges. The Bible is all metaphor, right?"

He was already trying to work her into a debate. *I'm too tired.* "No, Dan, actually I don't believe that at all."

"Ah, good. Then you *do* believe in ghosts."

"You're impossible," she conceded. "And where were you earlier? You missed dinner."

Dan laughed. "Yeah, but I'm sure I didn't miss much. What was it tonight? Swanson sliced turkey and gravy or Mrs. Paul's fish sticks?"

"Fried chicken. It wasn't bad."

"You're too kind, Venetia." He casually crossed his arms, looking at her. "I think Driscoll buys all that cheap food on purpose, to make us humble."

"Shame on you, Dan," Venetia only half-joked. "Half the world's malnourished, and twenty-five million starve to death every year. There are people in Africa who'd sell their souls for those TV dinners."

"I know, but they still taste lousy. So call me a phony, but when you all were eating *that* I drove into town and grabbed a double quarter-pounder with cheese. It was *great.*" He looked away in what seemed an averting gesture. "And you'd be doing me a big favor by closing the top of your robe some. I've gone all day without a single lustful thought but now . . ."

Venetia looked down at herself. Quite a bit of cleavage had been showing—she wasn't used to talking to men while in her robe. The key on her chain felt hot against her flesh. She tightened the robe. At first she felt embarrassed, then mad, but it passed instantly. "I guess that's pretty crass for a seminarist to take note of my bosom but then I'll admit that it was pretty honest to look away and tell me. Most guys wouldn't do that."

"Of course they wouldn't, and most guys aren't idiotic enough to want to be priests."

"I suppose the same can be said for women who want to be nuns," she said and then regretted it. *It's none of his business what I decide to do.*

But he went on, "Especially if the nuns are as attractive as you." He grinned at her in a side-glance. "And don't worry, that's not a come-on."

"I should hope not!" she laughed. "Not from a seminarist presently standing in a Catholic prior house!" The brazenness of his remarks didn't make her uncomfortable at all and she guessed that was because he struck her as very devout and genuine beneath the jokester veneer.

"Is your room okay?" he asked next, cooling the subject. "I'll have you know that I respackled and painted it myself."

"Well, you did a fine job. I'm quite happy with the room." But she was already feeling stifled again. "The only thing that's a bit much is the lack of air-conditioning. But we really shouldn't complain, though, right?"

Dan's casual expression hardened. "Why not? It's hot

as hell, and Driscoll's never going to get fans unless he can find them at Salvation Army."

"Mother Teresa didn't have fans in Calcutta," Venetia said.

"No, she didn't. And she was hot all the time." He nodded cynically. "Trying to make me feel guilty again, huh?"

"Only a little," she said and smiled. "Where's your room, by the way?"

He pointed across the atrium to the opposite corner. "Over there. Mrs. Newlwyn and her daughter share the room next to yours, and Driscoll sleeps downstairs."

"What about John?"

"Who?" Dan paused. "Oh, the gardener kid. He never spends the night. He lives with his adoptive parents in town. He's kind of . . ."

"Mrs. Newlwyn told me. An anxiety problem."

"But he's a good kid and he works like a mule."

Venetia looked over the rail. "And you said Father Driscoll sleeps downstairs?"

"Yeah, in the old prior's quarters, next to the main office. Figures—he's the only one in the joint with his own bathroom."

"He *is* the boss."

"Yeah, and that sucks, doesn't it?"

"I heard that!" the voice boomed from downstairs.

"Shit," Dan muttered under his breath. He and Venetia looked over the rail and saw Father Driscoll peering up from the atrium floor. He had a glass of milk in his hand and wore striped pajamas.

"Hi, Father. I was just joshin'. You know me."

Driscoll grinned, his short blond hair spiky from a recent shower himself. "Indeed I do, Dan. And you're right, it probably does suck that I'm the boss but it's good to know that at least Venetia recognizes the significance of an authority figure during a project like ours. Now if you want some advice from the boss, you might want to turn off your ratchet-jaws and get to bed. You'll need your sleep—you especially, Dan."

"Me especially?"

"Why, sure. Since you're the one who's going to be clearing out all the attic coves tomorrow. There are twelve of them, Dan, just for your information. Hope it's not too hot tomorrow."

Dan's frown seemed to radiate. "I'm looking forward to it, Father."

Driscoll smiled, mainly at Venetia. "Now, good night to both of you." He disappeared back to his room.

"Dig those groovy pajamas," Dan sputtered.

"He's right," Venetia said. "It's getting late—see you in the morning." She rushed toward her bedroom. She wanted to get away quickly because she was afraid she might laugh at Dan's embarrassment. "Too funny," she said to herself once back in her room. A breeze slightly cooler than before billowed the curtains. *That's nice. . . . I'll sleep like a log tonight.* She put her toiletries on the dresser, but—

Thunk.

Then, *clack!*

The room was suddenly dark. She'd accidentally bumped her suitcase with her calf; it tipped over and struck the ugly metal floor lamp, which then crashed into the corner. "Oh, what a pain in the . . ." She tiptoed to the end of the dresser, careful of any broken glass, and switched on the smaller lamp there.

"That's just great."

Not only had the floor lamp's bulb smashed, its metal shade had gouged some of the freshly painted wall. She quickly swept up the broken bulb, then righted the cumbersome lamp, and then . . .

She was squinting at the gouge.

What is . . . She scratched the blemish with her fingernail. *Is that writing?*

She rapped her knuckles against the wall. *That's not Sheetrock,* she realized. Then she tapped the gouge. *I guess they just put plaster over bricks.* She scratched a bit more of the gouge and could even see several layers of plaster or some equivalent sealant beneath, indicating a number of re-coverings over the years. But—

There was something else, too.

Some black lines at the deepest part of the gouge. *That is writing,* she deduced when she scratched some more.

It appeared to be three-inch-high black letters, either painted or perhaps inscribed with Magic Marker: RUS

Venetia couldn't imagine what it could be, and by now she was too tired to care. *Deal with it in the morning . . . and repair the damage.* She turned off the other lamp, heading for the bed. As warm as it was she elected to sleep nude, which she knew would be comfortable with the breeze coming in. However—

Oh my God! Not again!

Before she could even take off her robe, that now-familiar vibration bloomed in her stomach and began to crawl to her head . . .

And the awful voice returned:

"Don't be alarmed! This isn't a dream!" A fuzzed-over shriek, like a distant voice on an old radio. *"Don't go to sleep or the transmission will be severed! Venetia! I have very important things to tell you!"*

The last line drove that spike back into her brain like the worst headache of her life. She squealed, biting her lips; then her knees thunked hard against the bare floor.

"You're just a hallucination!" her throat finally ground out. Her hands vised her ears but there was no relief from the pain. "Go away! It hurts so much!"

The voice crackled back. *"Listen! Listen! Lie down and breathe deeply. Do not be afraid! Try to relax and the pain will subside. You have to trust me, there isn't much time. But* don't *go to sleep."*

Venetia flopped on her back and followed the instructions of the impossible voice.

"Breathe. Relax. Calm down."

The head pain as well as that throbbing nausea began to soften.

"Can you hear me?" the voice asked next in a lower tenor.

This is a hallucination or a nightmare, her thoughts warned her. *I'm not going to have a conversation with either.*

But then the discomfort slipped further away.

The voice wasn't lying.

"Can you hear me, Venetia?"

"Yuh-yes."

"We can only communicate when you're in a state of fatigue because your subconscious blocks are down and your brain waves are optimum. We lose contact if you fall asleep or come fully awake. Try to maintain your fatigue, try to stay semiconscious."

Her brow furrowed in the dark. "That doesn't make sense."

"I know it doesn't . . . because everything is opposite here. What makes sense to you makes no sense here. Your moon is white, Venetia. Ours is black. Your science is our sorcery; our logic is your madness. You have enchantments, we have disenchantments, and where your world strives for order, our world strives for chaos. Please understand, you must *understand."*

The pain was barely there anymore; her fatigue began to reach up. . . .

"Please don't go to sleep! Damn! How can I convince you?" Was there a sound like hooves on pavement? The voice seemed to speak to someone else. *"Don't worry, Ruth, it's just a Halberdier Squad looking for Broodren to chop."*

Ruth? "Huh?"

The voice sharpened. *"Your name is Venetia Barlow. You're a theology student from Catholic University and right now you're working for the New Hampshire Diocese at a place called St. John's Prior House. Am I right?"*

"Yes," Venetia said.

"How could I know that?"

"Because you're just my subconscious mind!" she almost yelled in reply. "My subconscious mind would know that, you moron!"

"All right . . . let me think. Turn on the light and look in the mirror. Look directly at the reflection of your own eyes."

She felt more of the haze embracing her. "Why?"

"Because then you could see me. If you saw me, you'd be convinced."

Now she yawned but the prospect also made her tremble a little. *It's just a stupid dream. . . .* "I don't want to see you, whoever you are." Then she giggled. "Oh, yeah, my subconscious."

"Venetia, my name is Thomas Alexander. I'm a Catholic priest from Richmond. I was working at an old abbey in Russell County—"

"So what?"

"—when I died. I died about ten years ago."

I really have to hand it to my subconscious, she thought loopily. *This is one bizarre dream.* "Oh, so you're dead, huh?"

"Yes, and you might be too if you don't believe me—" Another crackling pause as though something were distracting the voice. *"Ruth, can't you see I'm trying to talk here! Don't touch that! It'll bite!"*

"Who's Ruth?" Venetia slurred.

"My assistant. She's here with me too; her name's Ruth Bridges, from Collier County, Florida. Remember that."

"What on earth for?"

The voice seemed to pitch in and out again, like a radio station getting too far away. *"Look it up on the Internet, and look up my name, too. Then you'll believe me, and we can make some progress."*

"This is stupid, this is a dream. . . ."

"For God's sake, don't fall asleep!"

The trebled volume gave her heart a lurch.

The voice spoke again to this imaginary Ruth person. *"She doesn't believe me. She thinks I'm just a voice in a dream."*

Did a woman's voice reply? *"Then I guess you're fucked, huh?"*

"I know." Louder. *"Venetia, listen! You just knocked a piece of plaster out of the wall, right?"*

"Uh-huh."

"And there's a word underneath the plaster."

"Some letters," she groggily replied.

"Not just some letters, it's a word."

Venetia smiled in the dark. "Tell me the word because I haven't seen it yet. If you tell me the whole word then you can't be my subconscious. But you can't do that, can you?"

"The word is Eosphorus."

Now her mind ticked through the crushing fatigue. "That's not Latin, is it?"

"*It's Greek. It means torchbearer.*"

"Huh?" She was drifting again.

"*I knew it, we're losing her.*" The voice was getting tiny behind the crackling. "*She'll wake up in the morning and think it was all a dream. We're getting nowhere with this.*"

"Fuckin' sucks, man," the woman's voice seemed to say. "*You ever gonna tell me what the fuck this shit's all about?*"

Venetia was confused. "Where are you talking to me from?"

"*I told you yesterday.*" The man's voice returned with some clarity. "*I'm in a city called the Mephistopolis.*"

Meph— She struggled through the drowse. "Where's that?"

Wind seemed to sweep through the crackling pause. "*It's in Hell.*"

The voice was gone, leaving a swollen silence in the room and Venetia's eyes wide open. The dream's final words left her unpleasantly awake, like after watching a gruesome horror movie late at night. *This is so crazy.* But at least she felt much better than after her last bout with this. *Voices from Hell. Where's my mind getting this stuff?*

Just go to bed. Don't worry about it.

She couldn't recall the conscious impulse that triggered her next action. When her full awareness returned, the dresser lamp was back on and there was a pile of chipped plaster by the baseboard.

She'd used her nail file to chip, scratch, and gouge away a nine-inch-long area of plaster.

The word stared back in her face.

EOSPHORUS.

Chapter Eight

(I)

Ruth lowered the *Vox Untervelt* from Father Alexander's lips.

"So much for that," he said, discouraged.

"You think she didn't believe you?"

"We'll see. If she checks those details out, she might."

"Yeah, or maybe the only thing she'll check is herself . . . into a fuckin' psych ward.

"You have such a way with words, Ruth."

"And *why* is it so important that you talk to this chick?"

"In time," Alexander said, using his favorite reply. He still sat propped up on the Rot-Port public bench.

In time, my ass. . . . When Ruth looked down at some weeds growing up through the spongy sidewalk cracks—a rot-walk, really—she noticed sneering faces within the persimmon-colored flowers. She scuffed some of the rot growing there with her flip-flop, to reveal the pavement itself. There were chunks of bone, finger- and toenails, and teeth mixed with the concrete. *This place sucks.* A tree out in the rot-lawned park looked like a willow, but the tip of every leaf seemed to excrete some milky fluid. Clumps of what she thought were Spanish moss dangled from the thin branches, but looking closer she realized they were simply clumps of organic rot.

The priest caught her gazing at it. "A Seeping Willow. Stay away from the stuff dripping from the leaves. It'll get you pregnant with something that's . . ."

Ruth could imagine. She pointed to the *Vox Untervelt* around Alexander's neck. "So, what? We gotta wait another day for this chick to get tired before you can talk to her again?"

"Correct."

Ruth tried to remain focused on whatever arcane task was in the priest's head but the surroundings just unnerved her too much. "Man, can we just get the fuck out of this rotten place?"

"Come on, Ruth. At least *try* to tone down the language. It's ungodly."

"Fuck that shit, man." She indecorously spat, trying to to evacuate the taste of the District's meaty air. "Look. Even the *grass* is rot. Let's split."

"I know you hate it here, Ruth, but we're not done in Rot-Port yet," the priest informed. "Roll up my left sleeve."

Ruth gaped at him. "Roll it up over *what?*"

"Just roll it up."

She rolled the black sleeve up over a scabbed and grisly stump. Whoever'd chopped off his arms had only left about six inches of stump. "Why am I doing this?"

"What's it say? The calligraphy?"

The fuck's he . . . But then she saw it. A scarlet scar like the most deftly inked tattoo read: *1500 Block, Cadaverine & Pestiferous St. South.*

"It's right down the road. Strap me up and head *that* way," he said with encouragement, pointing his stump.

Ruth harnessed him up, still unbelieving of her plight. "You got directions written on your *skin?*"

"Yes. It was written by a twelfth-century friar who

worked in a scriptorium in Spain. He had a problem with lust so that's why he wound up in Purgatory. Writes beautifully, though."

This is the dumbest-ass bunch of shit. . . . Ruth hauled him down the hot street on her back, sputtering. "So where are we going now?"

"Women like to shop, right?"

"Yeah," she replied, stretching the word.

"We're going shopping now, Ruth. To get you some new clothes."

LILITH'S WOMENS- & DEMONSWEAR ANNEX #5315, the rot-framed sign read.

"What's this? A fuckin' Victoria's Secret in Hell?"

"Exactly," the priest said behind her ear. "It's a state store. They're everywhere."

"So it's, like, communism here? Everything owned by the state?"

"Oh, no, that's far too uniform for Hell. It's everything. Communism, socialism, anarchism, oligarchy, tyranny, and good old free-enterprise. When you throw them all together, *none* of them work. That's the way Lucifer wants it. And it makes the economy ripe for corruption and cleptocracy."

Ask a silly question . . . , Ruth thought. She pushed in through the fungus-stained glass door and was at once greeted by a smiling, lavender-skinned Succubus who wasn't wearing a stitch. Yellow nipples and lips contrasted the odd hue, and what should have been the whites of her eyes were maroon. She was bald and had a pair of tiny black horns on her pate. Canine teeth showed through the smile. "May I help you?"

"We're looking for a nice bra and miniskirt," Alexander told the pretty Demonness. "Provocative yet refined. I'm particularly interested in something from the exclusive Bloody Mary line."

The attendant paused. "That's the most expensive line in Hell, Father, and they only make one style of bra and one style of skirt."

"I'm aware of that. Are a thousand Hellnotes per garment enough?"

The smile sharpened. "Oh, yes." Her words seemed to come from everywhere but her mouth. "Follow me."

Ruth trudged behind, noticing the clerk's sleek physique and impeccable curves. "She's got a pretty good body for a . . . whatever the fuck she is."

"A Succubus, Ruth. A female Sex-Demon. You can tell by the eyes that she's First Caliph. That means she's a direct descendant of the Lilitu herself."

"Who?"

"Lilitu, otherwise known as Lilith. Various rabbinic texts define her as either Adam's first wife or the Demonic imposture he left Eve for in the Garden of Eden. She's a favorite of Lucifer, the Whore Mother of Hell."

"Shit, I think a guy I was in love with called me that once."

The priest chuckled. "What was your reaction?"

Ruth recalled the satisfaction. "I busted a fuckin' toilet tank cover over his head, then took his cash and sold his Corvette to a chop shop. The fucker."

The Succubus took them into a dressing booth, the curtain of which was comprised of what appeared to be linked ceramic triangles. When Ruth looked closer, however, she saw that the triangles were teeth.

"Teeth from Excre-Leeches," Alexander said. "That means this is a posh place."

"If you'll just give me a second," the Succubus said, and then—

"Hey! Hands off the goods, honey!" Ruth exclaimed. "Unless you want some black-and-blue to go along with your purple skin!"

The Succubus had opened her long-fingered hands directly over Ruth's melon-sized breasts. "I need to size you, miss!" she snapped back.

"Then get a fuckin' tape measure!"

"Ruth, relax," Alexander said wearily. "That's how they do things here."

"Jesus!"

"And I'd get a more accurate measurement," the Demonness added, "if you'd take off those ratty Living
World clothes."

"Ratty?" Ruth wanted to hit her. "I got these clothes at
Beach Access, where *all* the Florida celebrities buy their
beach clothes!"

"Ruth . . ." The priest sighed. "Just do what she says."

Oh, for shit's sake! Ruth unharnessed Alexander and
placed his torso on the seat, then—frowning mightily—
took off her T-shirt and cutoffs.

The Succubus' grin turned salacious; then she glided
her sleek hands over all of Ruth's physical contours.

*I can't believe I'm letting myself be felt up by this . . . this
horned thing!*

Maroon eyes paused over Ruth's very full breasts. Then
the Succubus hissed and left the stall.

Ruth laughed. "I love it! That purple bitch is pissed off
'cos I got better boobs than her!"

"Remember that pride is a deadly sin," the priest told
her from his nook. "Instead you might want to try being
grateful for your God-given beauty."

Ruth didn't want to hear it. She turned around and at
once felt uneasy. Her nude body felt as though it were
blazing. "I guess . . . I'm a little uncomfortable being in a
dressing room with a guy watching."

He smiled. "Especially when they guy's a priest, huh?"

"Yeah, a priest torso."

"But I must extend my compliments, Ruth. You look
quite good for thirty-nine."

"I'm only—" The objection collapsed. "Fuck. No point
lying to you."

"That's right. You fared very well for an adulthood of
reckless abandon. All that booze and dope, for over two
decades, with no discipline whatsoever."

"Make me feel like a million fuckin' bucks, why
don'tya?"

"I'm just making a point. Life blessed you with great
genes, and those same great genes will serve us well in
Death."

Was the priest staring at her?

"Hey, I appreciate the compliment and all, and I'm glad you like my body, but don't you get yourself worked up because there ain't *no way* I'm gonna do anything about it. Not with a talking torso."

"Don't worry, it's nothing like that. I'm a priest, which means I don't have sex."

"You've never been with a woman, ever in your life?"

"I've been with lots of women. Two hundred and sixteen, to be exact."

Ruth laughed. "What a male whore!"

"Don't laugh too hard, Ruth. During your stint on earth, you'd had sex with five hundred and forty-seven men."

"Bullsh—"

"And another seventy-six women. So your tally's got me beat by a long shot."

"Fucker. And you're faker than me anyway. Priests aren't supposed to have sex."

"I didn't become celibate until I got into the seminary. But before that? I was a sinner extraordinare. When I was in Vietnam, we'd go on leave to Bangkok and I'd hop from one bordello to another. Man, oh, man, was I a piece of garbage. But then I found God, and if you let Him into your heart, He forgives everything."

Ruth chuckled. "If He forgave everything, he wouldn't have dropped your ass in Purgatory instead of Heaven, would he?"

"Good point. There are catches."

"Yeah, that's real fuckin' fair. You're gonna get to Heaven one day, but I'm stuck here. And you can kiss my ass and so can God. It's bullshit, man. My sins are no worse than yours and you fucking know it."

"You're right, but there's a difference, Ruth. Every time you turned a trick or lied, cheated, or stole, or whatever . . . each and every time you knew it was wrong. But you were never sorry for it, were you?"

Ruth huffed. "No."

Alexander fell silent.

She jabbed a finger. "But you can bet your hypocritical

Catholic ass that I am now. But that doesn't matter, either, does it, holy man?"

"Quit crying, Ruth. Trust me, nobody gets the opportunity you're going to get if we pull this off."

She smirked with cynicism. "And what if we don't? What if we fuck up royally?"

"Then we're both in deep shhhhh . . . Deep stuff."

"And if we *do* pull it off, you go to Heaven?"

"Yeah. That's what they said anyway. And a thousand years late, you go to Purgatory . . . if you're a good girl."

Ruth glared. "You didn't tell me about that part. I'm not real good at being good."

Alexander smiled cockily. "A thousand years is *plenty* of time to redeem yourself and prove a worthy servant of God."

This just sounds like more and more jive, Ruth thought. But what did she have better to do? "So why are you buying me new clothes?"

"Because you need a job."

Ruth groaned. "I'm not good with jobs either, man. Conning people, ATMs, dope dealing, sure. But really *working?* You got the wrong girl."

"Actually, Ruth, you're the *perfect* girl."

"How the fuck do you figure?"

"Your own pride is the answer. You're not just good-looking, you're *great*-looking."

Ruth couldn't help but be flattered.

"The Human Damned weather fast in Hell. You're a cinch to get the job. With your body and this outfit, I can't see them not hiring you. Very few inhabitants can afford an outfit like this, only the very upper-crust of the aristocracy. Trust me."

She rolled her eyes. "What? A strip joint?"

"No, no. Just . . . trust me."

Ruth hated it when men said that. Did it matter that he was a priest? *Probably some secretary shit.* "Well, I'm just telling you. I've never held a regular job for long."

"Don't worry, you'll probably only be working this job for about an hour."

"What the fuck?" she said, dismayed. "You're spending two grand on clothes so I can work for a fucking hour?"

The torso's head leaned forward. "She's coming back! Keep your voice down!"

The tooth curtain clattered, and in walked the Succubus. She held up odd garments on a hanger covered with a plastic bag. "Turn around, *miss*. I'll dress you."

Ruth snatched the hanger away. "I'll dress myself. Now get lost, will ya?"

The Succubus scowled and looked to Alexander. "That'll be all for now, thanks," he said. She whisked out.

"How do you like that monster-dyke? I just might kick her can before we shove off."

"Not a good idea, Ruth. She's a state employee, and since she's also a Succubus, she'd more than likely suck your innards out through your mouth and consume them. Then she'd drain your blood for the shop's distillery, sell your breasts to a Body Boutique, pawn your ovaries to a Hexegenic Vendor, and trade what's left to the District Pulping Station."

Guess I won't be kicking her can.

"Try the bra on first," the priest suggested.

She held it up and gaped. "You gotta be shitting me!"

If Alexander had had hands, he would've been rubbing his temples by now. "Just . . . try it on."

Two hands twice the size of a human male's had been linked at the tips of the middle fingers. A glittery strap dangled off each wrist. Furthermore, the hands were covered with hair brown as almond skin, and from each fingertip sprouted a talon like a bear's.

"It's a Hand-Bra, Ruth," Alexander detailed. "Probably a Lycan-Pimp. All werewolves in Hell are either prostitutes or panderers."

Ruth held the bra away from her as though it were a flap of rotten meat. "A bra made of werewolf hands?"

"Yes, Ruth. And, please, keep your voice down. You can get a bit shrill—it's giving me a *big* headache. Now, just try it on."

"*I'm not wearing a bra made of fuckin' werewolf hands!*" she yelled, her face turning red.

Alexander closed his eyes, staving off an outburst of his own. After a few seconds, he said very quietly, "Ruth. I've explained over and over. Things are different here. They're opposite. You may be repulsed by the nature of that garment, but all the same, here in Hell it's high-fashion. It's *the* most expensive bra a woman can wear. You'll be admired. You'll be envied. More important, it'll further us on our mission."

"*Fuck the mission! I'm not wearing a bra made of fuckin' werewolf hands!*"

Alexander's torso almost flopped over at Ruth's cannonade of objection. "Stop being selfish. We're working for God right now—"

Ruth laughed gutturally. "Oh, well, in that case, *God* can wear the *bra made of fuckin' werewolf hands!*"

"And as I've told you, God will reward you for your service if we complete this mission. The fact of the matter is, if you refuse to wear these garments, you won't get hired at this place I'm taking you to. Then you'll have to spend eternity in this evil city."

Blackmail. *Oh my God I can't* believe *this bullshit!* She stared at the hideous brassiere for a while longer, contemplating the word *eternity*, then contemplating the stuff she'd seen in only one day of being in Hell.

Ruth ground her teeth and put the bra on.

"Perfect fit!" Alexander said.

The pads of the paws felt atrociously warm. And when she'd finished tying the straps, the furred fingers slowly constricted and began to gently knead her breasts.

Ruth didn't bother yelling anymore. It could serve no practical purpose. "These hands are still alive, aren't they?"

"Yep. They've been incanted with a Longevity Spell. Fifty-year shelf-life. Why do you think the bra cost so much?"

Ruth shuddered at the awful sensation.

"Now," Alexander said, "it's time to try on the Tongue-Skirt."

When Ruth finally walked out of Lilith's Womens & Demonswear Annex #5315, she felt more nauseous than the time she'd downed ten Jäger Bombs at the Beach Lounge in St. Pete and then followed them up with five tequila oyster shooters.

"You're a good, strong girl, Ruth," the priest said from her back. "Lots of resolve, full of self-sacrifice. I'm proud of you."

Fuck, she thought.

The Tongue-Skirt, by the way, was exponentially worse than the Hand-Bra. Stitched together from tongues of a variety of Demonic species, it, too, was still alive, each tongue quivering over Ruth's bare skin the instant she stepped into the skimpy garment. The tongues were mostly brown and black, but there were also a few pink Human tongues included in the living fabric.

"Thanks for not making me wear that evil shit out of there," she said, huffing along the spongy Pestiferous Street South. After the fitting, the priest had allowed her to re-don her Living World clothes. The new garments were put in a fancy bag.

"Don't want any denizens seeing you in the stuff," Alexander said. "They'd pulp us and steal the clothes."

Great. "And if somebody *pulped* us," she said wanting to get it clear, "we still wouldn't die?"

"No, we wouldn't. If our bodies were completely destroyed, our eternal souls would be reassigned into the nearest life-form. Look over there—that red tree."

Ruth saw some brownish-black thing swelling from the size of an avocado to the size of a grapefruit. Did it have little legs underneath?

"If your Spirit Body was completely destroyed," the priest went on, "your head crushed, your brain mashed, and your heart diced, then your soul would slip into that thing on the tree. It's a Caco-Tick. They like tree sap, but at night, they sneak into the Ghettoblocks and hunt for sleeping Humans. They sink tubules like dialysis needles into your brain stem and suck out all your spinal fluid. It's their favorite meal."

Ruth stumbled on, her flip-flops slapping soft pavement. Everywhere she looked—the rot-caked town, the hideous passersby, the bloody sky full of stinking black smoke—just made her sicker and sicker.

"Turn left here."

She saw a street sign that read PITUITOUS BLVD., and turned.

"And now are you ready for some good news?" the talking torso asked from her back.

"How good can it be in this fuckin' puke bucket of a town?"

"We're finished in Rot-Port. We'll never have to come here again."

"Cool!" Ruth's gait gained momentum. It *was* good news. "Where are we going next?"

"To—well . . . another District."

"Yeah? What's it called?"

"And it's pretty close, too."

"Cool, but what's it called?"

"There are other Districts we could go to in order to achieve the same purpose, but they're farther away. Big hassle to get to," the priest continued.

"I gotcha," Ruth said. She was starting to get annoyed. "But—"

"And I can guarantee that there's not a speck of rot in this District—"

Ruth stopped. Her blond hair flew when she jerked her head back. "What's the place fucking *called?*"

The priest paused on his harness of Demonic belts. Was he reluctant to tell her the next District's name?

"It's called Sewageton."

Sewage? Ruth thought.

"The Waste District."

"You fucker!" Ruth bellowed.

"But we'll only be there a little while," Alexander hastened to say. "There's only one thing we have to do. Then we can leave."

Ruth watched a steam-car full of Imps chug by. They were eating Demonic baby heads off sticks like candy apples. Sharpened spikes jutted from the vehicle's front grill.

For a moment, Ruth entertained the idea of jumping in front of it, and taking the priest with her. *But then I'd just turn into a fuckin' tick*, she remembered.

Utterly disheartened, she asked, "What do we have to do in *Sewageton* that's so important?"

Alexander beamed behind her. "That's the place where I get a new set of arms and legs."

(II)

"What a wonderful girl, so full of initiative," Mrs. Newlwyn complimented.

Venetia looked over her shoulder and saw the tall, statuesque woman striding out of the kitchen entry. "Good morning, Mrs. Newlwyn. I thought I'd get right to work after I got up." Venetia had taken it upon herself to resume the masking tape duties downstairs. She saw now that she was nearly to the last window.

"But you missed breakfast," the older woman paused to say.

"I know. I fell asleep later than I'd planned to." A semifib. The real reason she'd skipped breakfast was because last night's bizarre experience had stolen her appetite: the dream and, of course, the word on the wall beneath the plaster.

I was tired, that's all. I saw the word beforehand and just thought *the voice in the dream told me what it was.* Then, *Damn it.*

In spite of her conviction that it all *was* just a dream, she'd called her mother anyway.

And asked her to do a Web search of those two names.

Thomas Alexander, a priest from Virginia, and Ruth Bridges from Florida.

And it'll be nothing . . .

Mrs. Newlwyn offered a stern smile. "Don't let yourself get run-down, dear. All this hard work, in this heat? Don't take your youth for granted. It's one of God's greatest worldly gifts."

"I know," Mrs. Newlwyn." Venetia pulled off another strip of tape. "But I won't miss lunch, that's for sure."

"Okay, then." The older woman retained the stern smile and walked quickly back to her business.

"You'd think she was your own mother," Dan said, coming up behind her. He wore jeans, sneakers, and his black cleric shirt and Roman collar.

"Hi. And yeah, there is something maternal about her. I like her. She's like an old-fashioned schoolmarm."

Dan looked down the long wall. "You've finished taping all the windows. I was going to help you for a few minutes."

"Just a few minutes?" she joked.

"I have attic duty, remember?"

Venetia smiled at the recollection. "Yes, thanks to your rapier wit." She looked to her left and saw that no more windows needed taping. Then she noticed Dan. He appeared disconcerted. "How come you're not your usual slyly smiling self?"

He seemed to chew a thought, as if he didn't know whether to elaborate. "Just saw something funny last night."

"Funny?" She stowed the tape, brushed off her hands. "You're not laughing, are you?"

His eyes drifted to a window. "After I butt-faced myself in range of Driscoll's ear, I went to my room. Wasn't that tired so I read some of Paul's Gospel—easily the best writer of the Apostles."

"I'm partial to John but I do agree. Paul's expository skill blew everyone else away." She continued to note his odd expression. "So . . ."

"So I went downstairs to get some ice water. I was sipping it and checking out the bookshelves in the atrium when I heard a click."

She couldn't resist. "Don't tell me. The ghost."

"No. It was Betta coming in through the back door in the kitchen. She's sort of sneaking in, you know? Trying to be quiet and looking like she's in a hurry. So she slips upstairs and into her room."

"So she'd been outside, I guess."

"Yeah, but didn't we see her sneaking *down* the stairs earlier, when we were rapping on the stair-hall?"

"Yes, we did. I figured she was going to the kitchen to get some milk or something before bed. But she went outside instead. Kind of strange at that hour, but so what? She decided to go for a walk in the moonlight, I suppose."

"Yeah, maybe, but it was a long walk."

"What do you mean?"

"When she came back in it was several hours *after* we saw her go down the stairs. She didn't see me but I thought I noticed leaves and stuff stuck to her blouse, and the blouse was buttoned up one button off, like she'd been rushing. Hair kind of tangled up, too."

They looked at each other.

"Sounds like Betta's got a secret boyfriend she meets outside when everyone's asleep," Venetia ventured.

"Yeah, that's what I was thinking."

"All right, but, again, so what? Why shouldn't she have a boyfriend? It's probably that guy John, the yard guy. He's shy and so is she. Maybe they're attracted to each other."

"I was thinking that too, and her mother's kind of a stolid Bible-thumper, so it makes sense Betta would keep a lover secret from her."

"Right. Simple human sexual attraction—what most of the world is all about."

Dan chuckled. "Except for priests and seminarists . . . and girls contemplating the convent."

"So *that's* why you look bent out of shape? Betta's got a boyfriend?"

"No, no, that's not it at all. It was later . . . I woke up about two, could hear someone walking on the stair-hall. The floor creaks sometimes. I thought it was probably

Betta or Mrs. Newlwyn coming back from the bathroom or something. So I open my door a crack and look out. . . ."

"Was it her?"

"No. Someone else. It was someone else going down the stairs very slowly. Someone in a dark cloak."

"Come on. The ghost then? That's what you're telling me? I don't believe it and neither do you."

Dan kept looking out the window as he spoke, clearly at odds with something. "The figure continued down the stairs in total silence, but by the time it got to the bottom it was gone."

"You're a good actor, Dan, but not that good."

"I'm not bullsh— I'm not making it up," he said and finally looked at her. The disconcertion drew lines in his forehead. "I keep telling myself it was a dream but—"

"It felt real," Venetia said rather than asked. *Same thing with me . . .*

"Yeah. Anyway, I'm off to the attic coves. If I'm not back by sundown, send a search party."

" 'Bye," she said, and watched him shuffle off. *Yeah, he's really bothered by something.*

Only a minute later, more footsteps echoed through the atrium: Father Driscoll's. "Well done, Venetia," he said, admiring the perfectly taped windows. "I thought we'd be at it a few more hours before we could start painting."

"Hi, Father. I've been a busy bee, I guess."

"What's the old line? Idle hands?"

"Are the Devil's workshop," she finished.

"Exactly." A noise caught Driscoll's attention. He looked up to the second-story stair-hall and saw Dan on a ladder. Venetia did a double take when she noticed that Dan had removed his collar and black clerical shirt. *He's in . . . really good shape.* The stray thought sifted in her head. It actually annoyed Venetia the way her eyes kept flicking up at Dan's muscled chest and abdomen. *Stop staring at him—jeez!*

Dan didn't look happy as he fiddled with a ceiling panel.

"Don't have too much fun up there, Dan," Driscoll's voice boomed. "And try not to get too hot."

Dan looked down from the ladder, started to say something, but thought better of it.

Driscoll half-smiled. "Oh, and keep an eye out for rats."

Dan grinned back. "Father Driscoll, sir? I will bag every single rat in this attic and bring them all down just for you."

"Peace be with you, my son."

At last Venetia remembered something. *Oh, I guess I better tell him.* "Do we have any plaster or spackle?"

"Yes," Driscoll said, a cant in his voice. "Why?"

"I damaged one of my bedroom walls last night. I bumped the floor lamp and it fell over."

"Don't worry about it. It's hard to do any serious damage to these walls anyway."

"I know. Feels like they're all solid brick."

The priest nodded. "We'll take care of that later. Today I'd rather get these windows painted since you've finished taping them all." An abrupt clattering sound made them both look to the drapeless window, which was full of sunlight.

John, the yard boy, was pushing a large lawn mower around a weedy path.

"On second thought," Driscoll said, "why don't you start the painting in here. I'll go out and mow for a while. That kid's working too hard—he needs a break."

"Oh, let me do it, Father." Venetia said without hesitation. "I haven't introduced myself to him yet, and I'd love to get some real exercise."

"Venetia, it's *very* hot out—"

"I'm a big girl. I won't *faint*," she assured him. "Okay?"

Driscoll picked up a bucket full of brushes and a can of white enamel. "All right. But not more than an hour. God's got better things to do than protect the righteous from heatstroke."

Venetia laughed and rushed to the door.

But the heat *was* stifling. The instant she stepped outside, her skin began to mist with sweat. Her sneakers took her briskly around the cement path to the back of the building. Most of the grass was pale-green, and the huge area behind the house seemed paralyzed in heat and silence. "Hey, wait up!" she called out.

She jogged up. John froze in the middle of reaching for the mower's pull cord. He was taller than she remembered, and well-toned in spite of the overly thin physique. His blackish hair in need of a trim stuck out every which way.

"Hi, John. My name's Venetia," she said and stuck out her hand.

At once he seemed reserved, even shy. "Hi," he replied almost inaudibly. He shook her hand quickly and with barely any grip.

"It's nice to meet you. I only got here yesterday. Let me mow for a while—"

"You don't have to," he muttered.

"Father Driscoll wants you to take a break."

Now he seemed defensive. "Well, it-it-it's my job."

"I know that, John." She almost laughed. "But you're working really hard out here, so go take a break." She put her hands on his shoulders and guided him away from the mower. "You shouldn't have to do all the outside work yourself—we'll all chip in, okay? Go inside and relax, get a cool drink."

"Well, if you're sure . . ."

"I'm sure, John. See you in a little while."

He shuffled off, looking over his shoulder a few times. "Buh-bye . . ."

" 'Bye."

Wow, he really is shy, she thought. *Barely talks, and Betta doesn't talk at all.* Was Dan right about a secret romance going on between the two?

The mower started on the first pull and seemed loud as a prop plane. It wasn't self-propelled but that was fine; Venetia was enthused for the opportunity to get some exercise. *If only it weren't so hot!* she thought. The rear grounds looked huge now but she wasn't thwarted. She just turned the mower and pushed forward.

The loud machine plowed swath after swath. She used the stout brick toolshed as her starting point. It stood in the center of the backyard. She worked her way outward, mowing the grounds from the inside out. *This is even sort of fun.* The heavier splotches of onion grass disintegrated under the blade; dandelions exploded in endless white tufts. Humidity compounded the heat; she hadn't even mowed a quarter of the back before she stopped for a moment, rolled her short sleeves all the way up, then unbuttoned her blouse and knotted it at the midriff. Dandelion seeds, pulverized grass, and sundry grit stuck to her exposed skin. Several times she had to stop and wait for a toad to hop out of the cutting lane, and later she even saw a bullfrog. *Must be a pond around here,* she reasoned.

An hour later, she was baking and drenched in sweat, yet she felt invigorated. There were no leftover doldrums from last night's inexplicable dream. *Voices from Hell . . .* She grinned behind the mower's handle. *Now that's a Catholic nightmare if there ever was one.* And the writing beneath the plaster? *Big deal.*

When she approached the outer boundaries of the yard, she turned off the mower and pushed it into a cove within the front wood line. The sudden shade invigorated her. Just before she would sit down to rest, she heard a chorus of *rrrrrribit*s, and then looked aside. *There's the pond.* Nestled right among the high trees and complete with lily pads, the small pond shimmered like a dark mirror. Pairs of round, gold-flake eyes from submerged bullfrogs made her feel like a trespasser. Minute dots from water bugs appeared atop the water and radiated outward in radarlike circles. At once, Venetia felt serene and lulled by the frog songs. It was refreshing to see a slice of nature like this, untouched by human meddling.

Then she frowned—so much for being untouched. In the trees, just off the rim of the pond, she spotted empty beer cans and various other litter. *I'll get a bag later and pick it all up,* she resolved. And—

What are those *things?*

She moved closer and noticed a number of long white plastic tubes that she thought must be pens.

But she was wrong.

Squinting, she read: ORTHO-OPTIONS. *Applicators for contraceptive foam . . .* Venetia knew about all the various birth control methods, but suddenly she felt naive for this was the first time she'd ever seen such a thing for real. She couldn't imagine anything less passionate. *The woman has to dispense this stuff into herself before intercourse. . . .* It seemed even less passionate than condoms, but then she reminded herself, *These days, passion rarely has anything to do with it. It's just lust.*

But did she really believe the Church's stance, that birth control devices circumvented God's intent?

Venetia wasn't sure how she felt about that one. *No point arguing with the Pope. . . .*

She left the littered area and returned to the big ugly mower. She'd noted about a dozen of the emptied dispensers, plus lots of beer cans. *Yeah, they've got quite a party going on out here.* Of course, it wasn't her place to judge. But it did remind her of the deception of appearances. An eighteen-year-old introvert and a thirty-year-old mute woman couldn't have seemed more unlikely but then . . . *Love—and lust—will always find a way,* she thought.

She couldn't even remember the last time she'd had a genuinely lustful thought herself. Her few extra glances at Dan's shirtless body upstairs hardly counted.

Another thought crept up: *If I decide to* not *become a nun, what will my first sexual experience be like? And how grievous or venal a sin will it be if it's out of wedlock?*

She started the mower and pushed it back out into the heat. The machine's racket and the scent of fresh-cut grass cleared her head.

But another thought sideswiped her; more of an image than a thought. She imagined cool shower water teeming down on her nude body, then—

Oh, jeez . . .

A man's hands sliding up her sides and around to her breasts, a man standing behind her. She could also feel his nude hips against her buttocks, and the hard, warm column pressing against her. Then one of the hands slipped down slowly to caress her sex . . .

Oh, come on! I don't need this! Suddenly she was tingling, the sweat coming out of her only increasing the obvious state of arousal. What had caused the brief fantasy? Finding used birth control applicators? Was the discovery of these things and the beer cans a symbol of revelry and abandon that her psyche was juxtaposing with hard-line Catholic beliefs? *Just because I'm a Catholic virgin doesn't mean my sexual impulses are different from anyone else's.* But harmless as the fantasy was it annoyed her. It made her feel out of control, at the mercy of primality.

Looks like I'm done, she thought a little later. She was at the edge of the yard now, and could see nothing left to be cut. She turned off the mower just as she noticed Dan— still shirtless but now flecked with dust—striding across the yard.

"Driscoll wants you inside, says you've been out here too long. Come in and chug some water so you don't get dehydrated."

Venetia shook her head, mildly nettled. "I'm perfectly fine, Dan."

"Look, when a hundred and ten pound girl mows a half acre in this heat, she's going to be dehydrated."

"I'm actually a one hundred and *twenty* pound *woman*."

"Sure. Sorry. But just come in now. Boss's orders."

For the smallest moment, she caught Dan's eyes scanning her bare belly and glistening cleavage showing at the top of her blouse. Then he looked away.

"Where do I put the mower?" she asked.

Dan pointed to the brick shed in middle of the yard. "Right there. That's where the yard kid keeps everything."

For a second she toyed with the idea of telling him what she'd found near the pond. *Too gossipy,* she decided, thinking again of the importance of not making judgments about others.

"Come on, hurry up," Dan said.

"What's the rush!"

"Just come upstairs when you're back in." His expression changed to something half perplexed and half excited. "I found something pretty damn bizarre in the attic."

"What on earth is Dan so riled up about?" Mrs. Newlwyn remarked. Her old summer dress splotched by paint, she'd walked into the kitchen just as Venetia was getting a drink of water.

"Something he found while cleaning out the attic coves."

"Hmm," the tall woman contemplated. "But I wonder what they need brass polish for?"

"Brass polish?"

Mrs. Newlwyn pulled a can from the cupboard and grabbed a rag. "That's what they asked me to bring them."

"Let's go see."

They took the stairs up side by side. "You must be exhausted mowing all that grass."

"I don't know why everyone thinks I'm so fragile," Venetia joked. "I enjoyed it." She looked back down across the atrium. "Where's Betta?"

"She's out front, helping John."

Helping John? I'll bet she is.

The older woman glanced around with a satisfied gleam in her eye. "Slow but sure, we're getting this old place back to rights."

"I'll bet it doesn't take as long as Father Driscoll thinks."

"Down here," Driscoll's voice alerted them. He stood next to Dan beside the ladder. The ceiling panel up above had been taken down. The two men were inspecting something propped against the wall.

"What's that?" Venetia inquired.

"It's a very old painting," Driscoll said.

"It looks like . . . a painting of a Pope," Mrs. Newlwyn offered.

Dan got down on one knee to look closer. "Yeah, but

which one? The raiments this guy's wearing look almost medieval."

Venetia knelt right next to him, then felt the oddest reaction when looking. Something like a chill?

A great miter adorned the Pope's rather bulbous face, and the eyes seemed disinterested within hooded lids. A gold cross emblazoned the hat, while another hung around the nameless Pope's neck. He wore a white cope over a black cassock, both of which were flamboyantly piped. *Dan's right. It looks like the Middle Ages,* Venetia thought.

"He doesn't look very happy," Mrs. Newlwyn pointed out.

"The history of the Papacy includes some very unhappy times," Driscoll said.

"And this was in the attic?" Venetia questioned.

"Yeah," Dan said. "Much to Father Driscoll's disappointment, the attic coves were all pretty much empty—not much for me to do. But I found this in the last one—"

"The oil paint's cracked," Venetia observed.

"Uh-huh. This is just how I found it. No box, no covering. So many years of hot summers and arctic winters ruined it. It might've been worth money. They should've stored it better."

But Venetia wondered who *they* might be. "I wonder why they didn't hang it downstairs. There are at least a dozen papal portraits in the atrium."

"That's why we need the brass polish," Driscoll said. "See the name plate?"

Venetia saw it, at the bottom of the ornate but dust-caked frame. "Here, Mrs. Newlwyn, let me see that." She took the can of polish and rag.

She practically had her face to the floor. The small plate was black with tarnish. When Dan hunkered down right beside her, she received the impression that he'd stolen a glimpse down her cleavage, and when she glanced over to him, he quickly looked away.

"Be careful," he said. "Who knows how old the metal is. Too much polish might obliterate the name."

Venetia dabbed some polish on, let it sit a minute, then began to gently wipe.

"Can you read it?"

A name began to appear from left to right.

"It's . . ." She squinted hard. "Boniface."

"There were a bunch of Bonifaces," Dan said. "Isn't there a number?"

"Don't rush me!" Venetia gently buffed off the rest of the plaque. Then, in a voice so low as to be grim, she said, "Boniface the Seventh."

Dan chuckled. "Isn't that the one who died from gout?"

Venetia turned around but remained seated on the floor. "No," was her only reply.

Driscoll talked deliberately loud, and with that ever-so-slight smile of his. "Obviously Venetia got higher marks in her Papal history classes than you did, Dan. Venetia, enlighten our cocky seminarist as to the nature of Pope Boniface the Seventh."

Dan smirked.

"He was one of the worst anti-Popes," she said. "*The* worst, according to most historians. He murdered Pope Benedict the Sixth in order to be installed as Pope himself, but after only a month he was banished by the Holy Roman emperor, Otto the Second. When Otto died, Boniface—who was backed by corrupt, unscrupulous, and very *anti*-Christian Roman aristocrats—murdered the *next* Pope as well, John the Fourteenth—and was *rein*-stalled. If ever a Pope was pure evil, it was Boniface. A glutton, a rapist, a slave trader, and a robber baron—he was all those things. This guy was as corrupt as Nero, yet he sat on the Papal throne *twice*. He was even reported to be part of a secret Satanic sect."

"There you have it, Dan," Father Driscoll said, amused by yet another opportunity to rib his assistant. "And I'd say that you've answered your own question, too, Venetia."

She let out a grim chuckle. "Yeah. Now we know why *this* portrait wasn't displayed downstairs with the real Popes."

"But . . . why?" Mrs. Newlwyn asked now. "Why would there even *be* a portrait of this horrible man here?"

"Consider what Venetia said a moment ago," Driscoll commented. "Boniface was thought to be in a secret Satanic sect. Anyone?"

Venetia's eyes widened. "Amano Tessorio," she spoke up. "The architect for the prior house."

Dan nodded now. "Of course. For years while he was the Vatican's architect he lived a blasphemous double life—"

"As a member in a secret Satanic sect," Mrs. Newlwyn finished.

"So it's pretty easy to ascertain," Driscoll added, "that this portrait was something that Tessorio privately owned but never dared show anyone. I'll bet he came up to this attic to gloat over it every now and then while still on the Vatican payroll. Tessorio was a blasphemer hidden within the inner circles of the Vatican hierarchy itself—the ultimate offense to God."

A heavy silence hung in the stair-hall after Driscoll's bleak dissertation. Eventually, Mrs. Newlwyn uttered, "How . . . awful."

"Great grist for detractors of Catholic thesis," Dan offered. "It's hard to support the infallibility of the Church after so many anti-Popes."

"It doesn't mean the *Church* is fallible, Dan," Driscoll asserted. "Just humankind." He pointed down. "Now show Venetia and Mrs. Newlwyn the other one."

"There's another painting?"

"Not a *painting* . . . " Dan carefully slid the Boniface canvas aside to reveal a smaller frame of quality drawing paper.

"A sketch?" Mrs. Newlwyn guessed.

Driscoll nodded. "Probably drawn by Tessorio himself. Most architects are also excellent sketch artists, by necessity."

Venetia hunched forward again, then flinched. "It's . . . hideous. And I'm not sure why? It almost looks like—"

"A different rendition of the Boniface portrait," Dan said.

It was a fine-line sketch, detailed as the most intricate engraving—and indeed seemed to mimic the painting: a similar portraiture and outline, complete with the great miter, only now the cross was upside down. But the "hideous" part?

"The *face*," Venetia almost gagged.

"A mask, I suppose," Mrs. Newlwyn expressed.

Yes, now, the anti-Pope's face seemed more like a mask of white crust, with only crude eye holes and a gouge for a mouth.

"Read the inscription," Father Driscoll advised. "I'll bet anything it's Tessorio's handwriting, too."

At the bottom, Venetia read the fine cursive words:

In a Blood & Sumac Dream, my vision: E.D. Boniface.

"E.D.?" Venetia questioned. "What could that mean?"

"Who knows?" Driscoll said. "And it looks like a castle in the background, doesn't it?"

Venetia noted the intricate brickwork behind the appalling figure, topped by ramparts and a turret.

"A medieval fortress," Dan commented. "And check out the black sickle moon. That's *got* to symbolize something. The religious schism of those times, or the moral decay."

"A black moon for a black age," Driscoll added.

Venetia couldn't help but remain on her knees to inspect the strange artwork. It was true; she could see the tiny detail herself: a black sickle moon edging over the fortress wall.

Black, she thought. *Sickle moon . . .*

And the voice last night, her own dream . . .

Your moon is white, Venetia. Ours is black. . . .

Mrs. Newlwyn again: "What are those adornments, in the corners?"

I wish there was more light. . . . Venetia looked closer and detected cursive loops wrapped around each corner of the sketch.

Then—

"Wait a minute. Those aren't adornments," she noted. "It's more writing."

Driscoll leaned on his knees. "Can you make it out?"

Now Venetia had her face only a few inches from the drawing paper. "It looks like . . . *ash-shaytan*."

"What the hell is that?" Dan wondered.

"Hell is right," Driscoll said. He had a smirk for Dan's borderline profanity. "It's one of the Islamic names for Satan. Read the next corner."

"*Lux*," she began, and after more squinting: "*Ferre?*"

Father Driscoll looked down, hands on hips. "Come on, you both took Latin, didn't you?"

She and Dan traded glances, then almost simultaneously they both said, "Lucifer."

"Good. The third corner?"

"*Iblis*," Venetia and Dan said together. Dan looked up. "Isn't that *another* name for the Devil?"

"Uh-huh. *Pre*-Islamic. And the fourth corner?

Venetia read it, pushed back a sick feeling in her gut, then said, "*Eosphorus.*"

Chapter Nine

(I)

WELCOME TO SEWAGETON, THE BEAUTIFUL WASTE DISTRICT, the sign greeted them.

"Oh my . . . *god!*" Ruth howled when she looked around.

"I never said we were going to Disney World, Ruth."

"We're not going here!" she yelled over her shoulder. "We just left a town made of rot, but now we're coming *into* a town made of—of—" In utter disbelief, she looked around again, at the brown brick buildings, the brown brick streets, the dizzyingly high brown brick skyscrapers. "Oh my *god!*"

"Ruth, you're just making this harder and harder by complaining," Alexander said from her back. "I've already told you, each district exists in its own uniqueness. Rot-Port's made of rot. Osiris Heights is made of bricks of obsidian stone, to honor the Egyptian god of the Underworld, a place called the Chthonic Region. The Boniface District—which you'll be seeing later—was built with bricks made of baked blood."

"And this place is made with bricks of shit! It's disgusting, and it doesn't make sense!"

"I've told you over and over, everything is opposite here. That's part of Lucifer's design. This is just . . . the way it is."

"Well then *fuck* the way it is!" she bellowed. Several Polter-Rats scattered at Ruth's outburst.

"Just hold the line," the priest ordered.

Ruth thought of looking down as she walked along, to avert her eyes from the appalling look of the place, but even then she quailed when she noticed a detail within the sidewalk bricks. "Aw, man, the sidewalk's got *corn* in it. . . ."

"Be strong."

The next brown building took up the equivalent of a city block. Slim bronze pipes on the roof, like stovepipes, issued wisps of smoke that seemed pink. There were no windows.

THE GOETHE HALL OF AUTOMATIC-WRITERS, read the sign.

"What's *that?*" Ruth asked.

"Automatic-writers are one of Hell's favorite means of contacting people in the Living World," the priest explained. "And this, the Goethe Hall, is the most important one in the city. That pink smoke is the exhalations of the writers themselves. Specially trained Warlocks called Telethesists use intricate manipulations of telepathy. They go into a trance after inhaling the fumes of burning tree resin—a tree from which someone was hanged—while a human in the Living World is in an identical trance. Whatever the Telethesist writes is simultaneously written down by their earthly contact. It helps spread the influence of Hell on earth. The big deal these days is they contact novelists and songwriters. But they also use their craft to recruit myrmidons. . . ."

"I dropped out of school in junior high, man," Ruth griped, still wincing at the district's all-pervading stink. "Do I look like I know what that means?"

"A myrmidon is like a helper, Ruth. Only these helpers on earth exist to help Satan. Hitler was a myrmidon, by the way, and so were Genghis Khan and Napoleon."

"Napoleon—oh, the guy who invented the dessert?"

"They're famous figures of evil in world history, Ruth."

"World history didn't do shit for me so I don't give a shit about *it*."

Alexander tsked. "You should, Ruth, because some of what I'm saying involves you. For instance, a long time ago, there was a Pope named Boniface the Seventh. He was one of these myrmidons I'm telling you about."

"What, a *Pope* was in contact with some wizard in Hell?"

"Through a contract with the Devil, yes. Boniface is now a very high-ranking figure here in the Mephistopolis, and for quite some time he's been utilizing some of Hell's very best automatic-writers to contact some other myrmidons on earth, and it all has something to so with our mission."

Ruth winced when she spotted two construction Imps stirring what she first thought was a trough of cement. But it was a trough of something else. "And this chick you were talking to on that horn?"

"The *Vox Untervelt*, yes. That girl—Venetia Barlow—is the very keystone of our mission. If we can't convince her that we're genuine, then—"

"We're up Shit's Creek, right? And I'll bet this burg's really got one."

Father Alexander shook his head behind her. "Just try to listen more, Ruth. We've both got a lot riding on this."

"Yeah?" Ruth was getting fed up. "The only thing I've got *riding* right now is *you*—on my fuckin' *back*—while I'm walking through a town made of *shit*."

"Ruth, please remember. Try to have some Grace." He tried to sound hopeful. "And don't forget—with any luck, I'll have some new limbs in a little while, and you won't have to carry me anymore."

"Yeah, that I *really* have to see . . ."

Her flip-flops pounded on.

To passersby, the priest appeared as a second head on Ruth's shoulder. "Wait, wait," he said, as if alarmed. "Cross the street and cut through the next block."

"Why?"

"See those Broodren up there at the corner?"

Her eyes peered ahead. Several guffawing Demonic kids had congregated around a fire hydrant, and one of them had a big wrench. "Yeah, I see 'em. What about 'em?"

"Well, you know how kids in the inner city open fire hydrants during the summer to stay cool? Same thing here."

"Not *quite* the same thing," she snapped over her shoulder. "Kids in the inner city don't have horns and fangs."

"But it's all relative, Ruth. Just cross the street. We don't want to be anywhere near that hydrant."

Ruth slowed, thinking. "What's wrong with you? I'm burning up it's so hot here. Let's go cool off under that hydrant."

"Ruth. Think," the priest sternly suggested. "This town is called *Sewageton*. No water will be coming out of that hydrant, just diarrhea."

Ruth sprinted across the street.

"So where are we going now?" she half-sobbed.

"We're looking for Excreta Avenue. There's an urban event that's going to take place there soon, and we can't miss it."

"I don't even want to know."

"Good, because it's easier to see than to explain." He paused, looking off in the distance. "Oh, and here's something pretty disgusting."

"Then I don't want to know!"

"It's just more things that you *need* to know." The priest was losing his patience. "Knowledge is your best weapon, Ruth. You need to know the terrain of your enemy. Then you can operate more effectively. Like that, for instance. . . ."

Ruth stopped at the corner of a street called Ordure Lane, then spotted the sign on another multilevel brown brick warehouse that took up more space than just about any structure she'd ever seen. DISTRICT TANNING DEPOT #1.

"Ruth. You're looking at the largest tanning facility in

the Mephistopolis. It makes sense that they'd have it in Sewageton."

"Tanning like in tanning hide?"

"That's right."

But the smell coming out of the building's vents was abominable.

"I used to live with a guy in Florida who poached gator, and he'd tan the hide and sell it to dealers. But fuck! The chemicals smelled bad but not *that* bad. Jesus, that place smells like—"

"Take a look in the window."

Ruth hesitated, but then thought that maybe he was right. *The more I know about this fucked-up place, the better I'll be able to get along here.* She took one look through a stained window and saw vats so big they reminded her of water reservoirs.

"Every urinal in the district empties here, by the way. And as you can see, they also have an immediate source. Along the upper rims . . ."

Each huge reservoir was open-topped, and when she scanned the upper rim of each one, she saw—

Are those people?

"They're convicts," the priest continued. "In the Waste District, Human Damned who commit crimes don't go to the penitentiary, they come here."

"For what?"

"Take the Abyss-Eye and see for yourself."

Ruth reached around and grabbed the pendant, then held it to her eye.

"Oh, man! That's fucked-up!"

"That's how Humans serve their sentences here—by contributing to the supply."

She'd zoomed the Abyss-Eye on to one of several hundred Humans trapped in Iron Maidens that hung just past the reservoir's rim. Conscripts and Golems patrolled the rim in supervision. The Maiden that Ruth focused on contained a naked man whose hair and beard hung to his knees. A fat black tube led from the ceiling into his mouth. When Ruth took a longer view, she noted that thousands of such tubes fed thousands more of the Iron Maiden prisoners.

"Since the convicts are all Human, they can't die," Alexander explained. "No matter *what* you feed them. Polluted water is pumped through the tubes into their bodies so that they're constantly urinating, feeding the supply. Understand?"

"That's outrageous!"

"Um-hmm. So definitely don't commit any crimes in Sewageton, because *that's* where you'd spend your entire sentence. Ten years, fifty years, a hundred. Whatever. In Hell, convicted criminals are forced to contribute to the economy."

They're using people for piss generators! "Wait a minute! Wait a *fuckin'* minute! What's this got to do with tanning hide?"

"Watch. See those claws?"

Ruth looked again and noticed that every so often, a giant metal claw would dip from the ceiling and release scraps of freshly flensed skin. The scraps would fall into the vat.

"Human skin, Demon, Hybrid, fish skin, Gargoyle hide, Octo-Vulture—you name it. Flensing is big business in this District."

After the claw released its load, it shimmied to the other end of the vat, lowered, and a few moments later clattered back upward, its tines bearing scraps of still more skin.

"They alternate ends," Alexander said. "A fresh load sits in the vats for about a week, and then its removed for processing and tailoring. You see, Ruth, there's no tannic acid in Hell, but there's plenty of uric acid, an effective substitute. What you're looking at is essentially the most productive skin processor in Hell. The District's entire economy runs on it. Skin makes up ninety percent of all apparel in Hell. Only the very very rich own clothes made of fabric."

"That's the most fucked-up thing I've ever seen!" Ruth yelled, and jerked away from the obscene window. "You bring me into a town made of shit just to show me a piss factory!"

"Calm down, Ruth. You better get used to it. What you're seeing here is nothing compared to some of the things that go on in the Mephistopolis."

"Well I don't want to see any more!" Ruth was striding so fast that Alexander almost jounced out of the harness. "I want *out* of here. This is worse than that other fucked-up place—ten times worse!"

"Not much farther," he tried to console her. "Take a left at that Manburger stand."

Ruth glimpsed what looked like a hot dog cart on the corner like you'd see in any city. The only difference was that the vendor himself had a face that looked collapsed by a baseball bat and some kind of weird vegetation growing out of his ear. "You said hamburger, right?"

"No. Just . . . forget it."

They turned at the brown brick corner, under the EXC-RETA AVE. sign. "All right. What now?"

"Go to that alley. But watch for rats and Caco-Ticks."

Fuckin' great, she thought.

The stench that wafted out of the alley was positively worse than anything she'd ever smelled in her life.

"Just try to hack it, Ruth," the priest sensed her revulsion. "Set me down and pay attention.

Yeah, yeah. She did so, breathing through her mouth. "Man, do we have to be in the *alley?* It smells like a corpse's ass crack."

"We need a protected vantage point. For instance, if some Broodren or drug addicts saw a living torso sitting right on the street unattended, then they'd snatch me and sell my guts and blood to a fortune-teller, and the rest to a Pulping Station."

Ruth's brow popped up. "But you're not unattended. You're with me, and I've got this." She patted the clunky pistol on her belt.

The dismembered priest seemed reluctant to say something. "Look, Ruth. For this to work, you're going to be on your own for a few minutes. Into the fray, so to speak."

She glared down at him. "What the fuck are you talking about?"

"Sit down for a minute. Let me explain—"

"The sidewalk is made of *shit* bricks. I'm not going to *sit* on it. Now what kind of jive are you trying to pull?"

Alexander aimed his stump. "See that yellow line in the road?"

Ruth saw it beneath the feet of droves of Infernal citizens walking to and fro. The crowd parted every so often to let a steam-car chug by, or a Ghor-Hound driven carriage. "Yeah, a crosswalk. So fuckin' what?"

"It's not a crosswalk." Now his stump elevated. "Look at that sign."

The yellow sign with black block letters spelled CITY MUTILATION ZONE.

Ruth thought back. "Didn't you tell me about that before?"

"Yes. I lost my arms and legs in an MZ at Pogrom Park. There's another yellow line at the end of the street—everything in between is fair game. The Constabulary—sort of like a federal police department—always waits till rush hour to do this. More grist for the mill, you know?"

"No, I *don't* know." Ruth cocked her hip, continuing to glare. "Why are we here?"

"If my intelligence source is correct, in a little while a Nectoport will open at each end of the street, and—"

"A Necto-*what*?"

"Nectoport, Ruth. It's a sorcery-driven transportation device that folds space. The system was invented at the De Rais Labs. They run on pain."

"Pain?" This was getting harder and harder to comprehend.

"Pain, Ruth, derived from torture. Every district's got a Torture Factory. Let me put it this way—in the Living World they've got nuclear reactors and oil-burning power stations that generate electricity. In Hell, they've got Torture Factories. I can show you one later."

"I'll pass," Ruth said. "And how the fuck does pain—"

"Sorcerers invented a way of converting the energy that

fires between nerve cells into an equivalent of electricity.
But here it's called Agonicity and Electrocity. Humans are
the best fuel rods because they can't die. Anyway, that's
how the Nectoports work. Like the transporter on *Star
Trek*, only—"

"Only fucked-up?"

Alexander nodded. "It's a way for the Satanic police,
the military, and Lucifer's security forces to move around
quickly and without giving notice. You never see it coming until it's too late. National Mutilation Laws call for
these occasional slaughterfests. When it happens, you'll
see what I mean."

"What, you mean the cops can kill anyone between the
yellow lines?"

"Exactly. It's a way to keep the Pulping Stations full,
and more important than that, it helps maintain an overall air of terror, something that Lucifer insists on."

Ruth frowned back at the droves of Demons, Imps,
Trolls, and Human Damned filling the street. "Well if
they know they can be killed by walking between the
fuckin' lines, then why don't they just *not walk* between
the fuckin' lines?" she yelled.

"Because there hasn't been a Mutilation Action here in
decades. Same as the Living World, Ruth. People aren't
cautious. They're lazy."

Nectoports, she thought. *Agonicity*. She wondered where
it could possibly all end but then reminded herself that,
for her, it had only just started. Then another thought
jumped forward. "What's this got to do with you getting
new limbs?"

"That's how we're going to *get* the limbs, during the
Mutilation Action," the priest told her, then raised his
brow. "Or I should say, that's how *you're* going to get
them. When the Squads arrive, the first thing they'll do is
start hacking the crowd apart. That's when you slip into
the Zone, grab me two arms and two legs, and bring them
back."

Ruth looked down and laughed. "Bull-fucking-*shit*,
man!"

"Come on, Ruth. I can't do it myself for obvious reasons. And once I'm ambulatory again, you won't have to carry me. It'll only take you a minute." His gaze darkened. "Of course, you don't *have* to. You can walk away right now if that's what you want."

Ruth knew if she did that there'd be no Purgatory for her a thousand years from now . . .

"I'll do it . . . you *fucker*."

"Good girl. Try to get me arms and legs from an Usher—you know what they look like. But if you can't, go for Troll limbs or limbs from a strong Conscript."

Ruth chuckled. "Beggars can't be choosers, huh?"

Alexander raised his stumps. "You're quite right. Human Conscripts lead each Squad, and each Squad usually contains two Ushers and a half dozen demons of pretty much any species. I've heard that they've added Anneloks as well."

"What's that? Or . . . don't I want to know?"

"An Annelok is another experiment that came out of the Academy of Teratology, where they Hexegenically crossed Human genes with a species of Demon known as *Mephistus Annelia*—your basic Worm Demon. Since their brains are so small, they're very easily manipulated by Subordination Spells. The Annelok's got arms, legs, and an abdomen that look like giant earthworms. They can squeeze a Demon or Conscript to death in seconds. This new one's third generation, so watch out. It's almost as savage as an Usher."

Even Ruth's not terribly sharp mind caught the flaw. "Wait a minute. Ushers are those big-ass things with slimy grayish brown skin, claws, and faces like meat, right?"

"Yes."

"If they're the ones doing the mutilating, how am I gonna get any of *their* limbs?"

Alexander nodded. "See those four Imps over there?"

Ruth looked down the street and saw the four things sitting against a building. They wore rags, rotten shoes, and held out cups hoping for change.

"They look like homeless bums . . . except with horns."

"That's what they're supposed to look like. They are really Contumacy operatives—the Satan Park Sect. They're anti-Luciferic terrorist agents *masquerading* as homeless bums. They'll do a quick hit and run, take out several Ushers and Conscripts with their weapons, then slip away."

"What weapons? Those guys aren't carrying anything except cups for change."

Alexander smiled. "Just watch."

Ruth stood by, eyeing the bustle of pedestrians. Some big thing that looked like a giant jaw on two legs strode by. *That's fucked-up!* she thought. Then came a Human woman totally naked, but her skin was completely covered by grafted faces. *Get out of here!* Several creatures that looked part-reptile and part-Troll were playing some crapslike game on the sidewalk but with fingers instead of dice. *Hybrids,* she guessed. Then another Human walked by, but with four heads.

Fuck this shit, man. . . .

A fat clown approached her next. White makeup had been poorly applied in an attempt to cover up nests of some kind of parasite living in his cheeks. Frizzed orange hair sprouted from either side of his head, and he had a red rubber nose like Bozo.

"Awesome rack, baby," the clown said in a high, squeaky voice. "How much for a quicky?"

Ruth was appalled. "What do I look like, a whore?"

The clown chuckled. "Well . . . yeah. And I got money. Come on. A Brutusnote, all right?"

"Cram it, clown."

The clown shrugged in disappointment. "Oh well. Wanna squeak my nose?"

Ruth pulled the big sulphur pistol. "No. I wanna blow your ridiculous clown-ass back to McDonald's, and that's exactly what I'm gonna do if you don't move you're polka-dotted shit on down the road right fuckin' now!

The clown hustled away.

"You're a tough gal, Ruth," the priest said.

Ruth was still fuming. "Can you believe that guy? He thought I was a whore just by looking at me."

Alexander reserved any comment that may have come to mind.

Ruth kept looking around, over the tops of the brown buildings. The red sky churned, threaded by countless black plumes of smoke rising from every direction. Just past a leaning skyscraper, the windows of which were all upside-down crosses, Ruth saw a big patchwork balloon with a basket beneath lifting off. "Hey, look!"

The priest seemed disheartened. "Every now and then some poor soul manages to build a noble-gas balloon, thinking it'll take them to another Netherplane. Never does, though."

"At least they've got the balls to try," Ruth said, watching excitedly.

"And the stupidity. Something always gets them: Griffins, Caco-Bats, gunners in a Cloud Station, or—"

"Shit, what's that?"

In an instant, several squatty things sort of like apes seemed to climb down from black clouds via ropes. They swung toward the balloon basket, leapt inside, and attacked the balloon's pilot. Body parts were soon cast over the side as the things reveled on the balloon's rope.

"Or Gremlins," Alexander said.

Eventually one of the creatures got a claw up, and the balloon began to deflate. The Gremlins leapt back to their ropes and disappeared upward.

"You can forget about air travel here, Ruth. Unless you've got a Nectoport, you'll never get out of the Mephistopolis." Alexander tensed up, then jerked a glance at Ruth.

"Feel that?"

"Feel wh—" But then she did feel something. "Yeah, it's like—"

"It's a barometric pressure change," the priest informed. "Get ready. It means some Nectoports are about to open. Keep your eye on those four bums."

Ruth tried to but something kept dragging her gaze to

the street. There were a hundred residents in the Zone, at least, and most stopped, looking around in dismay because they felt something, too.

A shriek: "Oh my God, it's a Mutil—" but at the same time a louder sound began to resonate:

Sssssssssssssssss-ONK!

Then a terrifying *CLAP!* cracked in the air along with several blindingly bright flashes like a camera flash, only the light was gooey green. As more screams rose, Ruth noticed a light sort of hovering at either end of the Mutilation Zone.

"See those blobs? Watch. And *don't* step across the line until I tell you."

Blobs? Yes, now she saw what he meant. There were two green blobs of light that were shifting like something molten.

Ruth shrieked. "Holy fuckin' *shit!*"

A louder *CLAP!* resounded and suddenly the blobs had expanded into shuddering rims of the same gooey green light.

Rims, or, more appropriately, openings.

And through those two openings rushed a throng of armed Demons.

"Right and left flanks!" a Conscript shouted. "Cordon the Zone, then draw in. Strike first to disable. Cause maximum pain!"

The borders of the Mutilation Zone were quickly encircled by the first wave of slavering Ushers and a second wave of Anneloks. The later grabbed residents two at a time around the waist, then constricted their snakelike arms to sever spinal columns, while the Ushers used their claws—sharp as grappling hooks—to tear chunks out of the crowd. These flanks were followed by Conscripts and various armed Demons. Ruth could hear the eerie *whir*, like a threshing sound, as their swords, hewers, and great double-bladed axes blurred in the air to butcher anything before them.

More screams exploded. Limbs, heads, and blood of different colors began to fly.

"Ruth!" Alexander urged. "Watch those bums now."

Her eyes found them. The rag-draped Trolls had jumped up and seemed to be wiping something off with rags, in long up and down strokes, but the harder she squinted—

"There's nothing there! What are they wiping?"

"They're cleaning Sleath Tincture off their weapons."

In moments, like erasure in reverse, wooden hafts and long gleaming blades began to form beneath the strokes or their rags, eventually revealing machetes and axes.

"Wow! That's some fuckin' trick!" Ruth exclaimed.

And then the Trolls attacked from behind. They cleaved into the rear guard of Conscripts, their own weapons whirring as well. Now it was Conscripts' heads and demonic body parts that began to drop.

"Awesome," Alexander said.

"Reform!" a Conscript yelled. "Terrorists have infiltrated th—" and then his head shot across the crowd as a Troll pulled his machete across the shoulders.

"Get ready," the priest warned.

The sneak attack had caused the Mutilation Squad to fall into chaos. When Ushers tried to turn, their talons mistakenly gouged into the row of Anneloks, some of whom began to fight back.

"This is great!" Ruth celebrated. "They're fighting each other!"

"Retreat!" someone yelled.

"There they go," Alexander said. "The perfect hit and run."

The four Trolls who'd caused all this havoc in just seconds cut their way back to the sidewalk, where a white-skinned Gargoyle waited. The Trolls each grabbed a leather handle harnessed to the macabre beast, then— *Swoosh!*—the Gargoyle whisked up the side of the building and disappeared.

"Retreat and recover! Return to Egression Points!"

Conscripts were now hacking through their own troops to get back to the Nectoports. The green light began to intensify, and now a whistle was blowing. When

the flanks had collapsed, dozens of citizens had been able
to slip out of the Zone. Ruth guessed that more than half
had escaped.

Nevertheless, the other half hadn't, most of whom now
lay in pieces on the street.

"Go now, Ruth!" the priest ordered.

Fuck this shit, man! Ruth thought, sprinting over the
line. She spotted a pair of Usher legs just inside the yellow border, but when she tried to get them both under
her arm—

"Fuck!" she yelled. They were too heavy, and what
made it worse was that they were still moving. So she
grabbed each ankle and dragged them back to the alley.

"I need two arms, too, Ruth!" the priest's voice cracked.

"I can't carry all that shit at once!" she yelled back.
"These fuckin' things weigh a hundred pounds each!"

"Go! Go get me two arms now!"

Ruth rushed back, swearing under her breath. There
were severed arms all over the place, lots of them from
Ushers. She jumped at a final *clap!* and saw that the Nectoports had vanished, leaving many Ushers and Anneloks to fight amongst themselves.

They looked like they were having a good time.

Ruth reached forward and snatched up a severed Usher
arm, but—*Fwap!*—she immediately fell on her face when
her flip-flop slipped in a puddle of brown blood. *Shit!*

"Ruth! Behind you!"

It was Alexander. When she turned, sitting on her butt—
Oh my God! What is—

A glistening pink Annelok stood over her. It began to
reach down with arms like giant earthworms.

Ruth's instincts kicked in. She didn't even think when
she lunged forward. The flap of ragged pink meat that
hung between its legs in no way resembled genitals, but
she figured that's what it must be anyway.

So she bit the thing. Hard.

The Annelok shuddered, making a noise more like a
teapot boiling over. Ruth ground her teeth until the meat

between them detached; then the Annelok ran away, mewling.

Ruth spat the stuff out fast.

"Help me! Help me!" came a high-pitched voice she somehow recognized.

A gloved hand pawed her face.

It was the clown.

His legs had been cut off at the knees.

"Get me out of here!" the clown implored.

Ruth shoved his face away. *I hate fuckin' clowns.* She hopped back to her feet, grabbed another Usher arm, but—

"Hey! Stop that!"

Another Usher was trying to take a Demonic toddler away from its rotten mother. The toddler squalled.

Ruth threw the arm at the Usher and hit it right in the head. "Pick on someone your own size, ass-face!"

The mother retrieved her horned child and ran away.

Then the Usher turned toward Ruth. In the slits of its eyes, she saw a glint like lust. Its jaw fell open, revealing bloody, stalactitelike teeth, and then its huge, meaty hands opened, talons sparkling.

The thing lunged forward—

Bam!

Ruth hit the thing in the face with the sulphur pistol. The top of its head flew off like a Frisbee.

"Hurry!" Alexander yelled. "The Disposal Squads are coming!"

Ruth heard hooves pounding brick, then saw wagons approaching. She definitely didn't like the looks of the things driving the wagons. She grabbed two arms and ran back to the priest.

"Quick! Drag me and the limbs to the end of the alley! We can't be seen!"

Ruth did so, huffing.

Safely hidden in the alley now, Alexander said, "You did it, Ruth. You're quite a girl."

She sat down with a thump, no longer caring that the pavement was made of hardened excrement. "Did you *see* that crazy shit? I can't believe I ever got out of that meat grinder." She spat again, wincing. "Shit, I think I bit off a worm-man's dick!"

"You're a brave, brave woman, Ruth, and my intelligence source will be very happy about this."

Ruth sighed, suddenly exhausted. Had she wet her shorts in sheer terror? *Fuck* . . . "I need a drink."

"We'll be able to get one later. But for now, get the little foil tube out of my pouch."

Ruth kneed over and in the pocked pouch around his neck found something that looked like a crude tube of travel-size toothpaste.

"What the fuck's this?"

"Ruth, do you have to use the F-word every time you open your mouth?"

"Fuck yes!" she shouted at him. "And don't give me shit! I was neck-deep in monster guts out there!" She wagged the tube in his face. "Now what the *fuck* is this?"

Alexander smiled. "It's regeneration balm. There's only enough to reconnect four limbs, so use it sparingly."

"Reconnect? So that's it. I should've know it would be something fucked-up like that." She unscrewed the top, sniffed, then gagged. "So what do I do with it?"

"Squeeze a little onto your fingertip and rub it around the severed-end of each limb you got. Then just . . . hook me up. Do the legs first, 'cos they take more."

Ruth dragged both heavy legs over and applied the balm. While doing so, she noticed the end of the alley and saw the hopper-backed wagons rolling by.

"And try to keep your voice down. We don't want the Leperotics to see us."

I don't want to know . . .

Ruth dragged each leg to Alexander's stumps. "Wow, that's pretty cool."

The priest nodded, biting his lip as if in pain.

The connections were healed as Ruth watched. "So this shit is some kind of funky glue?"

"More like metaphysical solder. Hurts a little but it's working. Now the arms."

She applied a daub to the first arm, then paused and drew a long face.

"What's the matter, Ruth?"

"I—"

"What!"

Finally she admitted it: "I fucked-up. I thought I grabbed two Usher arms but . . . I only grabbed one."

"But I saw you bring back *two* arms after you got the legs. What was the second arm?"

Ruth held it up.

It was a severed Annelok arm, like a yard-long earthworm four inches thick.

The priest slumped. "Well. I guess it'll have to do. . . ."

(II)

"*Nemesis,* or more specifically *God's enemy*, is the best translation of the word ash-shaytan," Driscoll told them. They were walking down the stair-hall now, at Venetia's request.

"Does Eosphorus mean *torchbearer*?" she asked.

"Yes, torchbearer, light bearer, in Greek, and essentially the same thing in Latin, for *Lux Ferre.* Two more names for Satan, which I'm sure you can both comprehend as the diligent Christian theology students that you both are, right?"

"Oh, that's right," Dan offered. "Lucifer is still sometimes referred to as the Morning Star, or the Light of the Morning."

"Do you know why?" Driscoll asked.

"Because he was thrown out of Heaven in the morning," Venetia recalled. "In Hell, he's the Prince of Darkness, but before the Fall, he was the Angel of Light. That's why so many references to Lucifer involve a parallel reference to light."

"Very good. And according to some of the earliest Christian writers in the First Century, Lucifer fell in a westerly direction. The great light that was witnessed that morning may have been his wings burning." Driscoll smiled at them. "And I can guess what you both are thinking. . . ."

Venetia wasn't sure how much Biblical imagery was literal, but Dan spoke right up, with a hint of sarcasm: "Do I lack faith if I actually *don't* believe that part about the burning wings?"

"Not at all," Driscoll chuckled. "What our finite minds can't comprehend, we chalk up to the mysteries of faith. You'll be a priest someday, Dan, and Venetia may become a nun. The quality of your vocation doesn't depend on what you personally believe might be figurative or an abstraction. We'll find that out when we die. Until then, it's best to just live by the word of God."

The priest's remark set Venetia's mind at ease . . . but not all not all the way.

Then Dan said, "But atheists have a point when they condemn the mysteries of faith as a cop-out."

Driscoll shrugged. "They think what they want, we think what we want. And speaking of mysteries"—he shot Venetia an odd look—"*why* exactly have you insisted we go to your bedroom."

"Just . . . wait and see," she said.

When they got to the end of the hall, she led them all into her room.

"How bizarre!" Mrs. Newlwyn exclaimed.

They all saw it at once.

"Oh, yes," Driscoll recalled. "You mentioned knocking your lamp over—"

"It gouged the plaster," she said, "and I saw a few letters. So—"

"Curiosity urged you to scrape off the rest," Dan said.

"Yeah."

Eosphorus. The word stood out on the plasterless brick beneath the gouge.

"Who could've done this?" Mrs. Newlwyn asked.

"Tessorio, no doubt," Driscoll answered.

The tall woman continued, "And isn't it interesting that he would hide this word beneath the plaster of this room of the prior house and also write the word in the corresponding corner of his sketch."

Silence seemed to collapse on the four of them. They all looked at one another.

Driscoll said, "It's probably nothing but— Dan, get a hammer and a putty knife."

"*Great* idea," the seminarian said and excitedly left the room.

The room that would correspond to the word ash-shaytan was an empty bedroom. Dan met them there in a minute.

"Do I get the honors?" he asked.

"Go right ahead."

The hammer smacked the newly painted corner. The plaster fell out quickly, and after a few scrapes of the putty knife . . .

"How do you like that?" Dan said.

Ash-shaytan, read the bare brick.

And in the room that corresponded to the third corner of the drawing—Dan's bedroom—the words *Lux Ferre,* were revealed after a few more hammer blows.

By then it was no surprise when they found the word *Iblis* beneath the plaster of the fourth corner room.

Driscoll pinched his chin in thought. "Four names for Satan in the four corners of the house, and they also appear on four different corners of that sketch . . ."

"So what should we make of this?" Venetia asked. "It really is strange."

"And unnerving!" Mrs. Newlwyn added. "How appalling for a priest to write such words in a religious building."

"You know what *I* think?" Dan asked, eyes wide, as if to make a revelation. "I think it's just a bunch of devil-cult bullsh—BS."

"Though I can't say I agree with Dan's choice of words," Driscoll said, "I do agree with his conception of this. It's part of human nature to hunt for intriguing mysteries but nine times out of ten, there's no intrigue at all."

"So there's no real significance to these words being here," Mrs. Newlwyn ventured, "and also being on the drawing?"

"I don't think so."

A thought came to Venetia. "But isn't it at least possible that this might be connected to the murders that happened here? Satanic cults have been known to use murder as part of their rituals."

"Satanic cults are rarely serious, Venetia," the priest explained. "They consist of disgruntled youth and other misguided folk."

"Just looking for a new way to party," Dan added.

"Right. New Hampshire isn't exactly a haven for that sort of thing."

"No, but it was three hundred years ago," Venetia said.

Mrs. Newlwyn added, "And remember that there's a Salem, New Hampshire, just as there's a Salem, Massachusetts, and *both* have histories of witchcraft and devil worship."

Driscoll smiled and held up his hand. "I think that's stretching it a bit. It's all a cliché these days, Mrs. Newlwyn. I don't think I've ever heard of any Satanic cults operating in New Hampshire, and as for those regrettable murders? They were committed months ago. Tessorio died in the seventies. It's impossible for there to be a connection."

Venetia was inclined to agree.

They all looked to the window at the sudden sound of a car horn.

Dan peered out. "Looks like a limo from the diocese . . . with a monsignor's flag."

A fretful expression lengthened Driscoll's face. "It's that late already? I promised the monsignor I'd play golf with him!" Then Driscoll rushed out.

"How's that for church business?" Dan said. "And any time you play a monsignor, you have to lose on purpose."

They all went to the stair-hall rail and watched amusedly as Father Driscoll huffed across the atrium and out the front door, his golf clubs clattering on his back.

"Hey, where's Betta?" Dan asked. "I haven't seen her all day."

"She's out helping John with the hedges," Mrs. Newlwyn said.

That might not be all *she's helping him with.* Venetia kept the thought to herself.

"I better round her up to help me with the laundry."

"And I guess Dan and I will be spending the next few hours fixing the holes we just knocked in the walls," Venetia said.

"Piece of cake," Dan promised.

Mrs. Newlwyn made for the stairs. "See you both at dinner. It's hotdogs and beans night!"

As she and Dan meandered down the hall, Venetia was still at odds with the disturbing dream last night that seemingly told her the definition of the word Eosphorus and where it was located. *I saw it beforehand and forgot,* she told herself yet again. *Those nightmares about the voice simply confused me.*

It was the only thing that made sense, but why didn't she feel convinced?

Then they headed downstairs to get the plaster and paint.

"It's just creepy," Venetia commented, scanning around, "knowing that over thirty years ago Tessorio was hiding little homages to Satan in a prior house that he built specifically for the Catholic Church."

"Same as Black Mass in the Middle Ages," Dan said. "It was all done in secret. These congregations of heretics had to hide their reverence to the devil or else be hanged and burned at the stake."

"Do you think he did it in other buildings he constructed for the Vatican? All those beautiful churches and rectories?"

"It depends on when he lost his faith but sure, it's possible."

Another glance over her shoulder showed her the brooding portrait of the previous prior, Father Whitewood. He seemed to scowl at her as she descended the stairs.

"But as much as Driscoll steps on my tail, he's right about a lot of things. The devil-worship cults of today are just people who're screwed-up in the head, or looking for identity because they're social misfits, or—as in Tessorio's case—looking for a more flamboyant excuse to get drunk, take drugs, and have orgies. None of it's very serious at all."

Venetia half-smiled. "What about Lucifer's wings burning as he fell from Heaven? When you're a priest, what will you say if some kid in your congregation asks about it?"

"I'll say the same thing Driscoll said. It doesn't matter if it really happened or not. All that matters is God's word."

"And the figurative versus the literal?"

"Same thing. Do I *really* believe that a woman named Eve plucked an apple off the Tree of Knowledge and took a bite after God said not to? It doesn't matter. It's got nothing to do with how we live our lives and stay on the Holy Spirit's path."

Venetia wondered. Did it make actual sense, or was it just a bunch of hip Holy Roller talk?

Downstairs they began to cross the atrium toward the dropcloths, where the supplies sat.

"So you're not even a little creeped out by the fact that these two Catholic women—a nun and a clerical assistant—were murdered in this building only a few months ago?"

"No," he said at once, then paused. "Well, sure. A little."

"Then why *couldn't* a ritualistic cult have existed? Formed by Tessorio all those decades ago, and carried on by followers today?"

Dan grabbed some cans while Venetia grabbed some brushes and a trowel. "It's too far-fetched, Venetia. The state cops already investigated. It was probably a botched burglary by dope addicts. They broke in—"

"And then the two women surprised them."

"Right. Then the perps freaked out and killed them so

they couldn't be identified. It's a commonplace crime these days—this one just doesn't *seem* so because a nun was involved. The state police are convinced that the murders were random and not cult-related."

A man's voice startled them. "But that's not necessarily the opinion of the *local* police."

Venetia almost dropped her brushes. She and Dan eyed the stocky, goateed man in the sports coat standing across the atrium.

"Who are you?" Venetia asked.

The man smiled. "The *local* police." He flashed a badge. "Captain Berns. I'm with the Rockingham County Sheriff's Department, and I'd like to ask you a few questions. . . ."

Guess I scared the shit out of them, Berns surmised. "The door was wide open so I stuck my head in and heard you two talking."

The other two introduced themselves. The guy, Dan Holden, had a straitlaced look on the outside but Berns sensed a touch of the smart aleck on the inside. He had a Roman collar but when Berns addressed him as Father, the guy laughed and said, "Oh, no, please don't call me that. I won't be a priest for another year." *Whatever*, Berns thought. The blonde, Venetia Something-or-other, was all business behind the eyes and—*Jesus, what a bod. And stacked* . . . Berns didn't get the clothes, though: sneakers with a black skirt like girls wore at private school, and a blouse knotted up to show her bare stomach. She said she was a theology student, of all things.

"I heard this place was reopening," Berns told them, "so I came up." He looked around and tried not to frown. *What a mess*, he thought as he surveyed the drop cloths, paint cans, ladders, and covered furniture. He wasn't even sure exactly what a prior house was. "I understand that the guy in charge here is a Father Christopher Driscoll. Is he around?"

"Did you see a big black mafia-looking limo pull out of here a minute ago?" Dan asked.

"Yeah, at the end of the driveway."

"That was him, on his way to the golf course," the blonde said.

Berns looked at Dan. "So when he's not in, you're in charge?"

Dan chuckled. "From the church end, I guess you could say that, but the only thing I'm in charge of is cleaning up this dump."

Berns felt for him. Impulse kept tempting him to steal a glance at Venetia's cleavage. *Damn!* "Well, I really need to talk to someone who knew any of the previous staff. You know—last March, before the murders."

"That would be me then," Dan offered. "I knew everybody. Not very well, but—"

"Did you know the two women who were murdered?"

"Lottie Jessel and Patricia Stevenson—yes. And when I say I knew them, I mean I knew them enough to say hello to them. I was kind of like the diocese's errand boy. I'd drive up here once a month to fill Father Whitewood's supply orders."

"The guy who *used* to run the place . . ."

"Yeah."

"And then disappeared," Venetia added.

Berns nodded. "The state police talked to him, though. He didn't have anything to do with the murders, but he had sort of a—"

"Complete trauma-triggered mental breakdown?" Dan cut in.

"That's pretty much the case." *Well, this could be worse,* Berns thought. "Would it be too much trouble to ask you to come down to the county sheriff's station in town?"

Dan wavered. "I . . . guess not. Why?" He grinned. "Should I be getting uncomfortable?"

"No, no," Berns laughed. "We've apprehended another suspect. I'd just like you to take a look at her, see if it's someone you've ever seen up here before . . ."

"Sure." Dan tapped the blonde on the shoulder. "Why don't you come along, too? You haven't been to town yet."

"I guess the wall repairs can wait," she said.

Then they all went outside and got into Berns' unmarked car. *Wall repairs?* Berns wondered.

Dan let the blonde ride up front, which only teased Berns more. *Stop looking at her boobs!* Berns told himself. *I'm a cop for God's sake!*

It wasn't easy; she was *that* attractive.

"So, Captain," she inquired just as he was pulling off. "You said you've apprehended *another* suspect?"

"Yes. Last night—"

"And it was a *woman?*" Dan asked next.

"Correct. Susan Maitland."

"Never heard of her," Dan said. "And I'm sure no one by that name ever worked at the prior house, at least for the time I was going up there."

"It's probably an assumed name. We get a lot of drifters in port towns. They're sweating warrants in other states, or they get tired of raising their ten kids in the trailer so they just leave, abandon them. Not saying that's the case here. I just need someone from the prior house to take a look at her."

Venetia turned toward Berns. "Isn't it unusual for a *woman* to be a suspect in a murder case like this?"

"Oh, yeah, but it happens."

"And you referred to her as *another* suspect. . . ."

"A guy got busted several nights ago. He'd made it all the way up to Maine before they got him. That's two we've got now, but we believe there were *three* perpetrators, and you can call it a hunch, but I'm pretty sure the third one hasn't left town either."

Venetia cast an alarmed look back at Dan.

Oh, come on, give me a break! I'm trying to drive! Whenever Venetia turned to look out the window, Berns caught her breasts in the passenger-side rearview. "But it's kind of interesting, what you and Dan were talking about when I walked in."

"What? Devil cults?" Dan said, laughing.

"Right," was Berns' simple reply.

The silence left Dan and Venetia to stew. Finally Venetia ventured, "You mean the murders were part of a cult activity?"

"Well, let me just say that it's looking that way." Then he thought, *And it's also looking like you'll be sitting in the back when I drive you back to the prior house, because your tits in my rearview are gonna make me drive off the road!*

"That's shocking," she said. "What evidence do you have?"

"Well, at this point it's kind of confidential." Berns chewed on a thought. "But I can say that we don't believe the murders were random."

"Can you tell us why?" Dan asked. "It's not like we'll be blabbing to anyone."

"I appreciate that." Berns eyed the sigh: WAMMSPORT—3 MILES. *Didn't realize the prior house was so close to town. An hour's walk.* "Unlike the state police, we believe the victims were specially selected."

"Because of their vocation, you mean," Venetia said.

"Yes, their close connections with the Catholic Church."

Dan and Venetia traded another glance.

"Hence the suspicion of cultism," Venetia continued. "An anti-Christian motivation. One thing you might want to know, Captain . . . ," but then her words trailed off. She looked to Dan, as if seeking permission.

Dan picked up where she left off. "Just a little while ago we found some curious occult artwork in one of the attic coves at the house. One in particular is an old oil painting of an anti-Pope named Boniface the Seventh, among other things."

Holy shit, Berns thought. *I'll have to get technical services out there again. . . .* "Thanks. That could be of great interest. But for now, I'd just like you to take a look at this woman."

"Sue Maitland?" Venetia recalled.

"Right. Part of me is disappointed because she doesn't *look* like someone who might be in a sacrilegious cult."

"Neither did Boniface the Seventh," Dan offered with a smile. "He was a *Pope.* The Crusades and the Holy Inquisition didn't look like Christian undertakings either."

"I get your meaning," Berns told him. "Looks are deceiving. But here we are. You can judge for yourselves."

The small harbor town of Wammsport was suddenly before them as they turned off the winding country road that had taken them away from the prior house.

"Looks like a miniature version of Portsmouth," Venetia said, taking in the marinas and fishing docks. Old clapboard houses grayed by salt air and harsh winters leaned off rising roads.

Berns offered the only observation he could make without sounding too cynical. "It's quaint . . . on the outside."

But Dan already knew the town fairly well. "And redneck as hell on the inside."

"Uh, yeah." Berns parked in a reserved lot at a brick building along the main downtown road. A sign read, ROCKINGHAM COUNTY SHERIFF'S DEPARTMENT—WAMMSPORT STATION. In the past, Berns had had very few occasions to come here, but this was his second time today. "And it's nice and cool inside," he promised, showing them in. "Your tax dollars at work."

Dan and Venetia both sighed when stepping inside. Berns nodded to the officer at the booking desk and the watch commander, who both stiffened when they saw him. "Is she still in the interview room?"

"Yes, sir."

"Good. I'm taking these two back." Berns unloaded his Smith revolver and handed it to the watch commander. "We don't need them to sign in."

"Sure thing, sir."

"Something just occurred to me," Venetia said with some amusement. Berns took them down a shiny-floored but dark hall. "I've never been in a police station before."

"I have," Dan said. "This one, believe it or not. I got arrested when I was a juvenile."

Berns turned. "You're kidding me. What was the charge?"

"Pot."

Berns laughed and so did Venetia.

In the next room, Berns showed them to a long table

and some chairs. There was a window in the front wall
with a curtain on the other side of it. "Have a seat here,
and take a good look at her. You especially, Dan. I already
questioned her once today, so this time I'll keep it short.
The state police will be taking her for a more detailed interview tomorrow. I'll try not to keep you here too long."

"Keep us as long as you want, Captain," Dan said. "Venetia and I are in no rush to get back to the prior house—"

"Where there's no air-conditioning and no fans," Venetia added.

You can have that shit. . . . Berns left them and entered
the other room.

"You again. Officer Chuckles."

"I'll take that as a compliment, Sue—if that really is
your name."

Berns opened the curtain and sat down opposite a thin
woman in jeans and a baggy NASCAR shirt. Thick hair
hung just past her shoulders, a blend of auburn and black,
with split ends. "Did the photographer see you earlier?"

Her voice sounded rough. "No. What for?"

"To take pictures of your body."

The crows feet at the corners of her eyes deepened. "My
body, huh?"

"Identifying marks, such as tattoos. For your prison
file, Sue."

Smoke-darkened teeth showed behind her salacious
grin. "Don't worry. When your photographer comes, I'll
give him a *good* show."

"The photographer's a two hundred-pound woman, so
you can forget about sexual harassment."

"Shit."

Her face and arms were well-tanned but also a little
wrinkle-webbed: the look of someone who'd worked the
docks for a long time. She sneered up at the window.
"Who's on the other side?"

"Just some friends."

"Bullshit. You don't have any." She shot her middle finger at the glass.

"Friends from St. John's Prior House."

She only looked at him.

"So you're a boat cleaner, huh?"

"And painter, barnacle scraper, deck hand."

"We haven't been able to verify that yet. Which means you either get paid off the books or don't really do anything except sell crystal meth."

She gave a pained looked. "Hey, man, I don't go near that shit, and I lie to cops any chance I get, but I ain't lying about *that*."

Berns nodded, the tiniest smile tinting his face. "Well, tomorrow you're going to the *state* police, and they'll interview you a lot more thoroughly. They're not nice like me. They can even get a court order to inject you against your will with a drug called sodium amobarbital. Then you won't be *able* to lie."

"Oh, good, a downer. I like stuff that makes me mellow."

"I'll bet." Berns guessed she was midthirties but looked fifteen years older. "My point is, the state police don't like your kind."

She sat slouched but the remark brightened her eyes with amusement. "*My* kind?"

Berns whispered, "White trash."

"Just like you, brother."

Cute. "So it might behoove you to be forthcoming with information with me before they get their hands on you. I have a lot of power in this department. I might be able to cut you a deal. Like I did for Freddie."

"Who?"

"Freddie Johnson. He spun on you like a top."

"Bullshit. There's no way he could've known I was busting into his old place last night, so don't act like he blew the whistle on me. I know for a fact that he didn't."

"Well, thanks at least for admitting that you know him."

A thought seemed to trouble her; then she gave Berns the finger, too.

"So let's go over last night again. The police caught you burglarizing Room Three of the Wharfside Boarding

House on Fifth—Freddie Johnson's pad before he blew town."

"You talk so hip, *man*," she mocked.

"You betcha. But they talk hipper in general pop." Berns admired something about her redneck edge. "You're a gutsy gal, I'll tell you. Too bad you're not as smart as you are gutsy."

"What are you blabbering about?" she frowned.

"When you jimmied the window on Freddie's pad, you did it with the same knife you used to cut the throats of the two women at the prior house last spring. It still had some dried blood on it."

"Bullshit!" she exclaimed, leaning up. "I cleaned that fucker good!"

Berns' grin was wide. "Even heard of gas-chromatography, Sue? Or how about mass photo-spectrometry?"

She slumped back to her slouch, arms propping up the braless breasts that were probably quite full and appealing once but now just sagged.

"It's lock-solid evidence, Sue. Freddie's already confessed and implicated you."

She shook her head. "You're lyin'."

She's fried. He could tell. Sometimes when he pushed hard enough, they gave in, but Berns doubted that would happen here. *Drug burnout. But . . . a member of a Satanic cult?*

He wasn't getting any vibes. "So when you busted into his joint, you were looking for the forty grand"—he decided to play with her a little—"but Freddie screwed you out of it. He told me. Isn't that why he paid his rent three months in advance, so the landlord wouldn't know he was gone? *You* knew he was gone, though. He said he'd take his cut when he left town but would leave your end for you and the other guy. What was his name?"

She laughed sharply. "Man, you are so up the wrong fuckin' tree it's a riot." Then she leveled her gaze. "And you know what? Fuck it. Freddie was right. When the party's over, it's over."

"He said the same thing to me two nights ago in Lubec, Maine," Berns told her, getting his hopes up.

"I'm not gonna give up my friends, so you can forget about that. They're not even here anymore."

"Now *you're* the one bullshitting."

She gave him the finger again and grinned. "And as for the money—shit. Freddie always had money 'cos he was lucky. Pool, scratch-offs, craps. The fucker always had extra cash."

"The *fucker?* I thought you were all friends. Sounds like you don't like him much."

"I don't like him—he's a prick. But I do *love* him."

Redneck love, Berns thought. "Oh, one of those deals. He was your boyfriend."

"Yeah, or so he said. Cheated on me all the time."

"Back to the money—"

She shook her head as if Berns was stupid. "It wasn't about the *money*. After he blew town, we figured we'd wait a while for things to cool off before we broke into his old place. But it wasn't the money we were after. We didn't give a shit about it."

"We?"

"Yeah, fucker. We."

Berns intensified his expression. "And you didn't care about *forty grand?*"

"No, no. Something else, and you can't do shit 'cos someone else has it now."

Berns' mental gears began to excitedly spin.

"So it wasn't you who broke into the apartment. It was you and the other guy."

"Yeah. It was me and the guy.

"I see. And he got away but you didn't."

A long, huffy, "Yeah."

"Tell me who he is, and I can have your sentence reduced. Accomplice to a double homicide might get you life with no parole, especially when one victim was a nun. I might be able to rig it so you're out after seven years, if you're a good girl."

She jerked forward, animated. "You don't get it, do

you? We couldn't remember it all, all the instructions, I mean—"

Instructions?

"Freddie wrote them down but he made a copy. Took the original with him and left the copy here for us."

Berns appraised her. *I don't think she's making this up just to throw me off.* "The cops found an ashtray that had something in it—"

"Not an ashtray, a thurible."

Berns cocked a brow. "Well, this was an ashtray but there was no trace of cigarette tar or any drugs in it. They said it was something like resin. Burned resin. What's the deal there?"

"You'll have to find that out yourself."

"Sue, the ashtray's going to the big lab in Manchester. Whatever the stuff is, believe me, those guys will have it nailed. So why not just tell me?"

She waved a hand. "Naw. No point. You wouldn't get it."

Don't spin all your wheels at once, Berns reminded himself. "All right, back to the bust. It's very interesting what you're telling me. You got caught but the guy didn't. The guy got away."

"Right. When we heard the sirens last night, I deliberately stayed in the apartment."

Another bombshell. "You mean to distract the police while your accomplice got away with these ... instructions?"

"Yeah. It's a photocopy of something Freddie got. He called it a transcription."

A long pause seemed to dim the lights.

"They came from the other side," she whispered.

"The other side? You mean George Steinbrenner's office?"

Her lips pursed. "Huh?"

"Nothing. It's a baseball joke. So you sacrificed yourself so this other person could escape with these *transcriptions?* That's crazy. You've still got plenty of life left, but because you did that you could spend the rest of it in prison. Why sacrifice yourself?"

"Because some things are more important than life here." The words leaked from her throat very slowly. She seemed to be looking through him instead of at him.

"Life here as opposed to . . . life on 'the other side?' Hell? Is that what you mean?"

Now she was leaning on her elbows, the saggy breasts swaying in the baggy shirt. "You know Freddie. You know how he's always smiling. I'll bet he was smiling when you talked to him in jail."

"Actually, he was."

"And he was right. See, he knew, and that's why he kept saying it to us so much. *When the party's over, it's over.* Wanna know why?"

"Sure."

"Because there's a better party waiting somewhere else."

"In Hell? Is that what we're talking about, Sue?"

She said nothing.

"Sue, this is ridiculous," he finally said. "A devil cult? Come on. You look like the kind of girl who works her ass off all day in some manual labor job, sits in redneck bars every night getting drunk on draft beer, messing around with grizzly tough guys, and driving an old pickup truck with bald tires and dents in it."

She howled laughter. "You're right about everything except the truck. I don't have any wheels 'cos I can't get insurance."

"You're not a *devil worshiper!*" Berns said more loudly. "You're a redneck chick in a low-rent dock town!"

"Oh, man, you're such a riot!" She giggled hoarsely. "You don't get it and I don't expect you to. Freddie knew we were all at the end of the line—he could *see* it. They *told* him—"

They. The word seemed to echo in Berns' head.

"So that's why I stayed. That's why I took the rap and let Dougie beat the heat."

Berns immediately wrote *Dougie* in his notebook. "What's Dougie's last name?"

Finally it hit her. "Oh, fuck, man! Fuck you!"

"You've got nothing to lose, Sue!" he yelled back. "And you can believe this: the only party waiting for you is life with no parole in the state lezzie-block!"

She waved another dismissive hand. "Aw, but you know what? So what? Dougie's long gone anyway."

Bullshit. Berns remained convinced.

"And that ain't his real name anyway, just like Susan Maitland ain't mine. You want to know what I'm going to do the minute they put me in prison?"

"What's that, Sue?"

Her stained grin beamed almost like a light. "Find a way to kill myself."

Suicide pact, Berns wrote down next. *Freddie said the same thing,* he remembered.

Her mood shifted like a light switch being flicked. "Look, man, I don't feel like talking no more. I'm tired. Can I go back to my cell and sleep?"

"Yes, Sue. Do yourself a favor and change your mind. Don't protect this other asshole. Talk to the state prosecutor and he'll probably deal."

"Naw. Fuck it. I'm just tired. I want to go to sleep . . . and dream."

"About the other side?"

"Man, you *wish* you had dreams like me—like *all* of us."

"I probably *don't* wish that, Sue." The thoughts kept rolling over and over. *A suicide pact in a Satanic cult? These rednecks?*

"I'll be a baroness," she was murmuring now, her eyes closed. "And Freddie will be an arch duke. . . ."

"Good luck tomorrow, Sue," he said as he began to get up.

"Hey, man. Do me a favor?"

Now Berns saw her breasts in the loose shirt sitting on the table like two baggies full of water. "Maybe. What?"

"Tell Freddie I love him and can't wait to see him again."

Berns had to laugh at that one. "Sue, there is *no way* you're ever gonna see him again. Even if we get him transferred to a prison down here, it won't be anywhere near where you're going. Visitation between two convicts is simply not allowed."

She rolled her eyes as if his reply had been naive. "Yeah, yeah, sure. But tell him, will you?"

Berns turned at the door. "I'll tell him if you tell me what the stuff was in the ashtray."

She winced, her wrinkles growing intense. "Shit, man, I can't! Ask me something else!"

"All right." He stared her down. "What did you do with the blood?"

Her grin turned lewd. "We drank it."

"You're full of shit, Sue. Have a good time doing life. He opened the door.

"Wait! You're right. We didn't drink it. I was just pulling your leg." She raised two fingers to her mouth to denote fangs.

Then her voice got hoarse again, and this time her smile sent a chill up his spine.

"We *saved* the blood—"

"Saved it?" he questioned, incredulous.

"We saved every last drop."

Berns left the room quickly, while Susan Maitland yelled behind him, "You tell Freddie I still love him like you promised, you cop fuck!"

Chapter Ten

(I)

Even without the salt-mask, Boniface wasn't capable of showing fear in his expressions, not with most of the flesh gnawed off of his face. Maskless now, he looked upon his courtyard from the oculus window of his quarters . . . and shivered.

His own diviners were beginning to verify the same now: there was a blemish in his aura; there was an irregularity in the Flux.

The Exalted Duke was trying to distract himself with his favorite organic plaything, the court's Chief Soubrette, Voluptua.

"Like this, my most revolting lord?" she inquired, looking up from his broad lap.

Boniface felt nothing now, his eternal lust ruined by these new worries. Could it be her *look* that was growing insufficient? Voluptua was his favorite doxie, whom he reveled for most because she was nearly *all* Human, which was rare in this arena of enhanced Hybrids. Her large, over-full breasts, and skin unflawed as her last day alive in the Living World reminded him so much of all the worldly women—including nuns—that he'd ravaged on altars over a thousand years ago.

The Bi-Facial procedure amounted to Voluptua's only Luciferic improvement. Perhaps it was his love of dichotomies that dictated this singular preference. The erotic tinged by the nauseating; the beautiful flecked by the hideous.

Hence Voluptua's only surgical enhancement: she had two faces. The top face—which she almost always wore for her master's pleasure—was the face of a Putridox, a noseless thing from the Outer Sectors that had vertical eyelids, a vertical mouth set in a visage like curdled porridge, and lumpen cheeks freckled by abscesses. Each pock housed a Blood Maggot. It was perhaps the only face in Hell more revolting than Boniface's.

Boniface didn't want to admit that his loins were betraying him. He needed inspiration. "Entertain me, harlot." His corroded hand gestured toward the blackly shining Pasiphae, who stepped forth with a grin.

"Give succor to the Night-Mother, Queen of the Labyrinth," Boniface ordered. "I know full well that you love her."

Voluptua shuddered. "I love only you, my appalling master."

Boniface didn't care. "Yes, yes, but . . . give succor. It amuses me to watch."

She got up from his lap, her face so foul that even the Usher guarding the door turned away. On hands and knees, Voluptua crawled to Pasiphae, who stood with black hands on black hips, her gleaming black legs parted.

The Night-Mother sighed in bliss when Voluptua's repugnant mouth found the midnight black furrow of her sex.

"Yes," Boniface approved.

Pasiphae churned in place, her arousal swelling her breasts. Her ink black hands caressed her own curves as Voluptua's efforts grew more fervent. It wasn't long before the Night-Mother's release was imminent, and when black fingertips self-stimulated the gorged black nipples, it was milk as dark as crude oil that eddied out.

Then Pasiphae let out a silent shriek of bliss.

Boniface had grown partially aroused by the sight. *But I need more,* he thought. "Void yourself now, into the face of my whore," he ordered; then, to Voluptua, "Wouldn't you enjoy that, my love? Wouldn't you?"

"Oh, yes, my detestable lord," Voluptua answered with the greatest zeal.

Pasiphae parted her legs farther . . . then emptied her abyssal bladder into Voluptua's face. The stream of urine was black as pitch.

When the debasement concluded, Boniface, bothered by the stress of his worries, was still not ready to perform. Rather than admit it, he pretended not to care, instead grabbing Voluptua about the neck and thrusting her face out the window. Several shrieks were heard from below.

"Look, my love, out into my courtyard. Let your demented vision drink in the sight of my Involution as it nears completion."

The wench did so, her Human contours and hourglass figure more inspiring than any he'd ever seen, and—even better—the physical perfection spoiled by the Putridoxic face.

"Do you see?"

Vertical eyelids blinked over eyes like dark phlegm. In the courtyard the Unholy Carpenters had finished boiling the long lengths of Druid Oak, carved them into troughs, and bent them into exact geometric curvatures. From the yard's southeast corner, they began to join each length.

"It's lovely, my most unblessed lord," came her low but sugar-sweet voice from her vile mouth. "But I don't understand. . . ."

Boniface ran his foul hands down her sleek back and thighs. "Of course you don't, my dear, because you're an ignorant whore who has no capability of comprehension. Right?"

"Oh, yes, my great Exalted Duke. You're quite right. *Always* right."

"When the carpentry is finished, the trough will inscribe the most Unholy Spiral." A corrupt finger traced over the downy pubic mound in a corresponding spiral. "Tell me how beautiful it will be."

The Soubrette turned, her large-nippled breasts standing out in ardor. The vertical mouth replied, "It will be as beautiful as your own face, my great one," and with no hesitation the bosom lowered and her face came to his, and she kissed the lipless gouge that used to be his mouth.

Boniface's pallid flesh lay like something indescribable on the lead-trimmed bed. Only a Soubrette as well-conditioned as Voluptua could even stand to look at him without hemorrhaging. The Exalted Duke was *that* ugly. His genitals lolled, just as indescribable.

"And now, my most worthless trollop," he wheezed, "kiss me again, but with your *Human* face."

As a Bi-Facer, Voluptua's Human face was kept hidden beneath the scarf, the only garment she wore on these occasions. Her stomach flattened and her breasts rose as she straightened her stance, grabbed her long blond hair . . . and *pulled*.

So horribly lovely, Boniface thought, eyes raving at the surgical wonder.

The detestable face of the Putridox slipped over Voluptua's skull, and when it was pulled up sufficiently, it could no longer be seen, tucked back as it was under the shiny blond mane and now replaced by the same beautiful Human face she'd worn in the Living World.

Now her Human lips joined the monstrous Duke's, tongue roving unabashedly in the pitted cavity.

"And now . . . ," he demanded, "a final kiss—for your dear father, whose Spirit I personally sent to occupying the body of a dander flea." Then he raised the stick to which the severed head of Voluptua's biological father had been spiked. Its brain had long been evacuated and burned, while the flesh of its face now hung in rotten tatters.

Voluptua kissed the dead lips with just as much passion.

"Now be out of my sight, you useless property," Boniface said, "and tell Willirmoz that his presence is demanded."

"Oh, yes, my lord!" she replied and moved off. Several lower-scale Soubrettes appeared at once to dress the Chief

Odalisque back in her Tongue-Skirt and Hand-Bra, while still more re-dressed Boniface and replaced his mask. Voluptua and Pasiphae scurried off, hand in hand.

Waiting for the High Priest and Lithomancer, Boniface watched the Nicht-Mir—a mirror that was sacrifice-conditioned and served as an infernal surveillance camera that offered views of the fortress's most critical areas, including the Lower Chancel.

My Angels, he mused, watching the silver veins. The invisible Warding bonds could be seen laying grooves in the Angels' skin. They howled in the most mindless agony as the Archlocks and Torturians wielded their psychic torments: Heart-Pricking Spells, Psychic Branding, and Aura Toxins, all to further drive the pregnant Angels utterly insane but to leave their physical bodies unscathed.

Boniface watched the most pregnant of the six convulse as a Marrow-Boiling Spell was inflicted. Silent screams bulged the celestial eyes into embers of hatred; the paralyzed wings quivered on the semitangible slab, while the belly shined with so much agonized sweat.

So plump now; so ready to give up the wares of their tainted wombs to the Living World . . .

"A most holy sight, my lord." Willirmoz appeared, also looking at the mirror. "And so soon now, the fruit that is most perfect will be in your hands, ready to deliver to our ultimate Master."

Boniface's grub white finger pointed to the oculus. "And as you can see . . ."

The High Priest gazed out from blackened eyes. "The darkest miracle yet, my lord. The troughs designed to mimic the most blessed and unholy configuration in existence . . . is nearly complete."

The deplorable face of salt jerked up, "Yes, but none of it will be any good if it's sabotaged by our adversaries."

"It won't be, oh most detestable one."

"And you, the most proficient diviner in the Mephistopolis, doesn't even know who these adversaries *are* yet. So don't patronize me. I'm expecting the Divinations from your own Guild. Do you have them?"

The charred hand raised a scrolled stemma. "Of course, lord, as you so ordered."

"And?"

"The Rot-Port District is free of negative auric disturbances. The Vulgaressa reports that her forces have slaughtered several hundred Contumacy insurgents as well as dozens of suspicious stragglers."

The obscene meat of Boniface's heart went lax in relief. *Thank Satan. . . .*

But then the Wizard's tone changed, to something hesitant. "However I must also report, my most wretched master, that the latest Extipicisms have hinted that the threat may have moved through the Waste District, and is now headed out, to parts south."

South, Boniface thought, his dread hidden beneath the salt-mask. *That's us. . . .*

"And the Bloodmancers from Tepesville are inclined to divine that some counteroccult energy may be at work as well. Not necessarily in league with them, but . . . we must be cautious."

"Your honesty serves you well, Willirmoz," the Duke's voice fluttered. "Many lie to me when they bear bad news."

"But this isn't bad news, lord." The burned heretic leaned closer, with something like elation in his ruined voice. "My own private Divinations have divulged that these *adversaries* you so fear are but two pitiable members of the Human Damned—"

"What? Not Hybrids? Not Demonic?"

"No, Duke. And even more laughable, they are *Newcomers.*"

Boniface wanted to cry with joy.

"Even with Contumacy support, it is statistically and metaphysically impossible for a mere pair of Newcomers to infiltrate your great endeavor."

This welcome news refreshed the Exalted Duke; it made him feel five hundred years younger. "Your news makes me so joyous I could eat a newborn babe alive, and pick my teeth with his bones."

Boniface, indeed, was overjoyed—by the abstraction and, moreover, by the following reality. When Willirmoz snapped his dead fingers, the Sergeant at Arms stepped in the chamber bearing a newborn Hybrid on a silver platter.

Little chubby hands reached out, accompanied by a cheery whine. The infant blew happy spit bubbles from its tiny mouth, and in spite of skin like the rind of an avocado, the baby couldn't have been cuter.

"What a thoughtful Lithomancer!" Boniface rejoiced. "Come, my friend, and share with me in this delectable feast."

(II)

Venetia felt encircled by a black cloud; it was something about the *look* of the slim, weather-worn woman named Sue Maitland: the cast of her eyes, her poise and liquor-roughened voice. *A murderess,* Venetia thought, chilled. Was this really the Devil's manifestation of evil on earth? There was no relief from the feeling until Berns had exited the interview room. For a split second, the woman looked right at Venetia—even though she couldn't really see her—and smiled. Then the curtain was closed.

"Well," Dan said, "that about pegs my creepometer."

"Hard to believe," Venetia said. From the hall she heard Berns' voice addressing an unseen officer: "Call HQ and get a jail nurse. I want a suicide watch on her. If she offs herself while under county custody, my ass is grass."

Cop talk, she presumed. Rough and detached. *It's still a human life,* Venetia thought. A child of God ruined by the various taints of an ungodly world.

"That's one fully cooked psych-job in there," someone else said.

It was sad.

Berns returned to the observation room. "So much for that," he said addressing them both. Venetia doubted it was her imagination, but Berns kept taking quick glances at her. *Just like Dan. I guess they both think I'm hot.* The notion flattered her but only in an amused way. Venetia felt anything *but* attractive now, still muggy and grass-flecked from mowing the yard.

"That was very interesting," she told the brawny captain.

"Not to mention disturbing," Dan added. "And I wish I could tell you I've seen her before but I'm sure I haven't. If you've got a picture, I could show it to Mrs. Newlwyn and her daughter back at the house. They're from the area."

"And so is John," Venetia said.

"I can do that. Thanks."

Venetia pointed to the closed folder on the desk. "Captain, Dan and I were wondering—that folder says Stevenson and Jessel on it. Is that the case file?"

Berns picked it up guardedly. "Damn, I didn't mean to leave that there. Did you . . . look at it?"

"Well, no, but we'd like to."

"It's mostly autopsy photographs," the officer said. "Believe me, you don't want to see them. Especially you, Dan. You *knew* these women."

"Well, we'd still like to see them, sir," Dan said, "unless it's confidential or something. It might help us understand more about the case, since we *are* working at the murder scene."

Berns seemed flummoxed. "Well, since you asked . . ." He handed them the file.

Venetia found the macabre photos much less disturbing than the interview. She watched over Dan's shoulder as he flipped through. First was Lottie Jessel, the church custodian, who lay skinny and withered, with flattened breasts centered by nipples that looked like dried prunes. She was in her sixties. The other one was Patricia Stevenson—the nun. The nude body on the slab could've been a Playboy centerfold gone to sleep; Venetia was startled by how attractive the woman was even in death— buxom, curvaceous. The physique broke the stereotype that nuns weren't supposed to be attractive; then Venetia wondered how she herself might fare against the same prejudice.

Photos deeper in the stack grew grim: their bodies

Y-sectioned and yawning open, then two photos of the infamous incision rejoined by black staples. But on each photo the deep—almost black—gashes could be seen on the left side of either woman's throat.

"It doesn't bother us like it would regular people," Venetia said with cheery lift in her tone.

"Regular people?" Berns attention seemed to be alerted as Venetia let her hair down.

"We're hard-core Catholics," Dan said.

And Venetia: "To us these pictures are just dead meat. We celebrate Patricia and Lottie's ascendence into Paradise." She shrugged and smiled. "They're in a much better place."

"I sure fuckin' hope so." Then Berns winced. "Sorry. Can't help it sometimes."

"I suppose profanity is an occupational hazard for police." Dan laughed.

"It's a profane world," Venetia added. She tried to sit in a way that would offer less temptation to his wandering eyes; however, she wasn't offended at all, for it was obvious how hard he was trying *not* to look. If anything, she found him interesting and attractive. "We're curious about the comments regarding the blood, Captain."

"The official cause of death for both women was—and I hope you're ready for a mouthful—'multiple-organ system failure and cardiac/pulmonary arrest due to expeditious exsanguination.' It means their blood was drained, almost entirely. Strange part was there was no trace of blood in the rooms where the bodies were found."

"So they were murdered elsewhere," Dan said.

"Thought so until I read the follow-up conclusions from the state medical examiner. Something about the pericardial sack. I don't even know what that is, but the ME said there was still enough fluid in it to indicate that the women were murdered in the same place they were found."

Venetia's eyes narrowed. "And Sue Maitland said they *saved* the blood."

"Sounds pretty lurid," Dan said.

Berns led them back to the car. He seemed burdened but not necessarily by this. *How curious,* Venetia thought.

"It's more than lurid, Dan. There's an underbelly in our society that's really hard to figure. It's almost like there's a system to people's mental problems, like it's contagious." He chuckled and oddly offered Venetia the backseat this time. "But you'd have to be a cop to get what I'm saying. But then again, I guess priests see more of that than we do."

"I'm not quite a priest yet," Dan said, and got in the passenger seat. "But, yeah, I think I do know what you mean. People from bad environments tend to gravitate toward one another, and because they don't really have much hope for better things, they seize delusional solutions—"

"And the *occult* is one of them," Venetia said. "The lesser minds are the followers and the strong mind is the leader."

Berns looked over his shoulder with a surprised expression. "You know, that's *exactly* what the case is here. And we've got the leader is custody in Maine—that guy Freddie she was talking about. Between Freddie and Maitland, I think we'll get the rest of the answers we want."

Venetia's hair fluffed up in the car's air-conditioning, and began to chill her chest. As Berns pulled out of the parking lot, her gaze latched onto a figure hunched over a garbage can near the docks. *Another poor soul,* she thought. Matted gray hair hung down in a mop as his crabbed hands rummaged for anything edible.

Just as the car pulled away, the vagabond looked right at Venetia with yellowed eyes and snarled.

When they pulled into the front of the prior house, Berns said, "What's this? A delivery?"

Venetia leaned up between the seats and saw a large moving truck, with men taking boxes out of the back and rolling them into the house on dollies.

"I can't imagine what Driscoll would be ordering," Dan said.

"He didn't mention anything," Venetia added.

"Well, I better let you off here 'cos the truck is blocking the court." Berns shook hands with Dan, then turned toward Venetia. "Thank you both for your help. I'll be bringing that picture around soon, and I'd appreciate it if you could let Father Driscoll know that I'd like to talk to him as well."

"Sure thing," Dan said, and got out.

Berns' gaze loitered on Venetia's face.

She smiled. "Nice meeting you, Captain."

"Likewise. I hope to see you soon," but the reply sounded strained, until he grinned. "If you ever get a parking ticket, let me know. I'll fix it."

Venetia laughed and waved good-bye.

Dan was chuckling when the car was gone. "Looks like Deputy Dawg has a crush on Venetia."

"It seems so," she said, and thought, *But so do you.*

Driscoll came around the side of the house. "Where have you two been?"

"The cops," Venetia told him. "So far they've caught two of the murderers."

"What?"

Dan stood with his arms crossed, sweating again in the heat. "Yeah, the captain wanted us to watch an interrogation to see if anything rang a bell." A sly smile. "And he wants to talk to *you.*"

Driscoll looked perplexed. "If that's not the nuttiest thing . . ."

"And what's this delivery?"

The priest's brow popped up. "The good news is they're portable air-conditioners—*ten* of them."

"That's great!" Dan exclaimed.

"And the bad news is I don't know where the heck they came from."

"The diocese must've ordered them," Venetia said. "They don't want us dropping dead from heat stroke."

Driscoll slowly shook his head. "That's what I thought until I called them. They don't know anything about it."

"You're pulling our legs," Dan said.

"Wish I was. So I gotta tell these guys to load it all back on the truck. It's a wrong address or something."

"Who sent them?" Venetia asked.

"R. B. Electronics, the invoice says. Never heard of them."

"I have," Venetia said, and got out her cell phone. "It's my father's company."

Dan and Driscoll gave her astonished looks. "What would—"

"Hi, Mom," Venetia said into her phone. "Did Dad rent a bunch of air-conditioners and send them to the prior house?" She could see Dan and Driscoll standing frozen, listening. Even Driscoll had his fingers crossed.

"Oh, honey," her mother's voice shrilled. "When you told me you didn't have any, I *insisted*. As hot as it is? And he didn't rent them, he bought them. Tell Father Driscoll it's a church donation."

"I will, Mom. He'll really like that. We're all very grateful down here, because, you're right, it's *real* hot, and I just mowed half an acre in it."

"Your poor thing! You're not supposed to be doing that kind of work!"

"I actually love the exercise." Venetia didn't say anything about the apprehension of Sue Maitland. *That would just bend her out of shape.*

"Just don't overdo it, dear."

"I won't—"

"Oh, and there's another delivery coming, too," Maxine Barlow added.

"What is it?"

"A surprise. Call me when you get it!"

"Okay, Mom." But Venetia's thoughts fluttered back. "Oh, and did you—"

"I'm just about to start that Web search you asked me to do, though I'm still a bit mystified about it."

The voices in the dream, came the unpleasant recollection. But she was sure they were just figments of a stressed imagination. *I just have to know,* Venetia told herself. Then it wouldn't be able to bother her.

She rang off with her mother. "Well, Father Driscoll. You're to consider the AC units a donation to the Church. And my mother mentioned something else to be delivered but didn't say what."

"That's a *big* donation," Dan pointed out. "Those units are pretty high-end."

"I'm sure they are if my father ordered them."

Driscoll smiled with satisfaction. "Charity comes from the heart of God . . . and remind your father that every penny of his expenditure can be deducted as a charitable contribution."

"I'm sure he's aware of that," she chuckled.

The priest appeared to be musing now. "And it serves as a steady reminder to us, of the words of James: 'Every act of giving, with every perfect gift, is from above.' "

Dan had a challenge in his eyes. "And I'll bet you can't name this verse, Father: 'Freely we have received, so freely we must give.' "

Driscoll frowned. "Gospel According to Matthew. Come on, Dan. You know better than to try and stump me."

"But, Venetia, like I was saying," Dan went on, "every act of giving is terrific, but come on. These units must've cost a fortune."

Venetia shielded her eyes in the sun. "Well, my father's a very generous man, and he's also very rich."

Driscoll held up a finger. " 'He who giveth in abundance, receiveth in abundance.' Name it, Dan."

Dan rolled his eyes. "You *would* quote from noncanonical scripture, but of course it's *Tobit,* Chapter Four, I believe."

"You guys sound like two jocks arguing baseball statistics." Venetia laughed. "But to answer the parts of your question that St. Matthew's Gospel didn't: My father patented some kind of computer processor and circuit board a long time ago."

"So now he's rolling in the dough?" Dan asked.

"Yep."

"And it's our good fortune," Driscoll said. "Because last night I thought I was beginning to cook."

Dan glanced over. "But didn't you say something about *another* delivery?"

Just as Dan had spoken, another truck pulled into the court. The side panels read OMAHA STEAKS.

Like little kids at Christmas, Venetia thought with a smile. Driscoll called the entire group together and led a prayer thanking God—and Venetia's father—for the much appreciated gifts. The portable air-conditioners were rolled to everyone's rooms and required nothing in the way of installation save for positioning a vent hose out each window. Then they all retreated to the kitchen to help put away the gourmet food: vacuum-sealed and flash-frozen T-bones, filet mignons, ground sirloin, and ribs, as well as pounds of jumbo shrimp, king crab, and stout South African lobster tails.

"Well this most certainly is a surprise," Mrs. Newlwyn enthused. She and Betta scurried for place settings and broiler pans.

"Yeah, the TV dinners weren't exactly cutting it for me," Dan added while he and Venetia arranged everything in the freezer.

Driscoll smiled sarcastically. "Come on, Dan. A Catholic trooper like you?"

"Let's just say that I dig the fact that Venetia's father isn't as tight as the New Hampshire Diocese."

"I'm glad you *dig* that fact, Dan. And thank you for volunteering to *dig* the flower beds tomorrow."

Dan glared over his shoulder. "When did I volunteer for that, Father?"

"Why, just now, of course. You'll make a *fine* priest . . . someday."

Venetia smiled at their banter. But she also found herself wondering if she was getting paranoid, especially after noticing Captain Berns taking strained glances at her earlier. *Maybe it was just incidental,* she thought, *and Dan, too.* She thought she'd caught him taking similar glances several times, but now he didn't seem to. *I'm either paranoid or just a little too high on myself.*

John was setting the table for everyone, and Venetia *was* sure he was eyeing Betta quite a bit more than incidentally.

Or maybe I'm just jealous of Betta's body, she joked to herself. *I wonder if she'll be making another rendezvous with John tonight. . . .*

Venetia got her mind off these trivial things. "Dan, I was wondering—maybe we should've mentioned to Captain Berns about the names we found beneath the plaster today."

Now Dan cast an awkward glance at Betta while she stooped to get a pan out of a lower cabinet.

How do you like that guy! Venetia thought.

"Yeah, that's a good point," he answered. "The murders took place here, and Berns is confident that the suspects are part of a Satanic cult."

"Did he really say *that?*" Driscoll asked.

Both Mrs. Newlwyn and Betta stared at Dan.

"Sure did, but he doesn't think it's a very serious endeavor—"

"Not like the thing Amano Tessorio was into," Venetia added.

Driscoll gave a puzzled look. "What do you mean?"

"Judging at least by what you told me, Tessorio was a genuine hard-core Satanist, rebelling against the Church in secret."

"These rednecks who did the murders," Dan said, "are just lowlifes in a fake cult, delusional, a follow-the-leader kind of thing."

"Let's hope so," Driscoll replied. "But I've got to tell you—the whole business, I mean, this police officer I've never heard of coming here . . ."

"And wanting to talk to *you,*" Dan prodded.

"Oh, I look forward to talking to him and hearing what he has to say about these arrests—the Diocese will definitely want to know. But . . . where was I when he came?"

"Golfing." Dan frowned.

"I used to golf," John unexpectedly commented. "But just . . . the miniature kind."

"That's probably what Father Driscoll was doing, too," Dan said, "and just isn't telling anyone. He wants us to think he's Tiger Woods."

"Oh, Dan, please. You're more than welcome to join us next time we tee up, but I have to warn you, we play for ten bucks a hole. That's a bit out of your league, isn't it?"

"Not interested," Dan said. "Betting's a sin."

These two really are a riot, Venetia thought, but a minute later she was almost offended when Betta dropped a pot on the floor. This time she stooped so severely, her cotton panties became all too apparent, and Dan, John, and even Father Driscoll all took a long look. *Would you look at these sexist pigs!* Venetia thought.

Just then her cell phone rang. "It's my mother. Be right back." She slipped out to the atrium.

"Hi, Mom. Did you—"

"I hope you all enjoy the steak and seafood."

"Believe me, Mom. It's all much appreciated. Please thank Dad for us. But did you—"

"I'm finished with those searches you wanted."

Venetia felt very confident. "Nothing, I'll bet."

"Oh, no. It was very interesting."

Venetia's throat went dry. "You mean these people really exist?"

"Exist*ed*, honey," her mother corrected. "But I still don't understand why you're interested in—"

"Mom, please! What did you find?"

"Father Thomas Alexander. He became a priest after returning from several combat tours in Vietnam—he even won some medals. He wrote several books about the modern clergy, and evidently he was quite a respected counselor for the Richmond and New Jersey Dioceses. At his last post, he was the special assistant to the chancellor of the Richmond Diocesan Pastoral Center—some kind of a big wheel, I guess."

Venetia could barely talk. "And he's . . . dead?"

"Yes, dear, he died of a heart attack in Russell County—

that's southern Virginia—twelve years ago. He was forty-five years old."

A fog seemed to swirl about Venetia's mind. *Impossible. I know I'd never heard of him before, or that other person. . . .* "What about the other person, Mom. Ruth—"

"Ruth Bridges."

"Was she a nun?"

Maxine Barlow laughed. "Hardly. There were a lot of court dockets and arrest notices on her. She'd been arrested a number of times in four different states for prostitution, drug possession, check-kiting, and the like. That's why this whole thing is so strange, honey. Why would you have me search for information about a priest and a prostitute?"

Venetia began to feel sicker and sicker. "Never mind that, Mom. She's dead too, I take it."

"Oh, yes, I've got her obituary right here from the *St. Petersburg Times.* Ruth Bridges died of unspecified causes at a place in central Florida called Fort De Soto Park. She was thirty-nine years old. There's even a picture here. She's blond and pretty but . . . well, pretty in a trashy sort of way."

Venetia felt a sharp headache coming on. "When did she die, Mom?"

"Two days ago."

Chapter Eleven

(I)

At least I don't have to carry his ass around on my back anymore, Ruth thought.

The priest walked with confidence now, on two stout, muscular Usher legs, and the right arm, which came from the same species, flexed awesomely beneath the tacky gray-brown skin. It was the left arm that was the problem: a jointless hose of pink meat.

"Look, man, I'm sorry about the arm. I did the best I could."

"It'll be all right," the priest replied. His splotched, three-toed feet with claws left nicks in the cement with each step. "And I guess I should be happy with this." He shot a quick pose with the right arm, eyeing a bicep the size of a melon.

"What a stud. How about the other arm? Can you control it?"

"It takes concentration to fire the proper nerves," he told her. "Anneloks have a different kind of central nervous system—remember, they're just man-shaped worms." He slit his eyes, seemed to focus on a thought, and then the long tube reached straight up into the air.

"That's not bad!" Ruth exclaimed.

He looked embarrassed. "I was trying to scratch my chin. But if I keep practicing, I think the Annelok arm may come in useful. I've seen them crack stone pillars just by wrapping an arm around it."

Ruth's gaze scanned the dark street. "I'm glad we're not in that shit-town place anymore—"

"Sewageton," the priest corrected. "We're in a subdivision now. We won't be going to the next chartered District until tomorrow."

"So what are we doing now?"

"Making a pickup."

More pavement—made of crushed bones—stretched down the long street. Streetlamps on every corner glowed scarlet.

"Here we are." Alexander's monstrous legs strode sure as machinery when he stepped into a transomed entrance. "Keep your fingers crossed."

The transom read THE BTK MOTEL.

At the front desk, a Human woman with a halved face looked up. She had roofing nails in place of teeth.

"I'd like to rent Room thirteen, if possible," Alexander said. "I like lucky numbers."

The woman nodded and whatever she said came out garbled from her split jaw. When she gave the priest the key, Ruth noticed that all of the fingers on both of her hands had been whittled free of flesh.

"Why Room thirteen?" Ruth asked, following him up a spiral staircase.

Alexander whispered, "To pick up something that's been left for us."

"By who?" Then she reflected. "Oh, this intelligence source."

The priest nodded.

On the landing a female Troll with a cleaning cart was picking up chopped body parts. "Kids these days," she complained. "They get into such mischief."

Ruth frowned at the pointed tail hanging from her skirt.

"This is the Mengele Suite." Alexander unlocked the door and showed her in. "Nicest room in the motel."

Ruth switched on a Femur-Lamp and immediately looked appalled. "This is the *nicest* room?"

Bloody bandages comprised the wallpaper. The dresser was a pocked metal cabinet like something she'd expect in a doctor's office, and in the drawers were surgical instruments caked with blood. The bed was a mattress lain atop an operating table fitted with leg- and wrist-cuffs. In the opposite corner sat an iron chair with similar cuffs, and a coal bed beneath the seat.

Alexander's huge feet thumped in. "It's named for Josef Mengele. He was a Nazi doctor who experimented on captives. He'd regularly perform surgeries without using anesthetic, particularly brain surgery. The pricier rooms in any motel will always have a special motif to drive the rates up."

"Is that shade—"

"Human skin? Of course." Alexander raised the window shade and looked out. "So are the lamp shades. The mattress filling is hair, and see that curtain of beads?"

Ruth saw the strings of beads adorning the doorway to the bathroom, but the beads were teeth.

Fuck that shit, man. . . .

"If you think this is bad, you should see the Ivan the Terrible Suite at the Hilton."

Ruth groaned when she looked out the window. On the street two Broodren were dragging innards out of an old woman with a shopping cart, cackling like monkeys. When a Caco-Bat flew by, it looked right at Ruth and smiled.

"What are you doing?" she squealed when she saw the priest standing on the bed. The fist on his Usher's hand was almost as big as a bowling ball—

Thunk!

He punched a hole the size of a sewer lid in the ceiling.

"Who do you think you are, Van Halen?" Ruth gaped at the hole. "You can't trash the room! We'll get busted."

"Don't worry about it, Ruth. We'll be long gone before anyone finds out." The snakelike Annelok arm pointed at her and then curled inward. "Come up here, I need your help."

Ruth climbed uneasily onto the bed. Her eyes bulged when he grabbed her hips and raised her head and shoulders up into the hole.

"Hey! What am I—" Her head felt swallowed by darkness. "I can't see shit, man! Bring me down!"

"Light one of the matches you got at the convenience store and look around. We're looking for a pack of Hectographs."

Ruth railed. "How the fuck am I supposed to know what that is?"

"It's like a deck of cards. Stop complaining for a change and do it."

Pain in my ass. She pulled out the pack of matches, lit one—

And screamed.

When the match light flared, she was looking at a severed head lying on its side. It was a man, and he was smiling.

"Hey there," the head said.

"Holy shit!" she screamed down to Alexander. "Let me down!"

"Oh, sounds like you found a Talker, huh? I know it's a little unnerving at first—"

"*Unnerving?* There's a head cut off up here and it's talking to me!"

"Wow, you're really pretty," the head told her. "My name's Pete. What's yours? Let's go out sometime."

"Let me down!" she shouted again to the priest. "The head's name is Pete and it's asking me out!"

"Ruth, animated severed heads are all over the place in Hell. They're like tumbleweeds in the West. Now, be nice to the head and ask it where the Hectographs are."

Be nice . . . to the head?

"Oh, I know what you're looking for," the head named Pete told her. "Some Contumacy guys were up here a few days ago."

"So where are these Hecto-things?" she asked, trying not to look directly at it.

"Show me your breasts and I'll tell you."

She stared. "Fuck you! I'm not showing my boobs to a *head!*"

Alexander groaned below. "Ruth, just do it. You used to do it in Florida every night for free drinks. What's the difference?"

Ruth sighed at the question.

"Come on," the head asked. "Please?"

Ruth pulled up her top for a few seconds, then put it back down. "There, now you've seen them. So where're these things?"

The head grinned. "Give me a kiss and I'll tell you."

You fucker! Ruth grabbed the sulphur pistol and—

Bam!

The head burst to bits.

I hate it when guys lie to me.

Alexander's voice grew weary. "Ruth, can you find the Hectographs?"

"Oh, here they are." She reached out. "They were right behind the head the whole fuckin' time."

Alexander lowered her back down.

"If you can't control your awful language, Ruth, at least try to control your temper. We could've used that head for more information."

"Fuck the head! And I got your damn Hecto-whatevers, so stop bitching at me!"

The operating table bowed when Alexander sat on its edge next to Ruth. "Hecto*graphs*, Ruth. Hell's version of photography. Here, they use gold nitrate instead of silver nitrate and tin salt instead of silver salt."

"Oh, pictures. Like from the drugstore!"

Alexander nodded, and rubbed his temples with the huge hand.

"So this intelligence source of yours who you won't tell me anything about . . . she stashed this here for us?"

"Yes, or I should say she had some operatives in the Contumacy stash them."

"Contumacy . . . Oh, yeah, like those dudes at the Mutilation Zone, anti-Satan people."

"Exactly. Terrorists in reverse." Alexander slipped one Hectograph from the pack but held it back without showing it to her. "But first you must understand the next part of our mission."

Ruth leaned back on the bed, stretching her tan legs as she yawned. "Sounds like we're spies."

"That's pretty much what we are. We're field agents, so to speak, for a cause that exists in opposition to the Mephistopolis and all Satanic endeavors. So—" Alexander scowled when he looked over. "And don't fall asleep, Ruth! This is important!"

She flapped a hand. "I'm listening."

"There's a Grand Duke here named Aldezhor. He's very important because he's Lucifer's personal messenger. Ever heard of the Archangel Gabriel, God's messenger?"

"No."

Alexander shook his head. "Well, this Demon Aldezhor is the *Devil's* messenger. And the most important cryptograms in Hell are all delivered by him."

"Aldezhor," Ruth droned.

"It's his job to process all of Hell's most crucial communications without being detected by the Contumacy."

Ruth seemed confused, her fingers laced behind her head. "That's his job?"

"Uh-huh, and it's *your* job to wait on him."

Ruth winced over. "What do you mean, *wait* on him?"

"Wait on him in a restaurant," Alexander said. "And when you bring them their meals, you take a peak at the cipher."

Ruth leaned back up, annoyed. "How the hell am I gonna do that?"

"By distracting them." Alexander cocked a brow at her. "And I think you know what I mean. I didn't buy you that racy outfit for nothing. The Tongue-Skirt and Hand-Bra will make you the most unique waitress in the place . . . those and your overall looks, of course."

"Thanks," she grumbled.

"There's another reason why those clothes will help out, too, but we won't go into that now. Let's focus on one thing at a time." He nudged her to regain her attention. "You see, every day at lunch a Chevalier from the Department of Diabolic Encryptions brings Aldezhor the daily cipher from Manse Lucifer to Fortress Boniface. And that next note has something very important on it. Something we need to know."

Ruth flopped back on the bed, hands over her face. "Oh, man, this is so confusing! Manse Lucifer? Demons eating at some restaurant to pass messages? It's fucked-up, man!"

"Just continue to do as I tell you and follow my lead, and this'll all work out."

"I don't even know what this Aldezhor guy looks like," she complained. She was trying to get comfortable on the odd bed.

"That's what these are for." He held up the pack of Hectographs and showed the top card to her. "When you see this guy come into the restaurant, you do everything in your power to get his table."

Ruth held up the card. It looked like a regular color picture from a photo lab but had fuzzy borders, the image having been burned onto some weird photographic emulsion.

Goose flesh rose on her arms when she looked at the image.

A head disproportionately large—and queerly angled—jutted from shoulders that were wide yet somehow also gaunt. Two protrusions curved outward from the slablike forehead.

Horns, she realized over her fatigue. *Sharp ones.*

But even more disconcerting than the Grand Duke's physicality was simply the way it looked: all dark. Not black, not brown, just . . . dark.

"Aldezhor is a Scaedurian," Alexander told her. "That's a species of Subcarnate."

"It almost looks like he's made of shadow."

"That's because he is, and he also . . ."

Alexander's words petered out when he saw that Ruth had already fallen asleep.

(II)

One thing Venetia hadn't taken much of in college was psych. But her own troubles had sparked her concern, which led her back to a section of bookshelves reserved for psychology and psychiatry.

Maybe I'm overreacting, she thought, *or maybe it is more than fatigue. . . .*

One book seemed accessible—*Psychiatric Spirituality: A Guide for Catholic Clinicians*. She was hunting for causes of hallucinatory symptoms, but found mostly incomprehensible psych-speak: ego-syntonic hallucinosis, erotogenic ideas of reference, ketoacidosis and stage four sleep maladaptations. *This is depressing*, she thought; the terms all had definitions that were scary . . . and all rooted in forms of schizophrenia and psychosis. Then she flipped a page and saw:

> *Aural Hallucinotic Hypnagogia: The hearing of noises and/or voices during the semiconscious state immediately preceding sleep. More often, symptoms are connected to stress and fatigue, while the content of the aural activity may reflect the individual's personal worries. Catholic clinicians are well-used to otherwise mentally healthy patients experiencing aural hypnapompia, particularly in the twenty- to thirty-year-old age group. Even the most mentally sound Catholics experience observations and ideas that challenge faith; hence the symptoms. In fact, all forms of mild hypnagogic and hypnapompic imagery are periodic and normal, particularly among those who are 1) in the twenty- to thirty-year-old age group, and 2) on the verge of committing to a clergy-related vocation.*

Venetia nodded to herself. *On the verge of committing to a clergy-related vocation . . . That's definitely me.* A few of the last lines in the text seemed most reassuring of all:

> *Aural Hallucinotic Hypnagogia must never be con-*
> *fused with serious clinical hallucinosis. The "voices"*
> *that the individual hears are merely a form of precur-*
> *sory dream fragments and usually of no pathologic sig-*
> *nificance.*

Venetia sighed in relief. *How do you like that? I'm* not
crazy. She put the book back on the shelf and looked out
the window. *I wonder, though,* she thought. *Did I ever re-*
ally believe that two people in Hell were talking to me? The
fact that Thomas Alexander and Ruth Bridges did indeed exist was harder to explain, but still . . . *I could have*
read about Alexander in the Catholic Standard *a long time*
ago and just forgot. Same thing with the woman. So what if
she only died two days ago. I probably half-heard it on the
news.

When she turned, she noticed the edge of a slip of paper slightly sticking out between other two books. She
withdrew it.

A handwritten note. And . . . what is this?

> *She is beautiful in her skein-weave of darkness. It is*
> *horror which flows through her veins of ghostly dust,*
> *and horror that fills her eye sockets. This is but another*
> *unblessed personage I will be enthralled to meet at the*
> *fortress some day: Pasiphae, the Night-Mother, the Slut-*
> *Mother.*
> *Her pretty feet are but dark fog, her cunt a night-smile.*
> *In her excitement, black milk oozes from her ebon bosom.*
> *She is the Guide, and only she can lead the Privileged*
> *through the labyrinth below the fortress, to the heart of*
> *Satan's endeavor: the Lower Chancel.*

Venetia stared astonished at the blasphemous scrawl.
What is this doing in a Catholic prior house? she asked, but
then immediately recalled the secret nature of the man
who built it. *Tessorio . . . I'll bet he wrote this.*

More:

*The breeze, over the scarlet night, continues to sigh.
Chatterings from the overseers of the dead? Or messages
from her world, from her black haven in the Mephistopolis?*

Oh, how long to join her!

*For surely the Slut-Mother, the Guide to the Pith, will
lead me through the Fortress Gates to my lord Boniface.*

That name—Boniface—struck a black chord in Venetia's mind. *The worst of the anti-Popes, a murderer and blasphemer . . .* Clearly, Tessorio had a fixation with Boniface:
the unlikely portrait that Dan found in the attic, along
with that macabre sketch. Tessorio had hidden this odd
scribbling amid the books, which begged Venetia to
consider: *I wonder what else he might've stashed around
here.*

Between two old volumes (*Visual Thinking* and *Preter-
Naturality & The Human Mind*) she discovered another
sheet of paper, filled with more handwriting that was undoubtedly Tessorio's. But it wasn't from a tablet; the
scrawl had been written on the back of a yellowed store
receipt. It read:

*Begin fast at 6 am on Oct. 30, be sure to bleed yourself.
At midnight, begin channeling incantation.*

Channeling? Incantations? This was even stranger than
the first sheet . . . until she gave it more thought. *All right,
the guy was a nut. He worshiped the Devil as a means of rebelling against the Church. He probably drank a lot and took
drugs in secret. And he believed in crap like this.*

And fasting? Bleeding oneself? This was all part of
corny ritualism from the Middle Ages. She also knew
they were techniques involved in inducing trances.

She flipped the paper and read the receipt. It was from a
place called Hull's General Store, dated October 26, 1964.

*Four days before the thirtieth, and the morning before Hal-
loween.*

Tessorio seemed to be preparing for something. *Fast-*

ing? Bleeding? A ritual? Venetia wondered with a smile. *A meeting of the coven when at midnight Halloween has arrived.* Venetia knew there was no way she might even partly believe in such things; nevertheless, she had to ask herself, *What was this ritual for? Did it involve "channeling," a means of receiving information from the dead?*

She pushed it from her mind.

"Dinner'll be ready soon, and tonight, it'll be a *superb* dinner." The voice startled her. It was Father Driscoll, emerging from his downstairs office. He rubbed his hands together dramatically. "God bless your father for such generosity."

"It smells like Mrs. Newlwyn is broiling some lobsters."

"Yes—God *bless* him."

Venetia smiled at the priest's overstatement. "You sound like you've never had lobster."

"On *my* pay?" Driscoll laughed.

Venetia walked over to join him, yet without thinking she asked, "When did the actual building of the prior house begin?"

"November 1964, I believe." He walked by her side toward the kitchen. "Oh, yeah, now I'm sure that was it. I remember reading it in my prospectus. Construction began on November first, in fact. All Saints Day."

The day after Halloween, Venetia thought.

(III)

Berns dreamed of counterclockwise spirals, and he dreamed of buckets of blood. The daymare lolled on through his head such that some aspect of his sleeping psyche feared he'd dropped into a vortex of mad dreams from which he would never rouse. The dream was silent, Daliesque, running with stark images and blocked out shades of black. Colors seemed to bleed.

Behind closed, quivering eyes he was shown rather than saw rough hands gripping knives that slid through pale throats to the bone. Nude bodies shuddered as racing hearts emptied their lifeblood through the knife slits.

All the while, Berns thought in the grimmest consterna-
tion: *Where is the blood? What are they doing with the blood?*

Words droned in the background like a chant, but in
some language he'd never heard. *"Exos spiratum, Lux
Ferre, in aeternum . . . ,"* then things even less intelligible.

And the final image, crisply erotic, obscene: a woman's
flat abdomen quivering on a table as a tattooist's hum-
ming needle inscribed the design in threadlike waves of
crimson—the decorated rectangle with the spiral inside
and arrows pointing inward from three corners, and then
the dream quaked in an eruption of screams. Berns now
saw *himself* standing naked beside a torrential waterfall of
blood. When he looked down at himself, he saw the same
tattoo on his own abdomen. . . .

Berns woke up at the desk, his face glazed in sweat.
Had he shouted in his sleep? Someone was knocking on
the office door, loud.

"Come in."

The county booking sergeant looked suspicious. "You
all right, Captain?"

"Yeah. Why?"

"I was knocking . . . for a while."

Berns admitted it. "I fell asleep. Haven't gotten any
down time for a couple days."

"Sure, sir. But I wanted to let you know that you got a
call—"

An instant image snapped in Berns' mind: the glowing
face backed by bright blond hair. "Is it Venetia Barlow?"
he asked without thinking.

"Who?" Another suspicious frown. "It's a sergeant
from Lubec, Maine. Says its urgent. Line one."

"Thanks," Berns grumbled. "Berns here," he said into
the phone. A flash of vertigo stalled him: the notion of the
strange tattoo on his own stomach as though Berns himself were a member of Freddie Johnson's murder club.
"Sergeant Lee?"

"Yes, sir," came the voice over the line. Lee's tone
sounded hesitant. "I—"

"Something wrong, Sarge?"

A sputter. "I'll just have out with it. I fucked-up, Captain."

Berns' mental gears were just grinding up. "The judge wouldn't delay Johnson's arraignment?"

"Oh, no, he signed right off on that. Won't matter now, though. Freddie Johnson is dead."

Berns went rigid at the desk. "How the hell . . . Don't tell me he killed himself."

"He killed himself, Captain. Just like he said he would. Last night I put a drunk in the lockup two cells down from Freddie's. He's a regular, you know? Harmless. Once a month he downs a bottle of Black Velvet and out go his lights. The guy was passed out all night and all day today. . . ."

"And?"

Lee gulped through a pause. "I guess he came to and—well, Freddie talked the guy out of his belt and he slid it across."

Shit. Berns wanted to clunk his head against the desk. But as his emotions simmered, Freddie Johnson's words came back to him.

When the party's over, it's over. . . .

Susan Maitland had said the same thing, and again, Berns thought, *Suicide pact. Only problem is, Freddie Johnson wasn't suicidal.*

"I'm really sorry, Captain," Lee said. "With anyone else I wouldn't think twice about taking a guy's belt and shoelaces, but like I said—"

"The guy was the town rummy, you've probably known him for years, and he's never been any trouble."

"Yes, sir. I'll assume all responsibility."

There was no reason to stew over it. "Forget it, and look at the bright side. One less scumbag in the world is a good thing. Probably saved the taxpayers a hundred grand in custody and court costs. We already busted an accomplice—Freddie's sometime squeeze. The state's interrogating her now—we'll probably get more out of her than Freddie anyway."

"Good," Lee said. "Now I don't feel so bad. But I do

have something for you that might be helpful. We went over Freddie's room again like you asked and found some stuff. He hid it pretty well."

"He probably thought you'd stop looking when you found that forty grand in cash."

"Exactly what I thought, but . . . well, it's some weird shit we found."

Berns wasn't surprised. "Like what? Oh, let me guess. An ashtray?"

"No, but—" Lee paused, as if subtly bothered. "We found this weird glass bowl—made of *black* glass—and it had some burned stuff in the bottom. And a can of Sterno."

"And the stuff in the bowl wasn't cigarette tar or pot?"

"No way. We're sending it to the state lab but I'm pretty sure we already now what it is—tree sap."

"Tree sap?"

"That's right, Captain."

"How do you know?"

"Freddie had cut off some branches from a scarlet sumac tree, brought them into the room, and had them hanging over a plate. He was collecting the sap. Then I see this sticky burned stuff in the black bowl—"

"And figure it's got to be the same thing," Berns finished, but just didn't get it. Susan Maitland had referred to her ashtray as a thurible, which Berns had quickly looked up in the dictionary. *A vessel or censer in which incense is burned, especially during rituals,* he recalled.

"That's fucking *weird,*" Berns said.

"Oh, no, Captain. *That's* not the weird part. It's everything else we found. One of those lined yellow notepads. The top pages had all kinds of off-the-wall stuff written on them, all in Johnson's handwriting."

"What did he write?"

"Well, the first sheet was a drawing of that bizarre design that he also had for a tattoo."

Berns felt a stab of queasiness, remembering his dream.

Lee continued, "And the rest? Well, just wait till you see it."

"Writing?" Berns blinked. "*Instructions* of some kind?"

"I don't know *what* it is, Captain. Something in some foreign language I guess. Looks like Johnson's handwriting, but—"

"A redneck crabber with no education probably doesn't know any foreign languages."

"Right."

Berns stared at the wall, thinking. *Maitland said Freddie had copied some* instructions *and left them for her and the other accomplice. This stuff that Lee found must be the original copy.*

But if they were instructions for ritual murderers, what use could they be now? *The murders already occurred, last March at the St. John's Prior House. . . .*

"Do me a favor, Sarge. Before you book those papers as evidence, I need you to scan them and e-mail the file down here."

"I've already sent my guy to the county to use their scanner," Lee said.

"Thanks."

Lee's voice seemed to drift for a moment. "You want to know what bugs me the most, Captain? Don't know why, but it just does. When I found Freddie hanging in his cell . . ."

"Yeah?"

"He was stone-cold dead but he still had that same happy-go-lucky grin on his face, gold tooth flashing and all."

"I believe it. You heard him, though. He wanted to be dead. 'When the party's over, it's over,' he said."

Lee uttered a dark chuckle. "Well that redneck scumbag ain't partying now."

"Or maybe he is. In Hell," Berns said and rang off.

The office seemed queerly smaller after he hung up; he felt encroached upon. *Tree sap*, he thought, and lit a cigarette. *What the hell was he doing burning tree sap in a glass bowl?*

Chapter Twelve

(I)

"What is that? Trees?"

"Druid Oak. They use them for the sap," Alexander said as the chain gang of various Demons and Human Damned dragged the tree down the noxious street. "They're taking it there." He pointed to a wide gray building of uneven bricks, topped by a smoking chimney. At once Ruth's eyes began to water.

"In Hell, they use Druid Oak and Eldritch Pines. The counterpart in the Living World are sumac trees and shrubs, cashew trees, staghorns. It's because the sap is similar—it's poisonous to varying degrees. Bet your eyes are watering now, huh?"

Ruth frowned, nodding.

"Remember the Goethe Hall? It's like I was telling you in Sewageton," the priest went on, thumping forward on his monstrous legs. "Every District has its own hall of automatic-writers."

The sign on this building read THE MOZART HALL OF AUTOMATIC-WRITERS.

"Let's go and look in the window," Alexander urged.

Inside were a hundred tables, and at each sat several scriveners writing manically on pads of parchment. The room was smoky like a pool hall, and at its center was a great stone fireplace. An iron cauldron rested above the flames; within, Ruth could see bubbling sap. The bubbles broke, releasing the occult fumes to be breathed by all. Golems guarded each door, their faces of lifeless clay somehow sentient. Eventually Ruth noted that all of the scriveners were chained to their chairs.

"The smoke from the sap is a trance-inducer. The scriveners breath it, and with the help of a variety of Transpondence Spells and amplified Hex Fluxes, they are able to maintain psychic contact with counterparts on Earth, who are breathing similar fumes."

Ruth felt as confused as she was bored. "And whatever these people here write down—"

"Is simultaneously written down by a Human counterpart in the Living World, mostly cult members and genuine Satanists."

"But what are they writing?"

"Incantation instructions, spell sequences, archival material," the priest said.

"Okay, that's all very fuckin' interesting," Ruth told him, "but I don't really give a shit. I'm starving. Let's get something to eat."

Alexander frowned disapproval. "Ruth, this is important. You need to understand these details. It just so happens that our entire mission *exists* because an automatic-writer in Hell has been delivering instructions to cult members near the place where Venetia is right now. One of them was the very same man who built the St. John's Prior House a long time ago, and he was a Vatican architect."

Ruth tried to act interested. "Like a long distance phone service . . ."

"That's right, Ruth. A communication line between the Living World and Hell."

She followed the sturdy-legged priest, her mind trying to comprehend all the things she was learning. Leather-winged birds roved in the bloodred sky. In this collapsing subdistrict, Ruth noticed more homeless bums and Demons, and more prostitutes. A shapely Lycanymph with champagne blond fur tapped by on high heels and grumbled at Ruth.

"Hairy bitch," Ruth sniped. "She's just jealous of my bod, like that purple asshole at the lingerie shop."

"Keep your voice down," the priest warned. "Don't start trouble. This isn't the place for it."

Ruth grimaced at a severed face in the gutter, then sped up when the face grimaced back. "What's so special about this place?"

"Coleridge Avenue. It's a big dope hub."

"They have drugs here?" she asked with a spark of enthusiasm.

"They sure do, and they're a thousand times more addictive than the stuff in the Living World. One bang and you're gone for eternity. It used to be Zap was the biggest drug in Hell; the junkies would inject it straight into their brains by shoving needles up their nostrils, but that's old hat now. Look."

Ruth tracked his gaze, to a state shop that read SCALP-ING ANNEX. Hollow-eyed Human Damned stood in a long line at one door, while more trudged out of a second door, only these latter persons left minus their scalps.

"Scalping? Fuck! They're scalped as punishment for doing drugs?"

"No, no," Alexander explained. "They're *selling* their scalps for drug money. Right now the big drug on the street is L A—that's Lovecraftic Acid. It's so addictive that they don't even bother keeping the Retox Centers open anymore. Nobody *ever* gets off L A. They start by smoking it, then shoot it, and eventually they sell their scalps to expose the outer-cranial blood vessels. One drop of L A on an open blood vessel gets you the best high." Then he pointed to another shop across the street, from which a smiling She-Demon in a shaggy fur coat emerged.

"Naturally, every Scalping Center has a cloak maker's nearby. Efficiency in commerce."

ALEXANDRA ROMANOV'S—FURS FOR A SELECT CLIENTELE, the sign read.

Ruth didn't have to wonder what became of the scalps once they were sold.

"And there's a long-term L A addict," the priest pointed out next. "The stuffs wears you out. Lucifer particularly likes it when *Humans* become addicted, because then their misery is eternal."

Ruth gasped when she saw the ramshackle *thing* sitting in the alley. It was a man, or at least she thought so, his scalp long gone. When he looked at Ruth he did so with empty sockets, so he'd clearly sold his eyeballs, too. Even his heart was gone, sold for more drugs. Sparrow-sized mosquitoes crawled over him, siphoning blood, and from the holes where his ears used to be, thin red-tipped tentacles squirmed. When he opened his mouth to scream, another, longer, tentacle wormed out.

"Let's get out of here!" Ruth pleaded.

"Relax. We're almost there."

"There as in where?"

"The fringes of Boniface Square—the upscale restaurant block." The priest shot her a smile. "Time for you to get to work."

Ruth groaned to herself. *I can hardly wait.*

(II)

After dinner, Venetia found herself back in the atrium scouring the bookshelves. Father Driscoll had responded to her comment at the table about finding strange notes stashed between some books, possibly written by Amano Tessorio, like this: "It undoubtedly was," Driscoll had told her over a chunk of lobster tail shiny with butter. "Tessorio hid lots of notes and scribblings in the books."

"Why would he do that?" she'd asked.

Driscoll shrugged: "Because he was a weirdo closet-Satanist who was probably half-insane from tertiary syphilis."

His response had made her feel naive, but it also left her curiosity inflamed. What else might the former Vatican architect have left secreted in the prior house?

At first, the endeavor seemed ludicrous (there were thousands of books in the atrium, perhaps tens of thousands) but within fifteen minutes—

I don't believe it!

Stuck between two books of essays by Thomas Merton, she found another yellowed sheet. It read: *Ablissa, Eylla, Azusis, Belith, Gesmary, Tzaella.*

Names, obviously. Were they Biblical? *How bizarre,* she thought. Then: *Another one!* but she could only smile at herself when she discovered an ad clipping from an old newspaper, which read: COME ONE, COME ALL! TO HOLY TRINITY CHURCH FOR THE ANNUAL WAMMSPORT CLAM BAKE! SATURDAY, JULY 14TH, 1975!

I guess I'm getting carried away with this stuff, she thought.

"Wow, I really love those air-conditioners your father bought us," Dan was saying as he approached.

"He's a generous guy, even for an oddball."

"And that lobster for dinner? That was some spread." Dan dug some keys from his pocket. He'd removed his black shirt and collar in favor of a clean T-shirt. "Let's split. Driscoll wants me to pick up some extension cords, and . . . there's a Red Sox game. He said I could take the Merc."

Venetia felt disheveled and messy, but . . . *I wouldn't mind getting out of here for a while.* "We're going to a baseball game?"

"No, no, it's on TV. There's a bar in town," the seminarist announced with some relief.

"I don't drink. Do you?"

"I have a beer or two—that's no big deal. Besides, Big Daddy Driscoll said I could."

Driscoll's voice boomed from the upper stair-hall. "And if Little Daddy Dan gets pulled over in my Mercedes while driving intoxicated, he won't have to worry about *ever* becoming a priest."

They both looked up and saw Driscoll smiling down.

"Caught again," Venetia laughed. "You really do have a big mouth, Dan."

"Tell me about it."

Dan spent the entire drive into Wammsport smirking at himself. As dusk approached, the air cooled down and the fading sun painted brilliant orange steamers over the water. "Driscoll's such a pain in the butt, you know that?" he said when they parked at the city dock. "Treats me like a punk."

"But it's only because he wants you to become a good priest," Venetia offered.

Dan was about to gripe further when he did a double-take. "I don't believe it—come on."

Perplexed, Venetia followed him across the street to a grocery store parking lot. *What's he need here?* she wondered, but even stranger was his urgency. In the lot's corner she saw an attractive, thirtyish woman sitting in a lawn chair before the opened back doors of a step van. The side of the van read HOLY GROUND HOMELESS SHELTER— SHOES, CLOTHING, AND CANNED FOOD PLEASE. The woman in the chair immediately recognized Dan and stood up.

"What a surprise," came a soft Southern drawl. The woman was pretty in a startling way: well-curved, leggy, with a warm smile and aquamarine eyes. Bronze blond hair streaked with caramel fell over shoulders that were bare and tan; she wore a string-strapped halter and cutoff jeans. Lying against the swell of her bosom was a cross.

"Diane, it's so good to see you." Dan hugged her. "I'm surprised you remember me, as little as I ever saw you."

She smiled coyly. "Nuns *never* forget handsome seminarians," she replied. "Not that I'm a nun anymore."

"That's too bad." At once Dan seemed troubled. "This is Venetia Barlow. She's helping restore the prior house. Venetia, Diane Elsbeth."

"Nice to meet you," Venetia said, her curiosity already hair-triggering. *This is one of the nuns who fled the prior house after the murders.*

"Venetia is considering the vocation," Dan said.

"I'm glad to hear it." Diane sounded sincere. "It's just that . . . it wasn't for me."

"Why?" Venetia asked too readily. "The murders scared you off?"

Dan immediately raised a brow, while Diane fell sullen.

"I'm sorry, it's none of my business," Venetia corrected. "Rumors are usually never true anyway. I apologize."

Diane struggled over a pause. "Rumors?"

Damn. I should never have said anything, Venetia thought.

"The ghost stuff, Tessorio, and all that," Dan said.

The attractive woman idly scuffed her flip-flops on the pavement. "It's got nothing to so with that dreary prior house. The reason I quit the Sisterhood is because I'm not a strong enough servant of God."

"That's a bunch of crap," Dan abruptly disagreed. Then he winked. "You'll come back."

"I doubt it." The woman's eyes fluttered. "But don't worry, I'm still a Christian. I still go to church. I've got a day job and I do this at night. God is good to me."

"I'm glad," Dan said.

Venetia was nearly grinding her teeth. *God, I wish she'd talk about what happened. . . .*

"How's Ann doing?" Dan asked.

Diane's expression turned glum. "She's lost."

"No one's ever really lost," Dan offered, but it sounded feeble.

Then Venetia ventured, "Why do you say she's lost?"

Suddenly the woman looked depressed and exhausted. "I really don't want to talk about it, but . . ." She smiled right at Venetia. "Do you know the story of Jesus and the Widow's Mite?"

A strange shift of subjects. "Of course. The twelfth chapter of Mark," Venetia said at once. "When Jesus was asking for alms, a destitute widow gave Him her last two mites—or leptons—the equivalent of half a cent."

Diane's smile beamed. "Exactly," She stuck out a donation can.

"I *knew* she was still Catholic!" Dan jested.

Venetia put in a twenty-dollar bill, chuckling. Just then a station wagon pulled up, and a man and his kids got out, bringing boxes of canned goods.

"It's been good to see you, Dan," Diane said, parting. "Go with God."

"You too."

Diane's eyes locked on Venetia's. "I'm sure you'll be a devout nun. Good luck."

Venetia watched her walk away. "Thanks . . ."

"Well, it happens sometimes," Dan said, leading Venetia toward a drugstore.

"Nuns become disillusioned, sure. But because of murders?"

Dan bought some extension cords. "She'll be back."

But he was obviously perturbed; Venetia saw it at once. "Where are we going now?" she asked when he crossed the street away from the car.

He pointed to a low brick building whose sign read AB-NEY'S BAR & GRILL.

"Oh, that's right, so you can watch your baseball game."

He grinned over his shoulder. "Or maybe that's just an excuse."

"Excuse for what?"

He didn't answer, just led her in.

What a dive, Venetia thought. Low lights and smoke-thick air drew over a long black bar with cigarette-burned stools and a jar of pickled pig's feet every yard. Pool tables stretched along the back.

Dan plopped down on a stool.

"Can't we get a booth?" Venetia queried.

"Not unless you want to sit down on a used rubber," he chuckled. His eyes gestured the handful of broken alcoholics and yahoos sitting around. "As you can see, this isn't exactly the cocktail lounge at the Four Seasons. There are more teeth on the floor than there are in the mouths of the patrons."

Venetia sat, shaking her head at the cynical whimsy.

"Ah, there it is," Dan said of the baseball game on a high TV. "So, what, the only alcohol you consume is at Communion?"

Venetia laughed. "I've only been drinking age for a few

months. I have a glass of champagne on New Year's—that's about it."

Two rednecks guffawed at each other near the pool tables.

"I'll take two Wammsport Lagers," Dan told a barkeep who had to be eighty, and to Venetia: "What do you want?"

"Coke, please." She frowned when the keep set two beers before Dan. "That's what I call two-fisted drinking. You ever thought of seeing a counselor? The priesthood has a high rate of alcohol abuse."

Dan rolled his eyes. "I worked in the *attic* today. I'll bet it was a hundred and twenty degrees. Don't be judgmental. Besides, Christ imbibed, and so did the Apostles."

"Yeah, Dan, but they didn't order beers two at a time."

"I deserve it anyway," he said without looking at her. "I work hard for God. I mean, come on, I've taken a vow of *celibacy*, Venetia. With all that, I don't think God's going to get too pissed off if I have a couple beers."

"Let's hope not."

A squeal caused turn them to their heads. A trampish woman at one of the pool tables laughed hoarsely, bantering with the men. She wore raggy but tight jeans and a loose blouse that made no secret of braless breasts. "Come on, boys. Who's got the balls to rack 'em?"

"Redneck Central," Dan said.

"Such grace for the impoverished."

"I was only kidding, Venetia." He smirked back and drained a third of a beer in one sip. "I'm actually grateful for this wonderful day."

"Really?" she said.

"We got a lot of work done, your father gave us air conditioners and lobster tails, and"—he jabbed at finger at the TV—"the Sox are up on New York by two. Diane's right. God *is* good."

"I think God's a little bit busy to watch baseball."

He shot a wide-eyed look at her. "You don't know that."

Venetia smiled. But when he drained his first glass in

two more sips, she had to ask. "Dan, you're drinking like a longshoreman. What's bothering you?"

"Nothing. I'm just thirsty."

"Baloney. Diane is my guess," she asserted. "It shook you up to learn that she'd quit."

He stalled, looked at her, then slumped. "Yeah, I guess you're right. Professional hazard—we both know that. Some people just can't hack it, and that's a shame."

"It could happen to us, too," Venetia said, "but I'm not afraid of the possibility."

Another pause, another sip. "Maybe that's the problem. Maybe *I* am."

Venetia could not think of anything to say. She watched him decompress in silence, eyeing the TV. She was about to speak but then Dan's gaze snapped up. "What a rip-off! The big dumb lummox just hit a three-run homer!"

"It's just a game," she said. "And kind of a silly one at that. Big men swinging a stick at a ball and then running around."

"No, no, Venetia. Chicks just don't understand. . . ." He frowned. "And look at you. You're sitting there with your soda pop like Mother Teresa—only a million times better looking—in the middle of a bar. Would you *please* have a drink. We're two clerics in the midst of regular people."

Regular people, she mused. "You're really edgy today. I didn't know men got PMS."

Dan laughed.

"But if it makes you happy . . ." She ordered a beer. *I guess one won't turn me into a drunk.*

The lager was rich and strong; her brows rose over the first sip. But when she looked again, Dan wasn't watching the TV, he was looking over toward the pool tables.

More ruckus rose. The loud girl in tight jeans was lining up a shot, and as she did so, the V of her blouse hung low, affording any man looking a clear view of her bare breasts.

So that's what he's looking at. The observation depressed

some tiny part of her. *All day yesterday he was looking at me . . .*

"Come on, Jimmy. Put your money where your mouth is," her raucous voice cackled. "If I drop this shot, you pay forty for a blow."

Her roughened opponent laughed openly. "You're on, babe. And if you *miss* it, I get one for free."

Forty for a—Venetia's concentration tightened.

An explosion of laughter rose when the woman sunk the shot. "Shee-it," muttered this Jimmy person. He followed the woman out the door, reaching for his wallet.

"Dan, I know I'm pretty naive about some aspects of the real world," she began, "but is that woman a prostitute?"

The wizened barkeep hacked laughter and walked away.

Venetia's face reddened. But when she looked to Dan for an answer, she saw that his forehead was in his hand. "What's wrong?"

"This day is turning to crap real fast." He cleared his throat. "Yes, that woman is a prostitute . . . and I just now recognized her."

Venetia stared at him.

"It's Ann McGowen," Dan told her. "The second nun who left the prior house after the murders."

The shock seemed palpable. *My God . . .* "Diane wasn't kidding when she said Ann was 'lost.'"

"Going from nun to bar-whore is about as lost as you can get." Dan ordered two more beers.

He knew her, Venetia realized. *Probably not well, but still . . .* How depressing. She was about to comment on the second order of beers but then retracted the idea.

Soon the bar got loud. More roughneck crabbers barged in, bringing boisterous talk and sleazy work- and drink-worn women. *Dan's right. These are the regular people.* The reality turned her sullen.

Evidently Dan's team was losing; he kept cursing at the TV. Venetia wasn't sure, but the beer she'd only half-consumed seemed to be giving her a pleasant buzz. She began to people-watch, wondering if *any* of the revelers believed in God.

"Danny! You're kidding me!"

Venetia turned to see that Ann McGowen had returned from her illicit rendezvous. Beer-breath gusted with every word. She'd snuck up behind Dan, was hugging him, then smacked several wet kisses on his neck.

"Hi, Ann," he said.

"No black shirt and Roman collar. That's a good sign." Now her hands slid around his chest.

"Oh, don't worry. I'm still a seminarist, just out of uniform today. I've been working at the prior house."

"I heard some new priest took over Whitewood's post, and there's a crew up there fixing the joint up, picking up where we left off." Now her hands slid to his waist, practically to his crotch.

Dan introduced her to Venetia.

"Wow, I can tell *you're* Catholic just by looking at you. Guess you're my replacement, huh?"

"In a sense," Venetia said. "I'm helping clean up the prior house for college credits."

Ann McGowen's eyes shot brazenly to Venetia's bosom. Then she smirked.

This woman does not *like me . . .*

The former nun was whispering too loudly now into Dan's ear. "You wanna know something? Last year when you'd come to the prior house every Friday to get Whitewood's invoices, that was about the only thing Diane and I ever looked forward to."

Dan looked confused. "Why?"

"Why?" she cracked another laugh. " 'Cos you were the only good-looking man we ever got to see!"

"That's . . . nice of you to say. . . ."

Venetia could only guess that Dan was severely uncomfortable.

Ann whispered lower now. "You're not a priest yet, you know. Come outside to the car with me," and then one hand cupped Dan's crotch.

He pulled the hand off immediately. "I've already done my vows, Ann. Gimme a break."

"Shit. We could have some fun." She gave him a last

hug, deliberately pressing her breasts against his back. But then she pulled off. "Buy me a drink, Danny."

He jigged a hand at the barkeep. "Get her whatever she wants."

"You're a sweetheart." This time she gave him a wet kiss on the lips. She ordered a pitcher. "Lemme know if you change your mind."

"That won't happen, Ann, but I hope you change yours," he said. "God wants you back."

Ann's drunken expression soured. "Bullshit. God doesn't give a fuck about me, and he doesn't give a fuck about you or Little Bo-Peep sitting next to you, or anyone—"

"You're wrong—"

"But thanks for the pitcher," and then the woman walked back toward the pool tables.

Dan gulped his third beer. "Jesus."

"Am I being judgmental if I say that's sad?"

"That's *really* sad, Venetia."

"Why don't you skip the fourth beer," she suggested, "and let's get back to the prior house."

"It's bottom of the ninth. Just give me three outs."

Venetia knew that, now, he was using the baseball game as a blinder. Ann McGowen continued to cavort about the pool tables, rubbing up against any man in proximity. Several minutes later, though, she walked to the ladies room.

Venetia waited another minute, then went right in behind her, thinking, *This might be a big mistake.*

"Oh, the Catholic Cutie Pie," Ann sneered when she emerged from a stall.

"I—I wanted to ask you something—"

"Bullshit," the woman said. She leaned against the wall and lit a cigarette. "You think God's gonna give you brownie points for coming into a bathroom in a redneck bar and trying to preach to me?"

"I didn't come in here to preach," Venetia said, her heart rate rising.

"And I'll tell you—since I'm fucking *sure* you want to

know." She blew smoke into Venetia's face. "Sister Patricia and Lottie Jessel were two of the kindest, nicest, and most faithful people I've ever met in my life, and then God let some psycho cut their throats. Any God that could let two women *that* innocent be murdered is *fucked-up.* I don't want any part of your *God.*"

"Ann, the evil in the world is *our* burden. God's got nothing to do with it." She roused her nerve. "That's the worst excuse I've ever heard, and a weak, selfish reason to leave the Church."

Ann's bloodshot eyes leveled. She flicked the cigarette in the sink, and—

Venetia almost shrieked, the woman moved so fast. Ann was suddenly squashing her against the wall, licking her neck, and whispering. "Yeah? Yeah? And what about desire?"

Venetia shuddered, afraid to the point that she was petrified.

Ann kept her pinned against the wall with surprising strength, her hands sliding up under Venetia's blouse to knead her breasts through the bra.

"Stop!" Venetia gasped.

But the woman just licked her neck more intently. "You tell me, you little tease—what kind of God would give His flock desire and then demand that they repress it? Hmm?"

Venetia finally snapped out of the rigor and tried to push the woman off, but when she did so, Ann's assault only intensified.

"Hmm, honey? What kind of God does *that?*" Then she licked right across Venetia's pressed lips, trying to force in her tongue. Now Ann's fingers had pushed up the bra cups. Venetia squealed when the intruding fingertips clamped down on her nipple and pinched.

Powerless, Venetia gagged, "Stop it or I'll scream."

"No, you won't," and then Ann slipped one hand up Venetia's skirt, then down her panties. . . .

Venetia tried to scream but found her throat locked up. She grabbed Ann's wrists and with all her strength, fought to keep the marauding hands at bay.

"You're strong for a little girl." But the woman didn't back off. "I'll make a deal with you, and remember that lying is a sin." The drunken eyes bored into her. "You look me in the eye and swear to God on High that you don't want to fuck Dan. You tell me that you're not sexually attracted to him, tell me that you have absolutely no lust for him and never have. You *swear*, bitch. You swear to *God*. And if you do that, I'll go back to that fuckin' house with you, and I'll put my habit and cross back on."

Venetia met the woman's glare . . . and wilted. She didn't say anything.

Ann backed away, rescued her cigarette from the sink. "What the hell did you come in here for?"

Venetia wiped a tear from her eye. "I . . . wanted to ask you something. Mrs. Newlwyn said that the murders aren't the only reason you and Diane left the prior house."

A mocking laugh. "Mrs. Newlwyn, that big dyke? And how do you like that horny nutball daughter of hers?"

Venetia's heart was still racing. "She said the place is haunted. Is it?"

Ann blew another plume of smoke. "Gimme twenty dollars and I'll tell you."

I should just leave, Venetia thought, but instead, she gave the coarse woman a twenty-dollar bill.

"Yeah, Bo-Peep, it sure as shit is."

"And you've seen the ghost?"

For the first time, the drunken woman turned stolid. "Yeah. Three times. Diane saw it too, and so has Mrs. Newlwyn and her kid. On the stair-hall, in the atrium, and sometimes outside."

"Who is it?"

Ann's eyes thinned. She cocked a hip. "You really want to know, don't you?"

"Yes."

"Tessorio. Who did you think? He was really a Satanist, did you know that? And I mean a *real* one." She leaned closer. "He built that place for a *reason*, and it had nothing to do with God. It's some kind of *plan*."

A plan? "What are you talking about?"

"That's what Whitewood told me, and I believe it. And I can tell you this—he knew more than he was telling about that place, and I'll bet whoever replaced him does, too."

Venetia tried to assess the remark but felt bewildered.

"I never really believed in ghosts until I took *that* assignment. But I do now." In stages, Ann McGowen's hard veneer began to crack; her lower lip trembled. "It walks around at night and poisons our dreams. . . ."

Now Venetia felt pinned against the wall by something intangible.

"And there's a voice. . . . You'll hear it."

Venetia gulped, then admitted, "I already have."

"It's Tessorio," Ann said, but now her resolve was crumbling. "He tried to coerce us to go into the basement. He wanted us to do something there. But now? He'll want *you* to do it."

Venetia felt staggered. "I didn't know there *was* a basement. . . ."

"There isn't." Then Ann McGowen banged out of the restroom.

Night had fully fallen by the time they left the bar. Venetia tried to lighten the mood by jesting, "Gee, I can't wait to *never* go there again."

Dan nodded. Instead of going back to the car, he insisted they sit down on the docks. "Trust me, you'll like it . . . the sound of the riggings slapping the mast posts."

They sat down on opposing benches off a short pier. The sound was dreamy: the weird chime of all those sail ropes striking the masts of the hundreds of boats in the marina.

"It's hypnotic," she said.

"Yeah."

The big adrenaline rush from the bathroom had dissipated. She let a sea breeze sift her hair. "Shouldn't we be getting back? Why did you want to sit here?"

"Atmosphere," he said, and to Venetia's shock he produced a cigarette and lit it.

She gaped. "First you chug four beers in an hour, and now . . . you *smoke?*"

He flapped a dismissive hand, exhaling through a satisfied smile. "Relax, Mom. I smoke one a month. And we were in there more than an hour."

"Not much more."

"A couple beers and one cigarette a month is a pretty lame vice."

An excuse, she thought, but then realized she was being judgmental again, which she guessed was as bad a sin.

He chuckled smoke, eyeing her. "But for the life of me, I can't imagine what *your* vices are."

Venetia could think of no reply. She didn't tell him anything that Ann had done or said in the ladies' room, and now that the edgy confrontation was over, she began to manage the events of the night fairly well. *Addiction, bad luck, and bad environment are just more aspects of the real world. It's just the Devil's way of trying to separate us from God*, she reasoned, hoping she really believed it. *Some of us succumb, some don't.*

But she felt bad for Dan. "I'm sorry for your friends, especially Ann."

"Shit happens," he sputtered, looking at the cigarette tip. "And they weren't really friends—I'd just see them every now and then. The one I saw the most was Father Whitewood."

The comment rekindled a snippet of the bathroom conversation. *Whitewood.* And what else had Ann said?

He knew more than he was telling about that place, and I'll bet whoever replaced him does, too. . . .

"How long has Father Driscoll worked for the New Hampshire Diocese?" she asked.

Dan seemed more focused on smoking than anything else. "Huh? Oh, not long. He's done a lot of different things for the Church, all over the world."

"How does he . . . *seem* to you?"

"Seem?"

Venetia wasn't sure what she was asking. "He strikes me as keeping a lot to himself. Do you get that impression?"

"Of course, 'cos I know a little bit more about him than most." Dan let a plume of smoke spew from his nostrils and be carried away. "Driscoll has sort of a cryptic reputation."

"Why?"

"Because he took sequestered classes in Rome and Avignon."

Venetia squinted at the response. "I've never heard of 'sequestered' classes."

Did Dan smile in the dark? "It means they're secret, stuff the Vatican doesn't want the world to know it's still teaching."

Venetia studied the answer. In a sense he'd just corroborated her own query, hadn't he? *Maybe Driscoll really is hiding something.*

A clatter resounded at the front of the pier; when she looked she noticed a dock bum rummaging through a garbage can.

"I guess we should be good Catholics and buy him a sandwich."

But Dan had already stood up, and he seemed to look astonished at the vagabond. "Wait . . . here," he insisted.

What's he—To Venetia it seemed that Dan *recognized* the bum.

She watched him stride down the pier. *Now this is odd*, Venetia thought. She couldn't hear with any detail, but Dan was talking to the raddled man, who stood stoop-shouldered in a greasy black rain jacket and ratty sneakers. The jacket's hood was up, leaving only a shadowed oval for a face.

When Dan handed over some money, Venetia thought she heard the bum say, "God bless you, Dan. And be safe."

Then the bum shambled off, bowed and limping.

"Let's get back to the prior house," Dan suggested when he returned.

"You know that man," she said.

Dan spewed the last of his cigarette smoke and flicked the butt. "Yeah, I sure do. Or I should say I *used* to know him. He's not the same guy anymore."

"Who is it? Not a relative I hope."

"Nope." He dug out the keys and headed for the car. "It's Father Russell Whitewood, the priest who ran the prior house for the last twenty years."

Chapter Thirteen

(I)

Ruth noticed smoke rising from sewer grates along the road—Spirochete Avenue—but when she looked closer she also saw fingers wriggling in the gaps. *Eww* . . . "How much longer?"

"We're taking a shortcut," the priest told her, thundering ahead. "This is Satan Park."

"Oh, that sounds like a place I want to go," she complained.

"Don't be frightened by the name. Satan doesn't live there anymore. He can't."

"Why not? He runs this whole fucked-up city, doesn't he? You'd think he could live anywhere he wanted."

"Not here. It's an eyesore to him now. It reminds him of his greatest humiliation." The priest glanced back at her. "But with any luck, our mission will succeed . . . and he'll *never* be able to live it down."

Alexander's big, gnarly Ushers' feet splashed through a pool of blood, some of which speckled Ruth's face.

"Hey!"

"Oh, sorry."

Ruth wiped the blood off on the sleeve of her pink YUCK FOO T-shirt. *Fucker . . .* "I thought we were going to this restaurant so I can land a job and wait on this Aldezhor dude."

"He's no *dude,* Ruth. He's a powerful Grand Duke, with machination powers. But we're cutting through Satan's Park because . . . I want to show you something."

Ruth wasn't enthused. *I'm sure it'll be fucked-up, like everything else around here.* She paused to look at a very large ant on a tree—then she shrieked when she noted a human face on the insect. When the face stuck its tongue out at her, she swatted it with her flip-flop.

"Quit fooling around and listen." Alexander frowned back at her.

Ruth wasn't sure but it seemed that just ahead, the scarlet sky wasn't quite as scarlet, and—

Is that . . . fresh air I smell?

"Do you know what the theory of relativity is, Ruth?"

Her not very evolved intellect cogitated. "Oh, yeah, some law that was discovered by that Einstein guy. He was, like, the smartest guy in the world, but then he got tired of being an egghead and opened a chain of sandwich shops with his brother."

Alexander groaned. "In a nutshell, Ruth, the theory of relativity proves the existence of the propagation of space and time: the only thing in the universe that can never stop is the passage of time."

Ruth was scrutinizing her fingernails. "Do they have nail polish in Hell?"

"Oh, for God's sake, Ruth. Listen. This is important. In Hell, it's the opposite. Time is *not* a constant. What we have in the Mephistopolis is the theory of *ir*relativity. What this means is that in certain circumstances, things that have already happened have not yet occurred."

"Gimme a break!" she yelled. "Why do you think I dropped out in seventh grade?"

"I don't expect you to understand completely because the theory is designed to *not* be understandable. But we know enough about it now to use it to our advantage. It's just something I want you to think about while our journey continues."

Ruth guessed her period was on. "I'm sick of listening to bullshit! And you know what? I'd say there's a *really* good chance that I'm *not* going to spend a whole fuck of a lot of time thinking about the fuckin' theory of irrelativity, because shit that's already happened stays in the past!"

Alexander stopped and raised his brows at her. "Ruth, that's great! You get it! I've already told you, everything is opposite here. So how does that apply to what you just said?"

Ruth whined; her brain hurt. "I don't know! Shit in the future is already behind us?"

"Yes! Well, that is, some of it. You can never tell *what* exactly—because time, in Hell, in *inconstant*. You're getting it!"

Fuck this shit, man, she thought. *I just want some fuckin' nail polish 'cos my nails look like shit.*

"And if time is no longer a reliable unit of measure, and if everything is opposite here, explain *that*." The priest pointed upward with a fat taloned finger.

Holy shit . . .

Just moments ago, Ruth had noticed a lessening in the sky's hue of crimson; now she shielded her eyes—against sunlight in a modest but irrefutable aperture of blue sky.

"Sunlight! Like on earth!"

"Yes, Ruth. And if everything is opposite here . . . how can this be?"

Ruth's eyes sparkled at the glorious site. *Real sunlight* was bathing her face. "I guess, I guess," she tried to answer, "uh, something got . . . fucked-up?"

Alexander's frown indicated his disapproval of her choice of words, but he said, "That's good enough. Something happened here once that contaminated the constant environment of the Mephistopolis, but remember that, here, contamination means *purification*."

"So what happened?"

"Look down now . . ."

Ruth had been too busy looking at the circle of beautiful blue sky that she hadn't even noticed what the impossible sunlight was shining on. Her eyes dragged down—

"The fuck is *that?*"

She was looking at a pile of rubble the size of the largest pyramid in Egypt.

"It used to be Lucifer's home, the tallest skyscraper in history. It was a 666-floor building called the Mephisto Building."

"Looks like somebody did the job on it."

"Exactly. A Human Being gained entry to Hell and became sanctified through an act of Holy Martyrdom. She sacrificed her own life in that building, in God's name. The result was a fissile atomic reaction, almost the same as a nuclear bomb going off. It turned the entire building into a pile of junk in two seconds," the priest related.

"Wow. It's a bummer that the guy who did it is dead now."

"Not a guy," Alexander muttered.

"What?"

"But that doesn't matter. The suicide sanctified the most unholy plot of land in Hell. It's purified forever. Nothing evil can ever exist there."

Ruth considered the situation and chuckled. "I'll bet that pisses Satan off big-time."

"Yep. Satan's former domicile is now that only sanctified perimeter in Hell. But as you can see, it's not a very big perimeter." He offered her a cunning smile. "We've got something up our sleeves, though, that can create another sanctified zone that will just grow and grow."

"How?" she asked.

"In time—I don't want to overwhelm you." His stout gray legs flexed as he began to approach the virtual mountain of rubble. "Come on, I need you to read something."

Read something? Ruth couldn't imagine what he meant.

As the got closer to the pile, Ruth nearly swooned at the surge of fresh air. The sun on her face brought a delight to her heart unlike anything she could ever remember. Then—"Flowers!" She rejoiced when she saw the bright multicolored blooms growing between slabs of concrete the size of cars. Ruth had tears in her eyes by the time they reached the edge of the debris.

But what had he said? *He's got some plan to sanctify more land in Hell?*

"Remember that Spanish friar I mentioned?" he asked.

"Oh, the guy who wrote all that shit on your skin?"

"The calligrapher, yes. Well, he ran out of room so he had to inscribe some information on my back."

Ruth saw with some alarm that every square inch of the priest's torso was covered with the scar-tissue scribbling. Even his back.

"Most of the writing is in Enochian or Zraetic, which you won't recognize," he informed. "Just look for six weirdo-looking names in a row. They should be glowing."

Ruth spotted it at once, for they were indeed glowing in a soft whitish blue light, like luminous paint. She slowly pronounced them:

"Ablissa, Eylla, Azusis, Belith, Gesmary, Tzaella."

"Perfect. You've found them. Now—are the names glowing?"

"Yeah." Ruth ran a finger across the flesh-embossed script, and found the letters strangely cool. "It looks like that stuff they use on watches to make the hands glow in the dark."

"Whitish blue light?" the priest asked, concerned. "Not dark red?"

"It's whitish," she began, but then her eyes widened. As she looked at the line of strange glowing names, they—"They just changed! Now they're glowing in red."

Alexander nodded, lowered his shirt. "That means the time is getting closer. The Angels just lost their purity."

"Angels?" Ruth asked.

"Those names are the names of six very special Angels," the priest began, and led Ruth away from the glorious opening in the sky. "They're called Caliginauts. They're Holy warriors that infiltrate Hell and battle Lucifer's operations. That's *their* mission, to sneak into the Mephistopolis and . . ." He seemed to struggle for the right words.

"Fuck shit up?" Ruth offered.

Alexander frowned, as always. "Yeah, Ruth. These little skirmishes between Heaven and Hell have been going on for thousands of years." The desolate road darkened the farther they strayed from the mountain of rubble. "But these particular Angels are prisoners now."

"You mean they're in jail?"

"They're in a place worse than jail. They're in the Lower Chancel of the Fortress Boniface. I've already told you a little about him. A long time ago he captured these Angels, and he's been Unanointing them ever since. That's the reason we're here, and that's the reason their names on my back just changed from light to dark. It means their Unanointment Reversion is taking root. Originally they were Blessed and Holy, but after so much debasement they've lost their state of Sanctity."

"What's all that jive mean?" Ruth asked.

"It means we're very close to the time when the Involution will be charged."

"And what does *that* jive mean?"

"It's numbers and geometry, Ruth. In the Heaven the perfect number is seven but in Hell the perfect number is one less—six. The *geometric* equivalent to the number six is an angleless curved plane called the Involution. Think of it as Lucifer's lucky shape. Think of it as a *magic* shape."

When a Griffin flew by, a gust of wind mussed Ruth's hair. "This shit's too confusing, man. What's a shape have to do with Angels?"

"Because this shape—the Involution—is a Power Dolmen, and Lucifer's Warlocks have discovered various ways to harness that power. The Involution can be charged, like a battery, but instead of electricity it runs on the Deathforce energy of innocent blood. And it's the Involution that will—for lack of a better term—transport the six Angels from Hell to Earth. It's Boniface's job to do this, but he can't until the Angels have been properly deconditioned. That's why he's subjected them to rape, debasement, and torture for the last hundred years."

The last hundred years, she thought, annoyed now. "How

do you know it's been a hundred years if time doesn't exist in Hell?"

Alexander stopped and spun; he seemed overjoyed by her question. "You're starting to get it, Ruth—that's great! You're understanding information that deliberately *can't* be understood. Let me simplify. A Human life is a cycle— you're born, you grow up, and you die. And because the Human *soul* is immortal, every minute of your life is, too, on multiple planes of existence."

Ruth gaped at him.

He raised a monstrous finger. "Now, think of every minute of your life on Earth as a deck of cards. What Lucifer can do through his specialized sorcery is *shuffle* that deck to suit his needs. To change the chronological order of the manner in which your life transpired."

Ruth winced. "Why would he want to fucking *shuffle* every minute of *my* life?"

"Well, he doesn't. I'm just using you as an example. He's actually shuffling someone else's life, because it's part of his plan to gain a powerful ally in Hell."

Smirking ever harder, Ruth scratched her belly button. "So who's life *is* he shuffling? Yours?"

The monster-limbed priest seemed disappointed. "No, no, not *mine*. Venetia Barlow's."

"Who?" But then she blinked her awareness. "Oh, the chick you were talking to on that funky horn—"

"The Vox Untervelt, yes. If you keep in mind that it's impossible to fully understand the un-understandable, then you'll get it. Remember, every minute of someone's life is like a card in a deck. Yesterday, for instance, when we talked to Venetia Barlow on the Vox Untervelt, she hadn't even been born yet."

Ruth slapped her hands to her ears. "I don't know what the fuck you're talking about! You're making my head hurt with all this crazy shit!"

Alexander put his Annelok arm around Ruth's shoulder and led her onward. "Come on, Ruth, don't worry about it. Just do what I say and everything will work out."

"Good, just don't talk anymore of that whack-job theory of irrelativity shit, okay?"

"Okay." His giant feet plodded on. "Just as long as you understand that everything we're doing has already happened—"

Ruth groaned.

"—and ultimately our mission revolves around changing the future by interfering with the past."

"Fuck it, man," Ruth sputtered. *I give up. . . .*

"So now, back to something more comprehensible," the priest seemed relieved to say. The snakelike Annelok arm unrolled and pointed. "Can you see the next District there?"

A steam car full of rowdy Ghouls hooted at her when she stood on her tiptoes.

"Great legs, baby!"

Blow yourself, asshole. She was looking into the distance . . . and saw what seemed to be a long brick wall several blocks down. "The wall?"

"Yes. That's the outer verge of the Boniface District. The reason it's red is because the entire District is made of blood bricks, and it just so happens that that's where we're going."

"For my job?"

"Exactly."

Fuck, she thought. She didn't feel very good about this, especially after hearing all of his mumbo jumbo about the Devil shuffling time like a deck of cards. Past the next intersection, she saw a billboard that had no advertisements on it, but just a strange shape:

"What the fuck is that?"

Alexander gave her a poker face. "Ruth, do you really have to say the F-word *every time* you talk?"

"Huh?"

"Can't you just say 'What's that?' or 'What the heck is that?' or 'What in tarnations is that?' "

Ruth smiled. "Okay. What the fuckin' heck in fuckin' tarnations is fuckin' *that?*"

Alexander shuffled on. "You're hopeless. But to answer your profane question, that design on the billboard is the Involution."

"Lucifer's lucky shape?" she asked.

"Yes. You'll see those billboards all over the Boniface District. It's all non-Euclidean geometry, Ruth, though I don't guess you know what that means."

"You fuckin' guessed right," she laughed.

"Remember," he emphasized, "in the Living World, there's science, and in Hell, there's sorcery. Here symbols have power. That's why that spiral—the Involution—is so powerful."

Ruth squinted at his words. "What's it symbolize?"

"When Lucifer was ejected from Heaven," the priest explained, "he fell from the east, in a counterclockwise spiral . . . which formed the number six."

(II)

An intriguing day, at the very least. Venetia pondered its complexities in the shower, yet her thoughts kept dicing up, and she guessed the reason why was, *I think I'm kind of drunk. . . .* The one beer she'd had at the bar had snuck up on her now, buzzing her senses. *I really am a lightweight—drunk off one beer.* But it was Dan who worried her. A closet smoker and binge drinker? It seemed so. But now Venetia's own weaknesses began to intrude on more serious thoughts: she'd actually been jealous seeing Ann McGowen put her hands on him at the bar. *Doesn't make sense!* she insisted to herself while drying off. She'd be lying to herself in denying a physical attraction to him, but she also knew the attraction was moot; it was born of her instincts, not her spiritual self.

Just stop thinking about it.

The strong beer buzzed her so potently that she almost stumbled heading back to her room. Mrs. Newlwyn, crossing the atrium, looked up at Venetia's misstep, then acted as though she hadn't noticed.

"It's late. You should be asleep."

"I know, Mrs. Newlwyn," Venetia replied, and grabbed the stair-hall rail to steady herself. "The day got away from me."

"Evidently it got away from Betta as well. Have you seen her?"

"No, I haven't."

"She may have gone out for a walk. . . ."

Yeah, a walk right into the woods, where John is waiting. "Well, it is a clear night," she babbled.

"Pleasant dreams, dear," the tall woman said though her typical stiff smile.

"Good night."

Jeez! I almost fell flat on my face! Venetia thought when she got back to her room. Going from the warm stair-hall to her cool room shocked her; she even felt mildly dizzy. Had Mrs. Newlwyn noticed her tipsiness? Venetia let her towel fall to the floor, then lay back nude on the bed. *That's better.* She wondered if beds really spun, or if that was just a cliché. *I'm never going to drink again,* she vowed, taking deep breaths.

The AC unit hummed, and the cool air gusted and made her nipples constrict and instantly cooled the metal key between her breasts. Then an image rammed into her head quite uninvited: Dan's mouth on her nipple, sucking—

Stop!

But as soon as she banished the image, it was replaced by a more vivid one. Now it was Ann McGowen sucking her nipple, while her hand caressed Venetia's other breast—

These are useless, stupid fantasies, so stop!

And then the images alternated, until Venetia began to shiver. First Dan, then Ann, like that, back and forth, their warm nudity pressing against hers. Eventually, they were both upon her at once, Ann's nipples in her face, which

Venetia desperately inclined her head to suck, and Dan's mouth laving her sex, his strong hands parting her thighs. Her hips flinched when fingers delved in, and then she felt awash in obscure pleasures.

Venetia moaned at the brink of climax. *"That's it, baby,"* a rich, female voice intoned. Venetia's mouthed sucked the proffered nipple like a pacifier. *"Just lie back and come. Let Lottie get you off, then you can do me,"* and then a wet, clicking chuckle resounded.

After a delayed reaction, Venetia thought, *Lottie?* and then she opened her eyes and pushed the bare bosom out of her face. Her heart slammed once, then seemed to stop; it was no longer Ann McGowen and Dan who tended to her—it was Sister Patricia Stevenson and Lottie Jessel, both naked and pale as cream as they grinned at her, both bearing the great knife slits in their throats and the zipperlike lines of black stitches from their autopsy incisions.

Venetia screamed but no sound came out. The Patricia-corpse was trying to mount Venetia's face, her dead blue nipples puckered, while the shriveled sixty-year-old corpse of Lottie Jessel reapplied her blue lips to Venetia's sex.

"Have you gone to the basement yet?" one of them asked in a death rattle.

Venetia awoke, cringing. *Oh my God, that was disgusting!* She leaned up, sweating in spite of the room's cool air. *I fell asleep and didn't even realize it. . . .* Revolted, she jumped off the bed, donned her robe, and slipped out of the room.

She needed to get out. *Maybe I should ask for a different room,* she considered, skimming down the stairs. But that would sound inane. Father Driscoll would think she believed the room was haunted. *It was just a bad dream,* she convinced herself, but then—

She remembered. What Ann McGowen had told her in the seedy bathroom. *It walks around at night and poisons our dreams. . . .*

Weren't Venetia's dreams poisoned as well?

She stopped halfway across the atrium. She didn't know where she was going, but Ann had said something else too, something about the ghost of Tessorio urging her to go to the basement.

Consider the source. A drunk prostitute, a drug addict. *She was making it up, a scary story to frighten "Little Bo Peep."* Nevertheless, she spent the next half hour looking for a basement door but found none.

Outside?

Venetia was exhausted but admittedly too freaked by the dream to go back to her room. Without forethought, then, she was unlocking the back door with her key, then walking outside. . . .

A hot, starry night awaited her, with its nearly deafening chorus of crickets—the night seemed to *throb.* As her bare feet took her around the perimeter of the house, all the while she was looking down for a sign of some foundation-level windows, or a pair of slightly angled doors lying on the ground that would surely open to moldy steps leading down into a basement.

Thirty fruitless minutes later, she realized, there was no basement in this house. *What an idiot I am.*

She headed back to the kitchen door. A breeze puffed her hair but it was hot; she was already clammy again. The moon blurred in her eyes. At least the nighttime excursion had let her walk off some of the beer buzz.

She stopped just before the door. Had she heard a branch crack?

Her eyes darted toward the back of the property.

And she saw a shape, a white shape move between the trees.

Venetia laughed at herself. *Could this be the ghost of Amano Tessorio?*

Or was it just Betta, on another secret rendezvous with John?

She knew it was the latter, for she spied the movement in the same area as the cove.

Go to bed. Her search for the nonexistent basement had left her even more fatigued. But—

She slipped over to the wood line. *I am such a snoop. What is wrong with me?* She knew what she would see, so why was she doing this?

But no argument with herself sufficed. Venetia very carefully traipsed around the rim of the woods to the opening.

At once she heard rustling, then a moan.

Dan's a closet smoker and drinker, she half-jested. *Am I a closet voyeur?* She didn't think so; nevertheless, she admitted a subtle thrill. The secret onlooker. Moonlight dappled into the dell; white squiggles floated on the pond and just before it—

Venetia pressed her cheek against a tree, hiding half her face to watch with one eye. Betta—in her open white blouse—knelt before John, whose back faced Venetia. His bare buttocks flexed; it was clear what she was doing. John groaned, muttering, "Baby," then after another moment of this oral prelude, fell to his own knees to lie between Betta's legs. What took place was much more frenetic than "lovemaking"; it was primitive, animalistic, but even at this distance, Venetia could see the wanton passion in Betta's eyes. John thrust into her for a time, then stopped just as Betta's back was arching; then he was slithering down between her legs to pursue some oral titillations of his own.

Betta squirmed in the leaves, moaning, but otherwise unable to voice words of approval. Words were hardly necessary anyway. Betta continued to writhe along with her pleasure, while Venetia—

Her mind remained dead silent as she watched, but her hands began to trace her own body's curves through the robe. Hot sensations—that she knew were forbidden for a celibate—began to linger around her groin. All the while her vision strained through the moonlit darkness. . . .

Betta convulsed now, her gasps leaving no doubt that she was climaxing. "Like this now, baby," John's voice floated through darkness, and he was turning her around to hands and knees, and quickly reentering her. Betta's hair hung in the leaves as she let herself be taken, John's buttocks pumping and Betta's hanging breasts jumping with each thrust.

Venetia's eyes closed to slits. Her own hands had long since slipped beneath the robe to stroke her bare flesh, fingers pinching her nipples till she nearly squealed, her other hand cosseting her sex. The hot night—and its carnal sights—seemed to suck the sweat from her pores. Now the flood of pleasure wound through her nerves like twisting wires; she could feel the blood vessels beating in her breasts, could feel her nipples gorge, could feel—

She knew she was close to an orgasm, yet she also knew she mustn't let that happen. More of Ann McGowen's hostile words haunted her as her hands betrayed themselves: *What kind of God would give His flock desire and then demand that they repress it?*

Then her own words screamed, *I can't do this! It's a sin!*

And she stopped just before climaxing.

She stood paralyzed behind the tree, her heart beating so loud she was surprised Betta and John didn't heard it. When she looked back at them, they were finished. They were standing in each other's arms, kissing.

Then they parted.

Venetia froze. *They're going to see me! What am I going to say?*

John whispered some endearment and disappeared down the trail that would take him to town. Betta watched after him, a white ghost in the dark. Was she caressing herself while she watched? Eventually Betta turned around to nearly face the tree Venetia hid behind, and—yes—she very openly ran her hands up and down her bare flesh. Another gasp when her fingers slipped lower to tease her sex, as though she were trying to handle her post-orgasmic afterglow.

Then she left the clearing and headed back to the house.

At once the sweat of Venetia's excitement changed to the sweat of her shame. *Forgive me, God,* came her feeble prayer.

When she turned, her foot rubbed something. She looked down and saw—*A gas can?*

Yes. It sat at the base of some trees, but when she picked it up, she knew it was empty. *One of John's. Probably for the mower,* she thought. *But why leave it here?* She sniffed the end of the nozzle, expecting the aroma of gasoline, but smelled nothing. *Why'd he leave a brand-new gas can in the woods?* Then the answer became obvious. *He'd probably meant to take it to the shed but got a little sidetracked. . . .*

Venetia shuffled back to the prior house. She felt dirty. *Some aspiring nun I turned out to be. Masturbating in the woods.* It didn't matter that she hadn't finished. *Lust in the heart is the same thing as adultery—Christ said so.*

She lingered outside in the moonlight, giving Betta plenty of time to get to bed. What Venetia had witnessed only rubbed her face in what she was probably never going to have: mutual attraction and passion that led to sex. *God's testing me, that's it,* she tried to joke to herself, but it didn't seem funny to her. Eventually the night's cacophony of crickets drove her back into the house.

Inside she paused at the stairwell—she could hear the shower going upstairs. *Damn it—Betta must be taking a shower.* She didn't want to risk being seen so she waited in a chair beneath the stair-hall. She tried to focus on more halfhearted prayers, but fragments of Betta and John kept barging in, or her little fantasy of Ann McGowen and Dan. *Forgive me, God,* she thought again.

Was she jealous of Betta and John's passion for each other? She knew she had to be in some way. *Jesus, I'm a human being, I can't help it!* she tried to argue. It was intriguing, though, the dichotomy. Around others, John was shy and introverted. *But in the woods,* she thought, *he's a sexual animal, and so is Betta.* Could there really be that much wrong with it? Each of their inadequacies had brought them together. *I'll bet they even love each other,* she surmised, but again she felt that she was arguing with God. *What's wrong with that, if they love each other?*

Maybe nothing.

At any rate, Venetia knew that her next confession would be very interesting.

She could still hear the shower. *Hurry up, Betta.* Soon,

she was slumping in the chair, more exhaustion piling up. She tried to focus on paintings around the atrium, but they only turned to blurs. Her eyelids began to droop.

"Venetia! Venetia!" the tinny voice shrilled in her head. *"Don't fall asleep! It's Father Alexander, talking to you over the Vox Unterwelt! Please! Listen! And* don't *fall asleep!"*

The pain seemed to lance through her ears. *Not again!* Venetia doubled over out of the chair, to kneel—shuddering—with her head to the old throw rug.

A wave of something crackled through the terrifying words, like bad reception. Between the pain and the interference, she could only make out bits and pieces of the manic voice:

"—talking to you from Hell. Do you remember my voice from yesterday?"

"Yes," she croaked.

"This isn't a dream, this is for real!" and then another wave of distortion. *"—are six of them,"* and then *"—were Unanointed by an Exalted Duke in Hell whose name is Boniface—"*

The name snagged her through the pain.

But the voice grew louder. She knew she'd pass out. She could feel tears pouring from her eyes into the carpet.

"—of them, and it's almost time for them to be—" but she couldn't make out the next string of words, just something that sounded like *"transposed,"* and *"electrocution,"* or *"revolution,"* but then the crunching staticlike waves cleared and the shrill words continued,

"—Ablissa, Eylla, Azusis, Belith, Gesmary, Tzaella. Those are their names. And one of them—"

The next wave made Venetia feel as though her head had just been driven over by a truck.

"No! Please! Don't *fall asleep!"*

But it wasn't sleep that threatened her; it was pain-induced wakefulness.

"—six angels!" Then static. *"—six coffins!"* More static, then, *"—six bones!"* The mad voice spun around her head, and she thought the last thing she heard was this: *"—bones!*

Remember the bones! Venetia, for God's sake, remember to take one of—"

The voice ceased as abruptly as an ax-strike.

Venetia rolled over to lie flat on her back. "Thank God," she muttered, for the phalanx of pain, like metal barbs in her brain, disappeared. Her heart raced. *Calm down, it's over.* She dragged herself up, pulled her robe together. The shower could no longer be heard, so she straggled to the stairs. Behind her, the long expanse of the atrium stood in total silence.

Maybe I'm going crazy, she thought. *Maybe my sexual repression is making me mentally ill.* But any further thoughts snapped out of her mind. She was halfway up the stairs when a rigor of fear locked her joints up. Did her heart actually cease to beat?

At the top of the landing, a black-cloaked figure stood looking down. Within the hood was just shadow. . . .

It's not there. It's not real. . . .

Then the figure began to stride quickly down the stairs, arms outstretched for Venetia's throat, and that's when she fainted and toppled to the bottom of the stairs.

Chapter Fourteen

(I)

Alexander sighed and put the Vox Untervelt back under his shirt. Was he having his first genuine doubts about this mission? *Come on, God, help me out,* he thought.

But could God even *hear* him from the Mephistopolis?

He had no way of knowing if Venetia Barlow had received his latest communication. The Hex Fluxes seemed to spike whenever he engaged the Vox, and he knew what that likely meant: *Someone's onto us.*

The Boniface District shimmered all around him, the scarlet hue of the blood bricks so intense it seemed luminous. Even the municipal workers—Imps, mostly—wore blood-drenched overalls to keep with the District's theme. Alexander sat at a carriage stop across the street from the No Seasons Hotel, whose upscale infernal restaurant—The Alferd Packer Room—was thought to be the very best in Hell. Ruth—dressed in the pricey Tongue-Skirt and Hand-Bra—had been hired within a minute of speaking to the Demonic floor manager. Alexander peered through the glass, half-fretting. *Now if*

she can only manage to not get fired before Aldezhor arrives . . .
He'd already seen too many examples of her bad temper
and firecracker attitude.

He decided to wait a while longer before he went in himself; he figured he'd get a seat at the cocktail bar to keep an
eye on her. *Just be careful,* he reminded himself. *Grand Duke
Aldezhor always has a Bio-Wizard with him.* These practiced
occult scientists could often sniff out anti-Satanic detractors
by reading their auras. *And Ruth better not blow it, either. . . .*

He took another peek into the restaurant and he saw
Ruth competently taking orders at a table full of knot-
faced Viceroys from one of the Torturian Brigades. *Wow,*
he couldn't help but acknowledge. *Her boobs fill out that
Hand-Bra perfectly.* The Viceroys, too, couldn't keep their
rheumy eyes off her full-tilt body. Every so often the large
severed Werewolf hands that comprised the bra-cups gave
her breasts a squeeze, while the "fabric" of her Tongue-
Skirt slowly quivered over her hips and buttocks, still alive.

The priest cocked a smile. *I'll bet that's driving her batty.*

With some time to kill, he took a stroll, almost having
to shield his eyes against the District's glistening blood
bricks—every road, sidewalk, and building was made of
them. He'd heard that the blood bricks were enspelled to
make them stronger against enemy sorcery. At the end of
the street, he could see one of the foundries where the
blood was distilled down to paste and poured into molds.
Diabolical, the priest thought.

An extraordinary crush of aromas and odors hung in
the street like gas. Alexander was long since acclimated;
the District's main square was the restaurant hub, where
only the most posh denizens of the city could afford to
eat. Each street was lined with one noxious eatery after
another. He stopped at a bistro where something smelled
too good to pass up. "What's that, waiter?" he inquired of
a bow-tied Demon bearing a tray of steaming plates. "I
might have to order some."

"It's poached Goregator Bowel, sir," the waiter responded.

On second thought . . .

A shapely Demonness passed out fliers at the corner. She had slanted eyes and skin like the hide of a horned toad. Scaly fingers passed a flier to Alexander.

"Come to our grand opening, Father," she invited through an oriental accent. "Cockroach Gardens at Ninth Street and Emesis Avenue. Free order of Leg Rolls when you buy the special."

"What's the special?"

"Moo Goo Gai Puke."

"I'll . . . think about it," Alexander said and strode off. He didn't even want to *think* what his fortune cookie might say.

He made the round of Thrombosis Circle; then his stout, corded Usher legs stopped. *There he is.*

Valets with festering faces rushed from the No Season's portico to open the doors of a fancy steam car whose convertible top was fashioned by Human skin set with onyx stones.

Then a shadow shaped like a man—a man with horns—stepped out of the backseat.

Aldezhor. The Grand Messenger of Hell.

Instead of tipping cash, the Grand Duke tipped the valets with severed feet. Then the ink black shape entered the restaurant, with a jewel-cloaked Bio-Wizard behind him.

Alexander slipped to the front window, wide-eyed. *Come on, Ruth. Don't screw this up. If you don't get his table . . . we're finished.*

Oh, no, oh, no, Ruth thought, butterflies in her belly. *That's the guy. . . .*

The dining room became hushed when Grand Duke Aldezhor was taken to his corner table by a vampiric hostess.

Ruth had just pinned up a double order for Kidney Satay and Ghoul Marrow Stew when she noticed the Grand Duke's entrance.

Here goes . . .

"I'm taking Aldezhor's table," she asserted to her floor-mate, a saucy Hybrid with eyes like swamp scum. Her yellow skin had been creatively scarred with rows and rows of fanged Smiley Faces. She dumped some garbage into a grinder-chute that sounded like a tree mulcher when the leftovers hit the blades.

"You can kiss my Demon ass," the Hybrid flared. "Ain't no fuckin' way you get to wait on Aldezhor, moth-erfucker. You're the *new* girl, so you can fuck off."

Ruth froze at the retort. She even took a step back when the Hybrid smiled through surgically implanted Griffin talons where her teeth used to be.

Heart pattering, Ruth folded; she lost all her spark in a second or two. "Please. Can I have his table? Um—hey—I'll even pay you if you let me."

A slimy seven-fingered hand shoved Ruth by the face out of the server station.

"Big fake-tit blond bubblehead thinks she's gonna fuckin take *my* table when she hasn't even fuckin' worked here for a half a fuckin' hour?" The Hybrid laughed, blowing black spittle. "Silly bitch—yeah, you walk in here wearing a Tongue-Skirt and Hand-Bra like you're all that but you ain't nothin' but a motherfuckin' lowlife gutter-crawling motherfucker."

Ruth was appalled. *I don't believe it. This chick's got worse language than me. . . .*

"Don't like it? *Do* something about it," the Hybrid chal-lenged, and pointed a yellow finger right in Ruth's face.

Ruth *didn't* like it. "Get your finger out of my face or I'll bite it off."

The Hybrid gusted another obnoxious laugh. "You fuckin' dumb blond motherfuckin' bitch. I'll pop your fake tits and mop the Dumpster with your prissy face. Oh, and by the way, your mother's so dumb the last time she tried to rob a bank she blew the guard and tied up the safe," and then she jabbed her finger again.

Ruth bit the finger off and in one synchronous movement, yanked open the grinder chute, shoved the Hybrid in, and closed the door.

The blades whined.

Ruth spat the finger out. *Like I said, I'm taking Aldezhor's table. . . .*

Just about every male patron in the restaurant paused to admire Ruth's apparel, but like the professional she was, she ignored their comments—and even their offers to tip her—and rushed to Aldezhor's place. Set in the middle of the table was a petrified hand holding a card: RESERVED.

"Hello, Grand Duke. My name is Ruth, and I'm privileged to be your server today," Ruth said.

"What a comely tramp, my lord." The Chevalier at the Grand Duke's side smiled. He was from Lucifer's personal Cryptographic Unit, and was charged with hand-delivering Hell's most crucial operational messages. The Chevalier's skull was segmented, for all in his class were head-banded during infancy. "And so unworn for an infernal whore," he added.

Ruth ground her teeth.

The shadowy face of Aldezhor appraised her. "Indeed, Chevalier. Her harlot's body looks as fresh as though she'd stepped off the streets of the Living World a moment ago."

Close, she thought, forcing a smile. In the lobby, she noticed Alexander enter the lounge.

He looked a little nervous.

The Chevalier laughed. "Fresh, my lord, yes, but remember how deceiving are the looks of such immoral Human trash. Why, I'd wager the loins of a thousand men have been emptied into her privates."

"More like ten thousand, and for pennies per service," Aldezhor said, joining in the revelry.

Ruth wanted to upend the table and do a dance on their faces but when her eyes flicked to Alexander, who now sat at the bar, he very slowly shook his head no.

Don't blow a gasket, she ordered herself. *Don't let these two scumbags rock your boat.*

"Why, Grand Duke Aldezhor," she remarked, giggling. "You're as witty as you are handsome."

"No one gave you permission to converse with the Grand Duke!" snapped the Chevalier. "Now bring us a bottle of your best Chyme—*vintage*—and don't tarry unless you want to be skinned and packed in a salt box for time immemorial!"

"Of course, Chevalier." She smiled, thinking, *Jesus.* She went to the bar for the drink order, and didn't look at Alexander when she complained, "Man, those fuckin' guys are busting my chops so hard, I don't think I can keep my cool."

"You *better*," the priest whispered over a shot of creek water on the rocks, "because if you don't, being skinned and packed in a salt box will be the least of your worries."

"Thanks for the vote of confidence."

"And watch out for Bio-Wizard."

"Who?"

"The guy in the cloak watching over Aldezhor. He's scanning for hostile auras. Remember the Prism-Veil in Rot-Port? Same sort of thing only that guy's ten times more sensitive."

"Fuck . . ."

"Remember your mission. The note. You *must* see the note."

Shit, I almost forgot. "All right, I'll do my best."

With the tip of the Annelok tentacle, Alexander had slipped something out of his shirt: that ugly little pouch on a cord.

"The goodie bag. What's it for?"

"In case this doesn't go well." He looked quickly over his shoulder at Aldezhor's table. "And keep your voice down." Another nervous glance at the barkeep, who looked suspiciously similar to John F. Kennedy. "Don't speak directly to me. You don't know me, remember?"

"Yeah, yeah. But what's in the bag?"

"Shhh!"

"Quit chatter-boxin', bitch!" the barkeep snapped in a rich Massachusetts accent, "and stop botherin' my cus-

tomers unless you want your guts dragged out your ears."
The keep looked directly to Alexander. "Sir, is this
mouthy hosebag botherin' you?"

"Oh, no, not at all." Alexander winked at him. "She was
just asking me for the time."

The keep stalled, then slapped a hand on the bar, honk-
ing Bostonian laughter. "That's a good one, sir!" He set
down two dirty goblets and a bottle whose label read:
PINOT CHYMUS—A HEADY, ECLECTIC WINE MADE FROM THE
MOST SELECT HUMAN DUODENAL ENZYMES. "Now take this to
the Grand Duke's table, you piece of big-tit blond scum.
And there better not be *any* complaints about your service
or I will personally pop your gourd."

Ruth's lower lip quivered. *It's a good thing I don't have
that pistol on me right now.* She took the bottle to
Aldezhor's table and poured them each a glass. While the
Grand Duke and his Chevalier put their pinkies in the air
and sipped the yellow slop, Ruth thought over what she
had to do. *This Chevalier asshole is going to pass a note to this
Aldezhor asshole, and I'm supposed to take a glance at it. . . .*
More thoughts ticked. *And I gotta be careful of this Bio-
Wizard asshole 'cos he's got some psychic jive going on that
might rat me out.*

Ruth wasn't used to this kind of responsibility. "Is the
wine to your liking, sir?"

The Chevalier's banded head jerked up. "Yes, you detestable reservoir of carnal filth. But will you make the
Grand Duke wait *another* eternity before you see fit to take
his lunch order?"

Oh, how I would love *to comb this fucker's hair with a two-by-
four,* Ruth mused, then smiled. "What would you like, sir?"

"What I would *like* is you in an iron maiden roasting
nude over a coal fire—"

"But only after being stuffed with bay leaves and
onions," Aldezhor added.

"And covered with a nice macadamia nut crust," the
Chevalier finished. "But, lo"—he paused for effect—
"that's not on the menu, is it?"

He and Aldezhor tremored with laughter, along with everyone else in the dining room.

Hardee-har-har, Ruth thought. They sounded like donkeys hee-hawing. But again she sucked it up and just smiled, bearing her pen and order pad. "You gentlemen are just *so* funny."

"Of course we are, trollop!" the Chevalier snapped. "The Grand Duke would like the Chimichurri Gargoyle Tenderloin in Truffle Cream, and I will have the Braised Broodren Gallbladder Pie." He pointed a multijointed finger. "And be quick about it, you pitiable intercourse-soiled daughter of filth!"

The insults were wearing Ruth out, and the quivering Tongue-Skirt and frisky Hand-Bra only amplified her bad humor. "Coming right up, Chevalier." She turned to the cloaked Bio-Wizard, who stood aside from Aldezhor, still as a chess piece. "Anything for you, sir?"

Spittle shot from the Chevalier's lips. "That's a Bio-Wizard, you brainless blond waste of space! Only the dimmest wit in Hell doesn't know that Bio-Wizards don't eat! Hare-brain! Moronic Human trash!"

These fucking guys! She wished she still had her old pickup truck so she could tie them both to the trailer hitch and go for a long drive.

Ruth curtsyed to the motionless Bio-Wizard. "My apologies, sir." But before she rushed off to place the order, she took a split-second glance into the Wizard's hood, and saw a face that was nothing but a smoking skull.

Yuck!

Aldezhor's shadow-boned finger tapped her arm. It felt like a prod of ice. "That's quite a fetching outfit, miss—typically only worn by the most lauded odalisques—and I must say, your flawless body does it justice. I'll be sure to have *you* wait on me every time I'm here."

Finally! A compliment! "Why, thank you, Grand Duke." Though she couldn't see his eyes, she could feel them crawling up her almost nude body. *Yeah. Men are all the same, even in Hell*, she deduced. *Just a bunch of horny assholes.*

Aldezhor's words fluttered up. "May your beauty be as eternal as your Damnation."

"You have such a way with words, Grand Duke." *How do you like that. The monster's got the hots for me.*

Ruth rushed in the order and waited at the end of the bar, a seat down from Alexander. She tried to sluff off the ceaseless insults but just got madder. "Those guys are busting my hump," she whispered.

"I know," he whispered back. "Just grin and bear it."

Her teeth ground. "I don't think I *can.* They're laying it on thick, especially that pumpkinhead-looking mother-fucker."

A She-Ghoul with implants bigger than Ruth's waltzed by with a tray of roasted spleens. "Newcomer scum," the monster sniped under her breath. "I see you over there sucking up to the Grand Duke, but let me tell you, there's no way he'll have anything to do with Human shit like you."

Ruth swung her fist—but Alexander's Annelok arm caught it before it could make contact.

"None of that! You're going to blow the whole deal."

Ruth just ground her teeth some more as the slim Ghoul slinked off. *Keep it cool. Keep it cool.*

The priest looked disgusted with her. "And you're not paying *any* attention at all."

"Huh?"

Alexander leaned right into her ear when the barkeep wasn't looking. "The Chevalier just passed Aldezhor the note! Now get over there and distract him enough so you can read it before he puts it away!"

Distract him? Ruth didn't have a clue what he meant, and creativity under pressure wasn't a strong suit. The Werewolf hands squeezed as she moved briskly to the table.

Aldezhor's hand—like a glove of compacted black gas—was holding up a small piece of parchment. "Excellent." He regarded the Chevalier. "I'll rush this over to Boniface when we're done eating." Then he began to put the note beneath his cloak.

Without forethought, Ruth slipped her bra up. She touched Aldezhor's cold shoulder just as he was about to put the parchment away.

The Chevalier's segmented face went beet red. "How *dare* you put your filthy prostitute hands on the Grand Duke! I'll have them cut off!"

But Aldezhor's faceless face was looking right at Ruth's bare bosom.

"Why, that's most . . . impressive," he muttered.

She looked at the Chevalier. "Don't blow a gasket, sir. I just thought I'd offer the Grand Duke a lap dance while he's waiting for his lunch."

"You ridiculous impudent disgrace to all Humankind!" the Chevalier screamed. "You are lower than the lowest filth to ever exist in Hell! How *dare* you presume that Satan's Grand Messenger would have *any* desire to be in proximity to the likes of you!"

Aldezhor held up a shadowy finger. "Silence, Chevalier. The fact is I'd *very much* enjoy such a delightful spectacle."

We're good to go, Ruth thought and got to doing what she did best: enticing men with her body. The dining room fell silent as she slowly danced around the Grand Duke, churning her hips and tracing her hands across his black chest. Even Alexander was looking on. Ruth expertly spun a leg over Aldezhor's head, simultaneously edged her butt up on the table, then shot both legs up in a V. *There's an eyeful,* she thought. In more synchronous movements, then, she slithered forward facing him, and sat in his lap. *Jesus, this guy's colder than a snowman,* she thought. Now her bare breasts were right in his incorporeal face.

Got to get a look at that note now. . . .

She stood up, spun another leg over his head, and again sat herself in his lap, only this time with her back to him. Hands on knees, she slowly ground her buttocks into his groin.

The note lay opened right in front of her.

VII.VII, it read.

Remember that . . .

When Ruth finished her dance, she turned and bowed

to uproarious applause. Grand Duke Aldezhor slipped a thousand-dollar Hellnote into her waistband.

"That was marvelous," he gushed.

"Thanks for the tip, Duke. Oh—be right back. Your lunch is ready." She traipsed off, quickly grabbing her pen and writing *VII.VII* on her thigh.

"Harlot!" the Chevalier yelled. "In the name of Lucifer, stop right this instant!"

I guess he means me, she thought, but when she turned around, she almost fainted.

The Chevalier was aiming a sulphur pistol right at her face.

"Come forward!"

"What did I do wrong?" she said, astonished. She edged back to the table, noticing that creepy Bio-Wizard leaning over as if telling Aldezhor something.

"You're under arrest for anti-Satanic thoughts and terrorist premeditation," the Chevalier said.

"The fuck?"

Aldezhor stood up. "Conscripts! Fetch a cranial retractor at once."

The Chevalier smiled down the bead of his pistol. "Our Bio-Wizard has interpreted your psychic aura, harlot, and has discerned an act of subterfuge and treason."

"The fuck?" Ruth repeated, dismayed.

Helmeted Conscripts clattered into the room, and one handed the Bio-Wizard an iron device that looked like a closed bear trap.

"Remove her brain without delay and deliver it to the Psychical Sciences Center for analysis," the Grand Duke ordered.

"Brilliant suggestion, Grand Duke," the Chevalier added. "The mediums there will be able to read her treacherous brain like a book, and extract all of its heretical secrets."

The full force of the predicament finally socked home. *Holy shit! These assholes are going to take my brain out of my head!* In the background somewhere, she thought she heard a strange steady tone, almost like a bell, and as the Conscripts reached for her, Ruth began to scream—

"So, when are we gonna get to this funky restaurant?" Ruth complained. She and Alexander walked leisurely down a glowing redbrick sidewalk.

The priest smiled at her. "Believe it or not, Ruth, we just *left* the funky restaurant."

Ruth stopped and leaned against a wall below a poster of that weird design she'd been seeing—the spiral in the rectangle. "What?" she said. "I'm supposed to get a job at this joint so I can read some secret message passed on to this Aldezhor guy."

"You already did." The priest waved her into a scarlet alley. "Come on. You have to change clothes. You'll attract attention on the street, and after what just happened, we don't need attention."

What the fuck is he talking about? But before she could object, Alexander slipped his tentacle around her waist and urged her into the alley. More shock slapped her when she looked down at herself. She was wearing the Tongue-Skirt and Hand-Bra. She winced when the Werewolf hands gave her breasts a squeeze. "This is fucked-up, man! I don't remember changing into this!"

"You don't remember a lot, Ruth." The priest sat down in the corner, his Usher legs runneled with muscles. "In fact, nobody in the restaurant does. Because of this." He held up a metal implement that looked like a fork with only two tines. "Remember my goody bag?" He gestured toward the puckered pouch around his neck. "This was in it."

Ruth rubbed her eyes. "It looks kind of like a tuning fork that guitarists use."

"Good guess. It's a Regression Fork. It regresses the memory of anyone who hears it. We almost got nailed in the restaurant but once I struck this fork"—he winked at her and put it away—"it worked like a charm and we got out scot-free."

"I don't remember *shit*," Ruth asserted.

"Neither does anyone else who was there when I rang the fork."

Something clicked in her head. "Then how come *you* remember?"

He opened his wide, three-fingered hand, displaying two pebbles. "Earplugs."

Ruth's breasts heaved with a great sigh. "So you're telling me I've already read this note, this super-important secret message?"

"Yes, Ruth. You simply don't *remember* reading it. Pull your skirt up over your left thigh."

"Why?" she challenged. "I *knew* you were a perv."

"Ruth, just do it."

With obvious distaste, Ruth pulled up the Tongue-Skirt's quivering hem.

"There. See?"

Written on her thigh was *VII.VII.*

"That's perfect!" he enthused. "Now we know exactly when the Involution will be initiated."

"Huh?"

Alexander rose. "I'll explain as we go. But for now, you need to change—"

"Fine with me!" she rejoiced and yanked the hairy bra off. "I've been dying to drop this stuff in the garbage."

Alexander put the bra in a bag. "Not so fast. You'll need to wear the outfit one more time. It's very important."

Fuck, she thought. She reached to slip off the grotesque skirt but—"Hey!" She found the thousand-dollar Hell-note in the waistband. "How'd I get this?"

"You don't want to know." He handed her the cutoff shorts and pink YUCK FOO T-shirt. "Put this stuff back on and let's go."

Ruth stepped out of the skirt and as she stood naked before the monster-limbed priest, she caught him looking at her very intently.

"You don't have to *stare*, you know."

"Trust me, Ruth. I'm not lusting after your body."

Yeah, right. "Then what are you doing?"

"It's just amazing," he said, "how closely your body resembles someone else's. . . ."

(II)

Where . . . am I? Venetia thought when she awoke in a room that clearly wasn't hers. And when she leaned up—
"Oh my God . . ."

The back of her head throbbed with pain.

"Relax, dear. You're in Father Driscoll's room."

She recognized the soothing voice at once: Mrs. Newlwyn's. Then the matronly woman's face focused above her, along with two more—John and Betta.

"Why am I in Father Driscoll's room?" Venetia finally managed, and leaned up. She was wrapped in her robe.

"We found you this morning at the bottom of the stairs," a firmer voice cut in. Father Driscoll's face now appeared, along with Dan's.

The memory slammed back, and her eyes shot wide.

"What happened?" Dan asked.

That voice again.

I'm talking to you from Hell, it said.

But what else? *Something about bones—six bones? Six coffins? And a strange word,* she recalled. *Electrocution? Plus the same names on the list I found. And—*

She remembered the cloaked figure on the landing coming for her.

"You look like you've seen a ghost," Dan said trying to jest.

Maybe I have, she thought.

Then something worse jagged into her head: an image awash with sensations. *It must've been something I dreamed. . . .* Of course. She'd dreamed that the cloaked figure had proceeded to perform oral sex on her. . . .

Mrs. Newlwyn and Betta helped her sit up on the bed.

"We brought you into my room," Father Driscoll told her, "because it's downstairs." He touched her shoulder. "Venetia, did you fall down the steps?"

"I . . . ," she began. *I guess I did.* "I'm fine. I may have tripped at the bottom."

"I think I should call a doctor."

The idea alarmed her. "No, no, I'm all right, just a headache."

Driscoll frowned toward Dan. "It looked like you were *passed out* at the bottom of the stairs. Dan admitted that you'd both been drinking last night."

Dan cut in quickly, "But I also mentioned that Venetia only had one beer. It didn't seem like a big deal."

"Of course not, Dan," the priest said sarcastically. "A girl barely twenty-one—who *never* drinks—chugging a beer on a hot night after working in the heat all day."

"Look, if you want to blame me, go ahead. I'm sorry. I didn't think one beer would hurt. I told her to order it."

Venetia shook her head. "It's nobody's fault but mine. The beer may have buzzed me a little but I'm certain I wasn't drunk. I think I may have fallen asleep in the atrium—"

"Why in the atrium?"

"I couldn't sleep so I went outside for a walk." She flicked a quick glance toward John and Betta. "I took a walk in the woods, then came in and found I was really tired." She rubbed her face. "Lord, I feel so stupid. I came in and sat down and I think I fell asleep. I had . . . a nightmare. It's one I've had before—I dream I hear a voice."

"A voice?" Mrs. Newlwyn asked.

"A voice from Hell, telling me weird things."

Dan tried—and failed—to buffer the comment with some levity. "At least it was a good *Catholic* nightmare."

Driscoll frowned.

"And then I dreamed I saw this ghost everyone's talking about—the cloaked figure."

Mrs. Newlwyn's face blanched, and so did Betta's.

"Venetia," Driscoll said like a father to his little daughter, "there's no such thing as ghosts."

Well . . . he doesn't look happy, and I can't say I blame him. Venetia felt like an imbecile, shaking the whole house upside down with ghost stories. *I hope he doesn't tell my parents.*

The priest seemed to be thinking. "All right. You got tipsy—thanks to Dan. You had a bad dream. And you may have fallen. I'm responsible here, so I have to make sure you're all right."

"I am," Venetia implored.

"You're certain you don't want a doctor?"

"I'm positive."

"All right, but there's one other thing."

Everyone else was looking at her with a hushed concern. Eventually, Mrs. Newlwyn said, "We're worried . . . about the position we found you in."

Venetia sensed the tall woman was testing an uncomfortable detail. "My *position?* What do you mean?"

"When Betta and I found you, you were unconscious at the bottom of the stairs, and your robe was off. Your . . ." Another moment of hesitation. "Your legs were parted."

Driscoll stepped in. "We just want to make sure you weren't raped."

Astonishment broke over her. "That's ridiculous." *My robe must have come off when I fell. That's all I was wearing,* she thought. "There was no way I was raped, Father."

"Even with the new locks, this house would be easy for a professional thief to break into," Dan said.

And Driscoll: "Are you sure you locked the door when you came in from your walk?"

The key around her neck felt chilled. "I'm positive." Venetia couldn't believe all the concern she'd caused, but before she could answer, someone rang the doorbell.

"John"—Driscoll looked to the yard boy—"go and see who that is, please."

"Okay, Father," he said and went off.

All eyes returned to Venetia. "I wasn't raped," she said.

"We could take you to the hospital for an examination," Dan said.

"That's ridiculous. I would *know*," she asserted without stating outright that her hymen was intact.

Driscoll nodded, adding, "We could at least ask the police if there have been any sexual assaults in the area lately."

"That would be crazy," she scoffed. "We don't need to mention this to the *police*."

John came right back in.

"Who's at the door?" Driscoll asked him.

"The police," John said.

(III)

The scrawny kid who answered the door came back a minute later and said, as if insecure about something, "Um, uh, Father Driscoll says you can come in."

"Thanks," Berns said and stepped inside to an atrium that was walled with books and full of sheet-covered furniture.

"They're all in his office." The kid's hair was sticking up and his T-shirt was flecked with grass. *Yard boy,* Berns thought, but when he looked up to the second-story stairhall he thought he saw a woman in a white robe rush into one of the rooms. *Was that Venetia?* He caught a glimpse of bright blond hair but that was it.

"You can wait here, sir," the kid practically stammered. "Father Driscoll will be with you in a minute."

"Okay, thanks."

Berns sat in an old armchair by a high window with newly painted trim. He thought, *What a way to start the day.*

He'd been driving up to the prior house when the radio call had come in: "Two-zero-zero, do you copy?"

"Roger."

"We just got a message from central commo at state HQ."

What the hell do they want? Berns wondered, taking the wooded road up the hill. *Sue Maitland's in their custody now.* "What is it?"

"Susan Maitland committed suicide in her cell about an hour ago," the dispatcher informed him.

Berns almost drove off the road. *First Freddie Johnson, and now her! My only suspects are all killing themselves!*

"According to the state security director, she died by self-inflicted blunt trauma to the head."

"How the fuck is that possible?" Berns complained, violating radio protocol with the profanity.

"See banged her head against the cell wall until she died. But at least it was after the state did their own interview. They said they'll send you the transcript by five."

"Great," Berns sputtered. "Two-zero-zero over and out."

And now here he sat, in this dreary prior house. *Pissing in the wind again.* He figured anything was worth a try.

At least Maitland proves I was right about Freddie's accomplices not leaving town. He was the heavy so it makes sense for him to have left. But the others didn't.

Why?

Because they still need to be here? But if so . . . for what?

Another ritual. Maybe the two in March were just the beginning of something. . . . He mulled over the idea.

Eventually Dan appeared and took him to a downstairs office where he met a tall man in an identical black shirt and Roman collar. "I'm Father Christopher Driscoll," the man said.

Berns shook his hand. It struck him that Driscoll had a firm, "priestly" voice, but his face—and blond Marine Corp crew cut—made him look like anything but a priest. "Captain Ray Berns, Father."

"I'm sorry I missed you yesterday. Dan told me about the interview with the murder suspect." Driscoll's height made him seem cramped in the small white office. "How is the case coming?"

Berns could've laughed. *Yesterday, great. Today, not so good.* He elected to not mention that both of his material suspects were now dead. "We're making some headway," he said. "And the reason I'm here—" He hefted his briefcase. "I'd like to show you some things because, to be honest, I don't have a clue. I'm hoping that religious guys like you might shed some light."

Driscoll smiled. "The 'religious guys' are at your service, Captain."

Berns opened the case and without thinking asked, "Where's Venetia?"

"She may be down later," Driscoll said in an almost guarded tone.

"She's not feeling well," Dan added.

Keep on track! Berns scolded at himself. "The reason I need your consultation, Father, is because we believe the March murders were perpetrated by a—for lack of a better term—a suicide cult that practices Satanism." At once Berns winced at his own choice of words. "I know that sounds hokey but—"

"Why hokey, Captain?" Driscoll countered. "For the two thousand years that Christianity's been around, there have been sects that exist in total rebellion to it. God is love, God is life; hence, an antithetical cult who adheres to the opposite. Their god—Lucifer—is not love but hatred, and not life but death." Driscoll seemed content with the prospect. "In other words, Satanism is nothing new. It's always been here; it's just harder to see in these modern times."

"I appreciate your open mind, Father." Berns could've laughed. "That's not quite the response I've gotten from the diocese."

Driscoll waved a hand. "Don't worry about those sticks in the mud."

Dan chuckled.

Suddenly the door clicked open and Venetia slipped in. "Hello, Captain. Hope I'm not intruding."

"Not at all." But when he looked at her, with all that blond hair down, and the thrusting bosom, he could've keeled over.

"I think it's a case of the more the merrier," Dan interjected.

Berns was instantly distracted from withdrawing his materials from the briefcase. He wanted to look right at her but could only steal glimpses. *Holy Moses, she's beautiful.* Her apparel made her appear half-trashy and half-chaste: flip-flops and bare legs, her white blouse knotted to expose her midriff, yet the frumpy black skirt and cross glittering in her cleavage. He finally focused. "What I've got here are copies of some papers that were found in Freddie Johnson's domicile in Maine. That's where he fled to after the murders." He removed the printouts that the Lubec PD had scanned for him. "This isn't Latin, is it?"

Venetia and Dan stood on either side when he placed the sheet on Driscoll's desk.

They all peered down at the rushed scribble whose first line read:

1) *Zvaetlot srrpoyssuzc foedf du puzvmwuv an wiffew treeg untl!*

"No," Driscoll, Dan, and Venetia said all at once; then Venetia added, "And it's not Old English, Frisian, or Norse."

Driscoll was squinting. "I have no idea *what* that is. It looks like gobbledygook."

"Maybe that's exactly what it is," Dan suggested. "Maybe it's just a bunch of bunk scribbled by a crazy drug addict—this Freddie guy, perhaps. Or Sue Maitland."

Driscoll mulled it over. "Delusional people often pursue their delusions with great detail."

"These people *think* they're really worshiping Satan," Venetia suggested, still scanning the pages. "Maybe they created their own language to accommodate the fantasy."

"Crazy people do crazy things," Driscoll said.

"But Freddie Johnson wasn't crazy," Berns corrected. "We gave him every psych test in the book."

Venetia's cross dangled when she leaned over farther. "Forget about what language it is. Each paragraph is numbered. Like a list of some kind."

"A list of instructions," Berns told her. "That's what Maitland implied."

Dan said halfheartedly, "Instructions for a devilish ritual designed to appease Satan." Then he chuckled.

No one else laughed, and Berns thought, *Buddy, you just might be right.*

Venetia looked to Berns. "Captain, Freddie Johnson was the ringleader, right?"

"Yeah, that much we know for sure. The boss of the cult, or whatever you want to call it."

"Did anyone ever ask him outright?"

"Ask him what?"

"If he was a Satanist."

Good question. "Yes. And you know what he said?" Berns whipped out his pad of notes. "He said he was an 'Eosphorian.'"

Venetia, Driscoll, and Dan all looked at each other without a word.

"Why do I have this feeling everybody knows something I don't?" Berns asked.

"Follow us, Captain," Venetia said. "We'll show you."

What the hell? They took him upstairs and showed him each corner room, and the weird words written beneath the broken plaster: *Ash-shaytan,* in one room, *Lux Ferre,* in another, then *Iblis,* and finally, *Eosphorus.*

"Four different names for Satan," Driscoll told him.

Berns was confused now. "Freddie wrote these names?"

"That's the interesting part," Driscoll said. "No. They were under plaster forty years old."

"And Johnson was only in his thirties," Berns said. "So this cult . . ."

Venetia leaned against a dresser. "Maybe this cult has existed for all those decades, and Freddie and Sue were just the most recent recruits."

Sounds nutty, but she's got to be right, Berns thought. "This is so weird. It's almost like this *building* has some specific significance to the cult."

"And that's not all," Driscoll said, and then explained the history of Amano Tessorio.

"A Vatican architect who practiced devil worship in the closet." Berns felt waylaid.

"He secretly adorned the building with homages to Lucifer," Venetia added. "Built-in desecration."

It was difficult to process the information. Berns held up a finger. "Ah, but there's one more thing I need to show you." He led them back downstairs to Driscoll's office.

"This," he said. He pulled out the last sheet from the Lubec file: the sketch.

"Any of you got an idea what this might be?"

"A design," Dan said, "that looks . . . occult."

"That's exactly what I thought, and everyone else who's seen it." Berns looked harder. "Freddie and Sue Maitland had the same diagram *tattooed* on their lower abdomens. Originally I thought it must be a logo for some heavy metal band."

Driscoll ventured, "But it's probably the logo for Freddie's cult."

Berns nodded. "I asked him what it was and he called it 'the Involution.' It's a geometric term—the spiral. I've never seen anything like it."

Venetia was staring, her face going pale. "I have."

Chapter Fifteen

(I)

"That's it?" Boniface was astonished. "It's so . . . meager."

Pasiphae—the raven black regent of the Labyrinth—had just led in the nine-foot Golem, whose moldering clay hand clasped the arcane device. The lifeless monster placed it on a gem-studded stand just before the Pith, where the six angels—pregnant and insane—squirmed in naked turmoil.

Willirmoz' char-crisped face smiled within the hood. "Meager in only *appearance*, my repugnant lord. It's the only one of its kind, and it's a thousand times more accurate than even the latest-generation Occult Sensors. It's the ultimate safeguard for when the Involution is charged and the Pith is insolvent."

"I see," Boniface uttered, but he really didn't. *Best to leave these technical matters to the technicians.*

The device was called the Smoke-Light: a glass cylinder framed by iron. It looked like a lantern the size of a soup can—very small. Beneath the stand on which it sat was a candle made of infant fat.

"The Smoke-Light's glass chamber holds the smoke

from six burned Human hearts," Willirmoz explained, charred fingers interlaced. He lit the candle beneath. "Behold how it works, my diabolical prince."

The Wizard stood back as the lantern's chamber began to glow. Boniface could see the strange smoke swirling within. *Fascinating,* he thought a moment later. The light that now poured off the object tinted the entire stone-walled room.

The light was black.

"It's beautiful," the Exalted Duke admitted, "but I still don't understand."

Willirmoz stepped closer. "Were there an infiltrator here, his intentions would be betrayed by the obsidian light, my lord. The light would turn white around his aura. The device instantly detects any thought, notion, or motivation that is hostile to Lucifer. Charmed objects, too, and Power Totems would be similarly detected."

Boniface's dry eyes scanned the populants of the Lower Chancel: Golems, Ushers, Conscripts, and the oil black Pasiphae. The light around them all was brilliantly black. "But everyone here is a servant of Lucifer," Boniface objected. "How do we really know it works?"

Willirmoz' grin sharpened as he snapped charred fingers. Pasiphae stepped up, her bare breasts shining black as the light, and withdrew something from a small box.

"Here is a detestable relic from a terrorist we caught sabotaging an Electrocity Station recently," the High Priest explained.

When Boniface glimpsed the trinket that dangled from Pasiphae's sleek fingers, he winced as if bile had flooded his mouth.

It was a crude tin crucifix, and during the instant it was revealed, the light around it glowed white.

"Put it away," Boniface groaned. "It's making me sick."

Willirmoz nodded and the obscene object was removed from view.

"So you see, my hateful lord?"

The Exalted Duke had to catch his breath, huffing through the salt-mask's mouth slit. "Indeed, Wizard. It's

works perfectly." At once the decayed lump that was
Boniface's heart beat with joy. *With the Smoke-Light, no one
who may be plotting against us can possibly taint our plans.*

"You've done well, Wizard, and you will be rewarded,"
the Duke promised.

"But now, my lord," the Lithomancer spoke, "it's nearly
time."

Pasiphae led the priest and the Exalted Duke out of the
chamber, the Smoke-Light's indescribable glow glittering
behind them.

Oh, so soon, Boniface thought.

(II)

"Yeah, Mom. You remember, the convenience store,"
Venetia was saying into her phone. She sat in the passenger seat of Captain Berns' unmarked police car.

Venetia's mother sounded duped. "Convenience store,
honey?"

"Yeah. Not a 7-Eleven but something else."

"Oh, yes." Maxine Barlow connected the dots. "Where
you fainted."

"Right. Could you ask Dad exactly where it was?"

"Of course . . ."

"It'd really help if she knew what road," Berns said in
the interim. "There're convenience stores everywhere.
Super-7s, Qwik-Marts, 7-Elevens."

"All I know is it was right off the highway from Con-
cord," Venetia told him. "It was on our way to the prior
house."

"We'll find it," the captain said.

Her mother came back on the line. "The Qwik-Mart on
Brewer Road, he thinks."

"Thanks, Mom," Venetia said and relayed the info to
Berns.

"But . . . why do you want to go to a convenience store,
dear?" her mother asked.

"Oh, we're just driving around," she said and then was

surprised by how easily she'd lied. *I can't tell her I'm helping the police with the murder investigation. . . .* "For sodas."

"Oh, well . . . are you feeling all right? Had any more
spells?"

"Just a little one, last night, but it's no big deal."

Alarm tensed Maxine's voice. "You should've called me
immediately! I don't like this. You're not sleeping well,
you're having these spells, and now this awful murder
business. I still am your mother, you know. I've a mind to
come there right now and take you out, get you to a doctor
for a checkup."

Another can of worms. "Mom, please," Venetia groaned.
"I'm all right. It's just the heat, plus I'm still burned out
from finals. I'll be home soon anyway."

"Well . . ." Her mother stewed. "I'm just worried."

"Don't be. Everything's fine. But I have to go now. Tell
Dad I said hi."

"Of course, honey."

"Love you, Mom—"

"Call tomorrow!"

"I will, I will." Eventually she managed to end the conversation. "Worried mother," she said to Berns.

"Can't say I'd want my kid working in a place where
there'd been murders, either," Berns offered from behind
the wheel.

Venetia saw his point but she also felt that this new discovery was somehow exciting—that bizarre drawing of
Freddie Johnson's, the spiral in the rectangle.

She had immediately remembered seeing the same
thing scrawled in the bathroom of the convenience store,
just before she'd passed out that day.

And now we're checking it out.

She could see his gun butt in the shoulder holster as he
turned onto a wooded road. This was a thrill, especially
for a college student who'd been buried in libraries for
two years.

"What exactly do we do when we get there?"

"First, see if the design is still there, then ask the employees if they have any idea who drew it. I've got pictures of Johnson and Maitland to show them. Any connection is something to go on." Suddenly the cop seemed fatigued. "The person who drew it might know the perpetrators or even *be* one."

"And might live close by."

"Right. It's all I've got right now. With Johnson and Maitland dead, we've got no direct information sources. Sometimes it's the little things that solve big crimes."

"It could be someone who works there, too," Venetia said.

"That would be even better, which is why I'll try to get a list of all the employees over the last year or so and run checks," Berns said, as he dragged his eyes off her legs.

He's something. . . . She didn't feel at all threatened, though, or even offended. *It makes me feel good,* she admitted to herself, *especially for a girl who's probably going to be celibate all her life.* But the topic suddenly soured in her head. For whatever reason, the dream-snippet resurfaced, with the image—someone greedily performing oral sex on her as she lay naked and unconscious at the bottom of the stairs.

Ugh . . .

"Here's the place." Berns' voice severed the awful recollection.

QWIK-MART, the sign buzzed. Only a few cars sat in the lot.

As Venetia followed Berns in, she asked, "At Father Driscoll's office, you said that Freddie had a name for the diagram—"

"Right. He called it the 'Involution.' The spiral. It's a geometry term."

Venetia felt hesitant. *Will he think I'm stupid if I say this?* She shrugged. "I'll tell you something nutty—I think I heard the same word in a dream."

"Really?"

"Last night."

"And that's too much of a coincidence, right? You dream the word last night and then I walk in today and use the same word." He offered a lenient smile. "You must only *think* you heard the word before, like déjà vu and all that."

"I hope," she muttered.

The cool air inside sucked them in. Behind the counter stood a tall, muscular black man with a shaved head. He looked like a wrestler or one of those extreme fighters. "We're going to the bathroom," Berns bumbled, and flashed his badge. "Uh, police business."

"In the bathroom?" the black man questioned.

Venetia led the way. "There it is," she said. "I knew it wasn't my imagination." She pointed to the bathroom wall where the design had been penned.

"The Involution," Berns whispered, squinting. He produced a small digital camera and took a few pictures.

"What's going on in here?"

They both turned to find the black man filling the doorway.

"It's confidential pursuant to an ongoing homicide investigation," Berns said. "I'd appreciate your cooperation. Is the manager in?"

"That's me," the guy said.

"Any idea who drew *that?*" Berns pointed to the diagram.

The manager peered at it. "No, in fact I never noticed it, but then I'm not at this store a lot. I'm the district manager. I check each store every day, very briefly."

As the two men talked, Venetia found herself staring at the Involution; after several moments, the spiral seemed to be moving, and the arrows pointing in from the three corners looked as though they were lengthening toward the center.

Venetia blinked. *I'm just tired, that's all.*

They all went back out to the register area. Berns asked, "Would it be all right if you showed me employee records over the last year?"

The manager crossed massive arms. "I'd have to call the boss about that. Isn't that a Privacy Act thing?"

"Only if you want it to be," Berns egged. "With or without a warrant, I'm going to have to question everybody anyway."

The manager's voice was articulate and reserved, not the tough-guy rasp Venetia would've expected, given his size. "What do you want to question them about?"

"Any nutball customers they might remember," Berns replied. "Weirdos, Satanic tattoos. Oh, and I'm particularly interested in someone named Dougie, or Douglas—"

"Dougie, you say?" the managed asked, lowering his voice. "You're not gonna believe this, but the guy working the next shift is named Dougie Jones, and he's in the office right now, clocking in."

Before the manager's words sunk in, Venetia screamed as a hand grabbed her hair from behind and dragged her backward. A split second later, there was a knife at her throat and a tense forearm around her waist.

"Don't be stupid, Dougie," Berns said. As fast as she'd been snagged, Berns had his pistol out, aimed right at the face behind Venetia's shoulder. "Drop the knife and let's talk."

"Bullshit, man!" spat the hot voice next to her ear.

Venetia's heart was thundering. In the front window's reflection, she could see herself wide-eyed and on tiptoes, and she could see the man behind her holding the knife.

Lean, wiry, midtwenties, black mop haircut. *That's the guy who was working the counter when I came in with Mom and Dad.* He even wore the same black HIGHWAY TO HELL T-shirt.

The forearm around her waist tightened; she tensed up even more when the knife point tickled her throat.

A stray prayer slipped through her mind: *Please, God. Don't let me get killed today. . . .*

"Your goose is cooked, Dougie," Berns said behind his

gun. "You're done. Freddie and Sue shit all over you—blamed you for everything."

"You're full of *shit*, man!" came the jagged voice. Spittle from Dougie's lips fell onto Venetia bare throat. "I heard your whole conversation from the office!"

"All right, fine." Berns' free hand opened outward. "Just . . . be cool. Let the girl go, and we'll talk this out."

Dougie laughed. "Freddie always said, 'When the party's over, it's over.' But you know? I've still got a little more partying to do first."

Every muscle in Venetia's body twisted when her captor's hand slid up and kneaded a breast.

"Cut that shit out, Dougie," Berns warned.

"Why? It's fun. Did the same thing to the nun, *after* we drained her blood."

Don't faint, don't faint! Venetia told herself. A moment later, she was grinding her teeth when Dougie's free hand jacked up her skirt and pawed her crotch through her panties.

"Don't be a scumbag, Dougie. And don't make me do something you'll regret a hell of a lot more than me."

"The only thing you're gonna do is drop the gun and kick it over here, or else I'm gonna peel this bitch like a banana." Dougie paused, as if in consideration. "Or better yet, I'll cut her throat just like we did the nun and that skinny old bat." Then he positioned the knife so that its tip was pointing right into the side of Venetia's neck.

Please, God, she prayed.

Venetia's next scream resounded simultaneously with the ear-splitting *bam!* that cracked through the store. A muzzle flash blinded her as the bullet incredibly shot the knife out of Dougie's hand.

Dougie flew backward, then—

THWACK!

The manager's croquet ball–sized fist smacked Dougie's temple. Dougie crumpled to the floor, out cold.

Venetia nearly fainted when it was over. She braced herself against a stack of soda cases. *Thanks, God,* she thought. *I owe you one.*

Berns waved gun smoke out of his face, then chuckled when he looked down at Dougie. "Looks like that ass-hole's party ended a little sooner than he planned."

A dozen county cops responded within minutes. EMTs checked Dougie—aka Douglas B. Jones—and cleared him for transport. Berns' unlikely shot hadn't even nicked Dougie's hand; it had struck the knife and ricocheted. *A miraculous shot,* Venetia thought in the strange aftermath of radio squawk and blank-faced police.

"Keep him in *our* holding cell for processing," Berns ordered his uniforms. "We're keeping this case—to hell with the state." Berns glanced at a dismal Dougie, who was handcuffed and propped up by two more police. "I want a cop watching him at *all times.* No bullshit. This guy's a potential suicide."

The pair of officers exchanged odd glances.

"Just do it," Berns emphasized.

"Whatever you say, Captain," one of them replied.

"And . . . wait." Berns was suddenly animated in the post-shooting lull. "Hold him." He was reaching for Dougie's belt.

"Fuckin' pervert," Dougie snapped as Berns' hands un-buckled his belt and undid his jeans. "This is harass-ment." The black-haired punk glared at one of the cops holding him. "This guy's molesting me, man!"

"Just shut up, Dougie." Berns seemed uncomfortable but resolved just the same. "I gotta make sure."

What's he doing? Venetia wondered.

Berns lowered Dougie's jeans to just above the pubis. "There. I knew it."

Venetia's eyes widened. At once, she recognized the creepy diagram tattooed on Dougie's lower abdomen.

"The Involution, huh, Dougie?" Berns said, then re-buckled the prisoner's pants.

Dougie grinned defiantly. "Don't know what you're talkin' about."

"What is it? Exactly?"

"Kiss my ass."

"You're an . . . Eosphorian, too, Dougie?"

Dougie stalled, then blinked. "Fuck off."

Berns nodded. "Take him to the hospital for a full checkup, then lock his ass up in our holding cell."

"Yes, sir," a cop said.

Dougie was hauled outside to a patrol car.

"Coffee and doughnuts on the house," the immense manager said. Venetia noticed her hand trembling when she took a cup.

"Thanks for cleaning that guy's clock," Berns said.

The manager laughed. "I always thought he was a weirdo but, you know, he never called in sick and was never late."

Berns bit into a jelly-filled doughnut. "You can hire him back five hundred years from now when he gets out of prison."

Venetia steadied herself in the aftershock. "It just occurred to me, Captain, but you saved my life."

"Probably not," came Berns' modest reply. "A few more minutes and Dougie would've probably calmed down and given up."

Probably, Venetia thought with a shudder. *But God did answer my prayer. . . .* "Thank you just the same. That was some shot, though."

Berns chuckled. "I never would've taken it if I wasn't a hundred-percent sure. I got no wife, no kids, nothing else going on, so in my spare time I practice at the range. It's second nature."

Venetia admired his confidence. But her heart was still beating weird after the adrenaline dump.

"You look a little wobbly. I better get you back," he said.

She didn't argue. They bid their farewell to the manager and then were back in Berns' unmarked.

"What a difference a split second makes, huh?" Berns remarked from behind the wheel. "I'm the one who should be thanking you. If you hadn't remembered seeing the diagram on the wall, none of that would've happened and Dougie would still be at-large. A half hour ago I didn't have a case anymore 'cos my only two suspects were dead. Now, thanks to your memory, the case is solved."

Venetia hadn't thought of it that way, but it did make her feel better. *I almost peed myself but at least it was all for something beneficial.* "So you feel the case is genuinely solved?"

"Sure. There's no reason to think that there are any more accomplices to the March murders. Too much corroboration from Freddie and Maitland. But we'll grill Dougie big-time, too." Berns paused in reflection. "It doesn't really matter to the case but . . . I'd really like to know what it was all about. The diagram, the Eosphorous stuff, those instructions in whatever language they were in. Just to know."

"Probably just three messed-up people living a delusion," Venetia suggested.

"Yeah," he conceded. "Hey, do you mind if I stop by the substation real quick before I take you back? I'll just be a couple minutes."

"That's fine," she said, almost half asleep now in the seat.

"Once they bring Dougie back from the hospital, I have to make *damn sure* I have a suicide watch on him."

"You really think he's suicidal?"

"Yeah, because Freddie and Sue didn't seem suicidal but they knocked themselves off anyway. They even *told me* they would. I can't have the same happening to Dougie."

Suicide cult. The words thumped in her head. *A Satanic one . . .* It all seemed unreal, or so distant as to have no meaning, like reading of such things in the papers and just thinking, *Oh, how strange.*

But here it was, right in her face.

A phantom sensation from the knife-point continued to prick her neck, and she shuddered when she recalled the feel of Dougie's hand mauling her breast and crotch.

Berns parked in front of the Wammsport substation. "I'll be back in five minutes," he promised.

"Mmmm," she said. She was closing her eyes. *I'll just take a nap while he's inside. . . .*

The half-sleep felt luxurious after being terrorized at

the store. *Thank you, God.* . . . But it was true, she *could* have been killed, easily. She saw calm blackness behind her eyes. Her window was open, and she could feel a gentle breeze caress her face.

But then the strangest image flitted into her head: a wristwatch—was it hers?—but the hands were spinning backward, then forward, the day and date doing the same, until it got to the point where each second was a time hours off of the second previous.

Another image smacked: her naked body sprawled unconscious as a cloaked figure hunched between her legs. . . .

Bile flooded her stomach—

Then the tinny voice crackled and whined like an old-time radio transmission: *"You must find the Pith! You must find the bones! Venetia! Venetia! There's nothing you can do to stop the pouring of the blood!"*

Venetia gasped like someone just saved from drowning.

"You must find the Pith! You must find the bones! Do you hear me? Do you hear me? This isn't a dream! You must bring one of the—"

She roused with a silent shriek on her lips, and at once found tears dribbling down her cheeks. "Oh, my God, what is *wrong* with me?" she squealed. Her fists churned in her lap. *I must have a tumor in my brain or something.* What else could cause such vibrant hallucinations over and over?

When Venetia opened her fists—

What . . .

A piece of paper lay crumpled in one of them.

Someone put this in my hand . . . while I was asleep.

Groggy, still teary-eyed, she squinted at the crabbed scrawl:

> *Embrace your strength, as I have not. In my cowardice, I am no longer worthy to serve God. Take heed not to be sacrificed by mistake. Only you can rightly enter the Pith.*

"This is crazy!" she muttered and jumped out of the car. The note blew away. *Someone's messing with my head!* The main drag paralleled the docks. A block down she saw a bum hobbling across the street. *Him!* she realized. *Father Whitewood!*

"Wait!" she shouted, tramping down the sidewalk. Passersby gaped at her flight. "Father Whitewood! *Damn it*, would you *wait!*"

The man straightened, a smudged face peering at her from the hood of the greasy raincoat. He stopped, fist tremoring as if challenging himself, and for a moment it looked as though he would turn and come toward her.

"Damn it to hell!" Venetia swore.

Instead, this bum—the former prior of St. John's Prior House—got onto a bus and rode away.

"Come back!"

In the bus's rear window, the withered face gazed back at her; then the old man made the sign of the cross.

Chapter Sixteen

(I)

"It's going to be very soon," Alexander said, holding a weird brass crescent to the sky.

Ruth didn't even know what "it" was yet. "How soon?"

"Well, since there's no time here—" He shrugged, keeping his eye lined up on the device. "I'll only be able to tell from this. Don't worry, I'll know."

Ruth frowned. She sat next to him on a bench of long bones at the end of another alley. "What is that thing anyway?"

"Know what a sextant is?"

"Fuck no."

The monster-armed priest shook his head. "It's like a sextant, Ruth, a thing boaters used to use to chart courses by looking at the stars. This is a *Moon*-Sextant, though." He displayed it: a crescent of brass which—now that she thought about it—was shaped exactly like the black sickle moon that hung in the sky. "You line it up so the points are parallel to the ground and check the distance between the moon's points and the sextant's points. Here the moon never changes phase but it does change *pitch*. That's the closest you get to measuring time in Hell. The reading you snagged off Aldezhor was seven-point-seven. There's a gauge on this thing. Right now we're at seven-point-three. I'll just have to keep checking once we're inside."

Ruth scratched her armpit, wishing for a shower. "Inside *where?*"

"There," the priest said. His Annelok arm pointed toward a massive building several blocks away. "That's Fortress Boniface."

"It's so . . . bright," she said, shielding her eyes. Like everything in the District, it was made of those funny red bricks that had a weird glow, but this structure was the brightest. Each brick burned like fuzzy red neon against the darker scarlet sky.

"The blood bricks are Hexed very potently," Alexander explained. "Hence, the glow. It's one of the most important buildings in Hell and likewise one of the biggest targets for anti-Satanic terrorists."

"Like us?" she said.

"Like us, Ruth. The Hexing makes the bricks even stronger, so no one can break through them. The only way in is through the front door."

Ruth laughed. "And you think they're gonna open it for *us?*"

"Not for us, Ruth. For *you.*"

"I'm not going in there by my-fucking-self!"

"I'll be right behind you." The priest winked.

This is so fucked-up, she thought. "Damn it, I broke another nail!" Then she gasped. From the ramparts of the fortress, she saw hoppers dumping charred and mangled bodies over the side. "Did you see that shit?"

"Unfortunately, yes. Before any interstitial rite, they murder scores of people. It's called a precursory oblation."

Ruth squinted. "Huh?"

"A demonstrative sacrifice that's not functionally related to the ritual," the priest said.

"I don't know what the fuck you're talking about," she mumbled for the millionth time.

"They torture, then kill people for an extra effect. Like icing on cake. I'll bet they're slaughtering a thousand people a day in there: burning, threshing, crushing," the priest morbidly continued. "Remember, only the Human Damned have souls, Ruth, but even the Hellborn have a Deathforce."

"Deathforce? Do I want to know what that is?"

"You *need* to know. Deathforce can be likened to psychic energy—in Hell, it's in every living thing, Human and Demon alike. And when you kill Humans, Demons, Hybrids, etc. en masse, the Deathforce is released all at once. It keeps the air charged with positive Satanic energy. It makes their rituals work better, the same way gas treatment makes your car work better. Get it?"

Fuck, she thought. "I guess so . . ." She paled again, as another hopper emptied more bodies over the fortress ramparts.

"When they're done, they dump the bodies over the side to be scavenged by the local populace," he finished.

It was ghastly. This entire world seemed to *exist* on horror and despair. *Why did I have to be such a shitty person in life?* she lamented. *If I weren't, I wouldn't even be here.*

Alexander unsheathed an impressive knife from the Satanic Navy belt: a sharp blade on one side, a saw on the other. "This should do the trick."

Ruth found herself unsettled by the image of a priest grinning at a knife. Her voice rattled, "What's the knife for?"

The priest seemed to contemplate his response. "It's like a lot of things, Ruth. There's good news and there's bad news. The good news is, we're on the last leg of our mission."

Ruth felt petrified. "What's, uh, what's the bad news?"

"We've got some dirty work to do first. It won't be pretty."

Oh, like anything in this fuckin' city is, she thought.

"And she should be coming down this street real soon," Alexander added.

"She? Who? Your intelligence source?"

"No, no, Ruth. It's someone awful." He handed her one of the Hectographs. "*This* is who we're waiting for."

Pretty hot broad, Ruth thought when her eyes went first to the woman's body. Tall, buxom, long legs, and perfect hips.

"Shit, she's wearing a Hand-Bra and Tongue-Skirt just like mine."

"Um-huh. It denotes great wealth."

Only then did Ruth look at the woman's face. "Oh, make me gag! Did you see this bitch's *face?*"

"Um-hmm. No *Cosmo* cover for her, huh? It's the face of a lower-order Demon called a Putridox. Probably the most revolting visage in the Mephistopolis."

Ruth almost threw up looking at it. The face looked like a splat of cottage cheese pocked with yellow spots. No nose, but eyes and a mouth that were vertical instead of horizontal. The eyes themselves looked like wads of smoker's phlegm. "This is one fugly bitch, man. I'm gonna have nightmares. . . ."

"She *is* a nightmare, Ruth. Her name is Voluptua, and she's very important."

Ruth couldn't look anymore. "How could someone with a face like that be important?"

"She's the personal concubine of Exalted Duke Boniface," the priest said.

When he flashed a quick Hectograph of Boniface, Ruth shuddered at the image of the inhuman salt-mask.

"Voluptua is the one who's going to get us into the fortress."

Hmm, Ruth thought. She looked back at the picture of the woman and noticed an oddity. "Why's she wearing a scarf? It's hot as shit here."

Did Alexander seemed disturbed by his next thought? "You'll see," was all he said.

All the while, something bugged her about the picture, and finally it snapped. "Hey, this ho's body looks a lot like mine."

Alexander handed her another Hectograph. "Here's

one of her naked, Ruth. Let me know when that steel-trap brain of yours starts to click."

Ruth was about to respond to the obvious sarcasm but—

The next picture showed Voluptua standing buck-naked on the Fortress ramparts, the horrendous white-lumpen face grinning as Ushers loaded a hopper with corpses.

Every physical feature of the woman's body bore a striking resemblance to Ruth's. They were nearly identical: breasts, nipples, navel, hip contours, and leg curves. *She even trims her pubies the same way I do,* Ruth thought.

"Her body looks so much like yours," the priest said, "she could pass for you."

Or me for her. That's when Ruth's steel-trap brain finally clicked. "You're shitting me, man! You want me to stand in for *her?*"

"Yes," Alexander said rather grimly. "You look just like her. Even naked, your bodily features are so similar you could fool those closest to her—including Boniface."

Ruth frowned so hard it hurt. "I might have the same body but—hello!—I don't have the *monster face* to go with it!"

"Don't worry about it, Ruth. It'll all work out."

Ruth couldn't believe it. "You're fuckin' shitting me, right? That's the big plan? We came all this way and did all this stuff for *that?* What kind of shit do *you* have for brains?"

"Quiet! Here she comes now," the priest whispered. "Come on, into the alley."

Ruth ducked in with him. She'd glimpsed a figure down the street. *What is he gonna do?* she wondered. Alexander stood with his back against the alley, the knife in his Usher hand, and his Annelok arm coiled.

A tapping came down the bright red street. *High heels,* Ruth edged an eye out of the alley. . . .

"How close?" Alexander whispered.

"Thirty feet," Ruth said. Voluptua sashayed down the sidewalk, blond hair flowing around her appalling visage.

The Tongue-Skirt shined, the wolf-hands firmly cupping the breasts so similar to Ruth's. And when she passed—

Snap!

Alexander's Annelok arm shot out, caught the woman around the neck, and hauled her into the alley.

Ruth stood back, appalled. The woman flailed on the ground, gagging. The priest muscled her down with surprising cruelty, his Demonic knees pinning her shoulders. All the while, the Annelok arm constricted like a boa.

Voluptua's lumpy white face began to turn blue, and the vertical eyes bugged. "Unhand me! I'm from the Court of Boniface!"

Alexander ground his teeth at the sight of her. "God, you're ugly."

You got that right, Ruth thought. Then she noticed that each of the face's yellow pocks was occupied by a tiny red worm.

"I'll have you sealed in a keg and steamed for eternity, you wretched heretic!" the monstrous face spat.

Whack!

Alexander rammed the butt of the knife against the top of Voluptua's head. Her flailing ceased at once; now she lay still, unconscious.

The priest gave Ruth a very dark look. "You probably don't want to watch this."

Ruth crossed her arms. "I don't wanna watch anything! I want to know what's wrong with your fucked-up brain to think that I can pass for her! You're pissing in the wind, man! It'll never work."

"Look carefully, Ruth." Then Alexander took off Voluptua's scarf, revealing a ring of crumpled flesh about her throat.

"What the fuck . . . ?"

"She's a Bi-Facer, Ruth." Alexander grabbed Voluptua's mane of blond hair and pulled.

The awful Putridox face stretched thin as it was pulled off the woman's skull; at the same time the queer folds of skin about her neck disappeared as a second face slipped over her skull.

"The bitch's got two faces?" Ruth nearly howled.

"Yep. The Putridox face was surgically grafted on top of her Human face. Anytime she wants to change faces all she has to do is pull up or pull down, like a stocking mask," Alexander explained.

Voluptua's Human face was pretty but . . . *Not as pretty as mine*, Ruth thought.

Now the first face hung as a flap of skin off the top of the skull. Alexander casually cut it off with the knife, explaining, "In the Living World they've got face-lifts, implants, and tummy tucks; here, they've got Bi-Facial surgery—very pricy. You can have any face you want sewn on top of your own—if you've got the money, and as Boniface's favorite whore, you can bet she's got plenty of that."

Ruth's stomach grew upset from some unbidden dread. When Alexander finished cutting the Putridox face away from the Human face, he shook it out like a piece of laundry, blond hair and all.

Alexander shot Ruth a cunning grin. "Got the gist yet, Ruth?"

Her voice sounded like gravel when she replied, "You want me to wear that face, don't you?" She blinked, staring cold. "That ugly-ass, gross-out, Demonic monster face."

"Yes, Ruth. Without you, we're done. You're our only hope, and it's the only hope for you, too. Do you want to go to Purgatory in a thousand years"—his Usher hand gestured the stinking, smoking city—"or do you want to stay here, forever and ever?"

Ruth gulped.

"Remember, Ruth, our minds are limited. God's is not. Sometimes we have to let ourselves be redeemed the hard way. Take your choice."

Ruth shimmied in place. "All right, I'll wear the fuckin' monster face. Jesus . . ."

"Good girl," the priest grinned, then—

Crunch!

He stepped on Voluptua's head with his Usher foot and

crushed her skull flat. The stunning body hitched once, then fell still.

Ruth wasn't sure but just as Alexander's foot squashed the head, a thread of blue-black mist seemed to waft up like smoke and then snake its way to a crack in the alley wall.

"Was that—"

"Her soul," the priest said. He looked at the crack in the wall. "I'm happy to say that Voluptua is now occupying the body of a Brick-Mite."

Next Alexander took the woman's Bone-Sandals off. "Put these on now, Ruth, and then your Hand-Bra and Tongue-Skirt."

Great, I get to wear that freaky shit again, she lamented. She changed quickly, and found the Bone-Sandals to be a perfect fit.

Next, Alexander passed her the severed face. "It's time, Ruth. Just remember what you're doing is for the forces of good."

Fuck that shit, man, she thought, then took a deep breath, winced—*Aw, Jesus, I can't believe I'm doing this*—and pulled the Putridox face over her head as though it were a ski mask.

Alexander put the scarf around her neck, then stood back and marveled at her. "Ruth, you look *exactly* like her. It's even better than I thought."

"Terrific," Ruth muttered. The new face felt like hot, wet meat against her skin.

"And like I said, I'll be right behind you the whole way."

"How?" she objected to the obvious. "Even if they don't make me as an imposter, they ain't going to let a *priest* into the fortress."

"Leave that to me," he said and then turned his knife around and began to saw off Voluptua's left hand.

(II)

Maybe there is a God, and He was protecting Venetia, Berns thought. He'd just dropped her off at the prior house and was heading back to the county substation. He hadn't even consciously squeezed the trigger when he'd shot the knife out of Dougie Jones' hand, and the truth was he rarely practiced at the range. *That was the luckiest shot in the history of police work.*

Hiding his own adrenaline rush from Venetia and the manager hadn't been easy; now his hands shook on the wheel. He wanted to go home and chill out but knew he couldn't. Dougie wouldn't be long at the hospital; Berns' priority now was making sure the punk was safe in his cell.

"Two-zero-eight, this is two-zero-zero," he said into his radio mic. "Give me an ETA on Dougie Jones transport, over."

Dead air answered him.

"Two-zero-eight, do you copy?"

Nothing.

The clowns must've left their Motorolas in the car. He tried another unit. "Two-zero-seven, this is Berns. Do you copy?"

Nothing.

I'm going to kick some ass today, he thought, riled. *Fuckers are asleep at the switch.* But fifteen minutes later, he was pulling into the station and noticed all three responding cruisers parked in the lot. *Well, at least they've already got Dougie back. They're probably securing him in the cell now.*

Berns strode in to the station.

The booking desk stood empty. "Sergeant Naylor!" he bellowed at once. "You better have a good reason for not being at the desk!"

Bern stood still. No one appeared from the file room; in fact, nothing could be heard in the station. *There should be eight or ten cops in this place right now!* He looked behind the desk—

"Oh my God . . ."

The booking sergeant lay crumpled behind the desk, a pulpy red crater in the side of his head.

Somebody capped him. . . .

Berns drew his gun, struggled through a sudden tightness in his chest, and proceeded down the hall.

The cop in the property room sat slumped at his desk, a fan of blood and brains splattering the wall behind him.

Dougie Jones, Berns thought and ran toward the lock up.

Another cop lay head-shot in the hall. The air seemed static; hairs rose on the back of Berns' neck when he stepped into the jail and found three more cops lying dead on the floor. Their brains had all been blown out.

"No, no, *no*," Berns groaned.

The jail cell that should've been occupied by Dougie Jones stood empty.

Chapter Seventeen

(I)

"It's called a Hand of Glory," Alexander explained, "a fairly notorious Power Relic." He held up Voluptua's severed hand. "Used to be a standard discantation would activate it, but only if it was the hand of someone good."

"Well that ain't her, according to you," Ruth pointed out. She sat huddled with him amid some ill-smelling yellow bushes, just a block from Fortress Boniface. This close, the scarlet castle looked as impenetrable as it did immense. *What if they don't let me in?* she fretted.

The priest admired the grotesque hand as though it were a unique gadget. "No, Voluptua was an atrocious person, a hater of God, and a servant to the most unholy lust. But I have brand-new Celestial Enchantment that will make this thing work better than they ever have in the past. I got it from—"

"Your intelligence source," Ruth broke in.

"Right."

"So what's this thing do?" She looked at the hand with skepticism. "It's a fuckin' cut-off hand."

Alexander's gaze sparkled. "It'll make me invisible."

"Bullshit," Ruth smirked.

She didn't like the way he smiled after her remark. Next he struck a match and roved the flame back and forth under the fingertips. To Ruth's amazement, each tip began to burn like a candle. "That's a neat trick," she said.

"Not as neat as this," he muttered as he pulled up his black shirt. He seemed to be inspecting his navel.

"Checking for lint?" she asked.

His finger trailed over the many cursive scars that now embellished his skin. "Here it is!" Then he recited, *"Um God per me invisus vi flamma."* He grinned at Ruth.

"What?" she retorted. "I'm supposed to be impressed?"

"Come on, Ruth, I'm invisible."

Ruth laughed good and hard. "You tool! It doesn't work!"

"Oh, I forgot, the umbric perimeter. Move back a few feet."

Ruth slid back over fallen leaves that looked like pieces of dead skin. One foot, two feet, three, then—

Father Alexander vanished.

"You gotta be fuckin' shitting me, man."

"Told you. And it'll last a long time with that new enchantment," his voice floated from nowhere.

Hand of Glory, Ruth mused. *I could've made a lot of money in Florida with one of those.*

"All you've got to do is approach the gate," the priest said, "and they'll open it. I'll follow you in. But first I need to tell you the rest."

"The rest?" Ruth didn't exactly revel in the sound of that.

"What you need to do once inside." His voice hovered around the bushes.

God, I wish I had a cigarette. But Ruth figured it was time to get serious. "It's got something to do with this chick you've been talking to on the horn, right?" she said.

"Venetia Barlow, yes. Venetia's not your typical twenty-one-year-old girl. She has a special attribute—she's a Chastitant, which means, one, she's a virgin—"

"Wow," Ruth remarked, impressed.

"—and, two, she possesses a state of corrupted perfection. Her desire to be Godly nullifies her capacity for evil."

Ruth sighed. "I'm not following you, as always."

"Don't worry about it." The priest's voice sounded aggravated. "For five thousand years, Lucifer has dedicated his existence toward one goal, and that is to achieve some sort of passage from the Living World to Hell, and vice versa, and he's succeeded in a number of ways—incarnation, subcarnation, spatial transposition, interstitial egression—but none of these methods effect a *permanent* exchange . . . until now. His Warlocks and Bio-Wizards have devised a technique known as Involuntary Redeposition. It involves intricate occultized oblations here and on Earth."

"Oblations?"

"Sacrifices. In other words. Lucifer wants to bring Venetia into Hell, and it's Boniface's job to do it for him."

"What's Lucifer want with Venetia?" A notion finally sparked in Ruth's head. "He wants to pop her cherry?"

Alexander groaned. "No, Ruth. He wants to bring her here by sending six defiled angels there first. One second later, over twenty years will have passed. Remember what I told you about time in Hell?"

Ruth rolled her eyes. "How could I forget *that* confusing shit?"

"In a little while, Boniface will initiate an Involuntary Redeposition in his courtyard, which will transport six insane angles to Earth. One second later, acolytes of the Devil on Earth will initiate their own Redeposition, which will transport Venetia here."

Ruth frowned. "And in that second, twenty years go by?"

"Roughly, yes."

"So then this Venetia chick goes from Earth to Hell. What then?"

"She'll be imprisoned and taken to Lucifer for Infernal Conditioning and Indoctrination. Because of her Chastitant status, Lucifer can corrupt her and turn all of her inborn Godliness into pure evil. He'll be able to use her as a weapon against all of his enemies in Hell. It would be the equivalent of giving nuclear bombs to terrorists in the Middle East. This is serious business, Ruth."

Satan can use her as a weapon? Ruth's mind ticked. "So that's it. Our job is to knock her off when she gets here, or fuck-up this Involution whatchamacallit so she *doesn't* get here."

"No," the faceless voice said. "But that's a good guess. It's our job to *make sure* she arrives here safely, at a place underground called the Lower Chancel. In it there's this slab of rock called a Pith. That's the Dolmen—or platform—on which the Angels are moved from Hell to Earth and Venetia is moved from Earth to Hell."

Ruth winced. "On a fuckin' *rock?*"

Alexander sighed. "It's a *magic* rock, Ruth, okay? A *magic* rock."

Should've fuckin' known. His sarcasm pissed her off. "Look, man. I don't know what the fuck any of this shit is you're talking about. All I *do* know is I get to get out of here in a thousand years if we pull it off. So let's just go do it, and you tell me the rest of the funky shit along the way."

Alexander's faceless voice sounded relieved. "Excellent idea. And on that note . . ."

Ruth stepped back into the umbric perimeter; Alexander was pointing the Moon-Sextant upward.

"Time to go to the fortress?" Ruth asked with some unease.

"Not quite yet. There's only one more thing to do."

Ruth sighed. "What's that?"

"Adopt a baby," the priest told her.

(II)

Even with ten live cops in the station now, it still sounded silent as a morgue. Berns had given his report to a state deputy chief named Moxey, who seemed young for the high rank and brawny as a fullback. "Six dead cops, but only five of them had their service pieces in their proximity."

"Which means Dougie Jones lifted one of them," Berns lamented.

"This isn't looking too good for you, Captain." The snide deputy chief looked back blank-faced. "This might be the worst police massacre in East Coast history."

"Tell me about it." Berns leaned against the booking desk as the six dead officers were taken out on stretchers. "I figured Jones wrong. Thought he was just a dumb fanatic punk."

"This was organized. He must've had an accomplice waiting around the station, which is damn near impossible."

"Not damn near. It *is* impossible," Berns insisted. "There's no way Jones could've contacted an accessory to let them know he'd been busted."

Moxey snorted. "Captain, somebody shot six veteran cops in the head. There's no way Jones could've pulled that off himself, even if he'd had a piece hidden on him." A glare. "You frisked him, didn't you?"

I ought to punch this asshole in the face, then quit. Fuck it. "He was frisked five or six times. He wasn't hiding a piece." Berns struggled not to shout.

"Got the playback loaded up, sir," a tech guy said from the security office. They walked back to the small room full of TV screens.

"Here comes the moment of truth, Captain," Moxey sniped to Berns then, to the technician, "Roll 'em."

He was playing back the surveillance tapes. "Screen One's the booking room, two is the hall, three's the jail anteroom," the tech said, and pushed a button. Berns watched the grainy screens and saw two cops taking a handcuffed Dougie past the front desk, where the booking sergeant sat. The sergeant smirked. They passed the property room, where another cop looked up from his desk, moved down the hall on the second screen past a third cop, then passed three more police waiting in the jailway on the third screen.

"Nun killer, huh?" one cop remarked. The cell door swung open. "Takes a tough man to kill a *nun*."

"You pigs can kiss my ass," Dougie said, smirking. "Come on, uncuff me." Then another cop shoved him.

"Shut up, punk. Big bad Satanist. What's the matter, your mommy lock you in a closet when you were little?" a cop said, then shoved Dougie again.

"Hey, that's assault! I got my rights!" Jones complained. All five cops chuckled.

Now the biggest cop unlocked Dougie's cuffs and prepared to put him in the cell. "You got anything to say, shithead?"

Dougie turned, grinning, before the cell door could be closed. "The only thing I've got to say to you . . . is this: *Stekk ceffaen mzeluum eoziforus . . .* "

Berns felt a knot in his gut. The screen jiggled a little; the camera was looking down from a high corner, and he could see the backs of all three police in the hall. They all just stood there, as if looking at Dougie.

One at a time, each cop calmly withdrew his service revolver, put it to his own head, and—

Berns flinched, gritting his teeth. Moxey rubbed his eyes. The three shots sounded unreal over the reproduction, and the muzzle flashes momentarily whited-out the screen. Two more shots were heard from the hall and property room.

Berns' eyes darted to the first screen. The booking sergeant looked drugged. Then he put his gun to his head and squeezed the trigger.

Dougie walked out to the booking room. He seemed to fiddle with something on the desk, then took the sergeant's gun. Was he whistling a tune? Lastly, he winked up at the camera and left the building.

"Holy mother of God," Moxey muttered. That accusatory edge to his voice was gone.

"There's our accomplice," Berns said, still in disbelief.

"*No* accomplice. Multiple suicide."

Moxey's lower lip trembled. "Captain Berns. How do you account for what we just saw?"

"Well, if I didn't know better, I'd say that Dougie Jones, a self-proclaimed Satanist, just initiated some kind of occult spell that made six of my cops blow their own heads off."

"That's ridiculous, Captain—"

"I know, sir. So how do *you* account for it?"

Moxey stared. "I-I-I . . . I can't."

Don't think about it, don't think about it, Berns reinforced over and over. *It's impossible, so don't try to figure it out.* He didn't believe in the occult; he only believed that other people did. Delusional people. Crazy people.

Instead, he stuck to objective tasks. He put out an immediate APB for Douglas B. Jones, and also sent his picture to every newspaper and television station in the region. Now he sat in his makeshift office at the substation, which had been restaffed by more county cops from Manchester. The bodies were all gone now, and the evidence section was finishing up.

Still, the atmosphere of death clung to the air. "I'm going out for coffee—be right back," he said, and walked out.

Four girls in bikinis traipsed down the boardwalk, but Berns didn't notice. An old man in a stained raincoat and rotten sneakers shuffled by, searching garbage cans. A dirty hand stuck out.

"God spake that charity will be rewarded in Heaven," the wizened voice begged.

Berns, oblivious, shrugged and gave him five bucks.

"May the Lord keep you and bless you," the old man creaked, and shuffled away.

He sure as shit didn't bless me today.

His cell phone ringing in his pocket gave him a jolt. UN-KNOWN NUMBER, the screen read. Berns answered it anyway. "Berns here."

"Hey, Captain . . ." The voice sounded as wiry as the description of the caller. "How'd you like my work back at your rinky-dink station?"

Berns suddenly felt melted to the bench he occupied. "Where are you, Dougie?"

"You'll find out but by then I'll be long gone." Then a laugh.

Berns' throat turned as dry as the sidewalk. "How'd you do it? I saw the security tapes." In the background he heard motor noise. *Bus station? Airport?* he wondered.

"You know how I did it, Captain." Dougie sounded as cocky as Freddie Johnson.

Berns stood and snapped, "What? The Involution, Eosphorus? Some Satanic shit like that!" He yelled, "Level with me!"

"You did a pretty good job." Dougie cracked a laugh. "But not good enough. That's why I'm moving on, taking our business somewhere else."

Passersby gaped as Berns stood red-faced, blaring into the phone: "*How'd you do it?* What? Don't say it was some Satanic spell, Dougie! Don't say it was some voodoo fucking bullshit!"

A reserved titter. "It was a Self-Annihilation Hex, Captain—"

"*Bullshit!*"

"But don't worry. I can only do one. I'm just an Underling. Freddie was the Myrmidon. When he martyred himself for Iblis and the Exalted Duke Boniface, some of his wisdom came over to me. It's a piece of work, Captain . . . when you're a believer. But the Hex was nothing. Know what else I inherited? The Power of Unholy Decryption. Now I can read the Intercessions myself."

"Don't give me that fucking occult bullshit, Dougie!" Berns screamed.

"And I have the copy, since that night we burgled Freddie's room at the Wharfside on Fifth—"

Berns' eyes shot wide. "Yeah, Dougie, and I have the original! Sue Maitland said they were instructions! Instructions for what? More nun murders? More *sacrifices?*"

"We call them Involutionary Oblations, Captain."

"And what language is it written in? Some gobbledygook Satan language you made up with your little devil club?"

Another titter. "Oh, you want to know so you can have it translated, huh? Well, you know what, Captain? Today's your lucky day. The Intercessions are written in Zraetic."

"What?"

Dougie roared laughter. "And don't hold your breath trying to find someone who knows it. I gotta split, Captain. I just jacked me a car off a pretty hot babe, had some fun with her, too—after I blew her head off with the gun I pinched from one of your guys—"

"Don't you hang up, Dougie!"

"You wanna know why you'll never catch me, Captain? 'Cos you don't believe in *anything*—"

"Don't hang up!"

"Hail Boniface—"

"Dougie!" Berns screamed.

"Praise be to Lucifer—"

Then Dougie hung up.

(III)

"Praise be to God," Dan said with a great grin after Venetia told him what had happened at the convenience store.

"Amen," Mrs. Newlwyn agreed. "The Lord, indeed, watches over His flock."

The three of them said a short prayer of thanks in the atrium. But Venetia was still shaking.

"I just can't believe it," she said. "And Captain Berns thinks the case is over now." Through the high, narrow windows, the sunset approached. *I just came very close to never seeing one again . . .* "I can't wait to tell Father Driscoll."

"Where is he?"

"I haven't seen him all day," Dan said. "But I know he said he had to go to the diocese."

"Well, he must be back—his car's out front."

Dan nodded. "He's around someplace. This morning he told me to set up the buffer to make sure it's working. For some reason it's my duty alone to buff the entire atrium floor tomorrow. But Driscoll never told me where the buffer was."

"I'll—I'll show you," John offered, crossing the atrium with some paint buckets. "It's upstairs in storage."

"Thanks." Then Dan caught Venetia's eye. "I'm going into town later tonight, if you want to come along."

That's his way of inviting me to that awful bar again, she realized. *He just doesn't want to say it in front of Mrs. Newlwyn.* "I'll pass tonight, Dan."

"Whatever. See you all later," Dan said to everyone, and followed John.

Mrs. Newlwyn seemed puzzled. "It seems that Father Driscoll isn't the only one who's made himself scarce."

"What's that, Mrs. Newlwyn?"

"I haven't seen Betta, either. She's been acting rather secretive lately."

Venetia held her tongue. *She's probably taking a nap 'cos she doesn't get much sleep at night. Ask John about that.* "I'm going to look for Father Driscoll. If I see Betta, I'll tell her you want her."

"Thank you, dear." The tall woman made for the kitchen, leaving Venetia in the darkening atrium. She wandered, checking the downstairs offices. *What do I tell Mom about this Dougie Jones business?* She dreaded the question.

Fatigue caught up quickly. Part of her wanted to take a nap; the terrifying ordeal at the store had sapped her. But still she felt impelled to look around. Every office she checked was musty and unoccupied. As she continued, she contemplated her strange encounter with the prior-turned-bum Father Whitewood. *Wish I hadn't lost that note,* she thought. But he was just a nutty old man. *The murders last spring must've pushed him over the edge, poor man.*

As she followed the wall to the next office, she noticed a book on the shelves that wasn't flush with the others. Instinct made her pull it out. *The Catholic Recipe Book!* was the title. *Meals for Godly Living!*

What could be more boring? she wondered. *Mrs. Newlwyn's probably been looking at it. . . .* Then her heart leapt when she withdrew a slip of paper from inside.

This is definitely no recipe.

Another note in Tessorio's hand. *A word list?*

The heretical priest had written:

*Sacrifant: a hellbound Human whose blood is let for
    specific—often transpositional—rites.*

*Myrmidon: an earthbound Believer who follows infernal
    instructions, often via automatic writing or channel-
    ing.*

*Chastitant: an "unspoiled" crossbreed whose purity
    overrides infernal instinct. Typically one of six. May
    be female or male.*

*Morte-Cisterna: a font, carafe, or other closed container
    in which Sacrifant blood is stored for precursory de-
    composition.*

Venetia put the yellowed sheet back, knowing by whom
it had been touched so long ago. It repulsed her like a
wrapper of something rotten. *More of Tessorio's madness*,
she thought, *which eventually touched poles with the same
madness forty years later.*

Were Freddie, Sue, and Dougie really new members of
an occult sect that Tessorio was once a part of?

The odds seemed astronomical but then she couldn't
deny the Eosphorus link.

And Driscoll hadn't been exaggerating when he'd told
her of Tessorio's fondness for hiding arcane notes amid
the atrium's thousands of books. Two shelves down she
found another one, entitled *Catholic Conspiracy & the Vietnam War.* The title was nonsensical but inside was an
older, more yellowed sheet of paper. It read: *The blood must
be voided through the throat.*

Venetia dropped the sheet, mortified. *There's another
link if ever there was one.* . . . The two women murdered last
March had had their throats cut. *By Freddie, Dougie, and
Sue*, she reminded herself. *More than four decades after Tessorio wrote this.*

The atrium windows darkened. She thought again of
her last spell or nightmare, or whatever. *You must find the
Pith! You must find the bones!* the manic voice had
shrieked. *Bones?* she wondered. And what on earth was a
Pith? Hadn't Whitewood's note also mentioned a *Pith?*

Yes. *Take heed not to be sacrificed by mistake*, the priest-turned-bum had scrawled. *Only you can rightly enter the Pith.*

Venetia shook her head. The entire event had been so bizarre. These spells; these voices that could only be the product of nightmare . . .

Nevertheless . . .

She stuck her head in Father Driscoll's office again but there was no sign of him. The portable AC unit hummed. She walked straight to a bookshelf and found a big dictionary and flipped to the Ps.

pith *n.* **1.** *Botany.* The soft, spongelike substance at the center of plant stems.

"That can't be it. Plants?" she muttered. But there was a second definition.

2. The central point or core of a crucial thing or event.

A pith, she reflected. *A center point.* The definition left her more confused. The central point of what?

The prior house itself?

The notion made her stomach hitch, but then she noticed another door she'd previously presumed was a closet.

It stood open now, yet didn't lead to a closet.

Another room, an office behind the office. How curious. A smaller, book-lined office with a desk and computer. The latter observation infuriated her. *He told me I couldn't go online with my laptop because the phone lines weren't working!* She could easily see not only a phone on the desk but another phone cable going into the back of the computer.

Her thoughts ticked. She was nervous, yet excited at the same time. *What would he do if he caught me in here?*

No answer came as she began to go through the desk drawers.

I have a right to. There's too many fishy things going on.

The top drawer contained a framed picture of Father

Whitewood, whose wise, healthful likeness bore little resemblance to the man now.

Uh-oh, she thought. Beneath the picture was a cross and chain, and a pistol.

Don't overreact. If I were in charge here I might want a gun around, too. After two murders?

She blinked fatigue out of her eyes. The bottom drawer contained nothing but a single manila folder. *I really shouldn't do this,* she thought, but opened the folder anyway. The top sheet was a newspaper clipping from *L'Osservatore,* which she knew was the Vatican's daily newspaper, but—*Just my luck*—it wasn't the English version, it was Italian, a language she wasn't well-versed in. It was dated October 25, 1985.

Just shy of my birthday, Venetia noted.

She flipped the page and found another newspaper clipping, this one in English, from *The Catholic Standard.* The article began:

> *VATICAN CITY—Today, with the Holy Father's blessing, the Vatican's Office of Permits and Licenses authorized a small-scale excavation of the Basilica's Holy Sepulcher. Several plots of Christendom's earliest Popes and Saints may have to be temporarily moved while engineers check for water seepage that could damage grave liners. Among the exhumed is an ossuary thought to contain the remains of St. Ignatius of Antioch. As to how long these holy remains would be out of their original resting places, the Office remarked, "They will be reentombed with every possible promptitude."*

Venetia stood in total befuddlement. *Why would Father Driscoll keep an article like this?* It made no sense.

But then the thought kindled: *Holy remains* . . . She gulped at the coincidence.

Bones.

Only one sheet remained in the folder. Venetia picked it up—

Her head spun. Her eyes went dry from not blinking. What she stared down at in Driscoll's desk was something else penned by Tessorio, but not notes this time. It was an old drawing:

The Involution.

The discovery nearly caused her to faint. *I don't believe it.* . . . Driscoll must have known about the diagram all along, yet acted like he didn't. And if that were the case, it could only mean . . .

Driscoll's part of the cult, too? Carrying on in Tessorio's footsteps along with Freddie and these others?

The revelations only made her more light-headed. She sat down at the desk, nearly in tears. *What is going on in this place?* But wouldn't complicity explain Driscoll's peculiar absence? Venetia rubbed more fatigue out of her eyes, thinking, *I should go get Dan.*

Then her teeth clacked together, as the familiar spike of pain pierced her ears, along with the half shriek of a voice, distorted like someone screaming through a blown speaker. *"Venetia! Venetia! For the love of God, can you hear me?"*

The manic voice filled her belly with prickly sensations. She put hands to ears but could still hear the voice:

"You must find the Pith! You must bring the bones! Can you hear me!"

"Yes!" she screamed. "Stop it! You're killing me!"

It was no exaggeration. This was the loudest she'd heard the voice so far, and with trebled volume came trebled pain.

"I can see everything you're seeing, Venetia! You're in Driscoll's office, aren't you?"

"Yes!"

"And you just found a copy of the Involution in his desk—"

"Yes! My god, leave me alone!" Was the flayed voice expanding the pressure in her brain? Would it split her skull open?

"It's not just a drawing of the Involution! It's the original guide Tessorio used while in contact with automatic-writers in Hell!"

Venetia began to convulse.

"Turn it over! Venetia! Turn the drawing over!"

If she appeased the voice, would the pain abate? Her hands blindly fumbled for the folder, found the last sheet, and flipped it over.

Through the agony-driven vertigo, she could see a different version of the Involution, this one much crisper, all straight lines and perfect angles, in blue ink. She noticed dimensions jotted down along each of the rectangle's four lines, and in the middle, where the spiral was, Tessorio had written the words *Atrium Floor.*

"It's not a drawing, Venetia! It's a blueprint! Tessorio built the prior house to the same specifications as Boniface's court-yard , and Boniface's courtyard is a Power Dolmen!"

Venetia fell out of the chair. *I've got to wake myself up, otherwise the voice'll kill me. . . .* She crawled for another door in the corner which stood half-open; she could see a light, a mirror, and a sink. A bathroom.

She could feel separate blood vessels in her brain beat with the voice's exclamation: *"It's going to be very soon, so be ready, and don't be afraid!"*

At the sink, she splashed water in her face; that and the final lance of pain jolted her to full wakefulness. *I'm going to have to go to a shrink or a hospital or* something!

She should probably call her mother, who'd insist on the same thing. The awful vibrations in her belly faded away in the next moments. For now, at least, she'd have to find Dan. . . .

She stopped when she turned around. On the floor near the bathroom, she noticed the most unlikely of objects: a wide-mouthed funnel.

"What on earth is that doing here?" she mumbled.

She leaned over, picked it up, then—

Her stomach nearly heaved. The funnel clattered to the floor.

My God, is that—

The funnel's mouth was glazed with something wet . . . and red.

She refused to let herself believe it was blood. That would be crazy. . . .

Next, she found herself in dead silence, staring at the closed shower curtain. *What am I thinking?* she thought. Her mind wanted to leave but instead she was seized by a modern yet very primal human instinct.

There's nothing behind there. . . .

When Venetia pulled back the curtain, she screamed, reeling backward, as—

Thwack!

An unseen blow struck her in the head from behind. The last thing her eyes registered before she blacked out was this: a very pale Father Driscoll lying crumpled in the tub, one side of his throat cut so deep he was half-decapitated.

Chapter Eighteen

(I)

"Good God, I hope she heard me that time," Alexander said, having just removed the Vox Untervelt from his lips. Scarlet buildings shimmered around them; in the distance, the blood brick foundries fumed smoke that somehow sparkled. Ruth and Alexander walked down a busy Demon-clogged street within the Hand of Glory's umbra, unseen by all.

"The virgin chick. She answered, didn't she?" Ruth asked. She was watching Maggot-Moths fly circles about some flowers with eyeballs for stamens.

"Yes, but does she believe what she's hearing?" The priest seemed to fret.

Ruth considered, *If I heard a voice that said it was from Hell, would I believe it? Not a fuckin' chance. I'd just lay off the dope for a while.* "And if she doesn't believe what you're telling her . . . what then?"

"Then we're—"

"Fucked hard and never kissed?"

Alexander nodded, frowning. "Try not to cuss, Ruth. Please?"

Fuck it. But Ruth did like the idea of walking unde-
tected; no one could see her now, not dressed in the expensive Hand-Bra and Tongue-Skirt, and wearing the
Putridox face that once belonged to Voluptua. The priest
stopped at a busy corner. "Well, here's Carnivorous
Boulevard and Apraxia Street, and there"—his Annelok
arm pointed—"is the adoption agency."

EVIL BABY ADOPTION SERVICES, read the sign.

"Can't say I dig the name," Ruth remarked, "but I think
it's pretty cool that childless couples in Hell can adopt a
baby to care for and love."

"Ruth, Ruth, Ruth. You don't understand anything yet,
do you?" Alexander complained. "People here don't
adopt babies to *raise* like they do in the Living World."

"Then what do they adopt them for?"

"To sacrifice to Satan. What did you think?" He passed
her the Hand of Glory. "Hold this, I'll be right back."

Ruth took the appalling hand with flame-tipped fingers.
"So what do *we* need a baby for?" she asked, distressed.

Alexander didn't answer; he simply stepped out of the
umbra and entered the agency.

As if shit couldn't be weird enough, Ruth thought. She
stood tapping her bone-sandaled foot, and a few minutes
later Alexander returned. Reentering the umbra, he held
in his arms a pudgy little baby with a big smile and big
wide eyes. He also had little horns, fangs like a wood-
chuck, and green and black-spotted skin, but that hardly
mattered.

"He's so cute," Ruth rejoiced, then paused. "I'm mean . . .
even though he's a *Demon* baby."

"Goo-goo, gaa-gaa," the baby blathered and burped.
Little pudgy hands reached up for Alexander.

"It's not as cute as you think," the priest said.

Next, the infant reached for one of Ruth's sizable
breasts. "I guess it's a *boy* baby, too, huh? And what do we
need a baby for anyway?" Ruth chuckled. "It's not like
we're gonna sacrifice it, right?"

Alexander gave her a grim look . . . as he pulled out his
knife.

"Bullshit, man!" she yelled. "I don't care if it *is* a Demon—it's still a baby, for fuck's sake!"

"Ruth, you don't understand, and we don't have time to bicker."

Ruth tried to yank the baby away. "No way, man! I don't care if I have to stay here for fucking-ever! Killing babies is where I draw the line."

Alexander's Annelok arm encircled Ruth's throat. "Give it back. Our mission will fail unless you let me do what I have to do," he said very slowly, and then the Annelok arm squeezed.

"Fuck you!" Ruth choked. Her eyes bugged. "You're as evil as everything else here!" Now she grabbed for the priest's knife, but as the pressure at her throat doubled, she collapsed to half consciousness.

She could only see through the dimmest vision as Alexander put the Demonic infant on the ground and—

"You evil motherfucker!" Ruth hacked.

—slit the baby's belly open. Astonishingly, the infant didn't shriek but instead just kept making cutesy baby noises.

The priest pulled something the size and shape of a soda can out of the baby's stomach. Then he helped Ruth up.

"Sorry I had to do that, Ruth, but you didn't let me explain."

"You just gutted a kid, you piece of shit!"

"It's not a kid. It only *looks* like a kid," he affirmed, and actually held her head and made her look.

"Goo-goo . . . gah!" the infant giggled and simultaneously deflated.

"What the *fuck* is happening?" Ruth asked.

No blood came out of the incised child, and instead of internal organs leaking from the knife slash, all Ruth saw was a mass of pulp that looked like uncooked ground pork.

"It's not a real baby, Ruth. It's a manufactured *thing* called a Hex-Clone, a product of occult genetic engineering. It's just a bag of cursed meat covered with Hexegenically engineered skin."

"A dummy baby?"

"Exactly. It's Hexed to sound and act like a baby, and it was planted in the adoption agency by more confederates of my intelligence source. And they hid *this* inside the Clone's belly." He wiped off the cylindrical object.

"Looks like some kind of lantern," she noted as she examined the implement's wire frame surrounding a glass jar. "Is that smoke inside?"

"Yes, but it's inert," Alexander explained. Beneath him, the Hex-Clone had deflated to a near-empty sack of skin, but the skull-less face still smiled. "Daa-daa!" it gurgled.

The priest frowned. "It's called a Smoke-Light," he continued, and looked up through the Moon-Sextant again.

"Smoke-Light? What's it for?"

"I'll tell you along the way—the gauge reads seven-point-six."

Ruth swallowed.

"We have to go now, Ruth," Alexander said, and led her down the shimmering block toward the entry road to the Fortress Boniface.

(II)

Venetia regained consciousness in moon-spattered darkness. When she recalled her discovery in Father Driscoll's bathtub, her muscles seized up . . . and then she realized that she'd been gagged and hog-tied. *I'm in the woods,* she eventually realized. The blow to her skull left her head throbbing so intensely that each throb threatened to push her back into unconsciousness.

Whoever murdered Father Driscoll . . . did this to me.

But who did it, and why?

Venetia's stomach tightened. *Oh, my God—not Dan. It couldn't be Dan.*

But confusion and terror made it too hard to calculate. *Have to get myself untied.* The woods she lay in seemed familiar, and when her eyes acclimated, she knew exactly where she was; she could see moonlight reflecting off the

pond. *This is where Betta meets John every night.* She
squinted further, then, and could see them. . . .

Just like the other times. They made frenetic love in the
leaves beside the pond. John was on top of Betta, thrusting.

Then the name clacked in her head—

John.

Who else could've dragged her out here but him? *Another accomplice in Freddie's cult,* she thought, *and a clever
cover. Pretending to be someone nearly retarded, a churchgoing "yard boy," always happy to do volunteer work . . .*

But did that mean Betta was in on it, too?

She seemed to be enjoying John's ministrations very
much.

Most of Venetia's sentience remained in chaos. The
cricket trills made it even harder to think through the
pain, and it occurred to her now that she felt dehydrated.
She struggled to remember. She thought it had been about
eight PM when she was knocked out.

How many hours had she been lying out here in the
woods?

She tried to sort facts: *John killed Driscoll—obviously in
league with the current members of the cult Tessorio formed
forty years ago, and he's obviously the one who knocked me out
and dragged me here. But—*

Something shriveled inside of her.

What's he going to do next? Who's he going to sacrifice *next?*

It was a concept as old as human civilization itself. The
blood of the "pure" spilled as an offering to the gods, and
more specifically—Satanists sacrificed *virgins.*

The two women murdered last spring had been chaste
and, more than likely, Father Driscoll was too. . . .

The four corners of the Involution gave Venetia the
grim suspicion that a fourth murder was almost certainly
on John's to-do list.

Me, Venetia thought.

"Aw, baby, I love you so much," John whispered in a
hot gasp. His hips bucked at the peak of his climax, after
which he collapsed on Betta. Betta, in turn, embraced him.

All the while, Venetia regained more of her senses.

They're going to kill me if I don't get loose on my own. More thinking: *There's a gun in Father Driscoll's drawer—if only I could get it . . .* And the car out front, the black Mercedes: *Are the keys on Father Driscoll's dead body?*

But now—

Venetia thought she heard something, but not from near the pond where John and Betta had had their fun.

The sound seemed to be behind her.

A creaking sound. Like an antique chair creaking, or the timber on an old boat.

Hog-tied, it was nearly impossible to flip over and see the source of the noise. But if she *did* manage to flip over . . . John and Betta might hear her struggles.

Either way, her predicament was bleak.

John pulled his pants back up, while Betta remained nude on the ground. As previously, Venetia could only see them as silhouettes, and now John was helping Betta get back up and put her blouse on.

"Come on, honey," he continued to whisper. "I have a surprise for you."

Betta's silhouette paused, and now she seemed giddy with anticipation.

"This way, by the trees . . ."

The silhouettes moved closer—

They're coming here! Venetia thought.

Then John switched on a flashlight. He maintained the lowest whisper. "Here's the first part of your surprise, honey—"

The light snapped right down into Venetia's face.

Betta made a noise as best she could: something like a gasp.

"That's Venetia. I tied her up and brought her out here . . . because she's *very important.*" A chuckle. "Unlike you."

In the fringes of light, Venetia could see a look of complete shock on Betta's face.

"But here's the *real* surprise." John's voice grew louder. "I did it just for you, Betta. . . ."

Next, the flashlight snapped upward, behind where Venetia lay.

Betta's mouth fell open in a silent scream.

Crack!

John hit Betta in the head with the flashlight. She collapsed right in front of Venetia.

John reached behind the nearest tree and produced a long length of rope with a noose at the end. It had obviously been preprepared. He calmly put the noose around Betta's neck, then began to yank on another length of rope. Each yank hoisted Betta a few more feet upward, until her feet dangled a foot above the ground. The body hitched for a few moments, then hung still.

Venetia tried to scream through her gag.

"That's it for her." The light was back in Venetia's face. Now the young man spoke at normal volume. "Guess you've got some questions, huh, cutie?" and then suddenly her gag was cut off.

"John, you evil bastard!" Venetia shrieked.

The figure behind the flashlight stalled. "John?" and then he cracked a laugh. "Fuck!"

Now that he spoke at normal volume, Venetia realized her error. It was a voice she'd heard before . . . but not John's.

Oh, God—it can't be . . .

"So you thought I was that dimwit geek who cuts the grass?" The flashlight turned up to the face. "Shit, baby, you're dumber than Betta."

It was Dougie Jones.

He grinned down, the light dicing his face with jet-black wedges.

"You're in jail!" Venetia shrieked. "I saw you arrested!"

"Yeah, and then I broke out." The pumpkin grin sharpened. "All by the grace of my god. You know him."

Venetia's eyes felt lidless.

"Eosphorus. Ash-Shaytan. Lux Ferre. Iblis. Lucifer, my Morning Star."

Venetia's mind whirred like a mouse on a wheel. "If Betta was in your cult, too, why did you kill her?"

He sniggered at the hanging corpse. "That mute bitch was just some squeeze on the side—she was never one of

us. I had her completely duped. Told her I worked at a
store in town and was going to community college. She
fell in love with me *real* fast."

"You led her on for . . . *what?* Just *sex?*"

"No, no, don't be stupid. For access to the prior house.
After the spring murders, they put serious locks on the
place. I needed her key—"

"So you discreetly copied hers," Venetia realized, "after
you became involved."

"Sure. Once a chick gets mushy for a guy, they're a
cinch to manipulate. Oh, sorry, you haven't seen the rest
of my work." Then he flipped her over and shined his
light upward.

Venetia's scream wheeled out into the woods.

Two more bodies hung by their necks, both naked, their
white skin nearly glowing in the moonlight.

Mrs. Newlwyn and John.

"More sacrificing?" Venetia dared ask.

"Nope. These are different—we call them precursory
oblations. Killing the innocent for kicks, you know? It
keeps the psychic energy around the house nice and dark.
We killed a lot of people in these woods—me, Freddie,
and Sue. Tortured 'em, burned 'em, even buried some
alive. Hitchhikers, bums, hookers." Dougie leaned over
and pinched Venetia's cheek. "It keeps the air *rich*—just
the way Boniface wants it. We do as he bids."

"Pope Boniface died over a thousand years ago."

Dougie shot her a surprised look. "You're a Christian,
for fuck's sake. Nobody ever really *dies*. Exalted Duke
Boniface is alive and well."

Venetia was working her wrists behind her back, pray-
ing they would come undone. *Keep him talking. Bide more
time.* "Tell me about the Involution, Dougie. I know you're
going to kill me, so go ahead and say it. You need four
sacrifices, right? One for each corner of the Involution?"

"Last spring we got the first two," he said. "The nun
and the old biddy. And you saw the third—"

"Father Driscoll," she croaked.

"Right. Another virgin. The fucker was celibate his

whole life, which was just what we needed. Chastity equals purity, and purity corrupted equals power to Lucifer."

Driscoll was the third, and I'm the fourth. She continued to twist her wrists within the lash. . . . "Why did you drag me out here? Why not just cut my throat and drain my blood in the prior house like you did the others?"

Dougie shook his head. "You don't know anything." Then he cut the bonds around her ankles and wrists and lifted her to her feet. "The actual sacrifices are much more critical than these precursory jobs."

Venetia couldn't believe he'd untied her . . . until he stuck a pistol in her ribs.

"So what are you waiting for?" She stumbled as he shoved her toward the clearing's exit.

He stalked along through the brambles, one hand girded about her arm. "Since you're not going to be around that much longer, I guess I can tell you." Dougie paused. "The blood needs to rot—"

"What?" Venetia almost gaped.

"Virgin blood alone isn't good enough. It has to be soured. It has to be corrupted before it's poured at the four font-points—"

Font-points, Venetia thought. *Each corner of the diagram . . . or each corner of the house.* "Font-points . . ."

"Any container will do," Dougie explained. "But the blood needs to rot for at least a day before the Involution can be charged, and it's not quite time yet."

Now he'd taken her out of the clearing and across the moonlit backyard, toward the house.

The blood has to rot for at least a day? "What time is it now?"

"A little past midnight."

"You knocked me out at about eight, right? So how many people have you killed in the four hours since then?"

Dougie laughed and squeezed Venetia's buttocks. "Hate to tell you this, baby. It wasn't four hours ago I jacked you out. It was eight PM *last night.*"

I've been unconscious all that time? It didn't seem so, but then it made more sense when she remembered what he'd said about the blood. "So Father's Driscoll's blood has had over a day to 'spoil,' huh?"

"That's right. We hid the Morte-Cisternas back in the woods—"

"Morte-*what?*" she interjected.

"The fonts. It's just a fancy name for whatever container we use to hold the blood. It's the blood, get it? The blood is what makes it all work. Always has, since Lucifer's Fall. Where do you think all that witchcraft and hokey folklore shit came from anyway?"

"The sacrifice of *virgins*," Venetia said. "The offering of chaste blood to Satan . . ."

"Uh-huh. It's all true, it just got all fucked-up and twisted around over the ages. There ain't no witches on broomsticks but there really *is* power in virginal blood. You just have to do it all right—" He squeezed her buttocks again. "Plus, you've got to have faith." Then he laughed some more.

He unlocked the back kitchen door with the key he'd copied from Betta's. A twinge of hope flared when Venetia remembered that Dan had gone to the bar last night. Maybe he'd gone tonight as well. . . .

Maybe he's back now . . . and Dougie doesn't know.

"Everything's ready now," Dougie said, more to himself. He seemed very satisfied. "I've brought everything inside. We just have a little time to kill is all."

Venetia wilted. Now Dougie was caressing her buttocks and thighs. "But if you rape me, I won't be a virgin anymore, Dougie."

"Oh, don't worry. *That* won't happen. But that doesn't mean I can't play with you a while. . . ."

He wedged his hand up between her legs. Venetia winced. Her blouse was torn open, her bra ripped apart at the cups. The rough hand suddenly kneading her bare breasts made her stomach quake.

"Yeah . . ."

But the molestation decreased once he got her into the atrium; at once he seemed distracted.

The huge room looked vacant now, to the extent that Venetia was taken aback. "You've been busy," she said.

"Yep. Took most of the day." Then he parted from her, looking out in awe. "It's beautiful, isn't it?"

All of the couches, chairs, and tables had been moved away to the atrium's outer edges; the large oval rugs had been rolled up and pushed aside, revealing the bare floor beneath. Even from this low vantage point, Venetia could easily make out the design.

Inlaid into the blond wood was the symbol—immense—set in much darker wood, and expertly carved.

The Involution, she thought.

Mahogany arrows pointed inward from three corners, while from the fourth—the southeast corner—sprouted the corkscrew spiral which came to an end precisely in the center of the atrium. Now that Venetia was looking at it from the left, it occurred to her just how clearly the spiral formed the number six.

"Tessorio inlaid the floor with the Involution over forty years ago," Dougie breathed, "but it still looks brand-new."

He was right. The darker wood inlays that formed the diagram's features seemed to shine beneath the old wax.

Dougie's voice resonated with awe. "Freddie would be so proud of me. . . ."

Venetia looked at him. "How could *Freddie* have gotten into this at all? Tessorio himself obviously founded the cult—"

"Right, and he built the prior house to the exact specifications as Boniface's courtyard. It was brilliant. See, Boniface's courtyard is a Power Dolmen."

The mad voice in her head had said the same thing. . . .

Dougie went on, "It's the only way to have the rites occur at the same time."

Keep him talking. "Rites? Plural?"

"Of course. When I charge the Involution, an identical rite will be underway at Fortress Boniface."

"In Hell," Venetia said, and thought, *Madness.* "But you

never answered my question. What's the link between Tessorio's cult from over thirty years ago and your cult today?"

"Freddie."

"What?"

"Freddie's mother was a junkie prostitute."

"So?"

"Freddie's father was Tessorio. Tessorio left all the instructions for Freddie after he died in the mid seventies—see, Freddie was blessed from the beginning. Eventually he brought me and Sue into the fold of Lucifer's congregation." Dougie's eyes turned bright on her. "Two Involutions—two identical Power Dolmen's—in two different worlds."

Now Venetia was seeing firsthand just how insane Tessorio had been. *The ultimate jinx—he constructed an occult temple with Church funds . . . and no one ever knew.* But as her eyes strayed along the room's long dimensions, she finally noticed. . . .

"Now I'm really confused." In the northwest and southwest corners sat two gasoline cans. "I thought this was some kind of *blood* sacrifice. You're going to *burn* the place down?"

Dougie chuckled. "Don't worry about what you don't understand," he said, and walked to the first can. "It's almost time now anyway. I told you before, the Morte-Cisternas can be anything—the name's pretty much just for show. It's the *meaning* behind it—and our *faith*—that gives it power."

The gas cans are the fonts, she realized. *The storage vessels for the blood.*

"These first two'll be *really* ripe—they've been rotting out in the woods since last spring." Then he unscrewed the top and laid the can down on its side.

The *blub-blub-blud* sound brought with it an appalling smell. What emptied from the can looked like black rice pudding. Stinking and shining, it laid in a lumpy puddle at the beginning of the first corner arrow.

"That's the blood from the nun—whew! Stinks, doesn't

it?" Then Dougie repeated the procedure with the southeast can, whose contents stunk just as badly. "And this is the old prune—but I'll tell ya, she went down kicking and screaming. And she had a Jersey accent, too, ya know? Between her prune-face and that accent, no wonder she never got laid."

Venetia could only stare.

Dougie walked outward toward the far corner. "If you try to run"—he showed her the pistol again—"I'll kneecap you. So don't be stupid."

The light was dimmer at this farther end of the atrium. Next to the corner pillar, she noticed another can. Dougie dumped it.

Blub-blub-blub . . .

"And that's Father Driscoll's blood," Venetia said.

"Yep. It's not as dark 'cos it's only been sitting out a day." He rubbed a finger in the foul puddle. "But it's spoiled enough. . . ." And then he grinned up at her.

It was in the southeast corner from which the great spiral sprouted. *That's the spot where* my *blood will be poured,* Venetia thought.

In the moment his back was turned, Venetia darted her eyes around. *There must be* something *down here I can use for a weapon!* The walkways beneath the overhead stairhall were all clogged with furniture now. If only there was a knife . . .

The kitchen's too far away, she reasoned. *He'd catch me before I got there.* When she glanced out the window, though, she didn't see the Mercedes, and this rekindled her hope that Dan was out somewhere—the bar, maybe. *And maybe he'll be coming back any minute. . . .*

But then—

It lay in plain view right on the windowsill between two heaps of furniture: one of the Red Devil razor-knives they'd been using to scrape excess paint off the glass.

Got to get over there . . .

She took a few slow sidesteps so as not to seem overt, but stopped when Dougie looked back over.

That's when then another question snagged her interest.

"So this is all happening *tonight?*" she asked.

"Yeah," he said, standing now at the southeast corner.

"But you said the blood had to spoil for at least a day."

"It has," Dougie said. Then he blinked and started laughing. "Oh, man, that's hilarious. You think *you're* the fourth sacrifant!" He shook his head. "How stupid can you get?"

He reached behind the pillar and produced something. Venetia squinted but couldn't make it out.

"What's . . . that?" she asked.

Dougie's laughter echoed through the atrium when he tossed the object across the long floor. It bounced, thudding, several times, and then wobbled to a stop just a few feet from where she stood.

Venetia didn't even scream this time; she just stared in the numbest dread . . . at Dan's severed head.

"You're crazy," she uttered. "You're a psychopath."

"Hey, sticks and stones . . ." Now he dragged out a fourth gas can, which had clearly been sitting in the sun all day along with Driscoll's. "Two virgin men in the same house. Shit, I couldn't believe it. You fuckin' Catholics really take shit serious." Then he unscrewed the cap and began to dump the blood.

(III)

He dumped the blood into the fourth corner of the courtyard by sliding the stone lid off the font and tipping it over. Then the Sergeant at Arms stepped back, looked up, and bowed to Boniface.

The Exalted Duke, peering down from the high wall, nodded back from behind his face of salt.

Within the smoking court, all Conscripts, Ushers, and Golems stood in the stillest silence. Sentinels on the high ramparts, too, watched in awe as the Hex-Flux about the Fortress amplified. The energy crackled so thickly it could almost be *seen.*

"The fourth and final Morte-Cisterna has been spilled, my most terrible prince," uttered Willirmoz.

Boniface watched through his eye slits, his gnawed face twitching with nervousness. At each corner of the courtyard, the four pools of sullied blood shined like hot tar.

"But nothing's happening," the Duke croaked.

Willirmoz smiled with burned lips. "Patience . . ."

Were the blood bricks of the Fortress walls glowing more deeply now? The richness of horror could be smelled in the air. Boniface felt the prickling waves course up his corrupted skin beneath his mantle and cloak.

"When must we descend to the Lower Chancel, wizard?"

"When the blood begins to move, my most sickening lord."

Boniface continued to look down. He was scared to the core of his demented soul . . . but he knew he must not show it.

"The blood isn't moving, wizard," Boniface's voice rattled. "If you have failed me, the scribes of Hell will be writing about your tortures for the next ten thousand years, so help me."

But Willirmoz' charred eyes beamed. "In that event, I would deserve it and worse, my lord, but . . . behold . . ."

Willirmoz pointed down to the southeast corner of the yard.

The pool of blood began to shudder, then . . .

Glory to Lucifer . . .

It began to *move.*

The finest crimson mist began to rise from the puddle's irregular surface, while the puddle itself shifted, as if struggling, and inched itself toward the end of the great spiral trough of hand-steamed Druid Oak. From there, the blood came alive, and began to slowly follow the trough's spiriferous contour.

Struck dumb, Boniface watched. The blood pools in the other three corners began to mist and shudder as well, and began to crawl in straight lines toward the Involution's center.

"You are the greatest Lithomancer to ever walk the Mephistopolis," the Exalted Duke gasped.

Willirmoz bowed. "As the cursed blood travels its

course, my horrendous lord, the more enriched the Pith will grow. We should adjourn to the Lower Chancel posthaste."

Boniface was practically vibrating with joy. "For this, my whore must be by my side to witness my greatness. Summon her at once."

Willirmoz' remarked, "The Barbican Guards have just now begun to admit her."

"Excellent. Order her to join us in the Lower Chancel."

"It will be done, great putrescent prince." The High Priest led Boniface toward the stone steps at which Pasiphae—the Night-Mother and Guide of the Labyrinth—waited to escort them deep into the charnel warrens below.

(IV)

The thirty-foot-tall fortress walls and the iron portcullis—topped by a row of punctured skulls—rose as gears clattered and chains chimed. A line of leech-skinned Ushers guarded one side of the great stone entry, while a line of Golems guarded the other side. Vile faces glared at Ruth.

"Man, this is so fucked-up," she whispered beneath the Putridox face.

"Go, Ruth!" Alexander whispered back from his sphere of invisibility. "Don't just stand there! They'll think something's wrong."

Something is wrong. Way wrong, Ruth thought as she stepped through the entry. The monstrous severed face pulled over her own sucked down hot against her skin. Ruth could tell that aspects of the face were still alive.

"Act like you own the place," the priest said from behind her.

She tried to seem arrogant as she sashayed down the walk. The Ushers and Golems bowed as she passed. When the portcullis slammed shut behind her, it was all she could do to not scream. A horned Conscript, in a helm fashioned from some warped Demonic skull, stood at attention and said, "Oh, great Voluptua, Chief Soubrette of

our master Boniface—proceed at once to the Lower
Chancel."

Ruth nodded briskly and walked on.

A few steps later, Alexander rejoiced, "We're in!"

"Yeah, but what now?"

"Just walk all the way around the courtyard. In the
northwest corner, you'll see a stone arch. There'll be a
woman waiting for you—er, well, not really a woman."

Ruth faltered, trying to appear elegant as she walked in
the Bone-Sandals. "If she's not really a woman, then what
the fuck *is* she?"

"A Primordess—a living subjectivity, Ruth—an unholy
notion made flesh. Her name is Pasiphae, and her body is
composed of primordial ooze—the black ichor of the
earth."

"Oh, I can't wait to meet her," Ruth grumbled, turning
into a neon scarlet courtyard that seemed hazy with mist.

"Remember the Greek fable of Theseus and the Mino-
taur?"

Ruth frowned. "No."

Alexander sputtered behind his umbrella of invisibility.
"Good God, Ruth. Didn't you pay attention to *anything* in
school?"

Ruth didn't bother answering.

"Pasiphae is the Guide of the Labyrinth. Only she
knows her way through the city's subterranean byways.
That's how the location of the Lower Chancel remains a
secret, so it can't be infiltrated. Don't screw up."

"I'm glad you have such fuckin' confidence in me."
Ruth felt the urge to complain further, but now her eyes
were riveted to the macabre spectacle in the courtyard.

The number of Golems, Ushers, and Conscripts standing guard must have topped a hundred. From one corner
she saw a great brown gutter shaped into a spiral that
must've encircled thirty yards, and from three other corners puddles of rank blood seemed to be lengthening
toward the center of the spiral.

"It looks like a giant version of those diagrams we've
seen all over town," she observed.

"The Involution. This is it. It might be the most effective transpositionary Power Dolmen in the history of occult science. Once the blood from each corner reaches the center of the spiral, a kind of doorway opens."

Ruth didn't like the sound of that. "A doorway between here—"

"And the prior house where Venetia is. But it's more like one of those *revolving* doors you see at big-city hotels. While someone goes in, someone else comes out."

The great courtyard stank of sweetness merged with rot, while the blood-bricks of the Fortress' walls seemed to hum within their mysterious neon. Ruth looked again and saw that the blood in each corner was moving slowly but resolutely toward the center, each puddle inching along the same way a snail moves.

Piles of corpses rimmed the yard.

Most disturbing of all, however, was the perfect silence that hung over the entire fortress.

Ruth forced her eyes away.

"One other thing about this Pasiphae woman . . . ," the priest spoke up.

"Yeah?"

"She's a lusty type, and she's rumored to have something going on with Voluptua on the side."

"Chicks who dig chicks," Ruth muttered. "You sure they're not from Florida?"

"I'm serious, Ruth. You're not contemplating the ramifications of my statement." The priest's bodiless voice seemed hesitant. "You might have to—you know . . . make out with her."

Ruth gagged. "Bullshit, brother! I already had to swap tongue with that pus-lady in Rot-Port! Now I've got to suck face with primal ooze?"

"*Primordial* ooze, Ruth," Alexander corrected.

"With a chick who's made from the black ick of the earth?"

"The black *ichor*, Ruth."

Ruth turned to face him . . . but of course saw nothing. "I oughta haul this monster face off and walk out of here."

"The Ushers would turn you into puree in two minutes. Now keep walking and don't make a scene. Otherwise we're both history."

Ruth fumed and continued to the next corner of the fortress. *The fucker waits till now to tell me that.* . . .

Next she thought she heard something like fabric tearing behind her. "What's that noise?"

"Nothing."

"It's not *nothing*. I just heard it. You tearing something back there?"

"Focus on your task, Ruth."

More aggravation. *He treats me like a kid.* But then she saw the stone arch, and something like a shiny shadow in the entry.

"That's her," Alexander whispered. "Act like you know her. And no talking from here on."

"But I don't know what to do!" she whispered back.

"Just follow Pasiphae—and shut up!"

She tried to steel herself. Conning people was nothing new to a grifter like Ruth. But could she con a denizen of Hell?

Pasiphae's grin seemed longing when her eyes met Ruth's. The Night-Mother's body looked like a cheerleader who'd been dipped in crude oil.

Make it good! Ruth urged herself.

She stepped right up to the blackly shining Pasiphae . . . and ran a finger adoringly down her cheek.

Pasiphae kissed her on the lips, then gently took Ruth's hand and took her down into the labyrinth.

(V)

They found the woman in some weeds behind a strip mall with a Laundromat, pizza parlor, and a seedy bar. She lay naked save for the few scraps of clothes Dougie had left; the sodium lights made her skin look yellow. Berns guessed midthirties; she had a decent body—*Why would Dougie pick a dog if he didn't have to?*—and pretty nougat brown hair. But her face . . .

She'd been shot in the head, and then her face had been further pulped by a nearby cinder block. Dougie Jones had also pulverized the fingertips with the same block.

"Bashed her face in just for kicks," Moxey, the state deputy chief, remarked.

"No, Dougie's smarter than that," Berns said. "No ID on the body, and no face or fingerprints? He wants to bide time. If we don't know who she is, we don't know the make and model of the car he jacked. A DNA probe'll take days, and she probably won't have it on file anyway. All we can do now is hope somebody reports her missing."

"And by then he'll have switched cars anyway," Moxey said, sneering, "if this guy's as smart as you think."

A squad of uniforms were around front asking proprietors and customers if they'd seen someone matching Dougie's description drive off at around the time of his phone call to Berns.

Eventually some evidence section men bagged the body and carried it off. "At least the damn phone company didn't shuck and jive about giving us the location of the phone," Moxey commented. "The turnoff to the interstate is just down the road. Jones could be in Ohio by now."

This guy's useless, Berns thought. They walked back around to the front of the stores, where more cops and detectives milled about, eerie shapes in the throbbing red and blue light. The medical examiner's van sat with its back door yawning open. "My hunch is Dougie only wants us to *think* that."

"What, that he left the state?"

"Sure."

Moxey's irate expression compressed. "There's the body." He pointed to the van. "There's the pay phone he called you from." He pointed to the phone. "And there's the exit ramp to the highway." He pointed down the road. "But you don't think he left the area? Come on, man, it's right in front of your face."

Berns sat down on a bench in front of the pizza parlor. His exhaustion made him feel hypnotized. "Freddie Johnson gave me the same jive—*swore* that his accomplices had left the state just like he did. Then I get the same bit from Sue Maitland. It's the only thing they lied about."

Moxey's collar was digging into his neck. "So you think Jones is still in town? Bullshit. I can't redirect a manhunt when all these facts are right in front of us."

Berns sighed. "Then you're making a mistake."

"I'm the one calling the shots here, Captain," Moxey snapped.

"Fine. Call them." Berns didn't want to argue. "Jones escaped on my watch, so it's *my* fuck-up. But I know these people—you don't. I talked to all of them. They acted like there was still something going on—something important to them. Dougie's still in town but he went out of his way to make us think he's not. That's what I'm seeing here."

Moxey's cheeks pinkened with suppressed irritation. "All right, we'll do it your way . . . and I'll probably wind up losing my job."

Berns laughed good-naturedly. "I'll be right behind you."

Moxey ground his teeth as he radioed in: "Central Commo, this is D.C. Moxey. Order all available units into Wammsport."

"Smart move," Berns said. The pizza smelled good but after seeing the Jane Doe's face, forget it.

Moxey glared down. "All right, Captain Berns. Any ideas where Jones might be right now? Like *exactly?*"

Berns stood up and looked out into the dim night. "Yeah, I've got an idea. . . ."

(VI)

Venetia had never seen anything so macabre in her life. The blood Dougie had dumped in the southeast corner seemed to *convulse* the instant it hit the floor, while the spoiled puddles in the other corners did the same.

Then the faintest crimson mist began to rise.

She felt it at once, a sensation—like static—prickly off her skin. Several strands of her hair rose as if levitating, and in her belly she noticed a distinct, unpleasant buzz.

Dougie's grin was exuberant. "Feel it?"

"Yes," she croaked.

"Freddie was right about everything, even the timing. The Involution is charging now, the power's building." He came forward with the pistol. "We'll have to go soon." He grinned. "But not just yet . . ."

Venetia could imagine what was next on his agenda. She stepped back into the shadows beneath the stair-hall, hoping she'd gotten herself closer to where she'd seen the razor. His hands were on her at once, spinning her around. Nauseousness rose when he bent her over the end of a couch that had been shoved aside; then he pulled her dress up and her panties down. He grabbed her ponytail and shoved down.

"I thought you needed a virgin," she choked.

"Oh, I do, but I'll be giving it to you in the back door, if you know what I mean. Your virginity won't be busted."

Oh my God . . .

She could hear him unzipping his pants, then felt the tip of the gun barrel stroke her bare buttocks. She could only hope that the excitement of anal rape would distract him enough for her to grab the razor, turn, and cut him.

"Now that's what I call a great ass."

His hands parted her buttocks . . . and she let her right hand creep to the corner of the windowsill. . . .

The razor wasn't there anymore.

She heard him expectorate, winced when she felt where it landed, but when she expected this invasion of her body to commence—

Nothing happened.

She heard a gasp.

What . . .

Venetia turned, bolted upright. Dougie stood behind her, shivering, his back arched. His hands seemed desperate, at his throat as blood gushed between his fingers.

When Dougie collapsed, she saw another figure right behind him.

Venetia froze in place.

The figure reached down, took Dougie's pistol—

Bam!

Venetia shrieked at the concussion. Dougie's shuddering ceased as half of his head fragmented.

Now the figure pointed to the atrium. . . .

Venetia followed with her gaze. The blood in the southeast corner was beginning to slowly follow the inlaid spiral, while the puddles in the other three corners were lengthening toward the center.

"The Involution is charging," a solemn voice informed her. The figure stepped into the light—Father Whitewood. "Follow me, child. It's time to go to the Lower Chancel. . . ."

"It's your destiny—a gift from God on High," he told her, taking her across the moonlit backyard. "You are truly, truly blessed."

Venetia followed, mainly because she felt compelled to, by something in her heart. She oddly felt no fear, just searing curiosity. "I thought they wanted to sacrifice me."

"No, no, child," Whitewood said. "Their success depends entirely on your staying alive . . . as does *our* success. They both hinge on the same thing."

"What?"

"Your successful entrance into the Pith. But we infiltrated their motives long ago. We thought it best to let Tessorio's sect commence with everything, and turn the tables on them without them ever knowing. A Trojan Horse. You."

"I don't understand, Father."

The old man smiled in the dim moonlight. "You don't need to. You need only have faith in the Lord God, your Protector and Redeemer."

I do, Venetia thought.

"It was Driscoll's job to re-bless the prior house after my cowardice caused me to abandon my post. The building's defenses are down since the murders. A respite home for reassigned priests was simply the cover story. It's not a prior house and never was. It's a tomb."

"A tomb for who?"

Whitewood's tired voice creaked like old timbers. "For

six angels who were debauched by Lucifer's confederates. They were raped and impregnated, and then via Satan's latest sorcerial sciences, sent here, to this house."

"Why here?"

Whitewood touched her shoulder. "Have patience and strength." Then he took her into the storage shed in the middle of the yard. *What could possibly be here?* Venetia thought, but then saw the oblong floor panel taken up, and the black maw leading down.

Stairs.

Whitewood snapped on a flashlight.

"Ann McGowen said that a ghost kept telling her to go to the basement—but there *is* no basement at the prior house," Venetia told him. "So *this* is what she meant."

The old man nodded. He led the way to the catacomb beneath the house.

"It leads straight back to the point directly beneath the center of the Involution," Whitewood informed. "There's a similar catacomb in Hell. Both lead to the Pith."

Venetia's curiosity pulled her along. The walkway was reinforced with cinder blocks but was very narrow. Whitewood continued, "One of the few upper hands the Lux Ferre has over God is the timelessness of Hell. He means to bring something from Hell into the world, and then take something from the world back to Hell. The sorcery merges two points at once. That's what will happen when the Involutions here and there are charged. For a few moments both Piths will occupy the same space. No one in the Living World has ever witnessed what you are about to."

Venetia shuffled along behind him; his crisp silhouette led the way. "What were you saying . . . about timelessness?"

"It's the most perplexing element of all—which is perfect logic from our enemy's standpoint. See, when the two Piths become one, some of that same timelessness will carry over to here. That's how it works. Here time is a constant, there it is nonexistent—therefore, when time's constancy on Earth mingles with the timelessness of Hell, time turns into a disproportion, and is therefore manipulable. You will see twenty years pass in one second, and in that second, you'll witness everything that occurred. Lucifer's sorcery will then be mincing time up into bits and mixing the bits around like dice in a cup."

"But what's his motive?" she asked.

"His motive is to transfer something hideous into our realm, and then take something blessed from us into *his* domain. It's something that he could forge into a great weapon." The old man slowed and looked back at her.

"This *something* is me, isn't it?"

"Yes."

They scuffled through the catacomb; spiderwebs snagged at Venetia's face. When she looked again, she saw that Whitewood was holding the pistol forward.

"What's . . . that for, Father?"

A hollow pause. "There may be a detractor waiting for us. Just remember to take one of the bones and hide it on your person."

At once Venetia remembered the insane voice. "But that's what I don't understand! What *bones?*"

"Shhh. We're here."

The Lower Chancel bloomed before them, a crude circular room walled by more blocks. Something glowed faintly—something with a red tinge—in the center. It looked like an irregular slab of stone.

"The Pith," Whitewood said. "When the blood in the atrium has fully wound its course to the center of the Involution, the Pith will be fully charged, and then . . . they will arrive."

"They . . . ," Venetia murmured. "These angels you mentioned?"

The old man nodded, then led Venetia into a small anteroom to the right. His flashlight froze on something in the corner.

Venetia's mouth fell open.

"When they arrived, they knew that mutual death was

their only resort," Whitewood's voice echoed in the chamber.

There they hung by their necks, the entire group of them. They hadn't decomposed as humans would, but had instead become mummified, their skin browning like leather. Hanging behind them, off bony webworks, were their once grand wings. Venetia could tell, by the remnants of their genitals, that they were all female.

"Suicide," Venetia muttered.

"Not quite. They knew we couldn't kill them—Humans can't kill Angels—so as they were hanging, they pulled each other's hearts out. It's the only way. They killed one another."

Closer inspection showed Venetia the rents in each of the being's chests, and each held in a desiccated hand a malformed lump that could only be a heart.

Utter confusion made her plead to Whitewood, "How can we be waiting for them to arrive when . . . they're already here?"

"Remember what I said about time and its inconstancy once the Piths are charged. Satan's ploy can only work in two stages. He is now going back in time to implement the second stage. Only then can he reclaim what was born here all those years ago."

Venetia felt more and more static prickling her skin. "What *was* born here?"

"It's time you saw for yourself." Then he took her into another brick anteroom off to the left. His flashlight pushed aside the shadows to reveal . . .

Boxes?

Concrete boxes—six of them—sat in a row, each a yard long, two feet wide, and two deep. *Coffins.* The word snapped into her head.

And atop of each sat a yellowed bone.

"The bones of St. Ignatius," she whispered.

"Yes, the most potent Power Relics that we could come up with. Once the Vatican realized what Tessorio had done, it was too late, so we entombed them. The bones keep the crossbreeds inside paralyzed. They've continued to grow, of course, but they can't escape as long as the Power Relics are present. Nothing evil can touch such a Relic." The old man stepped to the first coffin. "Help me, child. . . ."

The grating rasped in her ears as she helped push the first lid-half off the box.

Venetia almost keeled over when she got a look at the thing inside: a grooved face and warped bald head with flesh the color of mucus. The abomination filled the confines of the cement coffin, clearly growing from infancy until the coffin's walls prohibited further development. Venetia noticed breasts but also what appeared to be a hairless penis.

Senses reeling, she pushed back the lid.

"It's the offspring of an angel raped by a demon," Whitewood said in his lowest tone. "Each one is different, a variant abomination."

In the second box was a lithe, crushed thing as pale as butter with crystalline orbs for eyes. Between the broken spokes of its wings were folds of carnation pink skin. Lips the color of liver trembled, and between them sprouted disarrayed fangs.

"It's still alive, isn't it?" Venetia asked, shuddering.

"Yes." The response echoed. "They all are."

"Even in spite of what they are, how could you entomb them *alive?* How could ministers of the *Church* be that barbaric?"

Whitewood's shadow shifted on the wall. "We were terrified, Venetia. We didn't know what to do, so we followed the Vatican's orders. We had to become as ghastly as their creator. They can never escape as long as the Power Relics hold down the lids."

Venetia looked into the next three, one after the other. Whitewood was correct; they each displayed a variety of hybridized features, the hideous compacted into the beautiful. One seemed near-perfect, but for gelled-over eyes and bruise-blue wings sectioned by black veins. Another had perfect human eyes and nose but a mouth like a jackal, and the third—had it not been malformed by growing within the unyielding box—was flawlessly Human on one side and flawlessly monstrous on the other. One was male, one female, and the third both.

Did Whitewood step back when Venetia stooped over the sixth coffin? She had to see the last one, just to see them all before time was jerked backward and their tainted mothers rearrived in the Living World.

The lid grated till it was half off.

Venetia stared down.

It was empty.

"That one's yours," Whitewood intoned.

The luminous red mist was slowly intensifying. *Mine.* The word thumped in Venetia's brain. She could hear her own heart beating.

A heart only half Human.

"I'm one of them. . . ."

"Yes. You were the only one born perfect."

Now Venetia's mind overloaded.

"That's what makes you so valuable to the wards of Hell. Your Christian faith and willing chastity conquered your genetic heritage."

A heritage of evil, she thought. "And my true mother . . . is hanging over there . . . ?"

"No," Whitewood said.

Venetia's eyes bloomed.

Whitewood's voice sounded battered, and it was with the most secret whisper that he pleaded, "This was all foreseen, dear girl. Remember to do as you were bidden."

It was now impossible for Venetia to fathom *anything* . . . as another voice—a woman's—began to flirt through the underground chamber.

"Sextus rhytzum despiritae devorare—"

Whitewood collapsed with a groan, gnashed his teeth as if resisting an urge, then wailed. . . .

God in Heaven, Venetia thought.

Whitewood began to eat the flesh off his own arms. Blood smeared his face as grisly sounds smacked about the vault.

Before the crimson light stood the cloaked figure Venetia had already seen prowling the prior house.

Not the ghost of Tessorio, she realized now.

The cloak dropped to reveal Venetia's mother.

She stood nude, arms spread as if in jubilation. Sweat glazed her robust breasts, and branded just above her pubis was the Involution. "My dear sweet child," her voice resounded. On her face was a smile of rapture.

"But . . . the angels all killed each other," Venetia stammered.

"Yes, all but me—I was the last. They thought they could redeem themselves to God, but I chose to redeem myself to Eosphorus."

Venetia's eyes darted to the mass of hanged corpses. Only then did she notice the numerical fact: there were only *five*, not six.

"But . . . my father . . ."

"Your father was a Demon called a Coitasaurian," Maxine Barlow said. "The man you *thought* was your father—Richard—was just a dupe whom I machinated with Obsession Spells. I asked Lucifer to make him rich from his silly computer chips, and the money enabled us to raise you with ease. He did whatever I told him, never saw what I didn't want him to see. I cultured him for money and sex—that's all." Maxine seemed aroused just talking about it. "I burned him alive last night, by the way. And as for my wings?" Her mother turned to show her bare back . . . and the two clipped stubs at the shoulder blades. "I cut them off."

"So it was you haunting the house all this time," Venetia concluded.

"Helping make you ready for this unholiest of nights."

Venetia fell to her knees. "Why me?"

"Because you were the only perfect child, just as was prophesied."

Tears glittered in Venetia's eyes. "But why would Hell want *me?* I'm a *Christian.*"

"By your own free will, yes, dear," her mother sighed in bliss. "And once you are plucked back into the abyss, that same Godliness will revert to the opposite. You will be the first true wife of Lucifer."

Venetia gagged.

"You will be corrupted and despoiled, tortured and degraded, your willing virginity and faith in God cast aside for sport. The free will of your beliefs will be turned inside out, after which you'll choose just as willingly to disavow God and serve the Lord of Wretchedness."

Venetia was trembling on her knees.

The remains of Father Whitewood convulsed on the floor. By now he'd devoured all the flesh off his arms and legs, and was now digging a skeletal hand into his gut for more.

"What did you do?" Venetia gasped.

"A simple Anthropophagy Hex." Her mother looked down with glee; Father Whitewood was attempting to admit his entire liver into his mouth. "But in Hell, my beloved daughter, you will have such powers a *millionfold*."

"Why?" Venetia cried.

"Because after your debauchment and willing abandonment of God, you will be sent back here through the Pith—to bear Lucifer's son for the end of times. It's perfect."

Venetia wished she could shrink to nothingness.

Her mother stepped forward, the crimson light aglow on her glazed skin. "There, there, dear. For this you will sit in a far higher place in Hell than me. No being—Human or Demon—has ever been so privileged." The room's scarlet luminosity grew brighter, the static edge sharpening. "And consider the privilege, too, to behold the miracle of Lucifer's genius, to witness him molding time with his bare hands." Her mother's eyes beamed as a black aura formed around her head. "You're about to watch yourself be born. . . ."

Venetia's face was thrust forward when her mother grabbed her by the hair.

"Watch!"

The static maximized. Was it Venetia's imagination, or were the cinder blocks all around her *bleeding*?

"The Involution is charged!" her mother shouted in triumph. "The Pith is coming alive!"

Venetia felt something like a variation in gravity as the slab of stone seemed to become superimposed with a similar slab. . . .

"Glory be to he who was first cast out," her mother whispered.

An impulse dragged Venetia's eyes to her watch, whose hands jerked forward and back at random. The days and the dates, too, changed with each half second, and when she looked again to the Pith . . .

The hanging corpses were gone, as were the cement coffins. Instead, each blink of her eyes showed her another glimpse of what had happened over twenty years hence:

Six debased angels shuddering on the slab, all pregnant as if about to burst; each gravid belly shuddering, then collapsing, as the tiny monsters were disgorged; six angels moaning as they hanged themselves with no reluctance, and tore each other's hearts from their chest . . . all but one—Venetia's mother—who took herself down from her own noose, plucked up the one infant who was perfect, and ran off.

And the last blink:

Solemn priests placing the five squalling newborns into their coffins and sealing each lid with one of the bones of St. Ignatius.

The Pith throbbed in its light, standing empty now. When Venetia stared, she thought she could see *through* it, into a similar chancel of rock, while onlookers peered back—Demons beyond description—but one figure more hideous than the rest:

A man wearing a pope's miter, with a face of salt.

"It's time, my love," her mother beckoned.

Venetia rose to meet her destiny, yet the old priest's words haunted her: *Remember to do as you were bidden. . . .*

Venetia froze.

What *had* she been bidden?

And now, Venetia thought, *I have to go there. . . .*

When Maxine donned her cloak, Venetia grabbed the bone off the sixth coffin lid and stuck it in her pocket.

Then she and her mother stepped onto the slab and melted away.

(VII)

Keeping her cool wasn't easy as the anciently beautiful Pasiphae took her down through the labyrinth. The Putridox face felt even clammier in these humid warrens, and the tongues of her ghastly skirt seemed to slather with more voracity the deeper they went. Ruth's only relief was knowing that Alexander was close behind—and undetectable.

Finally she saw scarlet light flicker beyond a great stone archway. *This must be it—the Lower Chancel. . . .*

But Pasiphae didn't take her in; instead the abyssal woman stopped, her bottomless eyes reaching into Ruth's.

Oh, shit—that's right, Ruth recalled with no enthusiasm. *She's got a thing for me.*

She knew she had to make this good.

The shining, obsidian face drew close; at once Pasiphae's indescribable arms slipped around Ruth to embrace her. *I've made out with chicks before,* she reminded herself. *But not . . . monster chicks.*

Ruth did the best she could.

Cold lips were on hers, a cold tongue eager to probe. Ruth kissed the obscene woman back for all she was worth. . . .

Then Pasiphae recoiled, alarm on her night black face.

"She knows!" Alexander exclaimed. "Don't let her scream!"

Fuck fuck fuck fuck fuck fuck FUCK! Ruth thought. She latched on to Pasphae's throat and squeezed harder than she ever had in her life.

The effort choked off the shriek that would've betrayed them. Then—

Schulp-schulp-schulp . . .

Alexander's disembodied hand had shot out of the umbra to plunge a knife in and out of Pasiphae's belly. After a few more plunges, oil black organs fell forward along with a slew of tarlike blood.

Pasiphae, the Night-Mother, fell over dead.

"What the fuck happened?" Ruth asked, bewildered.

"I guess you don't kiss as well as Voluptua," the priest's voice presumed.

Ruth frowned.

"I can tell by the light—the Involution is almost charged, which means the Piths will merge—"

"When?"

"Any minute now. Get in there. Go to Boniface, and try to distract any of them from watching the Smoke-Light."

Then an invisible hand shoved Ruth into the archway.

Rude prick!

Ruth resumed her role, and followed a short corridor of blood bricks toward a wide, rock-hewn chamber in which scarlet light seemed to float like fog.

A Minotauress stood watch at this last entry, the sleek feminine physique rising to high breasts, which then converged into the head of a bull. Black beads for eyes looked down below sharpened horns.

"Stand aside," Ruth ordered. "The Exalted Duke is expecting me." Then Ruth walked in, Bone-Sandals clicking on the rock floor.

Holy fuckin' shit, she thought. *Look at this place.*

The mistlike light was rising. Helmed Conscripts stood round the chamber's perimeter, holding wickedly sharp weapons. She immediately saw the Smoke-Light. The modest metal-framed cylinder sat on a stand of some kind.

Right next to it stood a hooded Bio-Wizard.

That's the dude I've got to distract.

Beyond the Smoke-Light, however, was the chamber's most paramount feature: a warped stone slab that seemed to be half-aglow from some throbbing inner illumination. Ruth's stomach flipped when she saw what was taking place atop the slab.

Angels, she thought.

Six of them lay naked and squirming on the slab, some invisible force paralyzing them. Pain and horror distorted their faces as their swollen breasts and hugely pregnant bellies shuddered. Ruth paled as a higher ranking Conscript stepped between each of them and— *Sssssssssssssss*—put a branding iron low on their abdomens. When the sizzling smoke cleared, Ruth saw the configuration of the brands: The Involution.

This is some hard-core shit. . . .

Several Golems and slavering Ushers stood on each side of the slab.

"It's glorious!" a voice rattled.

And there he is, Ruth noted.

Boniface, short and squat in his white cloak and funny hat, stood beside another Wizard, watching the spectacle through the hideous mask of salt.

"The Involution is nearly charged, my lord," the Wizard boasted. "Soon the Pith will become subcorporeal." When he glanced over his shoulder at Ruth, she saw that his face looked like the bottom of a charcoal grill. "And my horrendous Duke, your Harlot has arrived to be by your side."

Ruth noticed a lustful joy through the mask's eye slits when the Exalted Duke glanced at her. A fat corroded hand waved her over. "Voluptua! My most rank and corruptible whore! Come to me and behold my greatness!"

Ruth groaned and went to him. When she took his hand as a lover would, she could've been holding the hand of a cadaver. Boniface at once turned to kiss her.

Ruth choked back bile and let her Putridox lips meet the mouth-hole of his mask. *This is a new low for me*, she told herself when a tongue like a strip of spoiled beef slid slimily into her mouth. She embraced him, playing the game, then felt something unspeakable harden against her thigh.

Fuck this shit, man. . . .

His hand plied her breast through the hairy bra-cup.

"You're always so lovely in these infernal garments," came his wet voice. The foulest stench piped from his mouth. "Only your despicability outweighs the beauty of your disgraceful whoredom."

Ruth was slack-jawed. *I guess that's a compliment.* "How . . . sweet, my great Exalted Duke," she whispered, but then she quailed when his dead hand began to slither up her Tongue-Skirt.

Acting like she enjoyed it was the most difficult thing she'd ever done.

"Pull up that putrescent visage," he breathed. "I must now kiss your *Human* face."

Ruth felt like a flowerpot had landed on her head. *What am I gonna fuckin' do now?*

Boniface stared. "Your obedience is not instantaneous? Do you wish to be quartered and eaten by Ghor-Hounds?"

"I'm sorry, my lord. It's just that I'm so aroused by the sight of you. . . ."

Boniface seemed pleased by the flattery; then he moaned when Ruth's hand went to his crotch.

"I just can't keep my hands off you, Duke. . . ."

For a moment, Boniface's mask blushed; then he reached to yank up her Putridox face—

"Exalted Duke!" the Wizard next to him exclaimed. "Put aside your lust for now! The Pith is fully activated!"

Thank you, God, Ruth thought. Boniface's wretched hand fell away from her as he turned to watch.

Ruth watched, too.

"Great Satan, let it be so!"

The scarlet light buzzed; then the Angels on the slab seemed to melt out of existence.

Is that it? Ruth wondered. But something else was supposed to happen now, wasn't it?

That Venetia chick . . .

Boniface had forgotten her, instead grabbing the arm of the Wizard next to him.

"Fire the Smoke-Light!" the Wizard commanded.

"Ruth!" Alexander whispered.

Fuck. Ruth ran to the Warlock by the Smoke-Light. "Let me help!" she said. The revolting magician was about to touch the oil lamp beneath with a burning twig. Ruth grabbed it, then—

"Oops! Sorry!"

She faked a stumble and knocked the Smoke-Light off its stand.

Did she feel Alexander's invisible form brush against her as she fell?

Boniface bellowed at the farce. "You clumsy, ridiculous, pox-ridden sow! You pitiful Human waste product!"

"Secure the Smoke-Light!" shouted the Wizard. "If it's broken, the Chancel will be vulnerable!"

Boniface was insane with anger. "I will have your blood replaced with the piss of Gargoyles, you useless trollop!" Then his hands wrung her neck.

"Calm yourself, Exalted Duke," fluttered the voice of the Warlock. He picked the Smoke-Light off the stone floor. "The Totem is intact." Then he lit the oil lamp and set the device back on its stand.

"I'll deal with you later, whore." Boniface shoved Ruth away.

Fuck you and *your mother*, Ruth thought.

What hovered off the Smoke-Light now was an illumination that was black yet somehow as bright as flashbulbs on a camera. It seemed to cover everyone in the room with a dark, glittering caul and seemed to stretch out fingers into the brighter crimson light coming from the Pith.

Then the stone slab seemed to *scream.*

Someone whispered, "Glory to Lucifer . . ."

Two shapes on the slab appeared like two things melting in reverse.

All of the chamber's occupants fell to their knees.

Ruth blinked, but when she looked again, the red light was fading, and on the slab stood a woman in a cloak and a younger woman—blond—in a black skirt and torn white blouse.

That must be her, Ruth realized.

"It worked, it worked, *it worked!*" Boniface blubbered with joy.

The two women seemed frozen at first; then they began to blink.

"The Chastitant is among us!" yelled the Wizard. "Conscripts! Seize her and shackle her at once!"

Several soldiers with chains rushed toward the Pith.

Bam!

The first Conscript's helmet blew off, along with half of his head. The other two flinched, then bowled over howling as a knife from nowhere plunged into their bellies.

"Infiltrators have switched the Smoke-Light with a fake!" the Warlock yelled, then a knife-slash appeared at his throat.

The Wizard pulled Boniface aside. "Someone must be working a Stealth Charm or a Hand of Glory. Ushers! Conscripts! Scythe every square inch of space in the Chancel!"

Pandemonium ensued as the servants of Boniface raised great hewers and sickles and began to systematically thresh them through the air.

Ruth tried to back up into a corner. She noticed that the two women on the slab were beginning to move, but she also noticed this: Boniface was staring right at her.

The squat, masked hulk barged toward her. "Something's amiss and I fear it starts with you!" he yelled. He grabbed her, yanked off her scarf, then—*shhhhlup!*—yanked off her Putridox face.

"An impostor! Cut her down in place!"

Ruth rammed both fists into the Duke's face; the mask fell apart in chunks.

"Oh, fuck you, man!" She shrieked when she saw the ruination beneath. "Your face looks like pimples on a Gorilla's ass!" She kicked him between the legs so hard they both fell over at the same time. Boniface howled. As Ruth fell, a great blade swooped down and just missed the area of space that her head had occupied a second earlier.

When the Usher raised its blade for a second strike—

Bam!

Alexander's sulphur gun split its head. Chunks of something like green goulash flew this way and that. But the remaining Conscripts and Demons were converging in a single line, their weapons blurring through the air.

Looks like this is the end, she realized.

Boniface croaked up at her, "Despicable heap of Human shit . . ."

"I'm glad you said that, you ugly fat fuck," Ruth replied, and stomped down hard on his face. The spiked heels of her Bone-Sandals sunk deep. After enough stomps, the face collapsed like darkly stained styrofoam. "And you've got a little dick, too!"

Alexander finally appeared, throwing aside the Hand of Glory. He rushed toward the Pith. "Venetia! The Power Relic! Now!"

The blond woman seemed to snap out of a trance; then she shrieked when she saw the chaos around her. The cloaked woman beside her looked about in disarray, then glared at Venetia.

"Venetia!" Alexander screamed. "Don't tell me you forgot the Relic!"

The cloaked woman lunged . . . just as Venetia pulled something from a pocket . . .

What the fuck is that? Ruth wondered, squinting.

Venetia had withdrawn some small unidentifiable *thing.*

Is that a chunk of bone? Ruth asked herself.

Then came a deafening shriek like wind through the highest mountain peaks—

"Holy shit!" Ruth screamed.

And everything turned white.

Some inchoate forced knocked Ruth across the chamber, as if she'd just been hit by a speeding truck. It was a concussion like dynamite going off, but without the explosion, just the inhuman shriek.

The preternatural force dropped Ruth hard on her back, slamming the wind from her lungs. She began to black out, but even on this verge of unconsciousness, the blinding white light prevailed. . . .

Ruth knew she was about to be destroyed. By now she truly did regret the outrageous sins of her life but still she thought, *What a ripoff . . .*

It seemed like hours had passed when her vision finally cleared. Her first sight upon coming to was a monstrous hand reaching down for her.

Ruth screamed—

"Relax, it's me," Alexander said. It was his Usher hand helping her up.

"Oh, fuck, man, you fuckin' scared the *fuck* out of me."

He bellowed right into her face: "Damn it, Ruth! Would you quit cussing!"

After all that shit, I deserve to cuss all I want. She took a moment to catch her breath. Memories returned like a steady drip. "What happened?"

"Look around."

The Pith sat inert—nothing more than a slab of rock. Askew piles of something white and sandy lay everywhere, but there were no signs of the Conscripts, Wizards, or Demons that had previously dominated the Chancel.

"Where did they all go?" she asked.

Alexander gestured to the piles. "Turned to salt—all of them. When Venetia secreted the Power Relic from the prior house to here, she brought something holy into an *un*holy perimeter. Any being motivated by evil has been—for lack of a better term—sterilized. With that bone, Venetia—via her power as a Chastitant—will be able to consecrate a great portion of the Boniface District, and more."

"You're fucking shitting me. . . ."

Alexander winced. "She's already up in the courtyard, doing the same as she did here. The Fortress Boniface will now become the first anti-Satanic stronghold in Hell."

Ruth noticed that the Werewolf hands and the tongues of her apparel had stopped moving. "Where's Boniface?"

The priest pointed to another pile of salt.

"Cool!" Ruth cogitated. *That chick with the blond hair*

sterilized all the evil out of the whole joint. "So does that mean we—"

"Succeeded in our mission? Yes. Let's go up now."

Where the stones of the labyrinth had once glowed crimson, they now glowed white. Ruth could've used some sunglasses. *This is cool as shit—the plan worked, and I get to go to Purgatory in a thousand years.*

The monster-limbed priest led Ruth through the labyrinth by following a long pink thread that wound its way back through the catacombs.

"You did that, didn't you?" Ruth guessed. "So we could find our way back out. You're a pretty smart dude!"

Alexander rolled his eyes.

"But where'd you get *pink* thread in Hell?"

"That's an astute question, Ruth."

Ruth's brow creased. "Hey. Where's my Yuck Foo T-shirt?"

Alexander held up the thread. "It's all I had on hand."

"You fucker! You used my favorite shirt!"

The priest moaned. "Don't worry about it, Ruth. Besides, you don't need to be wearing that shirt in front of the person you're about to meet."

"Who? That Venetia chick?"

Alexander didn't respond. Eventually he led them out of the last catacomb, into the courtyard.

"Wow," Ruth breathed. There were hundreds of piles of salt everywhere. The blood bricks had all turned white, each emitting a mild luminosity.

"Miraculous," the priest said, awed. "She's consecrated the entire fortress already." His eyes darted to the wide-open gate. "She's out in the District now."

"How much of the place can she consecrate with that bone?"

Alexander smiled. "Who knows . . ."

Ruth followed him outside the walls. "Hey. The place doesn't stink like it used to either."

"There'll be a lot of things changing in the District." Alexander's wide Demonic feet carried him to the first street. "And you get to be part of it. Venetia will need some assistance as she assumes her destiny. It's the perfect way for you to spend the next millennium while you're waiting to go to Purgatory."

Doesn't sound too bad at all, Ruth thought. But the worldly cynic in her kicked in. During her life, she'd been ripped off countless times on deals that sounded too good to be true: "How do I know that'll ever really happen, man? How do I know it's not jive?"

"In a minute, you'll see."

The fortress seemed to glow white behind her. As she looked down the block she said, "Check that shit out, man!" She could see Venetia slowly walking down the main roads just outside the fortress, a cloud of white light following her. The blood bricks whitened as she passed, and any Demonic being in her proximity immediately froze, then collapsed to a pile of salt.

"It's wondrous," Alexander whispered. "It all worked. . . ."

Ruth followed him without thinking much. "Where we going now?"

"Just looking for a puddle of water," the priest said.

The fuck? "A puddle? Why? Let's just go out there with Venetia—"

"You'll have plenty of time to do that later, but right now . . ." The priest stopped with a satisfied expression. At his feet was a puddle of dirty water. He just stood there, looking down.

"I'm getting pissed now, man," Ruth spoke up. "Why're you staring at a fuckin' puddle of dirty water?"

Alexander looked fretful. "*Shhh!* Of all the people you shouldn't cuss in front of, it's her."

Ruth's face screwed up. "*Who?*"

He pointed to the puddle. "Look. The charm is working, just like she said. . . ."

"You're scaring me now, man! What charm? That's no charm! It's a fuckin' puddle!"

Alexander winced yet again at the profanity. "Not like a *lucky* charm, Ruth. It's a charm like a spell. It's called a Transference Charm. Water's the best base to use for this kind of spell—even dirty water. It doesn't matter." A taloned Usher finger pointed down. "Look. See her?"

This guy's gone nuts all of a sudden. But when Ruth looked straight down into the puddle . . .

Holy shit . . . "Is that . . . a *face?*"

The image couldn't be denied. Indeed, what Ruth saw in the puddle was the face of a woman, but it clearly wasn't her own reflection. The face was pretty in an edgy way, and the woman had long shining black hair save for one gothy streak of white along the left side.

"Hello, Ruth," the image in the puddle greeted.

Ruth's jaw dropped.

"My name's Cassandra, and I'm speaking to you through a Celestial technology."

The woman's face in the image had a rim of light that made Ruth think of a halo. "A-are you like—an angel?"

"Something like that. I'm the intelligence source that Father Alexander told you about."

I don't believe this, Ruth thought. *I'm talking to a fucking puddle of water. . . .* "Where are you talking to us from?"

"That's unimportant, Ruth," the mysterious face said. "The important thing is you both succeeded and have proven yourselves worthy servants of God. You've both sufficiently redeemed yourselves, and I don't mean by working for us in exchange for a reward, but in *spirit*— when you weren't even aware of it."

"What do you mean?" Alexander asked, confused.

"By showing good will to Ruth, for instance, you sealed your redemption, Father. By assuming an extra burden that could lead to her own exit from Hell."

Alexander's brow popped up.

The eyes in the puddle looked again to Ruth. "And Ruth, you sealed your own redemption back at the adoption agency. You didn't know the baby was a Hex-Clone. You thought it was a *real* baby, and you were willing to risk your own reward by saving it. Remember?"

Ruth's memory reached back. *Yeah, I guess I did. . . .*

"Our Counter-Flux won't last long," Cassandra's image said, "so I have to make this quick. You both fulfilled the mission, so you'll both be rewarded as promised. I'm going to revoke Father Alexander's condemnation now, and Ruth, I'll revoke yours in a thousand years."

"How can you have the power to even *do* that?" Ruth's asked.

The image of the face seemed to stall. "It's been granted to me by a Celestial grace."

"Well then, if you have that kind of power, revoke *both* of us," Ruth urged. "Why do I have to wait a thousand years? You've got the power, so what's the difference?"

Alexander was rubbing his temples.

"My power has restrictions, Ruth," Cassandra answered. "Those are the rules—it's that simple. I'm only allowed to revoke one condemnation per millennium. If I could do two, I would—but I can't."

Next, however, Cassandra's eyes flicked back to Alexander, as if in expectation. "Something on your mind, Father?"

The priest looked at Ruth, then looked back at the face in the puddle. He stroked his chin with a large, monstrous hand. "Revoke Ruth instead."

"What?" Ruth snapped.

"Sure, why not?" Alexander reasoned. "Send her now, and *I'll* be the one to wait a thousand years."

Ruth gaped at him.

Cassandra's gaze drilled outward. "Are you absolutely sure, Father?"

The priest waved his hands dismissively. "Yeah, I'm sure. I'll make myself useful here, help Venetia, stuff like that." He chuckled. "A little extra redemption can't hurt, right?"

Ruth remained speechless.

"I'll ask one more time," Cassandra told him. "Are you *sure?*"

Alexander nodded.

Ruth's Tongue-Skirt and Hand-Bra flapped to the ground while Ruth herself disappeared. The priest wasn't sure but he thought he could hear her utter a few dissipating words before she was gone altogether: "What a cool fuckin' guy. . . ."

A wisp of smoke like glitter seemed to hang in the air momentarily; then it, too, was gone.

"You're a good man, Father Alexander," the face in the puddle said.

Alexander shrugged.

"I'll be in touch." Cassandra's eyes narrowed. "We have more work for you. . . ."

Before the priest could bid an awkward farewell, the face had vacated the puddle.

So . . . here I am, he thought with a relieving sigh. He flexed his beastly arms for no conscious reason. By now the entirety of Boniface Boulevard glowed white, as the Chastitant continued her scourge of consecration. But beyond—as far as he could see—the infernal city gushed smoke and screams, and through the black clouds before the black sickle moon, abominations soared on great leathery wings. Alexander knew that this city was endless and always would be, but now . . .

Now's my chance to change a little bit of it.

Overhead, directly above the former Fortress Boniface, the smallest rive seemed to appear in the smudged, scarlet sky, like a modest tear forming in filthy fabric.

Then a ray of sunlight strayed across his face.

Alexander strode forward then, thumping on inhuman feet, to join Venetia in her destiny.

Epilogue

Flashlights probed the dark wood behind the house. In spite of all the police, little was said after they'd found the two bodies—and all the blood—in the atrium. The only sound were crickets and the crunch of twigs beneath shoes.

More flashlights roved the rest of the backyard; Berns thought of monstrous fireflies.

"So what do you make of that giant spiral on the floor back at the house?" Moxey asked, if only to break the unnerving silence.

"It's an occult emblem. They called it the Involution."

"So what *is* it?"

Berns brushed a spiderweb off his face. "Wish I knew."

"And how the hell did these psychos get the blood to follow the course of the spiral? If they poured it out of the can, there'd be footprints."

"I don't know, sir," Berns replied, holding his annoyance. But Berns didn't think he *wanted* to know, either.

Moxey shrieked like a little girl when his flashlight veered upward onto three nude bodies hanging in the woods.

The ropes creaked.

"The housekeeper and her daughter," Berns said, "and the guy who took care of the yard."

All faces stared at the corpses.

"This is a real horror show you've got going here," Moxey said, trying to recover after his feminine shriek.

Berns smiled. "My county, my fault? It's your *state*."

Moxey smirked.

A distant voice from the yard called out: "Captain Berns! Over here!"

They strode quickly out of the clearing to where several more uniforms stood by a storage shed. Inside, a flashlight shined on an open floor panel.

"St-stairs," Moxey observed.

Berns led the way. A corridor of unadorned blocks seemed to lead back toward the house. The worst thought fluttered in his head. *Six people were staying at the prior house, and we've found five bodies. . . .*

Where was Venetia Barlow?

The corridor seemed to swallow them in narrowing darkness. The sound of foot scuffs echoed hard off the brick walls. Then—

"Shit," Berns said.

They all moved slowly into a large brick chamber. An odd stone slab sat slightly atilt toward the back. Flashlight beams danced around, a moving webwork of light.

Someone said, "This place feels like a crypt."

Moxey stood still, looking directly up. "You know, I'll bet—"

"I was thinking the same thing," Berns interrupted. "I'll bet this room was built directly beneath the middle of the atrium."

"Right under the center point of that spiral-thing . . ."

It was Berns' flashlight that found the anteroom to the left. He drew his gun and sidestepped in but found no one in wait, only six cement boxes. One was empty, its lid half-pushed off. But the other five had their lids on.

"Don't tell me those things are coffins," Moxey said.

"They're small for coffins," Berns noted. "And—"

They all noticed the odd white fragments sitting atop each lid.

"They look like pieces of *bones*," Moxey declared.

Yeah. Berns approached the fifth box as a cop in the main chamber yelled, "Hey, Captain, there's another room out here."

"Check it later. We need some help with these boxes." Berns removed the bone off the top of the fifth box. "Everybody grab a lid," he ordered. "Let's see what's inside these things. . . ."

SIMON CLARK

THIS RAGE OF ECHOES

The future looked good for Mason until the night he was attacked…by someone who looked exactly like him. Soon he will understand that something monstrous is happening—something that transforms ordinary people into replicas of him, duplicates driven by irresistible bloodlust.

As the body count rises, Mason fights to keep one step ahead of the Echomen, the duplicates who hunt not only him but also his family and friends, and who perform gruesome experiments on their own kind. But the attacks are not as mindless as they seem. The killers have an unimaginable agenda, one straight from a fevered nightmare.

ISBN 10: 0-8439-5494-9
ISBN 13: 978-0-8439-5494-4

RICHARD LAYMON

SAVAGE

Whitechapel, November 1888: Jack the Ripper is hard at work. He's safe behind locked doors in a one-room hovel with his unfortunate victim, Mary Kelly. With no need to hurry for once, he takes his time gleefully eviscerating the young woman. He doesn't know that a fifteen-year-old boy is cowering under Mary's bed....

Trevor Bentley's life would never be the same after that night. What he saw and heard would have driven many men mad. But for Trevor it was the beginning of a quest, an obsession to stop the most notorious murderer in history. The killer's trail of blood will lead Trevor from the fog-shrouded alleys of London to the streets of New York and beyond. But Trevor will not stop until he comes face to face with the ultimate horror.

ISBN 10: 0-8439-5751-4
ISBN 13: 978-0-8439-5751-8

EDWARD LEE

❱ SLITHER ❰

The trichinosis worm is one of nature's most revolting parasites. Luckily, these worms are rarely more than a few millimeters in length. But guess what? Now there's a subspecies that's thirty feet long…

When Nora and her research team arrived on the deserted tropical island, she was expecting a routine zoological expedition. But first they found the dead bodies. Now members of her own team are disappearing, and when they return, they've…changed. And is there any sane explanation for the lurid, perverse dreams she's been having? Indeed, there are other people on the island. But the real danger is something far worse.

ISBN 10: 0-8439-5414-0
ISBN 13: 978-0-8439-5414-2

THE BACKWOODS

EDWARD LEE

More than memories await Patricia when she returns to the quiet backwoods town where she grew up. A woman strangled half to death and buried alive. Children who scampered off to play, never to return. Men and women strung up and butchered for sport. Corpses dug up and bodies found—with parts missing. All these greet Patricia. All these and more...

Something from the darkest heart of the night is stalking her, while the town itself seems cursed by a nameless evil. Lust-filled dreams fuel deadly obsessions, the bodies pile up, and the blood flows. Black secrets are revealed and nightmares live in... *The Backwoods.*

ISBN 10: 0-8439-5413-2
ISBN 13: 978-0-8439-5413-5

- -

To order a book or to request a catalog call:
1-800-481-9191
This book is also available at your local bookstore, or you can check out our Web site **www.dorchesterpub.com** where you can look up your favorite authors, read excerpts, or glance at our discussion forum to see what people have to say about your favorite books.

DEBORAH LeBLANC

MORBID CURIOSITY

It seems like the answer to Haley's prayers. The most popular girl in her high school promises Haley that her life will change forever if only she performs certain dark rituals. And if Haley convinces her twin sister to participate, their power will double. Together they will be able to summon mystical entities they never dared dream of. But these are powerful, uncontrollable forces, forces that can kill—forces that demand to be fed.

ISBN 10: 0-8439-5828-6
ISBN 13: 978-0-8439-5828-7

OFFSPRING

JACK KETCHUM

The local sheriff of Dead River, Maine, thought he had killed them off ten years ago—a primitive, cave-dwelling tribe of cannibalistic savages. But somehow the clan survived. To breed. To hunt. To kill and eat. And now the peaceful residents of this isolated town are fighting for their lives….

ISBN 10: 0-8439-5864-2
ISBN 13: 978-0-8439-5864-5